Get into the holiday spirit with
acclaimed Christmas novels from
MARY HIGGINS CLARK
and CAROL HIGGINS CLARK

DECK THE HALLS

"In their first collaboration, mother and daughter have produced a holiday confection."
—*The New York Times Book Review*

"Mary Higgins Clark and daughter Carol Higgins Clark create a winning detective duo by teaming up favorite characters from their own respective novels. . . . An entertaining . . . Christmas treat."
—*People*

"Fans will greatly enjoy the pairing of two favorite detectives—and two popular writers—in a Christmas ornament of a book."
—*Publishers Weekly*

"For fans of either of the Clarks, this book is a real treat."
—*Bookreporter.com*

"Some delightful Dickensian characters."
—*Providence Sunday Journal* (RI)

"The authors have created a wonderfully unique cast of characters."

—*The Pilot* (Southern Pines, NC)

HE SEES YOU WHEN YOU'RE SLEEPING

"A cheerful holiday tale."

—*Richmond Times-Dispatch*

"These bestselling authors blend suspense with a heart-warming story. . . ."

—*Atlanta Constitution*

"A new spin on *It's a Wonderful Life* . . ."

—*Los Angeles Times*

"Consume in one sitting with a tumbler of hot mulled wine."

—*San Antonio Express-News*

"Blends suspense and redemption."

—*The Virginian-Pilot*

"A combination of slapstick and suspense [that] turns out to also be a tale of redemption and insightful observations on how our society has changed in forty-six years."

—*Toronto Star*

BY MARY HIGGINS CLARK AND CAROL HIGGINS CLARK

The Christmas Thief
He Sees You When You're Sleeping
Deck the Halls

BY MARY HIGGINS CLARK

No Place Like Home
Nighttime Is My Time
The Second Time Around
Kitchen Privileges
Mount Vernon Love Story
Silent Night/All Through the Night
Daddy's Little Girl
On the Street Where You Live
Before I Say Good-bye
We'll Meet Again
All Through the Night
You Belong to Me
Pretend You Don't See Her
My Gal Sunday
Moonlight Becomes You
Silent Night
Let Me Call You Sweetheart
The Lottery Winner
Remember Me
I'll Be Seeing You
All Around the Town
Loves Music, Loves to Dance
The Anastasia Syndrome and Other Stories
While My Pretty One Sleeps
Weep No More, My Lady
Stillwatch
A Cry in the Night
The Cradle Will Fall
A Stranger Is Watching
Where Are the Children?

BY CAROL HIGGINS CLARK

Burned
Popped
Jinxed
Fleeced
Twanged
Iced
Snagged
Decked

MARY HIGGINS CLARK

Deck the Halls

CAROL HIGGINS CLARK

POCKET BOOKS

NEW YORK LONDON TORONTO SYDNEY

Pocket Books
A Division of Simon & Schuster, Inc.
1230 Avenue of the Americas
New York, NY 10020

This book is a work of fiction. Names, characters, places, and incidents either are products of the authors' imagination or are used fictitiously. Any resemblance to actual events or locales or persons, living or dead, is entirely coincidental.

This Pocket Books paperback edition November 2010

POCKET and colophon are registered trademarks of Simon & Schuster, Inc.

For information about special discounts for bulk purchases, please contact Simon & Schuster Special Sales at 1-866-506-1949 or business@simonandschuster.com.

The Simon & Schuster Speakers Bureau can bring authors to your live event. For more information or to book an event, contact the Simon & Schuster Speakers Bureau at 1-866-248-3049 or visit our website at www.simonspeakers.com.

Cover illustration by Julie Scott

Manufactured in the United States of America

10 9 8 7 6 5 4 3 2

ISBN 978-1-4516-0935-6
ISBN 978-0-7432-1688-3 (ebook)

Acknowledgments

Now that the tale is told, we are frequently asked, "Was it hard to work together?"

The answer is "No." It was fun. By the time we got to the closing pages, we were so in tandem that if we were searching for a descriptive word, we often would come out with the same one in the same breath.

Of course the journey was made smoother by the help and encouragement of others.

And so we joyfully deck the halls for our editors, Michael Korda, Chuck Adams, and Roz Lippel.

A glittering ornament for Lisl Cade, our publicist.

Silvery garlands for Associate Director of Copyediting Gypsy da Silva, copy editor Carol Catt, proofreaders Barbara Raynor and Steve Friedeman, and at Dix!, Account Executive Kelly Farley, keyboarder Dwayne Harris, and proofreader Barbara Decker.

Candy canes for our agents Gene Winick, Sam Pinkus, and Nick Ellison.

A cup of cheer for our law enforcement ex-

Acknowledgments

perts, Sgt. Steve Marron and Detective Richard Murphy, Ret., New York District Attorney's Office.

A holiday kiss for Santa's helpers, better known as our family and friends, especially John Conheeney, Irene Clark, Agnes Newton, and Nadine Petry.

And a holiday greeting to our readers. May your days be merry and bright.

God bless . . .

*In the spirit of this shared journey,
we, Mary and Carol,
are dedicating this book to each other
with love.*

Thursday,
December 22nd

Regan Reilly sighed for the hundredth time as she looked down at her mother, Nora, a brand-new patient in Manhattan's Hospital for Special Surgery. "And to think I bought you that dopey crocheted rug you tripped on," she said.

"You only bought it. I caught my heel in it," the well-known mystery writer said wanly. "It wasn't your fault I was wearing those idiotic stilts."

Nora attempted to shift her body, which was anchored by a heavy plaster cast that reached from her toes to her thigh.

"I'll leave you two to assess the blame for

the broken leg," Luke Reilly, owner of three funeral homes, husband and father, observed as he hoisted his long, lean body from the low bedside armchair. "I've got a funeral to go to, a dentist's appointment, and then, since our Christmas plans are somewhat altered, I guess I'd better see about buying a tree."

He bent over and kissed his wife. "Look at it this way: you may not be gazing at the Pacific Ocean, but you've got a good view of the East River." He and Nora and their only child, thirty-one-year-old Regan, had been planning to spend the Christmas holiday on Maui.

"You're a scream," Nora told him. "Dare we hope you'll arrive home with a tree that isn't your usual Charlie Brown special?"

"That's not nice," Luke protested.

"But it's true." Nora dismissed the subject. "Luke, you look exhausted. Can't you skip Goodloe's funeral? Austin can take care of everything."

Austin Grady was Luke's right-hand man. He had handled hundreds of funerals on his own, but the one today was different. The deceased, Cuthbert Boniface Goodloe, had left the bulk of his estate to the Seed-Plant-Bloom-and-Blossom Society of the Garden State of New Jersey. His disgruntled nephew and partial namesake, Cuthbert Boniface Dingle, known as C.B., was obviously bitter about his meager inheritance. After viewing hours yesterday afternoon, C.B. had sneaked back to the casket where Luke had found him stuffing rotted bits of house plants in the sleeves of the pin-striped designer suit the fastidious Goodloe had chosen as his last outfit.

As Luke came up behind C.B., he heard him whispering, "You love plants? I'll give you plants, you senile old hypocrite. Get a whiff of these! Enjoy them from now until Resurrection Day!"

Luke had backed away, not wanting to confront C.B., who continued to vent verbal outrage at the body of his less-than-generous uncle. It was not the first time Luke had heard a mourner telling off the deceased, but the use of decaying foliage was a first. Later, Luke had quietly removed the offensive vegetation.

But today, he wanted to keep an eye on C.B. himself. Besides, he hadn't had a chance to mention the incident to Austin.

Luke considered telling Nora about the nephew's bizarre behavior, but then decided not to go into it. "Goodloe's been planning his own funeral with me for three years," he said instead. "If I didn't show up, he'd haunt me."

"I suppose you should go." Nora's voice was sleepy, and her eyes were starting to close. "Regan, why don't you let Dad drop you off at the apartment? The last painkiller they gave me is knocking me out."

"I'd rather hang around until your private nurse gets here," Regan said. "I want to make sure someone is with you."

"All right. But then go to the apartment and crash. You know you never sleep on the red-eye flight."

Regan, a private investigator who lived in Los Angeles, had been packing for the trip to Hawaii when her father phoned.

"Your mother's fine," he began. "But she's had an accident. She broke her leg."

"She broke her leg?" Regan had repeated.

"Yes. We were on our way to a black tie at the Plaza. Mom was one of the honorees. She was running a little late. I rang for the elevator . . ."

One of Dad's not very subtle ways of getting Mom to hurry up, Regan thought.

"The elevator arrived, but she didn't. I went back into the apartment and found her lying on the floor with her leg at a very peculiar angle. But you know your mother. Her first question was to ask if her gown was torn."

That would be Mom, Regan had thought affectionately.

"She was the best-dressed emergency-room patient in the history of the hospital," Luke had concluded.

Regan had dumped her Hawaii clothes out of the suitcase and replaced them with winter clothes suitable for New York. She barely made the last night flight from Los Angeles to Kennedy, and once in New York had paused only long enough to drop off her bags at her parents' apartment on Central Park South.

From the doorway of the hospital room, Luke looked back and smiled at the sight of the two women in his life, so alike in some ways with their classic features, blue eyes, and fair skin, but so different in others. From the Black Irish Reillys, Regan had inherited raven black hair, a throwback to the Spaniards who had settled in Ireland after their Armada had been destroyed in battle with the British. Nora, however, was a natural blonde, and at five feet three inches was four inches shorter than her daughter. At six feet five, Luke towered over both of them. His once-dark hair was now almost completely silver.

"Regan, I'll meet you back here at around seven," he said. "After we cheer your mother up, we'll go out and have a good dinner."

He caught Nora's expression and smiled at her. "You thrive on the urge to kill, honey. All the reviewers say so." He waved his hand. "See you girls tonight."

It was a commitment Luke would not be able to keep.

Across town, apartment 16B at 211 Central Park South was in the process of being decorated for Christmas. "Deck the halls with boughs of holly," Alvirah Meehan sang, off-key, as she placed a miniature wreath around the framed picture of Willy and herself accepting the $40 million lottery check that had changed their lives forever.

The picture brought back vividly that magical evening three years ago, when she'd been sitting in their tiny living room in Flushing, Queens, and Willy had been half asleep in his old club chair. She had been soaking her feet in a pail of warm water after a hard day of cleaning Mrs. O'Keefe's house when Willy came home, really bushed, from repairing a burst pipe that had sent showers of rusty water on the newly pressed clothes at Spot-Free Dry Cleaners down the block. Then the announcer on television began to read the winning lottery numbers.

I sure look different now, Alvirah thought, shaking her head as she examined the picture.

The brassy red hair that for so many years she had dyed herself in the bathroom sink had been transformed by Madame Judith, to a soft golden red with subtle shadings. The purple polyester pants suit had long ago been banished by her classy friend, Baroness Min Von Schreiber. Of course, her jutting jaw was the same, a product of God's design when he molded her, but she'd gotten down from a size sixteen to a trimmer size fourteen. There was no question about it— she looked ten years younger and a thousand times better now than in the old days.

I was sixty then and looked like I was pushing seventy. Now I'm sixty-three and don't look a day over fifty-nine, she told herself happily. On the other hand, she decided, looking at the picture, even dressed in that bargain-basement blue suit and skinny little tie, Willy managed to look handsome and distinguished. With his shock of white hair and vivid blue eyes, Willy always reminded people of the late, legendary Speaker of the House of Representatives, Tip O'Neill.

Poor Willy, she sighed. What bad luck that

he feels so rotten. Nobody should be stuck with a toothache during the Christmas season. But Dr. Jay will fix him up. Our big mistake was to get involved with that other guy when Dr. Jay moved to New Jersey, Alvirah thought. He talked Willy into getting a dental implant even though it hadn't worked last time, and it's been killing him. Oh, well, it could be worse, she reminded herself. Look what happened to Nora Regan Reilly.

She had heard on the radio that the suspense author, who happened to be her favorite writer, had broken her leg the evening before in her apartment in the very next building. Her high heel had caught in the fringe of a rug, Alvirah mused—the same kind of thing that happened to Grandma. But Grandma wasn't wearing high heels. She had stepped on a wad of bubble gum in the street, and when the fringe of the rug stuck to the bottom of her orthopedic sneakers, she went sprawling.

"Hi, honey." Willy was coming down the hall from the bedroom. The right side of his face was swollen, and his expression was instant testimony to the fact that the trouble-some implant was still killing him.

Alvirah knew how to cheer him up. "Willy, you know what makes me feel good?"

"Whatever it is, share it right away."

"It's knowing that Dr. Jay will get rid of that implant, and by tonight you'll be feeling much better. I mean, aren't you better off than poor Nora Regan Reilly, who'll be hobbling around on crutches for weeks?"

Willy shook his head and managed a smile. "Alvirah, can I never have an ache or a pain without you telling me how lucky I am? If I came down with the bubonic plague, you'd try to make me feel sorry for somebody else."

Alvirah laughed. "I suppose I would at that," she agreed.

"When you ordered the car, did you allow for holiday traffic? I never thought I'd be wor-ried about missing a dentist appointment, but today I am."

"Of course I did," she assured him. "We'll be there long before three. Dr. Jay squeezed you in before he sees his last patient. He's closing early for the holiday weekend."

Willy looked at his watch. "It's only a little after ten. I wish he could see me this minute. What time is the car coming?"

"One-thirty."

"I'll start to get ready."

With a sympathetic shake of her head, Alvirah watched her husband of forty-three years disappear back into the bedroom. He'll be feeling a thousand percent better tonight, she decided. I'll make some nice vegetable soup for dinner, and we'll watch the tape of *It's a Wonderful Life*. I'm glad we delayed our cruise until February. It will be good to have a quiet, at-home Christmas this year.

Alvirah looked around the room and sniffed appreciatively. I love the smell of pine, she thought. And the tree looks gorgeous. They had placed it right in the center of the floor-to-ceiling windows overlooking Central Park. The branches were laden with the ornaments they'd accumulated over the years, some handsome, some battered, all cherished.

Alvirah pushed back her large, round glasses, walked over to the cocktail table, and grabbed the last unopened box of tinsel.

"You never can have too much tinsel on the tree," she said aloud.

Three more days until Christmas, twenty-six-year-old Rosita Gonzalez thought, as she waited for Luke Reilly behind the wheel of one of the Reilly Funeral Home limos, standing near the hospital's Seventy-first Street entrance. Mentally she reviewed the presents she had bought for her five- and six-year-old sons, Bobby and Chris. I haven't forgotten anything, she assured herself.

She so wanted them to have a good Christmas. So much had changed in the last year and a half. Their father had left—not that that was any loss—and her ailing mother had moved back to Puerto Rico. Now both boys clung to Rosita as if they were afraid *she* would somehow disappear too.

My little guys, she thought with a rush of tenderness. Together, the three of them had picked out their Christmas tree last night and would decorate it tonight. She had the next three days off, and Mr. Reilly had given her a generous Christmas bonus.

Rosita looked in the rearview mirror and straightened the driver's cap over her waterfall of dark curly hair. It sure was a stroke of luck when I got the job at the funeral home, she thought. She had started working part-time in the office, but when Luke learned that she moonlighted as a limo driver, he told her, "You can have all the extra work you want here, Rosita." Now she frequently drove for funerals.

There was a tap on the driver's window. Rosita looked up, expecting to see the face of her good-natured boss. Instead she found herself locking eyes with a vaguely familiar countenance, which, for the moment, she could not place. She opened the window a few inches and was rewarded with a belch of cigarette smoke. His head darting forward, her unexpected visitor identified himself in staccato tones: "Hi, Rosie, I'm Petey the Painter. Remember me?"

How could I forget? Rosita wondered. A mental image of the brilliant chartreuse shade he'd painted the main viewing room of the Reilly funeral home in Summit, New Jersey, flashed through her mind. She remembered Luke Reilly's reaction when he saw it. "Rosita," Luke had said, "I don't know whether to laugh, cry, or throw up."

"I'd throw up, Mr. Reilly," had been Rosita's advice.

Needless to say, Petey the Painter's services had no longer been requested nor required in any of the three Reilly funeral homes.

Petey had gratuitously added bright yellow to the moss-green paint Luke had selected, declaring that he thought the place needed a little livening. "Relatives of dead people need cheering up," he'd informed them. "That green was really depressing. I had a little extra yellow paint in my car, so I threw it in for free." On his way out, he'd asked Rosita for a date, which she'd promptly declined.

Rosita wondered if he still had flecks of paint in his hair. She looked at him, but couldn't tell. A cap with earmuffs covered every inch of his head and shaded his narrow, bony face. His wiry frame was encased in a dark-blue storm jacket. The turned-up collar of the jacket grazed the graying stubble that shaded his chin.

"Of course I remember you, Petey," she said. "What are you doing here?"

He shuffled from foot to foot. "You look great, Rosie. Too bad your most important passengers never get to feast their eyes on you."

The reference, of course, was to the fact that Rosita sometimes drove the hearse in funeral cortèges.

"You're funny, Petey. See you." She began to raise the window but was stopped by Petey's hand.

"Hey, it's freezing out. Can I sit in the car? I need to ask you something."

"Petey, Mr. Reilly will be here any minute."

"This will only take a minute," he explained.

Reluctantly, Rosita threw the lock that opened all the doors. She had expected him to go around and get in beside her in the front seat. Instead, in a lightning-fast motion, he opened the back door of the vehicle and slid in.

Thoroughly annoyed with her intruder, she swiveled her head around to face him in the back of the limo, whose tinted windows shielded anyone seated there from the view of the outside world. What she saw took her breath away. For a moment she thought it was a joke. Surely that couldn't be a gun Petey was holding?

"Nobody's going to get hurt if you do what I tell you," Petey said soothingly. "Just keep a nice, calm look on your pretty face until the King of the Stiffs gets here."

A weary and preoccupied Luke Reilly emerged from the elevator and walked the short distance to the door of the hospital, barely noticing the Christmas decorations adorning the lobby. He stepped outside into the raw, cloudy morning and was glad to see his limo waiting near the end of the driveway.

In a few strides, Luke's long legs brought him to the car. He knocked on the window of the passenger side, and a moment later was turning the handle of the back door. He was inside and had closed the door behind him before he realized that he was not alone in the backseat.

Luke's unerring memory for faces, coupled with the sight of paint-flecked boots, made him realize instantly that the man sitting opposite him with the gun in his hand was none other than the idiot who had turned his viewing room into a psychedelic nightmare.

"In case you don't remember me, I'm Petey the Painter. I worked for you last summer." Petey raised his voice. "Start driving, Rosie," he ordered. "Turn right at the corner and pull over. We're making a pickup."

"I remember you," Luke said quietly. "But I prefer seeing you with a paintbrush instead of a gun. What's this all about?"

"My friend will explain when he gets in.

Nice comfortable car you got here." Again, Petey raised his voice. "Rosie, don't try any funny stuff like running a light. We don't want no attention from the cops."

Luke had barely slept the night before, and his mind was blurry. Now he felt somehow detached from reality, as though he were dreaming or half asleep, watching a movie. He was alert enough, however, to sense that this unlikely kidnapper might never have held a gun before, which actually made him twice as dangerous. Luke knew he could not take the chance of throwing himself forward in an attempt to overpower his captor.

Rosie turned the corner. The car had not quite stopped when the front passenger door opened and another man joined them. Luke's mouth dropped: Petey the Painter's partner in crime was none other than C. B. Dingle, the disgruntled nephew of the late Cuthbert Boniface Goodloe.

Like Petey, C.B. was wearing a cap with earmuffs that fit loosely over his balding head, and a bulky, nondescript storm jacket that covered his butterball-shaped torso. C.B.'s round, pale face was half covered by a dark, bushy mustache that had not been present at his uncle's wake the day before. Wincing, he pulled off the fuzzy disguise and addressed Luke.

"Thank you for being on time," he said cordially as he patted his lip. "I don't want to be late for my uncle's funeral. But I'm afraid *you're* not going to make it, Mr. Reilly."

Where are they taking us? Rosita agonized as, following C.B.'s instructions, she turned right on Ninety-sixth Street and headed for the FDR Drive north. She had seen C.B. at the funeral parlor only yesterday, had met him a couple of times before when he came to the funeral home with his uncle, who kept changing his mind about the plans for his last farewell.

Irrationally, she almost smiled, remembering that Cuthbert Boniface Goodloe had stopped in only last month to inform Luke that the restaurant he had chosen for a reception after his funeral had been closed down by the Health Department. She had driven Mr. Reilly, Goodloe, and C.B. to the Orchard Hill Inn, which Mr. Reilly had suggested as a replacement. Mr. Reilly told her later that Goodloe had painstakingly studied the menu, eliminating the most expensive items from his guests' future selections.

That day C.B., as usual, had been practically kissing his uncle's butt, which obviously had done him no good. Yesterday afternoon the viewing room had been filled with shocked but grateful members of the Seed-Plant-Bloom-and-Blossom Society of the Garden State of New Jersey—a group commonly known as the Blossoms—whose goal to spruce up every nook and cranny of New Jersey had just received a much needed million-dollar shot in the arm. The buzz was that Goodloe's dying words to his nephew had been, "Get a job!"

Had C.B. gone crazy? Was he dangerous?

And what does he want with me and Mr. Reilly? Rosita wondered as, even inside her gloves, her fingers turned to ice.

"Head for the George Washington Bridge," C.B. ordered.

At least they were going back to New Jersey, Rosita thought. She wondered if there was any hope of appealing to C.B. to let them go.

"Mr. Dingle, you may know I have two little boys who need me," she said softly. "They're five and six years old, and their father hasn't supported or seen them in over a year."

"My father was a crumb too," C.B. snapped. "And don't call me Mr. Dingle. I hate that name."

Petey had overheard. "It's a dumb name," he agreed. "But your first and middle names are even worse. Thank God for initials. Mr. Reilly, can you believe C.B.'s mom saddled him with a name like Cuthbert Boniface, in honor of her sister's husband. And then, when the old geezer passes away, he gives just about everything to the stupid Blossoms? Maybe they'll name a new strain of poison ivy after him."

"I spent my whole life pretending to like those stupid names!" C.B. said angrily. "And what do I get for it? Career advice three seconds before he croaks."

"I'm sorry about all that, C.B.," Luke said firmly. "But your problems have nothing to do with us. Why are we here, or more precisely, why are you and Petey in my car?"

"I beg to differ—" C.B. began.

Petey interrupted: "I really like that expression. It sounds so classy."

"Shut up, Petey," C.B. snapped. "My problem has *everything* to do with you, Mr. Reilly. But your wife is going to have a million ways to make it up."

They were halfway across the George Washington Bridge.

"Petey, you tell Rosie where to turn. You know the way better than I do."

"Take the Fort Lee exit," Petey began. "We're going south."

Fifteen minutes later, the car pulled onto a narrow road that led down to the Hudson River. Rosita was on the verge of tears. They reached an empty parking area at the river's edge, facing the skyline of Manhattan. To the left they could see the towering gray span of the George Washington Bridge. The heavy stream of holiday traffic crossing back and forth on its two levels only increased Rosita's sense of isolation. She had a sudden terrible fear that C.B. and Petey might be planning to shoot them and throw their bodies into the river.

"Get out of the car," C.B. ordered. "Remember we both have guns and know how to use them."

Petey aimed his revolver at Luke's head as he and Rosita reluctantly left the familiarity of the car. He gave the weapon a quick twirl. "I watched reruns of *The Rifleman* doing this," he explained. "I'm getting real good at twirling."

Luke shuddered.

"I'll be your escort," C.B. told him. "We have to hurry. I have a funeral to make."

They were forced to walk along the shore, past a deserted marina, to where a dilapidated houseboat, its windows boarded up, was anchored at the end of a narrow dock. The boat rocked up and down, as the river lapped restlessly against its sides. It was obvious to Luke that the worn and aging craft was sitting dangerously low in the water.

"Take a look at the ice that's starting to form out there. You can't be planning to put us on that thing in this weather," Luke protested.

"In summertime it's real nice," Petey boasted. "I take care of it for the guy who owns it. He's in Arizona for the winter. His arthritis is something awful."

"This isn't July," Luke snapped.

"Sometimes you get bad weather in July too," Petey responded. "One time there was a real bad storm, and—"

"Shut up, Petey," C.B. growled irritably. "I told you, you talk too much."

"You would too if you painted rooms all by yourself twelve hours a day. When I'm with people, I like to talk."

C.B. shook his head. "He drives me nuts," he said under his breath. "Now be careful getting onto the boat," he told Rosita. "I don't want you to slip."

"You can't do this to us. I've got to go home to my boys," Rosita cried.

Luke could hear the note of hysteria in Rosita's voice. The poor kid is scared stiff, he thought. Just a few years younger than Regan and supporting two children on her own. "Help her!" he barked.

Petey used his free hand to grasp Rosita's arm as, fearfully, she stepped down onto the deck of the swaying vessel.

"You're very good at influencing people, Mr. Reilly," C.B. complimented. "Let's hope you're as successful for the next twenty-four hours."

Petey unlocked the door of the cabin and pushed it open, releasing a dank, musty smell into the cold outside air.

"Whew," Petey said. "That stink'll get you every time."

"Move it, Petey," C.B. ordered. "I told you to get an Airwick."

"How thoughtful," Rosita said sarcastically as she followed Petey inside.

Luke glanced over at the Manhattan skyline, then looked upriver to the George Washington Bridge, taking in the little red lighthouse underneath. I wonder if I'll ever get the chance to see all this again, he thought, as C.B. pressed the gun in the small of his back.

"Inside, Mr. Reilly. This isn't the time for sightseeing."

Petey turned on the dim overhead light as C.B. closed the door behind them.

On one side of the small, shabby space was a seating area consisting of a Formica dinette table surrounded by a cracked, imitation-leather banquette; directly opposite was a matching couch. The furniture was all built-in units. A small refrigerator, sink, and stove were adjacent to the table. Luke knew that the two doors to the left probably led to a bedroom and whatever passed for a bathroom.

"Oh, no," Rosita gasped.

Luke followed her stare, and with dismay realized that two sets of chains were bolted to the walls in the seating area. They were the kind of hand and ankle restraints commonly used to restrain criminal defendants in courtrooms. One set was next to the couch, the other near the banquette.

"You sit here," Petey directed Rosita. "Keep me covered, C.B., while I put her bracelets on."

"I got everybody covered," C.B said emphatically. "You're over here, Mr. Reilly."

If I were alone, I'd take my chances and try to grab his gun, Luke thought angrily, but I can't risk Rosita's life. An instant later, he was sitting on the banquette, chained, with Rosita opposite him on the couch.

"I should have asked if either one of you cares to use the facilities, but now you'll just have to wait," C.B. said cheerfully. "I don't want to be late for my uncle's funeral. After all, I *am* the chief mourner. And Petey needs to get rid of your car. When we come back, Petey'll bring stuff for your lunch. I won't be hungry, though. My uncle paid for my meal today, remember, Mr. Reilly?"

C.B. opened the door as Petey turned out the light. An instant later the door slammed shut, and Luke and Rosita could hear the grating of the key turning in the rusty lock.

Trapped in the shadowy darkness of the swaying boat, they both remained silent for a moment as the reality of their precarious situation hit both of them.

Then Rosita asked quietly, "Mr. Reilly, what's going to happen to us?"

Luke chose his words carefully. "They've already told us they're looking for money. Assuming that's all they really want, I promise it will be paid."

"All I can think about is my kids. My regular baby-sitter is away until next week, and I don't trust the girl who's filling in. Her Christmas dance is tonight. She didn't want to work at all today, but I begged her to. She expects me home by three."

"She wouldn't leave the boys alone."

"You don't know her, Mr. Reilly—she won't miss that dance," Rosita said with certainty, a catch in her voice. "I've got to get home. I've just got to get home."

Regan opened her eyes, groggily sat up, swung her legs over the edge of the bed, and yawned. Her bedroom in her parents' apartment on Central Park South was as comfortably familiar as the one in the family home in New Jersey in which she'd been raised. Today, though, she did not take time to appreciate the charming ambience of the peach-and-soft-green color scheme. She had the sensation of having slept a long time, but when she looked at the clock, she was glad to see it was only a few minutes before two. She wanted to phone the hospital and see how her mother was doing, then catch up with her father. She realized that beyond the fact that she was feeling the effects of the news about her mother's accident and the hurried red-eye flight, she was filled with undefined anxiety. A quick shower might help me clear my mind, she thought, and then I'll get moving.

She put in a call to La Parisienne, the local coffee shop, and placed her usual breakfast order: orange juice, coffee, and a toasted bagel with cream cheese. This is what I love about New York, she thought. By the time I get out of the shower, the delivery boy will be ringing the bell.

The strong spray of hot water felt good on her back and shoulders. She quickly washed her hair, stepped out of the shower, wrapped herself in a robe, and rolled a towel around her head.

Ten seconds later, her face glistening with moisturizer, she answered the door for the delivery boy. She was glad he pretended not to notice her appearance. In his job, he's seen it all, she thought. But he did produce a sunny smile when she gave him a generous tip.

Moments later, the bagel unwrapped, the coffee cup in her hand, she phoned her mother's room. She knew the nurse had to be there, but no one picked up. The ringer is probably turned off, she thought. She hung up and dialed the nurses' station on that floor.

What seemed like several minutes passed as she waited for her mother's nurse to come to the phone. It was a relief to hear the friendly, professional, and reassuring voice of Beverly Carter. She had come on duty this morning, just as Regan was leaving. Although they had spoken only briefly, Regan had instantly liked the slim, fortyish black woman, whom the doctor had introduced as one of their finest private nurses.

"Hi, Beverly. How's my mother?"

"She's been sleeping since you left."

"I've been sleeping since I left," Regan laughed. "When she wakes up, tell her I called. Have you heard from my father?"

"Not so far."

"I'm surprised. But he did have that funeral. I'll give him a call. Tell my mother she can always reach me on my cell phone."

Next, Regan dialed the funeral home. Austin Grady, the second in command at "Reilly's Remains," as Regan and her mother dubbed the funeral homes, answered. His initial greeting, as usual, was suitably subdued.

"Austin, it's Regan."

The somber tone turned jolly. "Regan, hello."

Regan was always amazed at the way Austin could switch gears so rapidly, his demeanor of the moment dictated by the demands of his job. As Luke had observed, he was perfectly suited to this line of work. Like a surgeon, he was able to disassociate himself from surrounding emotions.

"Is my father there?" she asked.

"No, I haven't spoken to him since he called early this morning to send for a car. Your poor mother," he commiserated in a most upbeat tone. "What's going to happen next? And I know your father was really looking forward to the trip to Hawaii. I understand she tripped on a new rug you bought her in Ireland."

"Yes," Regan said quickly, guilt about her purchase washing over her again. As her best friend, Kit, always said, "Guilt is the gift that keeps on giving."

"Austin, my father told us he was going to be there for a funeral you were having today. Didn't he show up at all?"

"Well, no, but the service went beautifully. The old guy had been planning it for years.

Your father probably realized he didn't really need to come." Austin chuckled. "Right now the mourners are all enjoying a free lunch across town. The deceased left the bulk of his estate to the Blossoms. They're all at the restaurant, and they look like one happy group. They inherited enough money to buy sprinkling cans for every plant in the state of New Jersey."

"Lucky them," Regan said.

"Your father has a 3:30 dentist's appointment on his schedule. I don't think he'll miss that."

"Thanks, Austin." Regan hung up and dialed Luke's cell phone. After several rings his voice mail came on. As she listened to her father's voice telling the caller to leave a message, her sense that something might be wrong deepened. Her father hadn't been heard from in hours, even to inquire about her mother. She left a message for him to call her.

She sipped her coffee and thought for a minute. I can't just sit here, she decided. She glanced at the clock. It was now 2:35. She called the dentist's office to confirm that her father had not canceled his appointment.

"Please ask him to wait for me," Regan said to the receptionist. "I'm leaving the city in a few minutes, and it shouldn't take me more than an hour to get there."

"Will do," the receptionist promised.

Regan hurriedly dressed and dried her hair. After Dad has his appointment, we can do the errands together, she thought. Then we'll drive back to the city to see Mom.

But even as she pulled on her coat and ran down to grab a cab, Regan somehow knew that that wasn't what she would be doing this afternoon.

How long had he and Rosita had been locked up in the dark, chilly houseboat? Luke had no sense of time. It seemed like hours. They could have left the light on, he thought angrily.

After C.B. and Petey the Painter took off, Luke had tried to reassure Rosita. "Trust my hunch," he told her. "When those jerks come back, they'll tell us what they want. And when they get it, they'll let us go."

"But we can identify them, Mr. Reilly. Do you really think they can be that stupid?"

"Rosita, probably nobody else could be that stupid, but I believe it of that pair. It won't be long before we're missed. Don't forget, my daughter's a private investigator, and she'll have everyone looking for us."

"Just as long as someone takes care of my kids. I'm so afraid that ditzy baby-sitter will dump them with someone they don't know. My little guy, especially, is painfully shy."

"If there's one thing I'm sure of, it's that when Regan realizes we're missing, she'll check on your kids."

They hadn't spoken for a while. It was only about ten feet across the cabin to the built-in couch where Rosita was chained. Had she dozed off? Luke wondered. The lapping of the water against the sides of the boat made it impossible to hear any sound of movement from her.

"Rosita," he said softly.

Before she could answer, a thud on the deck startled both of them. The sound of the key grating in the lock dispelled Luke's hope that whoever was outside might be a potential rescuer.

The door opened. A somber trickle of light and a blast of cold air preceded Petey and C.B. into the cabin.

"How are our campers doing?" C.B. asked jovially as Petey snapped on the overhead light. "I hope you're not vegetarians. We bought ham and cheese sandwiches." Both men were carrying grocery bags.

It was with mixed emotion that Luke noted how small the bags were. Either they were planning to have them out of here in a short time, or there would be frequent take-outs from the local fast-food outlets in Edgewater.

"Either one of you want to go to the can?" Petey asked solicitously.

Luke and Rosita both nodded.

"Ladies first," Petey said. He released Rosita's hand and ankle shackles. "You can close the door, but don't get any stupid ideas. Besides, it don't have a window."

Rosita looked at Luke. "Could you lend me a dollar for the attendant?"

When it was Luke's turn inside the tiny cubicle, he considered his options and realized he had none. Even if he could overpower Petey when he was refastening the chains, C.B. would be standing with his gun trained on Rosita. *I have to play along with them*, he thought.

While Luke, Rosita, and Petey ate their sandwiches, C.B. sipped coffee. "I'm full," he said, looking at Luke. "That restaurant you suggested wasn't bad. The veal parmigiana was the best I've had in ages. Although I'm surprised I could digest my meal, having to look at those nerds from the Blossom Society. It was only the thought of you two back here that got me through."

"You could have brought me back some veal parmigiana," Petey griped. "I think this rye bread is a little stale. And he didn't put enough mayo on mine." He peered over at Luke's sandwich. "Let's switch halves."

Luke grabbed the second half of his sandwich and took a big bite out of it. He laid it back down on the wax paper. "Be my guest." Luke was inordinately pleased to see the disappointed look on Petey's face.

Petey looked at Rosita. "No dessert for the boss. You can have his Twinkies."

"I'd rather choke," Rosita snapped.

"Now that we're one big happy family, let's get down to business." C.B. crushed his empty coffee cup and stuffed it into the deli bag.

"Be careful, the pickles are still in there," Petey protested.

C.B. groaned and dumped the contents of the bag on the scarred Formica table.

"Don't get mad," Petey said. "I wasn't at some fancy lunch. I feel like I've been on a bus all day. Once I dumped the car at Kennedy, I had to take a bus to the Port Authority. Then I hadda wait for another bus to Edgewater. Then I hadda wait for you at the bus stop. You were too cheap to let me take a cab. *You've* been riding in a nice warm car all day—"

"Shut up!"

But Petey wasn't finished. "I had my four dollars ready to pay when I crossed the George Washington Bridge. Then when I'm waiting in a long line to hand it over, I discover there's an E-Z Pass on the floor of the car. I stuck it back up on the windshield and switched lanes fast. Some jerk almost plowed into me. He starts honking his horn like a crazy person. Then I saved you more money when I went over the Triborough Bridge. You should have noticed that E-Z Pass when you rode up front. I'm surprised at you."

C.B.'s eyes bulged. "You used the E-Z Pass? You moron! I took it off so they wouldn't be able to track us. Now they can check and find out where it's been used."

"Really?" Petey looked awestruck. "I'll be darned. What will they think of next?" He turned to Luke and Rosita. "C.B. is so smart. He reads a lot of detective novels. I never had much chance to read. Mr. Reilly, I know he really likes your wife's novels. I think one of them is even autographed."

"When you release us, I'll get him another one. And when is that going to happen?"

Petey reached for a pickle. "Explain our plan, C.B. It's so good. In a few days we're going to be on a beach somewhere with a million dollars in our suitcase."

C.B. interrupted Petey. "I'm telling you for the last time, Petey. Keep your mouth shut!" He pulled Luke's and Rosita's cell phones from the leather pouch where he had stashed them. "Mr. Reilly, it's nearly 4:30. We're going to get in touch with your family and tell them we want a million dollars cash by tomorrow afternoon."

Rosita gasped. "A million dollars?"

Petey piped in. "He's got viewing rooms all over New Jersey, and his wife sells a lot of books. Hey, C.B., maybe we should ask for more."

C.B. ignored him.

"I can guarantee my family will pay you the money," Luke said carefully. "But it's Thursday afternoon of Christmas weekend. I don't know how they'd be able to get it by tomorrow."

"Believe me, they can," C.B. said. "If they want to."

"He read it in a book," Petey volunteered. "Banks do things for important people, like opening their doors at all hours. And you're a real important person."

"But my wife is in the hospital," Luke protested.

"We know that. Where do you think we picked you up?" C.B. asked. "Now—who do you want us to call?"

"My daughter. She just got in from California. She'll get you the money." He gave them her cell phone number: "310-555-4237."

Petey started scribbling the number on a piece of paper he had torn off the brown deli bag. "Say that again"

Luke repeated the number slowly.

C.B. turned the phone on and began dialing.

"That implant came out smooth as silk," Dr. Jay assured Alvirah. "I have Willy on oxygen now. I'd like you to wait a little while before you take him home. He's still groggy."

"That laughing gas really knocks Willy out," Alvirah commented. "But he sure was looking forward to it. He's been in such misery."

"Well, give him a couple of days, and he'll be good as new. The prescription for antibiotics should clear up his infection." Dr. Jay's pleasant, bespectacled face broke into a smile. "He'll be able to enjoy the Christmas holiday. I know *I'm* looking forward to it." He looked at his watch. "I have one more patient, and then I'm on vacation."

"Any big plans?" Alvirah queried with her usual genuine interest in the comings and goings of her fellow creatures.

"My wife and I are taking the kids skiing in Vermont."

"Nice," Alvirah said, shaking her head. "When we won the lottery, I made a list of all the things I've always wanted to do in this lifetime. Skiing was one of them. But I haven't gotten around to it yet."

She did not miss the alarmed expression on

Dr. Jay's face. "I bet you think I couldn't do it," she challenged.

"Alvirah, I've known you long enough. Nothing you do would surprise me."

Alvirah laughed. "Don't worry. I won't crash into you on the slopes just yet. If the weather reports are right about a storm, you should have some great skiing."

"If it does hit, we'll already be there. We're leaving tonight." Dr. Jay looked at the door. "He's never late," he murmured more to himself than to Alvirah, then said, "I'll check on Willy and start to wrap things up around here."

As the doctor left the waiting room, Alvirah admitted to herself that she really had been worried about Willy—more worried than she had allowed herself to realize. Willy has always been so healthy, she thought. I won't even let myself consider that something could be seriously wrong with him. She was so deep in thought that the ringing of the office bell startled her. That must be the patient Dr. Jay is waiting for, she reasoned. She jumped up to answer the door as a buzzer released the lock.

Alvirah immediately knew that the slender, dark-haired young woman who came into the waiting room was not the patient Dr. Jay was expecting. She had clearly heard him say that *"he"* was never late.

She quickly sized up the newcomer— around thirty, very attractive, wearing a handsome suede jacket, jeans, and boots; obviously preoccupied. She smiled fleetingly at Alvirah as she looked at the empty reception desk.

"Everybody except Dr. Jay has gone home already," Alvirah volunteered cheerily. "He's waiting for his last patient."

Alvirah could see that the look of concern on the young woman's face immediately deepened.

Dr. Jay appeared at the doorway. "Hi, Regan. Where's your father? He's holding up my vacation."

"I was hoping to hook up with him here," Regan said.

"Well, he should be along any minute. I expected him half an hour ago."

"It's so unlike my father to be late."

"There's a lot of traffic out there," Dr. Jay said with a wave of his hand.

The expression on Regan's face, however, remained clearly troubled.

"Is anything wrong?" he asked her.

Regan walked closer to the doctor and lowered her voice, a useless exercise, since Alvirah Meehan could hear a mouse sneeze from three rooms away. "It's been kind of crazy," she began, and briefly explained about her mother's accident.

That's who she is! Alvirah thought: Nora Regan Reilly's daughter. Of course! I thought she looked familiar. She's a private investigator, just like me. Only she has a license. Alvirah sat up straight and cocked her head, praying they didn't move into Dr. Jay's private office.

"I thought I'd help my father do some shopping this afternoon after he saw you," Regan was saying. "Because we were planning to go to Hawaii, we don't have a Christmas tree or any food in the house."

I love Hawaii, Alvirah thought.

"What worries me," Regan continued, "is

that I can't reach my father on his cell phone, and he hasn't called my mother since he left her room at the hospital this morning. And now he isn't here. None of this is like him." Her voice was forlorn.

Uh-oh, Alvirah thought. She's right. Something's wrong.

"Well, let's wait and see," Dr. Jay said reassuringly. "He'll probably be here any minute. If he isn't, with all that happened today, it must mean that he simply forgot. He's obviously got a lot on his mind. I'm sure there's a logical explanation."

He looked over at Alvirah. "Willy should be ready to go in about fifteen minutes."

"Take your time," Alvirah said, grateful that Willy wasn't ready yet to walk out the door. She watched as Regan restlessly crossed to the window, looked out at the parking area, then sat in the straight-backed chair opposite the couch.

After a moment, Alvirah leaned forward. "I just want you to know that I've read every one of your mother's books and I love them. I was so sorry to hear about her accident. I can see you're worried about your father, but take my word, when something happens to a wife, husbands are useless. They forget everything."

Regan smiled slightly. "I hope you're right. I'm going to try calling him again." She pulled out her cell phone and dialed. "No answer," she said. "I'll try the hospital."

Let him be there or have called, Alvirah prayed as Regan spoke to her mother's nurse.

Regan put down the phone. "My mother is still asleep, which is good. My father hasn't called, which isn't." She stood up and once again walked to the window.

Alvirah wanted to say something comforting, but she knew there was nothing to be said. Had something happened to Luke Reilly?

Nearly twenty minutes later he was still not there.

"Okay, Alvirah, you can collect your patient," Dr. Jay said as he came down the hall, his hand under Willy's arm.

"Hi, honey," Willy said feebly.

"Take him home and let him sleep it off," Dr. Jay instructed. "And have a great holiday." He turned to Regan: "Any word?"

"Dr. Jay, I think it's obvious my father isn't going to make it today. I'll call a cab to take me to the house. I'm sure I'll catch up with him there."

"Don't you live here in Summit?" Alvirah asked, but didn't wait for an answer. "I know you do. It says so on the book jackets. We've got a car and driver outside. We'll drop you home. Come on, Willy."

Before she could protest, Regan found herself sitting next to Alvirah in the backseat of a sleek, black limo. Willy, his legs stretched out, his eyes shut, was leaning back on the opposite seat.

"I've taken driving lessons three times in the last three years," Alvirah explained. "The instructors always found excuses to pass me off on someone else." She laughed. "I can't blame them. You wouldn't believe all the parking cones I've flattened."

Regan smiled. She instinctively liked Alvirah and realized now that she had heard her name somewhere before. As the car pulled onto the main road, she said, "I feel as though I know you from somewhere. Your name is familiar."

Alvirah beamed. "I know you're a private investigator, and I guess you could say I'm kind of in your business. I've accidentally been around when the police needed help. Then I've written about what happened for the *Globe*. I'm what you might call 'a roving crime correspondent.'"

"Roving isn't the word," Willy volunteered, without opening his eyes. "Alvirah's always at full throttle, looking for trouble."

Regan laughed. "My mother sent me a couple of your columns. She enjoyed them and thought I'd be interested in the cases. She was right." Alvirah's coat was open. Regan leaned over. "Is that your famous pin with the hidden microphone?"

"I never leave home without it," Alvirah said proudly.

Regan reached into her pocket. "I'm going to try my father's office."

But there was nothing new: Austin Grady still hadn't heard from Luke.

With a sigh, Regan clicked off the phone.

For the next five minutes, Alvirah did a running commentary on the Christmas decorations of the various houses they passed. Finally Regan said, "That's our house up on the left."

"Oh, lovely," Alvirah breathed, craning her neck to get a better look. "A lot nicer than the houses I used to clean, I'll tell you that."

It was obvious that no one was home. The Reilly house, unlike its neighbors, was in total darkness.

The long driveway extended to the garages at the rear of the house. The chauffeur stopped at the walk that led to the front door.

"Let me go in with you while you check your messages, Regan," Alvirah said, a note of concern in her voice.

Regan knew what Alvirah meant. If there had been an accident, there might be a call on the machine. "I'll be fine, Alvirah. I can't thank you enough. You need to get Willy home."

Reluctantly Alvirah watched Regan go up the steps and disappear into the house. The car began to move slowly down the driveway. They were just turning back onto the street when the soft ring of a cell phone made Alvirah look around quickly. I don't have mine with me, she thought. Then she spotted it. The phone Regan had been using was on the seat next to her, its green light flashing.

I'll answer it, she thought. I bet it's her father. She picked it up and flipped it open.

"Hello," she boomed happily.

"Regan?" The voice was deep and raspy.

"I'll get her," Alvirah said, as she yelled for the driver to go back. "Is this her father?"

"It's a message from him."

"Oh, good," Alvirah shouted.

As Alvirah jumped out of the car and ran up the walk, she did not hear C.B.'s comment to Luke: "Whoever answered your daughter's phone has a voice like a foghorn."

Fred Torres hung up his uniform and closed the door of his locker with a decisive snap. "That's it for two weeks, Vince," he said to his partner. "It's anchors away for me."

"I wish I were going sailing in the Caribbean," Vince Lugano said as he pulled on a sweater. "While you're on deck with a beer in your hand, I'll be putting together a fire engine and a dollhouse."

The tiny lines around Fred's dark brown eyes crinkled when he smiled. "You love every minute of it," he said.

"I know I do," Vince agreed, looking with affection at the man who had become his best friend since they were sworn in as police officers in Hoboken, New Jersey, six years ago.

Fred was twenty-eight years old, just under six feet tall, lean and muscular. His olive complexion, dark hair, and general good looks made him the perfect target for well-meaning friends who just happened to have an available sister or cousin. He was about to begin his final term at Seton Hall Law School after the holidays.

Vince, the same age as his partner, was two inches taller and twenty pounds heavier, with sandy hair and hazel eyes. He had never been interested in anyone except his high-school sweetheart, whom he married five years ago.

"What time do you leave?" Vince asked.

"I've got an eight o'clock flight tomorrow morning."

"You'll be at Mike's party tonight?"

"Sure."

"See you there."

Fred had intended to drive straight home to his apartment in a small brownstone at the south end of town. But he impulsively stopped when he turned the corner that led to his street and spotted the dazzling array of poinsettias in the flower-shop window. It won't take that long, he assured himself as he went in and selected a plant. He had met Rosita Gonzalez at a party a month ago, and they'd gone out to dinner together a couple of times since. He had invited her to the party tonight, but she didn't have anyone available to baby-sit.

As he got back in the car, he smiled, thinking of her and remembering the night they had met. They both had arrived at that party at the same time. He had parked behind her. She had been driving a glistening black limousine. As they walked up the steps together, he introduced himself and said, "You certainly arrive in style."

"Wait till you see what I go home in," Rosita had joked. "Among my activities, I drive a limo. One of the guys I work with will be dropping off my car and taking this one."

When the party ended, Fred had walked her out to her twelve-year-old Chevy. "Just call me Cinderella," she said with a smile.

She seemed so young, with her long, dark hair and infectious laugh, that it was hard for him to believe that she was the mother of two little boys.

"Does Cinderella have a phone number?" he asked.

And now, as he found himself driving to her house, Fred wondered if this was such a good idea. There was more traffic than he had expected, and he hadn't begun to pack for his trip. He admitted to himself that showing up at her house might be sending Rosita the wrong message. He had no intention of getting too involved with anyone at this point. For the foreseeable future, he wouldn't have enough time to devote to a relationship—especially one that involves kids, he thought.

Rosita lived in a modest garden-apartment complex not far from Summit. The shortest day of the year was yesterday, Fred thought. I can believe it. At 4:30 it was completely dark. He parked in a visitor's space, went up the path, shifted the festively wrapped plant to one hand, and rang the bell of Rosita's ground-floor unit.

Inside the apartment, seventeen-year-old Nicole Parma was in a state of near hysteria. At the sound of the chimes, she rushed to the door. "Your mother probably forgot her key," she yelled to Chris and Bobby, both of whom were sitting cross-legged in front of the television set.

Neither one of them looked up. "Mommy

never forgets her key," six-year-old Chris said matter-of-factly to his younger brother. Only eleven months apart in age, they could pass for twins.

"But Mommy said she'd be home by now," Bobby said, his voice low and troubled. "I don't like Nicole. She won't play with us like Sarah does." Sarah was their regular baby-sitter.

Forgetting all of Rosita's warnings about not opening the door until she knew who was on the other side, Nicole flung it open. Fred did not miss her look of acute disappointment when she saw him standing there.

"Is Mrs. Gonzalez home?" He took a step back, not wanting to suggest that he would make any attempt to enter unless invited.

"No, and I expected her over an hour ago!" The answer was almost a wail.

"It's Fred!" Chris shouted, jumping up.

"Fred!" Bobby echoed.

Both boys were at the door, crowding past Nicole to greet him.

"That's Mommy's friend!" Chris told her. "He's a policeman. He arrests people."

"Hello, you two." Fred looked back at Nicole. "I just wanted to drop this plant off for the boys' mother."

The boys were pulling at Fred's jacket.

"I can tell it's all right if you come in," Nicole said. "Rosita should be here any minute."

"Mommy better be here soon," Chris volunteered as Fred stepped inside. "Nicole's freaking out. She's got to get ready for her dance tonight and doesn't want to look ugly 'cause she lovvvvves her boyfriend. Ha ha ha, Nicole."

If looks could kill, Fred thought, as the young girl glared at Chris.

"You brat! I told you to hang up the phone when I was talking before."

"Kissy, kissy, see you later, I can hardly wait." Chris made a loud smacking sound with his lips.

"Kissy, kissy," Bobby repeated, mimicking his brother's sing-song tone.

"Come on, guys," Fred said. "That's enough." He saw the tears shining in Nicole's eyes. "You're running late, I guess."

"Really late," she confirmed, as her mouth

quivered and the tears began to roll down her cheeks.

"Hasn't Rosita called?"

"No. I tried her cell phone, but there was no answer."

"She must be on her way home." The same impulse that had made him stop at the flower shop elicited the next words from his mouth: "Look, I've got some time. I can wait with the kids." He started to pull out his police ID. "You can see the boys know me."

Chris ran over to an end table and picked up a framed picture. It was a group shot taken at the party where Fred and his mother had met. "There he is!" he cried, pointing at the photograph and running over to Nicole. "That's him in the back row."

Nicole barely glanced at Fred's ID or at the good-times snapshot before she was out the door, one arm already in the sleeve of her coat.

"She's a pain," Chris observed. "All she did was talk on the phone with her boyfriend. Yuck."

"She wouldn't play checkers," Bobby said quietly.

"She *wouldn't?*" Fred said, his voice suitably incredulous. "I *love* to play checkers. Let's find a place to put Mommy's plant, then we'll see if you two can beat me. Red or black?"

When Regan opened the door, Alvirah waved the cell phone at her. "The call you've been waiting for!" she said breathlessly.

Regan grabbed the phone. "Dad?"

Without hesitation, Alvirah stepped inside and closed the door. I just want to make sure everything's all right, she told herself. But an instant later, judging by the look on Regan's face, she was certain that something was very, very wrong.

Instead of the voice Regan had been expecting to hear, she was chilled by a curt command, "You'll talk to him in a minute. Get rid of whoever is with you."

This isn't the police or a hospital calling, Regan thought. She made a snap decision to let Alvirah stay. Not that she would have had much choice. Alvirah's two feet were practically glued to the marble floor. But the concern in her eyes made Regan glad for her presence. "Thank you, Alvirah," she said loudly. "I won't keep you." She reached past her and noisily opened and closed the door.

That guy doesn't want anyone else to overhear what he's telling Regan, Alvirah thought. Yanking open her coat, she quickly unhooked the sunburst pin that she always wore, turned on its tiny hidden microphone, and handed the pin to Regan.

Regan's eyes widened at first, and then she nodded, realizing what Alvirah intended. "Let me talk to my father," she said as she held the sunburst pin next to her ear and the earpiece of the phone.

"Not so fast," the gruff voice snapped. "I've got a list of demands."

In the houseboat, Petey nodded his approval. "Kind of like a top-ten list," he whispered to Luke, with a friendly punch to his manacled arm.

C.B. glared at him.

"Sorry."

C.B. continued. "You must have one million dollars in cash by tomorrow afternoon. It must be in one-hundred-dollar bills, in a duffel bag. At six o'clock on the dot, and I *mean* on the dot, be in your car driving into Central Park at the Sixth Avenue entrance. You will receive a phone call telling you where to leave the money. Do not call the police if you want to see your father and his cutie-pie chauffeur again. Once the money has been received and counted, you'll get a call about where to pick them up."

"I want to talk to my father now," Regan demanded.

C.B. walked over to Luke and held the phone to his ear. "Say hello to your little girl. And tell her she'd better do as she's told."

It was with heartsick relief that Regan heard Luke's calm voice. "Hi, Regan. We're both okay so far. Your mother will know where to get the money quickly."

Before Regan could answer, C.B. pulled the phone away. "That's enough from you. It's Rosita's turn." He was at her side. "Say hello to Regan."

The words rushed out of Rosita's mouth. "Take care of my boys."

Again C.B. didn't give Regan a chance to respond. "Okay, Regan Reilly," he said. "We've got a date. Six o'clock tomorrow. Right?"

"I'll be there," Regan said. "But I have to talk to my father and Rosita again before I drop that money." Trying to keep the mounting fury out of her voice, it was her turn to ask, "Right?"

"You've got it, Regan." The line went dead.

"Beverly, I feel like nine miles of torn-up road," Nora told her nurse as she looked into the mirror of her small compact and applied lipstick.

Beverly Carter smiled. "You look fine, Mrs. Reilly," she said reassuringly, fluffing up Nora's pillows. "I'm glad you slept so long. You seem a lot better than you did this morning."

"I certainly feel better," Nora said, glancing at her watch. "It's 6:30. Let's turn on the news and see what else has happened in the world today."

"It's me," Regan announced as she pushed open the door which had been slightly ajar.

Nora's face brightened. "You're early. That's great. Where's Dad?"

Regan hesitated. "He's been delayed."

"Mrs. Reilly, I'll be outside if you need me," the nurse said.

"Beverly, why don't you go have dinner?" Regan suggested. "We'll be visiting for a while. Take your time."

When the nurse left, Regan closed the door and slowly turned around to face her mother. Her expression was troubled.

"Regan, what is it?" Nora asked, her voice suddenly panicky. "What's wrong? Has something happened to Dad?"

"Mom, I . . ." Regan began, searching for the right words.

"He's not dead, is he?" Please God, Nora thought, not that.

"No, no—nothing like that," Regan said swiftly. "I spoke to him a couple of hours ago."

"Then what? What is it?"

"There's no simple way to tell you. He's been kidnapped, and someone called me with a ransom demand."

"Mother of God," Nora whispered. She clasped her hands against her chest as if to shield herself from another blow. "How did it happen? What do you know?"

Regan hated to see the pain on her mother's face as she related the little she knew about Luke's disappearance: her attempts to reach him; her decision to go to Dr. Jay's office; the ride to their home in Summit with Alvirah Meehan, whose articles about crime Nora had sent to her; and finally, the call on her cell phone demanding the million-dollar ransom.

"If Rosita's with him, and he didn't make it to the funeral, then the kidnapping must have happened right after he left here this morning." Nora's eyes welled with tears. She looked out the window. It was impossible to believe her husband of thirty-five years was out there somewhere in that cold, dark night, at the mercy of someone who might at any moment snuff out his life. "We can get the million dollars. But Regan, we have to let the police in on this."

"I know. Alvirah is friendly with the guy who runs the Major Case Squad here in Manhattan. He would be the right person to call. That squad handles high-profile kidnappings. Alvirah is with me. She's waiting outside."

"Bring her in," Nora said, "but wait a minute. Who else knows about this?"

"Nobody except Alvirah's husband and his sister, who's a nun. She's staying with him right now. After the dental surgery, he's pretty out of it."

"What about Rosita's children? Who's minding them?"

"I got her phone number from Dad's Rolodex," Regan replied. "When I called, I spoke to a friend of hers who said he had just relieved the baby-sitter. I only told him that Rosita had been detained, but I could tell that he suspects something is seriously wrong."

"As long as the kids are all right for the moment." Nora took a deep breath as she tried to pull herself up on the bed. Damn this leg, she thought. To be trapped like this when every fiber of her being screamed for her to take some action. "Let's get Alvirah in here," she said. "We'll get in touch with her connection in the police department and then get a million dollars together."

Regan had scarcely opened the door before Alvirah bustled into the room, walked over to the bed, and gave Nora Reilly's hand a reassuring squeeze. "We're going to get your husband and that girl back safe and sound," she promised.

There was something about Alvirah Meehan that made Nora believe she could do just that.

"Last year I lectured at John Jay College about the case of a baby whose kidnapping I solved," Alvirah told her. "The newspapers called it the baby bunting case because I found the bunting the baby had been wearing when she was abducted from the hospital."

"I remember that case," Nora said. "That one was right around Christmas too."

Alvirah nodded. "Yes, it was. We got the baby back on Christmas Eve. Jack Reilly was at my lecture that day and invited me to have lunch with him. He's the grandest fellow, and so smart. Only thirty-four years old and already in charge of the Major Case Squad with the rank of captain." She reached for the phone. "He'll know how to handle this. He works out of One Police Plaza."

"Reilly?" Nora asked.

"Can you believe that? And he spells it just like you do too. I asked him that day if you were related." Alvirah waved her hand dismissively. "You're not."

Regan smiled slightly as she sat on the edge of the bed and closed her hand over her mother's outstretched fingers. Together they listened to Alvirah's refusal to take no for an answer.

"I don't care if he's not due back until Monday, " Alvirah was saying. "Nobody else will do. I want you to page him now. Here's the message: 'It is absolutely urgent that you call Alvirah Meehan immediately at . . .' what's the phone number here, Regan?"

"Give him my cell-phone number," Regan replied. "It's 310-555-4237."

Alvirah replaced the receiver. "Knowing Jack Reilly, I'll hear from him in the next ten minutes."

Eight minutes later the cell phone rang.

Jack Reilly did not even mind the particularly impossible traffic on the East River Drive. His suitcase was in the trunk, and he was headed for his parents' house in Bedford. It was evident that the usual one-hour trip would take almost double that time tonight. The holiday exodus from Manhattan was well under way.

Of his six siblings, he hadn't seen two of his brothers and one of his sisters since August, when they'd all been at the family home on Martha's Vineyard. Counting spouses and children, there'd be nineteen of them under the same roof for the next four days. I just hope we don't end up killing each other, he thought with a grin. The weather reports were indicating a heavy storm over the weekend.

He jammed on the brake. Despite the bumper-to-bumper traffic, the car on his right had made a sudden move and cut in front of him. "You'll get there a lot faster now, won't you pal?" he muttered, looking out at the mass of red taillights that extended as far as the eye could see.

Jack Reilly had sandy hair that tended to curl, hazel eyes more green than brown, even features with a strong jaw, and a broad-shouldered, six-foot-two body. Keenly intelligent, quick-witted, and with a sharp sense of humor honed by growing up in a large family, he had undeniable charisma. Both at social gatherings and at work, his laid-back presence somehow filled the room.

His easygoing manner disappeared, however, when he was on a case. The grandson of a New York police lieutenant, after graduating from Boston College he surprised his family by making the decision to pursue a career in law enforcement. In the twelve years that followed, he had risen through the ranks from patrolman to captain and head of the Major Case Squad. Along the way he also had picked up two master's degrees. His goal was to become police commissioner of New York, and few who knew him doubted he would make it.

His pager beeped. He had taken it off and laid it in the well of the car's console. He picked it up, glanced at the number, and was not at all happy to see that it was his office trying to reach him. Now what? he thought as he pulled out his cell phone.

Fifteen minutes later he was tapping on the door of Nora's hospital room. Alvirah ran over to open it. "I'm so glad you got here so fast!" she exclaimed.

"I was right by an exit on the FDR Drive," Jack said as he greeted Alvirah with a peck on the cheek. He looked past her and recognized the face of Nora Regan Reilly. He knew the very attractive young woman standing beside her had to be her daughter. He had seen that same anguished expression on the faces of the relatives of other kidnap victims. They wanted help, not sympathy.

"I'm Jack Reilly," he said as he shook hands with both of them. "I'm terribly sorry about what's happened. I know you want to get right down to business."

"Just the facts, ma'am," Regan said with a ghost of a smile. "Yes, we do."

I like him, Nora thought as he took out a notebook. He's solid. He knows what he's doing. With a pang, she watched Jack Reilly glance around and pull up the chair Luke had occupied that very morning.

Immediately after they made the phone call to Regan Reilly, C.B. and Petey put on their coats and hats. As C.B. gratuitously explained to Luke and Rosita, it was happy hour at the bar in Edgewater at which he had met Petey some months earlier.

"Yeah," Petey brayed. "And wouldn't ya

know, Mr. Reilly, we met because of you."

"How did I manage that?" Luke asked, an edge in his voice as he flexed his fingers and shifted the handcuffs to move them past his wrist bones.

"I'll tell ya. Talk about coincidence. A couple of weeks after I painted your viewing room, I'm sitting at Elsie's Hideaway, and there's C.B., sitting at the other end of the bar, drowning his many sorrows."

"You were in a pretty sorry state yourself," C.B. interjected.

"Yeah," Petey agreed. "I gotta admit. At the time I wasn't feeling so good about life myself."

"Losers," Rosita muttered under her breath.

"Huh?" Petey asked.

"Nothing."

"Come on Petey," C.B. said impatiently. "Let's go. The cheese and crackers will be gone before we get there."

"The crowd that place attracts—vultures, every one of them," Petey said, shaking his head with disgust. Hellbent on finishing his story, he continued: "So I said to myself, I've seen that guy before. But where? Then I said to myself, wowie—I know where. It was at that lively joint of yours, Mr. Reilly. Turns out he and that old buzzard of an uncle had stopped by while I was doing the paint job."

"What a beautiful story," Rosita said sarcastically.

"Yeah. So I bring my beer over, friendly like, and we got to talking." Petey's voice changed. "And he told me you were all making jokes about that nice color I painted your room—and after I'd mixed it special for you."

C.B. opened the door to the deck. "When Uncle Cuthbert took a look at that room, he said he'd rather be waked in a fun house."

"That really hurt my feelings," Petey lamented. "But it all worked out for the best." His face brightened. "If he and his uncle hadn't poked their noses into the room, I wouldn't have met C.B. And now we're gonna start a new life with your million dollars, Mr. Reilly. We'll be on the beach, meeting gorgeous girls and everything."

"Good for you," Luke snapped. "Does that

radio over there work?" He nodded his head in the direction of the little kitchen.

Petey glanced at the top of the refrigerator where a scratched and painfully old radio was perched precariously. "Sometimes. If the batteries are working." He reached up and flipped it on. "What's your fancy? News or music?"

"News," Luke said.

"There'd better be no bulletin about your disappearance," C.B. said darkly.

"I assure you there won't be."

Petey twisted the dial until he found an all-news station. The sound was raspy and tinny, but clear enough to be understood. "Enjoy," he said as he followed C.B. out the door.

After they left, Luke and Rosita listened to the traffic and weather reports. A nor'easter was making its way up the East Coast. According to the forecast, it would be in Washington, D.C., tomorrow and was expected to hit the New York area on Christmas Eve.

"Listen up, you last-minute shoppers," the announcer cautioned. "We expect between eight and ten inches of snow, high winds, and icy road conditions. So it would be wise to get all your shopping completed by tomorrow afternoon. On Saturday the roads are going to be hazardous, so play it safe and make plans to stay home by the tree."

"I was going to put up our tree tonight, with my sons," Rosita said quietly. "Mr. Reilly, do you think we'll be home on Christmas Eve?"

"Nora and Regan will make sure that the money is paid. And I really do believe these guys intend to let us go. Or at least they'll tell someone where to find us once they have the money in their hands."

Luke did not tell Rosita what was now becoming his greatest fear. Stupid as they were, C.B. and Petey would never disclose his and Rosita's whereabouts until they were safely beyond the long arm of the law. This probably meant they'd be heading to a country that would not extradite them. If we're still here on Saturday, Luke thought, this river might be loaded with chunks of ice that could easily tear holes in this rotting tub. It had already been an unusually cold December. A storm would pull the ice that had already formed up north down the river.

Three long hours later, C.B. and Petey reappeared, this time carrying bags from McDonald's.

"Elsie put out some spread," Petey rejoiced. "Normally, she's a Scrooge, but I guess miracles happen during the holidays. Although she did get annoyed when I tried to fix a little doggie bag for you two. That's why we picked up some Big Macs."

"Set it out for them," C.B. ordered. "Then get blankets and pillows from the bedroom. As soon as they eat and get settled for the night, I'm out of here. And you get a good night's sleep too, Petey. We've got a big day tomorrow."

"We sure do," Petey said, his speech slightly slurred thanks to Elsie's eggnog. *"Who Wants to Be a Millionaire?* We do! C.B. and Petey, New Jersey's finest! But who needs Regis? We've got Luke Reilly."

The length of the chains made it possible

for them to lie back, Luke on the banquette and Rosita across the way on the couch. For hours Luke lay awake. Petey's tumultuous snoring from the tiny bedroom reverberated through the drafty cabin, but somehow it was easier to take than the sound of Rosita crying softly in her sleep.

"I think we're all agreed," Jack Reilly said, summing up the hour they had been together in Nora's room. "Mrs. Reilly . . ." he began.

"Nora," she corrected. Maybe someday Mom, she thought with a quick flash of humor. Oh God, I can just imagine what Luke would say if I told him that in the middle of his kidnapping, I'm trying, as usual, to fix Regan up. *When* I tell him, not *if,* she corrected herself. But one thing was certain: Luke would like Jack Reilly.

"Nora," he continued. "We've canceled your private nurses. You might be getting phone calls here about Luke and Rosita, and the fewer people who know about this, the better. Now I want you to try and get some rest. If you think of anyone who might hold a grudge, for whatever reason, against you or Luke, or even Regan, call me immediately."

Nora shook her head and raised her hands helplessly. "I just can't imagine."

"I understand. Of course, we'll be checking into Rosita's ex-husband as well," he said, then paused. "And then again, this could just be someone who knows that you have money."

"That's why when the lottery commission asked me and Willy to do a commercial about how happy we are with all our money, I told them to go jump in a lake," Alvirah announced. "Of course, I'd already been on plenty of shows, but enough's enough."

"You're right, Alvirah," Jack assured her. "Nora, first thing in the morning, you'll contact your broker and arrange a million-dollar loan against your stock portfolio. You're sure they won't start asking questions?"

"It's our money," she said firmly. "Nobody tells us what to do with it."

Regan was glad to see that her mother's fighting spirit was returning.

"We'll alert the Federal Reserve bank to start assembling the ransom money," Jack said. Then he turned to Regan. "You and Alvirah are going to Rosita's home now to speak with whomever is baby-sitting her sons. You'll have to use your discretion about how much to tell him. Our people should have her phone covered by now. If this baby-sitter wants to leave, we can send a social worker over."

"I have the perfect person for the job," Alvirah said triumphantly. "Sister Maeve Marie. She works with Cordelia, Willy's sister. Maeve's great with kids, and she used to be on the New York City police force. And like Sister Cordelia, she can make the Sphinx look like a blabbermouth."

Jack smiled. "Good. And Regan, after checking out Rosita's home situation, you and Alvirah are going to meet your father's assistant at his office."

Regan nodded. At Jack's request, she had phoned Austin Grady and obtained the license number of the car Rosita had been driving, as well as the E-Z Pass account number. Jack had already called this information in to his office.

They had agreed that Austin had to be fully informed, but the only thing Regan had told him so far was that there was a serious problem. "He'll be waiting there for us," she said.

"You'll bring the car you'll be driving for the ransom drop back into the city tonight," Jack confirmed.

"Yes. My mother's BMW."

"One of my guys will meet you later at your parents' apartment on Central Park South. He'll take the car downtown to be bird-dogged."

All three women knew "bird-dogging" was the slang for placing an electronic device attached by a magnet under the car so it could be tracked by a helicopter. Another tracking device would be placed with the ransom money, so that once it was transferred, the money could be followed to wherever the kidnappers were taking it.

The hope, of course, was that the kidnappers would then lead them to where the hostages were being kept.

"Alvirah, let me have the recording you made of the ransom call," Jack said.

"I want a copy of it first thing in the morning," Alvirah ordered as she unsnapped the cassette from the back of her sunburst pin.

"Another brilliant move by Alvirah," Jack said with affection, holding up the tiny cassette. "Even if he tried to disguise it, we have the kidnapper's voice on tape, and our tech guys may be able to learn something from the background sounds."

As Alvirah beamed at him, he kissed her cheek. "My team will be waiting for me down at One Police Plaza." He touched Nora's hand. "Try not to worry too much." He turned to Regan. "We'll keep each other posted."

When he left, the room suddenly felt empty. There was a momentary pause, and then it was as though the three women had the same thought at once.

There was no time to waste.

It had been a busy day for Ernest Bumbles, president and chairman of the board of the Seed-Plant-Bloom-and-Blossom Society of the Garden State of New Jersey. He awoke in the morning to the happy realization that it wasn't all just a dream. Cuthbert Boniface Goodloe had indeed left virtually his entire estate to the society.

The joyous news had reached them only hours after dear Mr. Goodloe had breathed his last. Ernest had received a call from Goodloe's lawyer with "sad news and glad news," as he put it. "Mr. Goodloe is no longer with us," he said with a sigh, "but his association with the Blossoms gave him so much pleasure for the past three years that he has left virtually his entire estate of a bit over one million dollars to your society."

Ernest had been busy mulching his thistles in the greenhouse behind his home when his wife, Dolly, had come running out with the portable phone. A sufferer of severe allergies, she covered her face with a surgical mask whenever she entered the greenhouse.

"Bumby," she cried, her voice muffled, "a call for you. He sounds smart, so it must be important. A-choo."

Even with the mask, the mulch always got to her.

The reason Mr. Withers had phoned before Goodloe had finished knocking on the pearly gates soon became clear. It had been Mr. Goodloe's express wish that the Blossoms turn out in full force for his wake, his funeral, and the luncheon to follow. Needless to say, Blossoms all across the state had dropped their shovels, ripped off their gardening gloves, and gathered to mourn their now beloved benefactor.

In the emergency board of directors meeting called by Ernest before the services, one of the members pointed out that were it not for Luke Reilly, none of this would have happened. Three years earlier, Reilly had been feted as Man of the Year at their annual banquet, in recognition of the fact that his three funeral homes were a boon to the local floral industry.

The night of the award, Cuthbert Boniface Goodloe had been his guest at one of the tables Luke had been strongly encouraged to buy.

Goodloe had been so enchanted by the society's four-minute film on the positive effects of talking to your plants that he had signed up to become a member that very night.

At the meeting after Goodloe's death, they had unanimously voted that in recognition of Luke Reilly's networking skills, he would be presented a Blossom Society Proclamation at the post-funeral luncheon. Much to their disappointment, however, Reilly did not show up. His associate, Austin Grady, had informed them of Luke's wife's unfortunate accident.

Ernest was especially disappointed. He had wanted to put the framed proclamation— enscribed on the finest parchment money could buy and surrounded by dried flowers— in Luke's hands personally. He had looked forward with great anticipation to seeing the thrilled expression on his face when he unwrapped the proclamation and read the message.

TO ALL WHO READ THESE WORDS

Greetings and Salutations.
Be It Known That Luke Reilly,
By Virtue of Bringing Our Beloved
Benefactor
Cuthbert Boniface Goodloe
Into the Fold of the Blossoms,
Is now and forever,
By the Authority and Recommendation
of the Board of Directors,
Freely and Without Reservation,
A Lifelong Member of the
Seed-Plant-Bloom-and-Blossom Society
of the Garden State of New Jersey
With all its honors, rights
and privileges thereof.
Presented on this Twenty-second Day of
December, at the dawn of the Second
Millennium,
E Pluribus Unum

When he had not appeared at the luncheon, Grady had assured Ernest that Reilly undoubtedly would drop by the funeral parlor sometime in the late afternoon. Ernest went there at five, but still there was no sign of him. Grady urged him to leave the festively wrapped gift, but that was absolutely out of the question. There are few times in one's life, Ernest thought, when you get to see pure, unadulterated joy on the face of one's fellow man. If it was humanly possible to see Luke Reilly before he and Dolly left for her mother's house on Christmas Eve and to give him that gift in person, he was going to do it.

"Bumby," Dolly said as she poured him a second cup of coffee, "if you want to stop by the funeral parlor before we go caroling with my choral group, we have to hurry."

"You're right, as usual." He gulped down the coffee and pushed back his chair.

Twenty minutes later he was back in the office of the funeral parlor inquiring about Luke Reilly's whereabouts.

"I'm afraid he's been delayed," Austin Grady said.

Bumbles thought he detected a slight irritation in the other man's voice. He was tempted to explain the contents of the package, but to do so would risk spoiling the surprise.

"I'll be back," he promised.

"We close at nine," Grady warned. "That's only a little over an hour from now."

"Tomorrow morning then," Bumbles said cheerfully as he carefully picked up the package he had rested on a chair and disappeared out the door, fragments of the proclamation running through his head. ". . . Be it known that Luke Reilly, by virtue of bringing our beloved benefactor Cuthbert Boniface Goodloe into the fold of the Blossoms . . ."

Bumbles couldn't wait until the whole world knew just what Luke Reilly had done for them.

It was 9:30 in the evening when their car pulled up to the garden apartment complex where Rosita lived. Between them, Alvirah and Regan had worked out the scenario they would follow once inside. They needed to size up the man who was with the children. If he turned out to be very close to Rosita, they would tell him what had happened. If he was simply helping out till she got home, they would tell him they had Sister Maeve Marie ready to jump in a car and drive over from New York.

Nora had told them that Rosita's mother was now living in San Juan with the rest of her family. Jack warned that it would be unwise to notify any of them yet. "They can't do anything to help," he pointed out, "and it could create a terrible problem if word of this got out."

"Be careful," the driver warned as he opened the door and offered his hand to help Alvirah out. "It's pretty slippery here."

"He's such a nice man," Alvirah said to Regan as they walked up the path. "I felt funny

90

when I pushed the button that raised the partition in the car so he couldn't hear us."

"So did I," Regan said. "That's why I'm glad we're picking up my mother's car right after we leave here. We've got to be able to talk freely if Jack Reilly or anyone else calls."

Alvirah knew that by "anyone else," Regan meant the kidnappers.

The driver was right; there were patches of ice on the path. Regan tucked her arm under Alvirah's elbow to keep her from slipping.

At the entrance to Rosita's ground-floor apartment, they looked at each other for a moment, then Alvirah pressed her finger firmly on the bell.

Inside, Fred was sitting on the couch, a sleepy little boy on either side of him. Hearing the bell, Chris sat up. "Maybe Mommy did forget her key," he said in a tired, hopeful voice.

Bobby rubbed his eyes as he straightened up. "Is Mommy home?"

Fred felt his throat tighten. How many times in his job had he been the one to ring the bell, bearing news of an accident or worse?

Regan Reilly had been evasive on the phone. Was that what she was coming to tell them?

He experienced a fleeting instant of profound relief when he opened the door and realized there were two figures standing outside in the dark. The relief, however, was painfully short-lived. An older woman was standing next to the one he knew had to be Reilly. Perhaps a social worker, he thought with a sinking heart. If so, that means something terrible has happened to Rosita.

"Fred Torres?" the younger woman asked.

He nodded.

"I'm Regan Reilly."

"And I'm Alvirah Meehan," Alvirah said heartily.

"Come in," Fred said quietly.

Alvirah preceded Regan. She glanced around the room. Two little boys with dark hair were standing together by the couch, the expression in both sets of large brown eyes apprehensive and disappointed.

"Now which one of you is Chris and which one is Bobby?" she asked, a warm smile brightening her face. "Let me guess. Mrs. Reilly told me all about you. Chris is the oldest, so that must be you." She pointed to the taller of the two.

Chris smiled tentatively.

"I'm Bobby," the younger one said, moving closer to his brother.

"Where's Mommy?" Chris asked.

"Did you know that Mrs. Reilly broke her leg last night?" Alvirah asked, dropping her voice as though she were telling an important secret.

"Mommy told us this morning before she left," Bobby said with a yawn. "Mommy said that tonight we would make a card and send it to Mrs. Reilly."

"Well, Mrs. Reilly needs your mommy's help tonight," Alvirah said softly. "So she just wants you two to go to bed, and she'll be home as soon as she can."

"I want her to come home now," Bobby said, suddenly on the verge of tears.

"Mrs. Reilly is nice," Chris told him. "It's all right if Mommy stays with her when she's sick."

"But when do we get to decorate our tree?" Bobby asked plaintively.

"In plenty of time for Christmas," Alvirah assured them.

Regan had been watching. Alvirah knows exactly how to handle the kids, she thought. Walking over to them, she said, "I'm Mrs. Reilly's daughter, and I'm so glad your mommy is with my mother right now. Having your mommy there makes mine feel so much better."

"Then your daddy is Mr. Reilly," Chris said. "I like his cars."

"Especially the reeeealy long ones," Bobby added, yawning again.

"You know, I think both you boys look pretty tired," Alvirah observed, "and that's just the way I feel too."

Fred knew exactly what these two women were doing—they were reassuring the boys about their mother, then they wanted them out of earshot.

"Okay, guys, bedtime," he said, putting his hands around two small shoulders.

Bobby peered up at him anxiously. "You're not going to leave us, are you Fred?"

Fred bent down and looked into the two distressed faces. He hesitated, then said firmly, "Not until Mommy gets home."

While he was settling the boys in their room, Alvirah went into the tiny kitchen and put the kettle on the stove. "I need a cup of tea," she announced. "How about you, Regan?"

"Good idea. I'd love one." Regan glanced around the cozy yet slightly cluttered apartment. The brightly slipcovered couch and matching chair with their rounded arms and thick pillows looked wonderfully comfortable. A corner with shelves had been turned over to the children's videotapes and toys. But it was the sight of the Christmas tree, already in the stand, just waiting to be decorated, that clutched at her heart.

By the time the kettle began to whistle, Fred Torres had emerged from the boys' bedroom. "I promise I'll be right out here, guys," he said as he closed the door.

Alvirah poked her head out of the kitchen. "I'm making myself at home, Fred. A cup of tea?"

"Yes, thanks." He looked at Regan. "Tell me what's going on."

"What is your relationship to Rosita?" she asked.

"We've had a couple of dates." He pulled out his police ID. "I'm a cop. Rosita's in trouble. What is it?"

Alvirah came into the living room holding a tray. "I'll put it right here on the table. Why don't we all sit down?"

Fred sat straight backed on the edge of the club chair, Alvirah and Regan opposite him on the couch.

"Fred is a police officer, Alvirah," Regan said, then looked directly at him. "Rosita and my father were kidnapped sometime this morning. We believe it must have happened between ten o'clock, when my father left the hospital after visiting my mother, and twelve o'clock, when he was supposed to show up for a funeral."

She looked down at the cup she was holding. "At about 4:30, I received a ransom call demanding one million dollars by tomorrow afternoon. We've already met with the head of the Major Case Squad in New York."

Fred felt as though he had been punched in the stomach. "Kidnapped?" he said, his tone disbelieving, his face registering shock. He glanced down the hall at the closed bedroom door. "Those poor kids."

Alvirah turned to Fred and put her hand on the sunburst pin on her suit jacket; on the drive out to Rosita's apartment, she had inserted a new cassette. "Fred, do you mind if I record our conversation? Sometimes we say things that don't seem significant at the moment, but that really turn out to be significant later. In some cases I have worked on, listening to the tapes over and over has led to the break we needed."

"Go ahead," he said. Ignoring the cup of tea cooling in front of him, he listened intently while Regan and Alvirah filled him in on everything they knew.

"Do they have any idea who could have done this?" he asked.

"None at all," Regan said. "We think this is just about money, though. My father has no enemies that we know of."

"Did Rosita discuss her ex-husband with you?" Alvirah asked. "From what Nora told us, he's something of a ne'er-do-well who could probably use some money."

"I only met Rosita last month, at a party. We've been out to dinner twice. She didn't want to talk about him. Today the kids told me they hadn't seen him in a long time."

"He sounds like a real charmer," Regan said. "The police are going to be checking him out very carefully."

Fred shook his head. "I hope for the kids' sake he's not involved. Rosita didn't give any indication that she'd had any trouble with him lately. When we went to dinner, we talked about the usual things. She really likes her job." He nodded at Regan. "She said your father is the best boss anyone could have. And that he keeps his cool no matter what happens. But there was nothing she said that would indicate he was having any real problem with anyone."

Regan put down her cup. "When we leave here, Alvirah and I are going over to my father's office to meet with his associate. We're going to dig around to see if perhaps there are any business problems that could be relevant. It's possible the kidnapper is a disgruntled person, perhaps even a former employee, who has a grudge against my father."

"That's sensible, and it's almost the only thing you can do. The hardest part of a kidnapping is having to wait for the kidnappers to make the next move," Fred added angrily.

"I have to keep busy," Regan said matter-of-factly, as she and Alvirah got up.

"My sister-in-law is a nun," Alvirah told Fred as she gathered the cups. "There's a young woman in her convent, Sister Maeve Marie, who was a cop before she realized she had a vocation. Maeve is wonderful with kids; she can be here in an hour if you want to go home."

Fred thought about the party he was missing, the plane he was supposed to catch in the morning, the long-planned sail with his friends. All those things seemed so trivial now.

He thought about Rosita, her dark hair spilling on her shoulders, her warm smile as she joked. "Just call me Cinderella."

Not every kidnapping ended happily, he thought. In fact, many did not.

He shook his head. "You heard me tell the boys—I'm not leaving."

It had been said of Alvin Luck that his name didn't suit him. Fifty-two years old, with thinning brown hair, a slight frame, and an amiable but timid smile, he lived with his mother in a rent-controlled apartment on Manhattan's West Eighty-sixth Street. The author of twelve unpublished suspense novels, he eked out a living doing temporary jobs while waiting for his break in the publishing world.

Given the season, his current odd job was to don a red suit and white beard and ho-ho-ho his way through the toy section of a discount department store near Herald Square.

"Stop slouching, Alvin!" his boss screamed

at him regularly. "Santa Claus is supposed to have some authority."

You'd think I was working for F. A. O. Schwarz and not this junk shop, he often thought.

Alvin was not without spirit.

Nor was his lack of success in the publishing world due to a lack of diligent research. He had dissected every mystery and suspense novel that had appeared on the *New York Times* bestseller list in the last twenty years, and then some. He was a virtual walking encyclopedia when it came to the plots, characters, and settings used by hundreds of suspense and mystery novelists. He had filled notebooks with plotlines, and he consulted them regularly when working on his own stories. He had divided the plots into categories such as espionage, bank robberies, murder, extortion, domestic crime, hijackings, arson, courtroom drama, and kidnapping.

His only luxury was to attend writing seminars and mystery conventions, where he listened attentively to the sage advice of published writers and later tried to corner editors at the cocktail parties.

He had been getting ready for work on Thursday when he heard on the radio the news about Nora Regan Reilly's broken leg. Over the oatmeal that his mother prepared for him every morning, he had discussed it with her.

"Mark my words," he said. "Nora's next book will be set in a hospital. She'll make the best of this situation."

"Eat your oatmeal. It's getting cold," his mother admonished.

Dutifully, Alvin picked up his spoon and slurped the somewhat lumpy mixture. "I think I'll send her a card."

"Why not stick in the picture you took of that husband of hers at the last mystery-writers' dinner?"

"You're right. I did get a good shot of him," Alvin recalled. "But only one. In the other picture his head got cut off because he's so tall."

"I like tall men. Your father was a shrimp, God rest him."

"Maybe I'll put the picture in a little holiday frame and drop it off at the hospital after work. The store has some frames with nice Christmas sayings on them."

"Don't spend too much on it," his mother cautioned.

"They're on sale," Alvin said, a trace of irritation in his voice. "Nora Regan Reilly always talks to me at the cocktail parties and is so encouraging."

"Not like those editors," his mother had sighed.

Alvin went to work, looking forward to the surprise he was planning for Nora Regan Reilly. To his disappointment, most of the best Christmas frames already had been snapped up. He settled on one that said, I'LL BE HOME FOR CHRISTMAS . . . IF ONLY IN MY DREAMS. Considering how she's stuck in the hospital, it applies more to her than to her husband, he thought, but it will have to do.

To his disgust, there was no employee discount on sale items.

"What do you expect?" the salesgirl asked

as she popped her bubble gum. "They're practically giving this stuff away." She studied the frame before placing it in a bag. "Maybe that's not such a bad idea," she mumbled as Alvin carefully placed his wallet back in a deep pocket of the Santa Claus suit.

The evening-shift Santa Claus apparently had not made it down from the North Pole, and Alvin's boss told him he had to work until 8:00 P.M. That was when the sign went up that Santa was back in his workshop. By then, Alvin's ears were numb. He'd had enough of listening to the incessant demands hurled at him by an unending stream of children, all of whom seemed to take sadistic pleasure in plunking down on his boney knees.

"You don't look much like Santa," a number of the little darlings had said accusingly.

In all, it had been a long day, but that did not deter Alvin from making his planned pilgrimage to the Upper East Side. Since it was his responsibility to keep the Santa Claus suit pressed, he carried it back and forth to work. It was now neatly folded in a shopping bag, with the gift-wrapped, framed picture of Luke Reilly resting on top.

He had picked out a get-well card and written in it, "Nora, thought you'd like to have a pic of your sweetie." On a whim he signed it, "Your number-one fan."

Now he would have something to talk about with Nora Regan Reilly next time he saw her at a mystery-writers' event. He could reveal himself as the mysterious benefactor who'd sent her the nice framed picture.

Once inside the lobby of the hospital, Alvin noticed a gift shop, and in the shop window the word SALE caught his eye. Underneath the sign were perched adorable teddy bears wearing Christmas hats. He hurried in just as the shop was about to close. I won't tell Mother, he thought. But wouldn't it make it really special if a teddy bear is holding Luke Reilly's picture?

The saleswoman obligingly waited while he unwrapped the frame and stuck it in the arms of the teddy bear he had selected. She tied a huge Christmas bow around the box while Alvin counted out the exact change, which came to fourteen dollars and ninety-two cents.

Thanking her, he left the shop and went over to the reception desk. They assured him the package would go up to Mrs. Reilly immediately.

"Oh no, not until the morning," he said firmly. "I wouldn't want to disturb her. It's late."

"That's very thoughtful," the woman said pleasantly. "Have a nice holiday."

Alvin went out into the cold night air once again and walked up York Avenue to Eighty-sixth Street, to catch the crosstown bus. Glowing with Christmas spirit, he smiled cheerily at the passersby who were spilling out of restaurants and shops.

They all ignored him.

Jack Reilly's top assistant, Sgt. Keith Waters, as well as Lt. Gabe Klein, the head of TARU, the Technical Assistance Response Unit, were waiting in Reilly's office at One Police Plaza when he arrived there.

"Long time no see," Waters said laconically.

"You just can't stand being away from here, can you?" A handsome black man in his late thirties, with keen intelligent eyes, he radiated restless energy.

"It's you I miss," Jack said.

But the note of levity disappeared as they promptly got down to business.

"What have you got on the car?" Jack asked.

Gabe Klein began, "The records from E-Z Pass show that the car went through the Lincoln Tunnel into Manhattan at 9:15 A.M. That would be when the girl went in to pick up Luke Reilly at the hospital. At some point the car must have been driven back to New Jersey, because it crossed the George Washington Bridge into New York again at 11:16 A.M. Then it crossed the Triborough Bridge in a lane headed for Queens at 11:45 A.M. That was the last time the E-Z Pass registered any activity."

"That means they may have reached New Jersey before they were abducted," Jack said. "Or maybe they were abducted in New York and taken to New Jersey. Most likely the car has been dumped somewhere. Stretch limos aren't that easy to hide."

"We have a bulletin out for it," Keith responded, "but nothing's turned up so far."

"You put on a safeguard for prints?"

It was a rhetorical question. That was the first thing Keith would do in a kidnapping situation. If located, the car would not be touched until the lab technicians got there.

Now, in terse sentences, Jack filled them in on the rest of the details.

Both men made notes as they listened.

Gabe Klein, fiftyish and balding, wore glasses that perched precariously on the end of his nose, giving him a bookish, slightly vague appearance. To a casual observer, he looked like the kind of man who was unable to change a lightbulb.

It was an impression that was absolutely wrong—Gabe was a technical wizard and ran the highly sophisticated unit that had become a vital tool in the police force's crime-solving efforts.

"These are the phone lines we're covering, right?" Gabe rattled off the numbers Jack had phoned in. The Reilly home and apartment, Rosita Gonzalez's apartment, the funeral homes, Nora Reilly's hospital room.

"And if they call back on the daughter's cell phone, she knows enough to try and keep them on the line so we can pinpoint the location," Gabe confirmed.

"Regan is a private investigator in Los Angeles," Jack said. "She knows the drill."

"That's a break," Keith observed. "Then you think it's okay to have her drive the car to the ransom drop?"

"She's smart," Jack said shortly. And very attractive, he thought.

"When do we get to work on the car she'll be driving?" Gabe asked.

"She's bringing it in tonight. She knows we have to bird-dog it."

"We've alerted the Federal Reserve that we need the million by tomorrow afternoon. They're working on it," Keith informed Jack. "Does the family have any idea who might have done this?"

"Reilly's wife and daughter can't come up with anyone. Rosita Gonzalez has an ex-husband who's something of a troublemaker. His name is Ramon. Mrs. Reilly thinks he lives in Bayonne."

"We'll get on that," Keith said.

"Rosita has two little kids. Regan Reilly is going there now to check on them and to get a fix on whoever is with them. Then she's headed to her father's office to talk to his associate."

Jack looked at his watch. "It's a long story, but Regan met Alvirah Meehan today, and now she's involved as well. Remember her? She's the lottery winner who lectured at John Jay."

"Sure I do," Keith said. "She was the one who got that baby back when all the cops in New York couldn't find her."

Jack pulled the cassette from his pocket. "Well, she's still on the ball. She managed to record the ransom call."

Gabe stared at the tiny cassette. "You're kidding." He picked it up and held it in his hand. "Does she want a job? I could use her."

"She'll have my head if you don't make an extra copy for her. But first, let's hear this tape amplified. Maybe there'll be something in the background that will help us."

As the machine was being readied, Jack felt his frustration building. They could study the tape. They could put a tracking device with the money. They could bird-dog the car. They could look for logical suspects. But until they were following Regan's wired car to the point of contact with the kidnappers, they were mostly in a waiting game.

The phone on Jack's desk rang. He picked it up. "Jack Reilly." There was a pause. "Good work," he said decisively, then looked across the desk at Gabe and Keith. "They found the limo at Kennedy Airport."

At 9:30 that evening, Austin Grady locked the doors of the Reilly funeral home behind the last of the mourners of one-hundred-and-three-year-old Maude Gherkin, the local battle-ax. In his entire career as a mortician, he had never heard the expression, "It's a blessing," uttered more often or more fervently.

Four times since her hundredth birthday, Maude had been snatched from the jaws of death. During her final hospital stay, a home-made sign had appeared over her bed: DO NOT RESUSCITATE . . . NO MATTER WHAT. The doctors suspected it was the handiwork of her eighty-year-old son, who after Maude's fourth mirac-ulous return from the long white tunnel, had been heard to shout, "Aw, give me a *break!*"

Austin turned out the lights in the room where Maude was now resting. He sighed. Hard as they tried, they hadn't been able to get the sour expression off her face.

"Night, night, Maude," he muttered. But the little ritual he had with the clients at closing time did not bring a smile to his lips tonight—he was much too worried about Luke and Rosita.

Since Regan had phoned some hours ago, his suspicion that they had been kidnapped had become a near certainty. Why else would Regan have needed the limousine's license plate and the E-Z Pass account number? Why else couldn't she talk to him about it on the phone?

An hour later, when Regan arrived with Alvirah Meehan in tow, his suspicions were confirmed.

"The police have arranged to have these phones tapped," Regan said. "There's just a chance the kidnappers might call here."

They were startled by a sudden knocking on the window.

"What on earth?" Austin muttered as he recognized the face of none other than Ernest Bumbles, his nose pressed against the glass, who smilingly held up the package he had been carrying earlier and waved it at them.

Austin went over and struggled to raise the window.

"Sorry to bother you," Ernest said, clearly lying. "I saw your light was on and thought maybe Mr. Reilly was back."

This time Austin did not attempt to keep the irritation out of his voice. "He's not here! If you want to leave that package, I'll see that he gets it. Better yet, his daughter will take it home for him. There she is." He pointed at Regan.

Ernest stuck his head in through the open window. "I'm so pleased to meet you. Your father is a wonderful man."

I don't believe this, Regan thought.

Alvirah had turned toward the window so the sunburst pin wouldn't miss a word.

"I'm sorry I can't come in, but my wife, Dolly, is out in the car. She's not feeling that well. We were out singing Christmas carols tonight, and she strained her throat on the final fa la la la la la la la la of 'Deck the Halls.'"

That used to be my favorite Christmas carol, Regan thought. Not anymore.

"I'll be back tomorrow. I want to give this to your father personally. Bye now." Like a game show contestant who has failed to answer the final question, Ernest vanished.

Austin shut the window with a decisive snap. "That guy is a nut case."

"Who is he?" Regan asked.

"The head of some plant society," Austin said. "They honored your father a few years ago."

"I kind of remember that," Regan said. "He's active in so many organizations that he's always being honored."

Regan realized that she was played out. There was nothing more she could accomplish here at the moment. Austin had told her that there was absolutely no one he could think of who would want to bring harm to Luke. In his memory nothing unusual had happened at any of the three Reilly funeral homes.

"We'd better get going," Regan said. "I've made arrangements to stay in my mother's hospital room tonight, and I've got to get this car to Manhattan so the police can prepare it for tomorrow. Let's talk in the morning."

"Regan, I'll get here early and start going through the records from the last few months and see if there are any problems that I didn't know about," Austin promised. "I don't think I'll find anything, but it's worth a look."

As the three of them started to leave, Alvirah noticed the discreet sign bearing Maude Gherkin's name and an arrow pointing to the room where she lay in repose.

Alvirah crossed herself. "May she rest in peace. Did you ever hear the story of the woman who was passing Frank Campbell's funeral parlor in New York and had to go to the bathroom? She stopped in there and then felt she shouldn't leave without paying her respects to somebody. So she popped into a room where there were no visitors for the poor soul in the casket, said a quick prayer, and signed the register. Turned out it was in that guy's will that anyone who showed up at his wake got ten thousand dollars."

"Alvirah, you already won the lottery," Regan said, smiling.

"And believe me, you'd be wasting your time putting your John Hancock in Maude's book," Austin told her as they stepped outside and he shut and locked the door behind them. Hold down the fort, Maude, he thought.

Friday,
December 23rd

"Rise and shine everybody! Time to start our million-dollar day," Petey called out as he emerged from the bedroom, clad in striped pajamas, his toothbrush in hand. He switched on the overhead light. "This is sort of like camp, isn't it?"

Why doesn't that idiot just let us sleep? Luke thought. The last time he had looked at the illuminated dial of his watch, it had been 4:00 A.M. He had finally fallen asleep, and now he was being jolted awake for absolutely no reason. He squinted at his watch. It was 7:15.

He could feel the beginning of a dull headache. His muscles were aching from a combination of the damp, cold air and being forced to contort his body to fit on the narrow, short banquette. The increasing choppiness of the river was causing the boat to knock against the dock, increasing his overall sense of misery.

A hot shower, he thought longingly. Clean clothes. A toothbrush. The little things in life.

He looked across the cabin at Rosita. She had pulled herself up on one elbow. The strain she was feeling was clearly visible on her face. Her dark-brown eyes looked enormous, stark against the increasing pallor of her complexion.

But when their eyes met, she managed a smile and tossed her head in Petey's direction. "Your valet, Mr. Reilly?"

Before Luke could reply, there was a loud pounding on the door. "It's me, Petey," C.B. yelled impatiently. "Open up."

Petey ushered him in, taking the McDonald's bags out of his hands.

"And here comes the butler," Rosita announced softly.

"Did you remember to get me an Egg McMuffin with sausage?" Petey asked hopefully.

"Yes, you moron, I did. Get dressed. I can't stand looking at you like that. Who do you think you are, Hugh Hefner?"

"Hugh Hefner gets a lot of girls," Petey said admiringly. "When we get that million, I'm going to go out and buy a pair of silk pajamas, just like Hef's."

"If I left it to you, we'd never get that million," C.B. sputtered as he snapped on the radio.

He looked at Luke. "I was listening to *Imus in the Morning* on the way over. He put a call through to the hospital. Your wife is going to be on in a few minutes."

Nora was a frequent guest on the Imus program. Imus must have heard about the accident and phoned her. Luke sat up and leaned forward, desperately eager to hear her voice.

C.B. was twisting the dial, searching for the station. "Here we are," he said finally.

Nora's voice came through the static. "Hello, I-Man."

"Where are the hash browns?" Petey was poking through the bags.

Luke couldn't help himself. "Shut up!" he shouted.

"All right, already," Petey said.

"Nora, we were sorry to hear about your accident," Imus said. "I fall off a horse and you trip over a rug. What gives with us?"

Nora laughed.

Luke marveled at how at ease she sounded. He knew that she was feeling exactly as he would if the situation were reversed. But she had to keep up appearances to the rest of the world until this thing was resolved.

However it's resolved, he thought darkly.

"How's the funeral director?" Imus was asking.

"He's talking about you," Petey cried. "Whattayaknow!"

"Oh, he's just great," Nora said, laughing.

"He's yachting," Petey yelled at the radio, and slapped his knee, pleased as always with his own humor.

Imus was thanking Nora for the children's

books she had sent his young son. "He loves it when we read to him."

Luke had a moment of acute nostalgia, remembering how he and Nora had always read to Regan when she was little. When Nora said good-bye to Imus, Luke swallowed over the lump he could feel forming in his throat. Would he ever hear her voice again?

"Mrs. Reilly sent books to my boys for Christmas too," Rosita told him, her voice gentle. "She told me that Regan's favorite thing when she was a child was when you read to her."

And Regan had a favorite book, Luke thought, one book she always carried over to him. *"Read me this one again, Daddy,"* she'd say as she climbed on his lap. Oh my God, he thought, as he remembered which book that was.

Luke's mind began to race. He knew that C.B. had agreed to let Regan talk to him and Rosita this afternoon before she paid the ransom. Was there any chance he could somehow communicate to her a clue as to their whereabouts? Was there any way he could let her know that from where they were being held they could see the George Washington Bridge and the quaint red lighthouse perched beneath it?

Her favorite book had been about those two famous structures. Its title was *The Little Red Lighthouse and the Great Gray Bridge*.

"Bye, I-Man."

Nora hung up the phone.

"Good job, Mom," Regan said.

Both of them had slept fitfully through the night, Regan stretched out on a cot that the nursing staff had sent in. There were times when she awoke and heard her mother's light, even breathing, a sign that she was sleeping. Several times, though, she was immediately aware that Nora was awake, and they would talk quietly in the near darkness of the hospital room until sleep overtook one of them.

At one point during the night, Nora said,

"You know, Regan, they claim that at the moment you die, your whole life flashes before you. I have the oddest sensation that the same kind of thing is happening to me now, but in slow motion."

"Mom," Regan protested.

"Oh, I don't mean that I'm about to die, but I guess when someone you love is in grave danger, your mind becomes a kaleidoscope of memories. Moments ago I was thinking about the apartment Dad and I had when we were first married. It was tiny, but it was ours, and we were together. He'd go off to work, and I'd hit the typewriter. Even when I kept getting rejection slips, he never doubted for one minute that I was going to make it. When I finally sold that first short story, boy, did we celebrate."

Nora paused. "I can't imagine life without him."

It took a giant effort for Regan, who had spent most of the night reliving her own memories of her father, to say softly, "Then don't."

At 6:00 A.M., Regan got up, showered, and changed into the black jeans and sweater she had picked up at the apartment before returning to the hospital.

As she and Alvirah were driving back from New Jersey the night before, she had phoned Jack Reilly and learned that the limo had been found at Kennedy Airport. He told her it had been towed to the lab at the Police Academy garage on East Twentieth Street, where they were going over it with a fine-tooth comb, looking for clues to the identity of the kidnappers.

Regan knew from her own experience the kinds of painstaking tests they would undertake and the carefully defined procedures they would follow. They would check any unidentified fingerprints they might find against the millions of prints stored in the FBI computers. They would collect any traces of fibers or hair for analysis. She had been involved in many cases where a minuscule, seemingly innocuous object turned out to be the Rosetta stone that led to the solving of the puzzle.

Jack had also filled her in on what the E-Z Pass records revealed. ". . . which as you know isn't necessarily significant. They could have been switched to another car."

Regan looked at her mother's breakfast tray, which was virtually untouched. "Why don't you at least drink the tea?" she asked.

"Irish penicillin," Nora murmured, but she did pick up the cup.

News of her accident had resulted in a deluge of flowers from the Reillys' friends. After the first few bouquets had been placed around the room, Nora requested that the others be distributed throughout the hospital.

There was a tap on the door, and a smiling volunteer asked, "May I come in?"

She was holding a box tied with a bright Christmas ribbon.

"Of course," Nora said, attempting a smile.

"First delivery of the day," the woman said sweetly. "It was left for you last night, but the girl at the desk stuck a note on it saying it should be held until the morning. So here it is!"

Nora reached up to take the box. "Thanks so much."

"Don't mention it," the woman said. She turned to Regan. "Make sure she takes good care of that leg of hers."

"I will." Regan knew she sounded abrupt, but she was anxious to keep unnecessary people out of the room. If the kidnappers happened to call before the agreed-upon time, she wanted to be able to speak freely and to record the call with the sunburst pin Alvirah had lent her.

"I always keep a backup," Alvirah had explained as she thrust the tiny recording device into Regan's hands. "Even though the cops have your phone covered, with this you'll have your own tape of any calls that come in."

Nora was sliding the bow off the box.

"Bye, now," the volunteer smiled. She walked out leaving the door slightly ajar.

As Regan was closing it, she heard a gasp from her mother and spun around.

"Regan, look at this!" Nora cried, her voice panicked.

Regan hurried over and stared down at the now open package. Inside, nestled in the arms of a stocking-capped, fluffy brown teddy bear, was a picture of her father, wearing a tuxedo and smiling warmly. But it was the lettering around the tacky red-and-green frame that shot a cold chill through her body. I'LL BE HOME FOR CHRISTMAS, it read across the top. . . . IF ONLY IN MY DREAMS, completed the sentiment at the base of the frame.

There was an envelope in the box. Regan ripped it open. On an ordinary get-well card the sender had printed: "Nora, thought you'd like to have a pic of your sweetie." It was signed, "Your number-one fan."

"Let me see that." Nora took the card out of her hand. "They're threatening us, Regan!"

"I know."

"If anything goes wrong and they don't get the money . . ." Nora whispered.

Regan had already begun dialing Jack Reilly's number.

Jack had been up all night directing the frenetic activity that was the modus operandi of the Major Case Squad when involved in a breaking case.

The lab had lifted prints from the limo, and while there were many different sets to run through their computers, so far no match had been found. A few strands of polyester black hair suggested that one of the kidnappers had been wearing a disguise. The short length of the hairs indicated a fake mustache rather than a wig. The only other discovery of possibly great significance was a few tiny flecks of paint that had been found on the limousine's floor, around the brake pedal.

Suspicion for the abduction was beginning to center on Rosita's ex-husband, Ramon Gonzalez. A check with the police in Bayonne had revealed that he was well known to them. A compulsive gambler, he was rumored to be heavily in debt to local bookies and had not been spotted recently in his usual haunts.

Of potentially vital importance was the fact that Junior, his younger brother and fellow gambler, was a sometime housepainter. They shared an apartment in a run-down, two-family house. The landlord, who also lived in the building, said that he had not seen them in a couple of days and complained that they were behind in their rent.

Jack had notified the FBI and was now working in tandem with them. Besides the police helicopter, which would be tracking Regan's car, an FBI fixed-wing aircraft would be overhead, ready to follow the signals sent by the device planted in the bag with the ransom money.

Alvirah's tape recording of the call from the kidnappers had been run through an exhaustive audio analysis. The voice of the person who had made the ransom demand, as well as those of Luke and Rosita, could be heard clearly. The feeling was that the low and almost guttural tone of the caller was almost surely an attempt to alter his normal tones. Another man's voice could be detected in the background, although it was so faint that whatever he said had not yet been deciphered.

From analyzing the ambient sounds on the tape, they were able to ascertain that Luke and Rosita were being kept in a relatively cramped area near a body of water.

As Gabe Klein observed, "That really narrows it down—three quarters of the earth is covered with water."

Now, except for the intense manhunt for the Gonzalez brothers, the police were entering the waiting-game segment of the investigation.

Regan's call, however, changed that.

"I'm on the way," Jack told her.

Twenty minutes later, Jack was in Nora's room at the hospital.

"The logo on the box is from the gift shop downstairs," Regan told him.

"There's nothing in the picture that gives me a clue about where it was taken," Nora said.

"Luke and I go to a lot of black-tie affairs."

"By the time we realized what this was, our fingerprints were already on the card and the frame," Regan said.

"Don't worry about it," Jack told them. "If there are any other fingerprints, we'll get them. Do you happen to know what time the gift shop opens?"

"I already asked," Regan said. "Nine o'clock."

"How about if you go down there and speak to them?" Jack said. "See what you can find out about who might have bought this. We have to be careful not to let anyone think this is a police investigation."

"I thought I'd tell them that the person who bought the gift forgot to sign the card, and we wanted to be able to send a thank-you note."

Jack nodded. He looked at the bouquets of flowers in the room. "Nora, there's been publicity about your accident. This could, of course, be a somewhat macabre coincidence."

"I do get a lot of mail from people who

read my books," Nora acknowledged. "But isn't the sentiment on that frame too much of a coincidence?"

"Possibly," Jack admitted.

"In which case, it becomes a pretty grim threat," Nora said.

Regan was studying him. "Jack, you're leaning toward coincidence. Why?"

"Because Rosita's ex-husband is our strongest suspect, and from what I know about his type, this kind of thing is way too subtle for him. But then again . . ."

He shrugged and looked at his watch. "It's almost nine o'clock. Regan, why don't we go down to the gift shop together and see what we can find out? Then I'll take all of this downtown and give it to the lab."

He looked at Nora. "I know how upsetting this is for you. But it could be an important break for us. There may be fingerprints that will match up with some we've found in the car. If the frame wasn't bought downstairs, we'll try to trace it to where it was purchased. Perhaps someone in the gift shop will be able to give us a description of whoever bought the teddy bear."

Clearly on the verge of tears, Nora nodded. "I understand."

Jack turned to Regan. "Let's go."

Meanwhile, on the Upper West Side, barely a mile away from the hospital, Alvin Luck was bent over his bowl of oatmeal, still glowing with pleasure at the thought of the happiness his gift must be giving to Nora Regan Reilly, perhaps at this very moment.

He had wisely not broken his resolve to keep his mother in the dark about the purchase of the teddy bear. But his wisdom only went so far.

"What do you mean you didn't sign the card?" his mother badgered as she settled heavily into the chair opposite him. "Are you crazy? What were you thinking? She could help you get published. For God's sake, her editor is Michael Korda!"

"Will Mommy be home soon?"

It was the first question Chris and Bobby asked when they opened their eyes at 7:30. At least they slept well, Fred thought as he answered, "She'll be home as soon as she can."

On the shelf in Rosita's closet he had found extra sheets and a blanket and pillow, so he had bunked on the couch. It would have been more comfortable to stretch out on top of her bed, but he had found himself unable to do that. It felt almost as though it would be an invasion of her privacy.

He knew that the deeper reason was that everything in the bedroom conveyed a sense of Rosita's presence that was haunting.

A smiling picture of her with her arms around the boys dominated the top of the small dresser. There was a faint scent of perfume—a scent she had worn when he last saw her—emanating from the atomizer on her dressing table. When he had opened the closet door to find the bedding, the first thing he saw was her white silk robe and, peeking from beneath it, a pair of satin bedroom slippers.

Cinderella, he thought with a stab of pain.

Before he had settled on the couch the night before, he'd called Josh Gaspero, the friend he'd planned to meet. "Not home," he muttered to himself as Josh's machine picked up. "Figures. He's probably over at Elaine's having a Christmas drink with the regulars." The explanation he'd left had been brief. "Delayed on a special case. I can't discuss it. I'll try and catch up with you down there in a couple of days. I've got the schedule of stops."

Now he watched as Chris and Bobby went into the bathroom and reached for their toothbrushes without being told. When they began lightly splashing water on their faces, though, Fred decided to lend a hand. "As my mother used to tell me, 'You wash for a high neck,' " he said as he rubbed soap on a warm washcloth and took over.

While he made coffee, the boys got their own cereal and juice. "Please, will you make the toast in the oven?" Chris asked. "Our toaster broke, and we're not allowed to turn on the gas ourselves."

"Mommy gets really mad if we play near the stove," Bobby volunteered.

"Mommy's right," Fred replied.

Had the lab found anything significant in the limo? he wondered. By now they would have gone over it thoroughly. Alvirah Meehan had called him from her apartment last night and told him about the find. "Regan asked me to let you know. She said we'll keep you informed on anything that comes up."

As they were finishing breakfast, Sgt. Keith Waters from the Major Case Squad phoned. "Captain Reilly asked me to call you, Fred. I know what the situation is out there. Let me bring you up to date on what we have here."

He began with the results of the lab's inspection of the limo and the focus on Ramon Gonzalez and his brother.

"We're homing in on them. You're in place in Rosita's apartment. We want you to go through it carefully and see if you can find anything that would suggest that her ex was either threatening her or trying to get money from her. Keep your eye out for anything that would show where he might be hiding out now. You know the routine. We have a search warrant, of course."

Fred was aware that the boys were listening intently to his conversation, trying to figure out who was on the phone. "Will do," he said, "and if you see Rosita, tell her that the boys are being very good and are glad she's helping Mrs. Reilly."

"But tell her she has to be home for Christmas," Bobby cried out, dismayed.

"And ask her when we're going to decorate the tree." Now even Chris seemed to be about to cry.

"What are you going to tell them?" Waters asked softly.

"Sure, I'll be glad to," Fred replied heartily. He turned to the boys. "Mommy sent word that she's going to be really tired when she gets home, so she'd like it a lot if we'd decorate the tree for her today."

He saw the doubtful look on their faces. "I'm really good with the lights, and I can reach to the top. We'll save your favorite ornaments for your mom to hang when she gets home. How about that?"

"Good luck," Keith Waters said as he hung up the phone.

Willy was snoring loudly in the bedroom, and Sister Cordelia was fast asleep on the living room couch when Alvirah tiptoed into the apartment at midnight.

A newspaper was under Cordelia's hands, and her glasses were perched on the end of her nose. Alvirah had removed the glasses and newspaper, unplugged the Christmas tree, and turned out the lights, without disturbing her.

Now, over breakfast, the three of them comfortable in their bathrobes, she related everything that had taken place since she had phoned Cordelia yesterday and asked her to stay with Willy.

"The ransom drop is set for six o'clock tonight, and I intend to be in one of the unmarked cars following Regan," Alvirah declared as she spread a generous lump of butter on her English muffin.

Now that the troublesome dental implant had been mercifully extracted, Willy both sounded and looked more like his old self. "Alvirah, honey, I worry about you being in one of those cars," he began to protest, but then shaking his head, poured himself more coffee. "Useless," he muttered.

Cordelia, the eldest of Willy's six sisters, had entered the convent fifty-three years earlier, at age seventeen. Now the mother superior of a small convent on Manhattan's Upper West Side, she and the four nuns who lived with her spent their time tending to the needy in their parish.

Their many activities included running an after-school day-care center. Two years earlier, Alvirah had been the one to track down a long-missing child, who turned out to be one of the seven-year-olds in their charge.

After having been her sister-in-law for more than forty years, nothing Alvirah did could surprise Cordelia, and that included winning $40 million dollars in the lottery.

Alvirah and Willy had been most generous with their newfound wealth. As Cordelia put it, "They're the same down-to-earth people they always have been. Willy still comes running whenever any of our people need a plumber. The only difference in Alvirah is, now that she isn't cleaning houses anymore, she's turned into a first-rate amateur detective."

With her regal carriage and no-nonsense air, Cordelia inspired both trust and deference. She also had a way of getting immediately to the heart of the matter.

"Are those ransom drops usually successful?" she asked.

"More successful in fiction than in fact," Alvirah said with a sigh. "And the problem is that if something does go wrong, the kidnappers tend to panic."

Cordelia shook her head. "I'll get everybody praying. I'll just say it's for a special intention."

"We need all the prayers we can get," Alvirah said soberly. "I just feel so helpless."

"Honey, thanks to you they have the kidnapper's voice on tape. That could turn out to be a big help," Willy reminded her.

"Isn't that the truth?" Alvirah exclaimed, clearly cheered. "The detective gave me a copy of the tape last night. Let's listen to it." She got up, retrieved the cassette from her purse and reached into the mahogany cabinet in the living room for her special, highly sensitive tape player, yet another gift from her editor at the *Globe*.

She had spent many hours with her ear cocked to its speaker, listening for nuances in the countless conversations she had recorded in her relentless pursuit of justice.

Willy moved the coffeepot out of the way as she set the machine down between the empty bacon plate and the jar of imported raspberry jam.

She snapped in the cassette. "After we hear this, I'm going to get dressed and head over to the hospital. I told Regan I'd come by this morning. What a long day this is going to be for them. There's almost nothing to do now but wait until six o'clock tonight."

"I feel better today, so if there's anything they need for me to do, I'd be glad to help out," Willy offered.

"I'll call you from the hospital," Alvirah promised as she pressed the PLAY button.

The cassette made for grim listening. Willy's frown and the tightening of Cordelia's lips mirrored Alvirah's own sense of anger and concern.

"It's pretty straightforward," Cordelia said when it was over. "It especially breaks my heart to hear that young mother so worried about her boys."

"I'd like to get my hands on that guy," Willy said as he unconsciously punched his left palm with his right fist.

Alvirah was rewinding the tape. "I want to hear it again."

"Did you pick up something, honey?" Willy asked hopefully.

"I'm not sure."

She played it a second time and then again,

her eyes tightly closed. Then she turned off the machine. "There's something there that's ringing a bell, but I can't quite figure out what it is."

"Run it through once more," Willy urged.

"No, it won't make a difference right now. It will come to me later. It always does," she said. Frustrated, Alvirah got up from the table. "I can tell it's something important. *But what is it?*"

When Regan and Jack entered the gift shop in the hospital lobby, the carefully made-up fortyish woman behind the counter was yawning. Spotting them, she halfheartedly held up a carefully manicured hand to cover her open mouth.

"Excuse me," she said. "I'm so tired. All this holiday stuff has me aggravated."

"I know what you mean," Regan murmured sympathetically.

"At least you're standing here with a good-looking guy. I haven't had a decent date in months."

"Oh, we're not—" Regan began, but Jack nudged her and smiled at the saleswoman, whose name tag read "Hi. My name is LUCY."

"They told me to get a job in a hospital. You'll meet a lot of doctors. So I get myself hired here to help out for the month of December." She paused briefly as though unable to believe what she was about to report. "Not one doctor has set foot in this place since I started three weeks ago. They all go flying right through the lobby in their white coats."

"Oh dear," Regan found herself murmuring inanely. She cleared her throat. "Well, I'm sorry to bother you but . . ."

"Go ahead," Lucy said in a resigned voice as she picked up her Styrofoam coffee cup. "I'm all ears."

"We need to speak to whomever was working in here last night."

"You're looking at her. Why do you think I'm so tired?"

Regan and Jack exchanged glances. What a stroke of luck was the unspoken mutual thought.

Jack had put the teddy bear with the framed picture in a clear plastic bag he'd gotten from the nurses' station.

Regan held it up "We think this teddy bear was bought here last evening."

"Bingo."

"You remember selling it?"

"Bingo."

"Can you tell us anything about the person who bought it?"

"Please. Don't get me started. I let him in when I'm closing up, and he takes forever to pick out a teddy bear." Lucy pointed to the display of bears on the shelves. "Do you see any difference between any of them and the one you've got there? I don't.

"Then he reaches down into his shopping bag and pulls out the package that frame was wrapped in. So I stand here—after I've been on my feet all day—and wait for him to unwrap the package, just so he can use the paper again. Then he sticks the frame in the teddy bear's arms and asks me to rewrap the whole thing. So I put it in a box and tied it with a ribbon. Then he takes out his wallet and spends forever getting the exact change out of the secret compartment." She rolled her eyes.

"I can tell you one thing," Lucy concluded, "anyone who goes out with him better know the definition of Dutch treat."

"He paid in cash?" Jack asked.

She looked pained. "Isn't that what I just said?"

"How would you describe him?" Jack continued, a steely edge creeping into his voice.

She paused. "What's this all about anyway? Please don't tell me he's Bill Gates's long-lost brother."

Regan smiled reluctantly. "He left this for my mother, who's a patient upstairs, but he didn't sign the card. She wants to be able to send a thank-you note."

"That's weird," Lucy said, looking genuinely perplexed. "He seemed so pleased with himself, ya know, sticking the frame in the box with the teddy bear and all. I would have thought he'd have signed the card."

"I might be able to figure out who it is if

you give me an idea of what he looks like," Regan prodded.

Lucy scrunched up her face. "Not that great," she replied. "You know, around fifty maybe. Brown hair, not much of it, average height, a little wimpy."

"You say he was carrying a shopping bag," Jack said. "Did you happen to notice where it was from?"

She rolled her eyes again. "Oh yeah, I went shopping there once. I bought an outfit that fell apart first time I washed it."

"Where was that?" Regan asked.

"Long's. You heard their commercial? 'I'm longing for Long's.' I'll tell you one thing—I'm not longing for Long's."

"What time do you close here?" Jack asked.

"Usually 7:30. This week we stay open till 9:00. We want to get rid of all this holiday stuff. Once Christmas is over, you can't give it away."

It was obvious that there was nothing more to be learned from her. Regan and Jack crossed the lobby to the reception desk. The obliging clerk there knew who had been on duty the previous evening. "It's my friend Vanessa. Let me phone her."

Regan was dismayed to hear from Vanessa only the same vague description of the man who had left the package. "Did he by any chance mention his name or say that he was a friend of my mother's?"

"He didn't say anything except that he didn't want to disturb her last night."

Regan tried to keep her tone casual as she said, "I guess whoever left it won't receive a thank-you note."

"A mystery gift for a mystery author," Vanessa said brightly. "Tell her I hope she feels better."

Regan hung up. "She gave the same physical description, but unfortunately didn't add anything, Jack." She turned to the receptionist and thanked her for her help.

As they started to walk away from the desk, Jack pointed to the security cameras that ringed the lobby. In a low tone he said, "I'll get last night's tape. We should be able to pick him out with that big box he was carrying."

"Hello, you two." Alvirah's hearty greeting was unmistakable. Before they could respond, she spotted the object in Regan's hand. With a worried frown, she said, "There's got to be a reason you're carrying that teddy bear in a plastic bag."

"Let's go up to Nora's room," Jack suggested. "It's easier to talk up there."

Five minutes later, when they walked into her room, Nora was hanging up the phone. "I called my broker. The million dollars is being debited from our securities account and credited to Chase Manhattan. From there it will go to the Federal Reserve. I said I was making an overseas investment." She smiled wanly. "Pray God this is the best million dollars we will ever spend."

Jack nodded. "We're doing everything in our power to see that it is."

Together he and Regan told Nora and Alvirah what little they had learned about the donor of the gift. "There was nothing outstanding about him physically. He paid cash.

From what we hear, he certainly took his time, so he wasn't nervous. And he was carrying a shopping bag from Long's department store."

"Long's!" Alvirah exclaimed. "Before I won the lottery I used to 'long for Long's.' It's like most of those discount department stores. You have to wade through a ton of junk to find a bargain, but sometimes it happens. Most people see it as a challenge."

She glanced at the frame. "Yup, that looks like a Long's special. Do you want me to check it out for you, Jack?"

Jack knew that Alvirah was a master at ferreting out information. She had an almost uncanny way of getting people to open up. Why not? he thought. Later, if they could get a half-way decent image from the security cameras, he would send one of his squad out to the store to see if anyone there could ID the guy.

"I think it would be a great idea for Alvirah to go to Long's," Nora said.

For a moment, Regan considered accompanying her, then rejected the idea. The store would most likely be packed with last-minute shoppers. If the kidnappers called her on her cell phone, she'd barely be able to hear them.

There was something else. The look on her mother's face told her that she was needed here.

"I'll get started looking into the security tapes," Jack said.

"And I'm off to Long's," Alvirah announced, glad that there was finally some action she could take.

C.B. and Petey had had a busy morning. After breakfast, they left the houseboat and headed west to the isolated and rundown farm off Route 80 where Petey's cousin allowed him to keep his outboard motorboat.

As they rattled down the dirt road leading to the farmhouse, C.B. grumbled, "What a dump this place is."

Petey took offense. "It is my cousin's after all. And thanks to him, I've had a place to keep the boat that's going to collect our million dollars, Mr. Hoity-toity. Beggars can't be choosy," he admonished.

"Are you sure your cousin's away?"

"It's Christmastime, remember? Everybody's going somewhere, including us—huh, C.B.? I drove my cousin and his wife to the bus station a few days ago. They should be at my aunt's house in Tampa by now."

C.B. groaned again. "Don't talk to me about relatives."

"Do you miss your uncle?" Petey chuckled, as he jammed on the brake of his paint-stained pickup truck in front of the barn door.

C.B. did not deign to answer. If Uncle Cuthbert had done the right thing, I wouldn't have to put up with this moron, he thought. The closer they got to putting their hands on the money, the more nervous he became that something would go wrong.

He knew that the location he had chosen for the ransom drop was brilliant. It was just trusting Petey to get there in one piece that was the problem. But Petey had assured him that he could navigate the waters around Manhattan with his eyes closed—which C.B. figured was probably the way he usually did it.

They got out of the car, and Petey ran to open the barn door. "Ta-daaaah," he cried as he yanked a cracked and aging tarp from a decrepit boat, perched atop the trailer used to haul it to the water.

C.B. almost burst into tears. He hated his uncle more than ever. "Are you trying to tell me that thing *floats?*"

By now, Petey had scrambled up the side of the trailer and jumped into the boat. "If it had a sail, it could win the America's Cup," he yelled. He took off the painter's cap, which was his chapeau of choice, and waved it at C.B. "Ahoy, maties!" he cried.

"Get down here, Popeye."

Petey gave him the A-OK sign and scampered down. "This baby has really got the juice!" he bragged. "My cousin rebuilt the motor after I found it in a junkyard."

"Which is where it belongs. When was the last time that tub was in the water?"

"I went fishing that nice day in October," Petey said, scratching his neck. "Let's see, was it Columbus Day? Or was it the weekend after?"

"I bet it was Halloween," C.B. replied. "Let's hitch that wreck up to the truck and get out of here. It's freezing."

Petey started backing up his vehicle, his head stuck out the window as he urged C.B. to give him some guidance. "How much more room I got there, brother?" he yelled.

C.B. cringed. Before he could answer, Petey had clipped the side of the barn.

After several failed efforts, they finally secured the trailer and went bumping back down the road.

Petey blew his nose and dabbed at his eyes. "I may never see this place again."

"Consider yourself lucky."

C.B. pulled out his notebook, and they went over the plans for the evening. They'd lower the boat into the water in a cove Petey knew about, which was a half-mile south of the houseboat. They'd ditch the trailer there.

At precisely six o'clock, Petey would board the boat and steer it north on the Hudson, through Spuyten Duyvil around the top of Manhattan, to the seawall near the pier at East 127th Street. That was where Regan Reilly would be told to deposit the ransom money. It should take Petey about half an hour to get there.

C.B. would be stationed at the houseboat, and at six o'clock would make the first phone call to Regan Reilly, allowing her to speak briefly to her father and Rosita. He'd tell her to start driving through Central Park. Then he'd hang up before the call could be traced.

He'd rush across the George Washington Bridge and down the East Side Drive, calling Regan several more times along the way with instructions as to where she should drive next. "It's known as a delaying action," he explained to Petey. "In case she called the cops, it'll be harder for them to follow her from a distance. For all they know, we have her in sight."

The final instruction would be for Regan to cross Second Avenue at 127th Street and take the Marginal Street exit and drive onto the isolated dock. There she would be instructed to drop the duffel bag on the seawall and leave.

Once the drop was made, Petey would scramble up, grab the money, hop back on board, and then, with no time to spare, race down to 111th Street, where C.B. would be waiting in the car they had rented under a false name.

Petey would abandon the boat, which, thanks to the fact he never had bothered to register it, and that the motor had been bought in a junkyard, would be untraceable.

After that, they'd drive back to the houseboat and amuse themselves by counting their money until their flight to Brazil the following night.

"The storm they're forecasting better not screw us up," C.B. said, worried. "The sooner we get out of these parts, the better."

"*Arriba, arriba!* Cha-cha-cha," Petey sang,

tapping his hands rhythmically on the steering wheel.

C.B. decided the best way to cope with Petey was to ignore him. He pulled one of Nora Regan Reilly's early books out of his bag and turned to chapter eight, which was filled with his own notations.

"I just want to go over this again," he said, more to himself than to his partner in crime.

Austin Grady arrived at the office early Friday morning and immediately began reviewing the big appointment book on Luke's desk.

Starting with the present, he studied Luke's activities day by day, going back for two months. He found absolutely nothing that brought to mind any mention by Luke of a difficulty or problem.

The references to the lunches Luke had had with the late Cuthbert Boniface Goodloe brought an unconscious smile to Austin's lips and for a moment relieved the sickening tension that enveloped him. No bride ever planned her wedding with as much attention to detail as Goodloe had dedicated to his funeral, he thought.

Wanting to ensure a full house for his final good-byes, Goodloe had issued specific instructions. If he died on a weekend, the wake was not to be held until Tuesday. He wanted two full days and nights of viewing, with the funeral to be held on Thursday. That was exactly how it had happened.

"It takes time to notify everyone and get the obituary in the papers," he had said. God knows that plant society got plenty of notice, Austin thought—now we can't get rid of them.

The phone on his desk rang. "This had better not be that Bumbles guy," he muttered to himself. It was Regan. For an instant the sound of her voice gave him a quick hope that maybe she'd say that Luke and Rosita were safe. But, of course, that was not to be.

He told her what he had been doing. "I'm

going to keep at it," he promised. "I'm also going to ask some subtle questions around here to see if there's been a problem with any employee that didn't reach our ears."

"Thanks, Austin," Regan said quietly. "Who knows who could have done this. Right now the police are focusing on Rosita's ex-husband. Apparently he has heavy gambling debts, owed to the wrong people."

"That'd motivate you to get your hands on a million dollars any way you can."

"Of course, this could be the work of someone who's been mad at my father for the last ten years." There was a brief hint of levity in Regan's voice. "It's like what they say about us Irish. We forget everything except the grudge."

"Don't I know it, Regan," Austin agreed, thinking of his grandmother, who never forgave her cousin for "stealing her thunder" by scheduling her wedding two weeks before her own long-planned nuptials. Grandma went to her grave sixty years later, still griping about it, Austin thought. The fact that her cousin endured a horrible marriage did nothing to appease her.

"How's your mother doing?" he asked.

"She's hanging in there. I'll be here with her until late this afternoon."

He knew what she meant. "Give her my love, and take care of yourself, Regan."

"Will do," Regan said. "Talk to you later."

Austin had barely replaced the receiver when the phone rang again. He picked it up, the hope always in the back of his mind that it would be Luke's laconic voice saying, as he had at least a thousand times before, "What have we got going on there today, Austin?"

"Austin Grady," he said.

"Ernest Bumbles!" The voice grated through Austin like fingernails on a blackboard.

"Luke is not here," Austin told him firmly. "And no, I don't know when to expect him."

"I'll keep trying," Ernest said cheerfully. "Bye now!"

Luke and Rosita wrapped the thin blankets around themselves as best they could. Even though there was a propane heater, it did little to dispel the bone-chilling dampness of the drafty boat.

"If we get out of here, I'm taking my kids to Puerto Rico for a week," Rosita said. "It'll take me at least that long to warm up."

"*When* we get out of here, I'll send you all, first class," Luke promised.

Rosita smiled wryly. "You'd better watch your cash flow. Your bank account just went south a million bucks."

"You owe me half."

"You have some nerve!" This time Rosita genuinely laughed. "As C.B. keeps saying, ad nauseam, if you hadn't introduced his dear departed uncle to the Blossoms, he never would have changed his will."

"I couldn't get anybody to go to that dinner," Luke protested. "I had tables to fill!"

"Do you think Mr. Grady might make the

connection and have the cops check out our friend C.B.?" Rosita asked.

Luke decided to be honest. "I don't see why he would. C.B. kept his anger pretty well hidden at the wake, although I did catch him stuffing rotting foliage in his uncle's coffin after viewing hours."

"Are you kidding? Did you tell Mr. Grady?" she asked hopefully.

"Unfortunately, no," Luke said. "I felt kind of sorry for C.B. Over the years I've encountered a lot of understandably emotional people, acting out of character at the time of a death."

"Then he showed up at the funeral and the luncheon, and I guess behaved himself. Since you didn't make it to the funeral, they probably realize now that we were already missing. So no one would tie him to this," Rosita concluded.

Luke nodded in agreement. "They wouldn't have any reason to."

"I guess there's no way anyone would give Petey a second thought either," Rosita continued. "You being your usual unflappable self, Mr. Reilly, never even let on to him that you were less than thrilled with the job he did."

"I felt very flappable, but it was easier to pay him off and send him on his way. And you must admit, we did get a lot of laughs out of it."

"We sure did."

"That reminds me, Rosita. If you had gone out on that date with Petey, we might not be here."

"I'd rather be here."

Luke chuckled. "I'm forced to agree."

They fell silent for a few minutes; then Rosita said, "I wonder who's with my kids?"

"Regan will make sure they're well looked after."

"Oh, I know that," she said quickly. "It's just that they're probably with someone who doesn't know them, and it always takes a while for Chris and Bobby to feel comfortable with a new baby-sitter." She paused. "I'm sure they're missing me, but they're also probably mad that I haven't come home yet. They've had enough to deal with this past year and a half, with their father deserting them."

"Once you're home, things will be back to normal faster than you think," Luke said, trying to reassure her.

"What bothers me," she said hesitantly, as if she didn't want to vocalize her deepest fear, "is that it's so unbelievable that someone like C.B., who seems so ineffective, would plan and actually pull off a kidnapping. I can't help but wonder what else he's capable of doing, if he decides he doesn't want to leave witnesses."

Luke started to speak, then closed his mouth. There was always the chance the cabin was bugged. He wanted to tell Rosita about his plan to try to communicate to Regan that they were in the vicinity of the subjects of her favorite children's book, the one about the bridge and the lighthouse. He knew it was a stretch, but it was the only card he had to play.

Rosita was absolutely right. C.B. might be capable of a final act of vengeance.

Alvirah hurried past Macy's, heading for Long's department store, around the corner. The traffic had been so heavy she had gotten out of the taxi and jumped into the subway to get downtown. Despite the cold, last-minute holiday shoppers were out in force. Normally she enjoyed window-shopping, but today that was the last thing on her mind.

Alvirah knew that it would be almost impossible to track down the man who had bought the cheap picture frame, but still she was determined to try.

She barreled through the revolving door of Long's and then paused and looked around, getting her bearings. I haven't been here for a while, she thought. Truth to tell, I haven't missed it. But she remembered the layout as though it was yesterday. Men's Department first floor, just like every other store. Retailers know that men hate to shop. When you finally lasso them into the store, the clothes better be popping out at them.

Junk like the frame would definitely be in the basement. There was a line waiting to get on the down escalator. The woman ahead of Alvirah had three small children in tow and looked frazzled.

"Tommy, I warned you not to tell your brothers there's no Santa Claus," she hissed in the eldest child's ear.

"But there isn't!" he protested. "Ma, you don't think that joker in the toy department is really Santa, do you?"

"He's helping Santa out!"

"I heard somebody call him Alvin."

"Never mind," his mother said as she guided her children onto the steps of the escalator.

Precocious, Alvirah thought, amused. But then watching the mother with her children reminded her of the two boys in New Jersey, waiting for their mother to come home.

As they descended into the basement, a banner with the word SALE came into full view. The first floor had been crowded, but down here was a madhouse! Boxes of picked-over Christmas cards were now marked half price. Tables were piled with tree ornaments, Christmas lights, tinsel, and gift wrap. That frame had to come from here, Alvirah decided, when she spotted a counter straight ahead that was covered with a bewildering array of Christmas knick-knacks.

Alvirah's bargain-hunting years had left her with the ability to maneuver her body along sales counters without infuriating her fellow shoppers. It worked very well for her today. Within seconds she had found the section where boxes of frames were piled high, an example of each type open and on display. She spotted one that, at a glance, looked just like Nora's.

Excited, she reached around another shopper, lunged for the frame, and whipped out her reading glasses. JINGLE MY BELLS was scrawled across the top in gilt lettering.

"Jingle your own bells," Alvirah muttered, as with a snap of her wrist, she placed the frame facedown on the table. But when she picked up the one next to it, she smiled broadly. I'LL BE HOME FOR CHRISTMAS . . . IF ONLY IN MY DREAMS, it read. This was it!

Alvirah managed to catch the eye of the sales clerk, a good-looking boy who couldn't have been more than eighteen.

"I'll take this," she said, waving the frame at him.

"Let me see which one that is." He reached over and took it from her hands. "Oh, we've got plenty of those." He placed the sample back on the counter and took a box from the only large pile. It was stamped, "Made exclusively for Long's."

Good, Alvirah thought. That answers one question.

"I'm surprised there are any of these left," she said brightly.

He shrugged. "The others went like hotcakes. Not this one."

"Maybe you haven't had them on display long enough," Alvirah said hopefully.

"It seems like they've been there forever." He took her money and rang up the sale.

Alvirah's heart sank. This was like trying to find a needle in a haystack. "Maybe you can help me out," she said hurriedly, knowing the woman at her right elbow was starting to get impatient. "Someone dropped off one of these for my friend in the hospital last night, and the card didn't have a name on it. She feels terrible that she doesn't know who left it. You don't by any chance remember ringing up another one like this, do you?"

"You have to be kidding, lady. You know how busy we've been since Thanksgiving? I won't remember you in two minutes."

"I'll put my picture in one of these frames and send it to you," Alvirah retorted.

"Everything all right here?" a supervisor who appeared from out of the woodwork inquired.

"I was just talking to this nice young man," Alvirah said in a syrupy voice. "He was being so helpful."

"Keep longing for Long's!" the supervisor chirped and rushed off to troubleshoot elsewhere.

"I only fill in on this counter at breaks," the boy said quickly, obviously grateful Alvirah had not complained about him. "The girl who is here most of the time is off today. She'll be back tomorrow morning. We're opening at nine because it's the last day of Christmas shopping."

"What's her name?"

"Darlene."

"Darlene what?"

"Darlene Krinsky."

"She worked yesterday?"

"All day till closing."

"Thank you," Alvirah said. She'd give this information to Jack Reilly. It was the best she could do for now.

As she walked away, she heard the woman who had been at her elbow say loudly, "Thank God to get rid of Sherlock Holmes."

As the time for the ransom drop approached, the tension in the Major

Case Squad at One Police Plaza increased. Everyone who would be involved was in and out of Jack Reilly's office.

It had been a totally frustrating day. The prints they had found in the limo did not belong to anyone on record. The security-camera tapes from the hospital had proven basically useless. The man who had left the gift for Nora Reilly was of average height with slouching posture. When he had entered the hospital, he had been carrying the shopping bag cradled in his arms, virtually hiding his face. Only the back of his head was visible when he entered the gift shop, and when he exited, the huge bow on the box effectively shielded his face from the cameras.

Alvirah had reported on her trip to Long's department store. They had gotten Darlene Krinsky's address and phone number from the store's business office, but so far she hadn't been located. Not surprising, two days before Christmas, Jack thought. She's probably running around shopping, or partying. Not that he expected a talk with her would lead to anything. If that guy hadn't used a credit card for the teddy bear in the gift shop, it was doubtful that he used one for a frame that cost loss than ten dollars.

But the conversation with Alvirah did have one direct result. She was going to be riding in the backseat of his car tonight. He still wasn't quite sure how she had talked him into it, but as she pointed out, the only direct link they had to the kidnappers was the tape made because of her quick thinking. It was a fact that could not be denied.

At three o'clock, everyone involved in the ransom drop assembled in Reilly's office. Jack and his close friend, FBI agent Charlie Winslow, jointly ran the meeting.

In painstaking detail, they reviewed every aspect of what would be happening. There would be six cars in the mobile surveillance unit covering Regan Reilly as she followed the kidnappers' instructions. They would stay in touch by portable radios operating on a closed FBI frequency.

The tech unit monitoring Regan's cell phone

would immediately convey the instructions through the closed circuit to the mobile unit.

"Our agents have picked up the ransom money from the Federal Reserve," Winslow told them. "Tonight our aircraft will be overhead to track it, wherever it goes."

"You guys," Jack said, nodding to five detectives on the right side of the room, "will be eyeballing the Reillys' apartment building in case the kidnappers try anything as she's leaving the garage. Once she's on the street, you jump in your cars and join the mobile unit. Any comments?"

Dan Rodenburg, a seasoned police veteran of thirty years, shifted in his seat. "I don't like the idea of Regan Reilly driving alone in that car," he said flatly.

Neither do I, Jack thought. "We've thoroughly discussed it with her. She will not further endanger those two lives by having one of us hidden in the car. She was told to keep the police out of it. Regan knows what she's doing; she's a licensed PI of considerable note in California."

Charlie Winslow addressed the look of skepticism on Rodenburg's face. "We've made Regan Reilly an FBI special deputy for this mission. She'll be armed."

Jack continued, "Regan's car will be driven into the garage at her parents' apartment on Central Park South at approximately quarter to six. Regan will be waiting there. The duffel bag with the money will be on the front seat. She'll drive the one block to Sixth Avenue and turn onto the park drive at six o'clock.

Jack paused. "I shouldn't have to say this, but I will. It's just possible that one of you will have the chance to nail whoever makes the pickup. Don't do it. The safety of Luke Reilly and Rosita Gonzalez is what this is all about. Whoever grabs the ransom money may have a prearranged signal that if he isn't back by a certain time, get rid of the hostages. Unfortunately we've seen that happen."

He stood up. "That about wraps it up," he said. "As you know, we have an APB out for Ramon and Junior Gonzalez. Everything points to them."

Just as everyone was getting up to leave, the phone on Jack's desk rang. They all stopped, knowing that he had given orders to hold his calls except any that directly related to the case.

Jack picked up the phone. "Reilly." He listened. "Both of them? . . . Since Tuesday? . . . You checked all the phone records? . . . Big winners, huh?"

He hung up. "The Gonzalez brothers are living it up in Las Vegas, winning back the money they lost in Atlantic City. Which means . . ."

Charlie Winslow finished the thought. "Which means we haven't got any idea who we're dealing with."

Fred had managed to keep Chris and Bobby busy a good part of the morning by giving them the task of sorting the ornaments and untangling the Christmas lights. While they were absorbed in trying to beat each other at finding the most ornaments that needed new hooks, he quietly went through the apartment. It was a task he found unsettling., It was only the image of Rosita being held against her will that kept him searching for anything that would help bring her home.

It was clear that her life was an open book. The divorce papers showed that the decree had been issued almost a year ago. It granted liberal visitation to the father—something he apparently took little advantage of. The bank statements showed she lived within her means, and there were no dunning letters indicating overdue bills.

Casual questions to the boys about their activities and their mother's friends did not raise any flags.

From everything he could see, Rosita was not romantically involved with anyone and had little or no contact with her ex-husband. This confirmed his initial belief that Luke Reilly must have been the target for the kidnapping, and that Rosita simply had the hard luck to be with him.

At noon he drove with Bobby and Chris to his apartment and got a change of clothes. From there he took them to SportsWorld, an indoor amusement complex, where they had lunch and went on the rides. He kept his cell phone in his breast pocket the entire time. He knew that Keith Waters would call him immediately if there were any developments, or if anyone left a message on Rosita's phone.

They returned to the apartment late in the afternoon. Somehow it seemed to have lost its cozy, welcoming feeling. He could see the way the boys' spirits immediately began to wilt.

Tears began running down Bobby's cheeks. "I thought Mommy would be home by now."

Fred pointed to the Christmas lights and ornaments now in neat piles on the floor. "Come on, we've got to get that tree ready. We want to surprise her when she does get home."

"But we want to save some ornaments for Mommy to put up," Chris reminded him.

"Absolutely. Hey, does Mommy ever play Christmas music?"

"Oh, sure. Mommy loves Christmas music. We have lots of CDs," Chris informed him.

"I choose first." Bobby ran over to the stereo.

As the cheerful sounds of "Rudolph the Red-Nosed Reindeer" filled the room, the phone rang.

Chris raced to grab it, then, disappointment evident in his face, he said, "It's for you, Fred."

It was Keith Waters, calling to tell him that the Gonzalez brothers were no longer suspects. Not a big surprise, Fred thought as he hung up, but still a big disappointment. As the saying went, Better the devil you know. Gonzalez may be desperate for money, but he probably would not have murdered the mother of his children.

Were Rosita and Luke Reilly in the hands of sociopaths?

At 4:30, Nora said to Regan, "You'd better head over to the apartment. Give yourself plenty of time to get there."

Regan could tell how nervous her mother was getting. "I wish you weren't alone," she said.

"I'll keep busy." Nora reached into the drawer of the bedside table and took out her rosary.

"A lap around the beads," Regan smiled.

"A marathon around the beads," Nora corrected her.

Regan bent down and kissed her mother's forehead.

"Be safe, Regan." Nora's voice broke.

Unable to answer, Regan gave her a quick hug, then turned to leave. As she opened the door, she paused and looked back at her mother. "You know, Mom, there's another line that follows 'I'll be home for Christmas . . . ' "

" ' . . . you can count on me,' " Nora said.

"That's the one."

Regan gave her a thumbs-up and closed the door behind her.

L uke's eyes widened in disbelief when Petey emerged from the bedroom.

Rosita murmured, "Oh my God, I don't believe it."

"Surf's up!" Petey cried. He was moving somewhat awkwardly, weighted down by a full-body wet suit.

"Don't tell me the ransom drop is at a costume party," Luke said.

Rosita nodded. "And he's going as Jacques Cousteau."

"Watch your mouths!" a high-strung C.B. snarled. "There's nothing that says I have to let them know where to find you two."

"That wouldn't be fair," Petey exclaimed, blinking his eyes. He rotated his neck and shoulders. "This thing feels weird. I shoulda gotten it a size smaller."

Always leave room to grow, Luke thought.

"Quit griping and get your goggles and whatever else belongs to that getup," C.B. ordered as he pulled on his own coat and unlocked the door. "It's time to get out of here."

"Hey, wait a minute," Luke said, alarmed that he might not get the chance to talk to Regan. "You told my daughter she could speak to us before she hands over the money. Don't think she'll give it to you if you don't keep your end of the bargain."

"Don't worry," Petey said. "C.B.'s just giving me a ride down to my boat."

"Come on!"

"Okay, okay, don't rush me. I've got a lot on my mind."

They were gone.

But not for long. Ten minutes later, Petey was back. "Forgot the keys to my boat," he said almost apologetically. "Like I told C.B., it's what happens when you rush too much."

At 5:30 Alvirah changed into a comfortable pants suit and rubber-soled shoes for her role as a passenger in Jack Reilly's car, following Regan to the ransom drop. She fastened her sunburst pin on her winter jacket, "That recorder is going to be turned on from the minute I set foot in the car," she announced.

A concerned Willy eyed her sensible shoes. "Honey, if there's a foot chase, you're not going to try to get in it, are you?" he asked anxiously.

"Oh, gosh no, Willy. I couldn't keep up. But if for any reason we get out of the car, I don't want to break my neck. It's getting icy."

"As long as you promise to stay back, no matter what happens."

They went down the hall to the living room where Cordelia was waiting for them.

When Regan had phoned twenty minutes earlier, Cordelia had answered and spoken to her quietly.

"Is your mother alone at the hospital?" she'd asked.

"Yes," Regan had said. "Which bothers me a lot, but she was very adamant about not telling anyone, even her closest friends, about what's going on. She's so afraid of a leak to the media."

"She shouldn't be by herself," Sister Cordelia said firmly. "I'd like to volunteer to go over there. And I know Willy would too."

Five minutes later, Regan called back. "I thought my mother wanted to go this alone, but she says she'd welcome your company."

They went down in the elevator together.

The doorman hailed a cab for Willy and Cordelia, then turned to Alvirah.

"A friend is picking me up," she explained.

From the front door, she could see the garage of the Reillys' apartment building. At seven minutes of six, Regan drove out in the dark green BMW. "Godspeed, Regan," Alvirah whispered, as Jack Reilly's car pulled up to the curb. She ran across the sidewalk and slid into the back seat.

"Alvirah, this is Detective Joe Azzolino," Jack said, indicating the driver. He did not take his eyes off the BMW as he spoke.

"Nice to meet you, Joe," Alvirah said crisply. No small talk at a time like this, she thought.

The long block to Sixth Avenue, as native New Yorkers still called the Avenue of the Americas, was clogged with taxis and limousines, picking up and discharging people at the upscale hotels and restaurants that lined Central Park South.

They followed Regan's inch-by-inch progress. "This traffic is perfect for the timing," Jack said with satisfaction. "She won't have to worry about delaying too long at the intersection."

At precisely six o'clock, Regan turned left into Central Park.

A voice came over the FBI closed circuit. "Her cell phone is ringing."

"Have you got it straight?" C.B. asked as he drove down the narrow track that led to the cove where they had secured Petey's boat and hidden the trailer.

"Can a duck swim? Is the Pope Catholic? Do bears—"

"Don't do this to me," C.B. begged. "Let's go through it just once more. You are going to get on that termite-infested piece of wood you call a boat. You are going to watch the time, and at precisely six o'clock turn on the engine and leave."

"Shall we synchronize our watches, me matey?"

C.B. glared at him, then continued. "You will guide that bucket through Spuyten Duyvil, around the north end of Manhattan to the Harlem River—"

"Spuyten Duyvil is Dutch," Petey volunteered. "I think it means 'in spite of the devil.' Current is reeeeeally bad up there. Yup. But no problem for an old salt like me."

"Shut up! Shut up! *Shut up!* I gave you Rosita's cell phone to use—"

"Mr. Reilly's is much newer. You could have given that one to me. But no—"

C.B. braked so violently that Petey was thrown forward. "I could have had a concussion," he said reproachfully.

"To continue, I will call you at about quarter of seven. By then you will be in place, tied to the dock at 127th Street, next to the seawall. I will speak to you briefly. *Try* to understand that the location of a cell phone can be traced in less than a minute."

Petey whistled admiringly. "That's really fast. It's all about technology today, isn't it, C.B.? Me, I like things a little simpler."

"God knows you've proven that," C.B. moaned.

Even with the traffic along River Road, it took C.B. less than ten minutes to drive the half mile from the cove to the houseboat. Every time he made the final turn off the busy thoroughfare, he was acutely aware that a passing police car might trail a car driving down a road that led to a marina closed for the winter.

When they'd hatched the plan, it was Petey who came up with the idea of taking the houseboat he looked after at Lincoln Harbor, a year-round marina in Weehawken, to the isolated pier in Edgewater.

That part of the plan has worked, C.B. grudgingly admitted to himself, as he looked nervously in the rearview mirror. And the next time I turn onto this road, I'll have a million bucks in the backseat.

He made the turn, but drove at a snail's pace until he was sure there was no one behind him. Then he picked up speed for the remaining stretch to the parking area. Once there, he left the car and walked down the dock to the houseboat. The wind was increasing and the temperature dropping. The weather report he had heard on the radio had indicated there was still a chance the storm would blow out to sea.

I don't care where it blows, as long as by then, I've blown out of here with the money, he thought.

The footing was tricky getting on the houseboat. The current was pulling the vessel out, then slapping it back, hard against the dock. Who could possibly want one of these torture chambers? he asked himself as he tried to hoist his out-of-shape body from the pier onto the deck. There was one frightening moment when his legs were pulled into a near-perfect split, one leg on the pier, the other headed out to sea with the boat.

"You'd have to be Gumby to do this as a steady diet," C.B. wailed aloud as he finally got both feet planted on the deck. But this nightmare is almost over, he promised himself as he unlocked the door to the cabin.

Ten minutes later, at precisely 6:00 P.M., he dialed Regan's cell phone. When she answered, in his rehearsed, guttural tone he ordered, "Keep driving north. Your father and Rosita are fine. As a matter of fact, they even listened to your mother on Imus this morning . . . Isn't that right, Luke?" He held the phone up to Luke's mouth.

"I did hear your mother this morning, Regan." Let her get what I'm trying to tell her, Luke prayed. "I can just *see* myself reading your favorite book to you when you were little."

"That's enough!" C.B. said. "Here's Rosita."

"Regan, who's with my boys?"

Before Regan could answer, C.B. pulled the phone back. "Circle the park, Regan. I'll call you back."

He broke the connection. "I'm out of here," he told Luke and Rosita. "Wish me luck."

Her father and Rosita were still alive. The kidnappers were going to collect the ransom. Regan had not realized just how desperately she had feared that something would cause them to panic, and there would be no further word from them.

Circle the park. That was what he had told her to do. There was heavy traffic on the winding park road as far as the Seventy-second Street exit, where a steady stream of cars turned onto Fifth Avenue. Many others veered left to the West Side. Far fewer continued driving north.

Not good, Regan thought. With so little traffic, it will be easier to spot that I'm being followed. Near 110th Street the road curved west, then headed back south. The caller hadn't given her a time limit for the drive through the park, but neither had he said to hurry. He's probably smart enough to know that the cops can fix a location on a cell phone if it's on for more than a minute or so, she thought. That's why he barely let them say anything to me.

Dad heard Mom on Imus this morning, she thought. They had talked about the children's books Mom had sent to Imus for his son. But why did Dad talk about reading to me as a child? He must have *known* he only had a few seconds. And he mentioned my favorite book. Which one *was* it? I can't even remember myself.

She was passing the exit to Ninety-sixth

Street on the West Side. The traffic was picking up.

Last night Mom told me she kept thinking about the days when she and Dad were just starting out. She mentioned their first apartment and selling her first short story. Dad's obviously doing that same kind of reminiscing.

Regan blinked back the tears that started to well in her eyes.

She was passing Tavern on the Green. The restaurant, always brilliantly illuminated, was particularly festive with Christmas lights. When she was little, it had been a special treat to ride the carousel near the Central Park Zoo and then have lunch there.

She was at the southern end of the park, on a strip of road running parallel to Central Park South. She had made almost a complete circle.

The cell phone rang again.

"Sailing, sailing, over the bounty Maine," a goggled Petey sang as he steered his boat north under the George Washington Bridge. But then as the cold, wet air stung his exposed cheeks, he switched to the song he remembered from his first-grade play: "Oh, it's so thrilly when it's chilly in the winter—"

Clunk!

"Iceberg alert!" Petey yelled as the boat bounced up and down. Once again he switched tunes. ". . . my heart will go onnnnn." He had seen *Titanic* three times. If I'd been steering that baby, we'd have made it, he thought.

Petey felt free as a bird. It seemed as if he had the whole river to himself, and he was making great time. He patted the side of the boat. "I'm going to miss you when I'm in Brazil. We've had a lot of fun together. I sure hope the cops find you a good home."

He was almost at the top of Manhattan. "Spuyten Duyvil, here I come," he called as he veered off to enter the narrow tidal strait that connected the Hudson and the Harlem Rivers.

"Feels like I'm in a washing machine," he muttered as the swirling currents fought to twist and turn his aging craft.

"I made it!" he said triumphantly fifteen minutes later, as he tied the boat to the seawall at 127th Street, well hidden under the Triborough Bridge.

W here do all these people think they're going? C.B. fumed as he waited in a line to pay the toll at the George Washington Bridge. They should be home wrapping their presents. Of course, I'll be unwrapping mine in a couple of hours, he mused. The thought cheered him up.

He had written out the instructions he intended to give Regan Reilly. I hope you like to zigzag, he thought, because that's what you'll be doing until seven o'clock.

He checked his watch. It was 6:20. Time to

call Regan again, but not until he was out of the vicinity of the bridge. He wanted to be sure to get a clear connection.

As soon as he reached the Harlem River Drive, C.B. pulled out the cell phone. "Time to see the pretty trees on Park Avenue, Regan," he said when she answered.

"What do you think they're up to, Jack?" Joe Azzolino asked his boss as the kidnappers' instruction to Regan to head to Park Avenue was relayed to them from the eavesdropping base at headquarters. "Eagle" was the code name assigned to the operation.

"The obvious answer would be that one of them is tailing her and is trying to spot our cars," Jack said. So why do I have a gut feeling that they've got something up their sleeves that we haven't figured out? he asked himself. They were never going to be able to pinpoint the location of the cell phone. Both calls had been much too brief.

The next call came at 6:35. Regan was told to leave Park Avenue, go up Third Avenue, pull over at 116th Street, and wait.

Jack keyed his transmitter. "Eagle one to all units. Lay back. Give her a little room, but keep her in sight."

Ensconced in the backseat, Alvirah had been remarkably quiet so far, mainly because she had been trying to figure out something that had been bothering her for the last half hour. Finally it came to her, and suddenly she knew why it had struck a chord this morning when she listened to the tape of the kidnappers' first call. One of Nora Regan Reilly's early books had dealt with a kidnapping in Manhattan. In that story, the victim's wife was told to drive up Sixth Avenue from Greenwich Village and enter the park at Central Park South. It's the coincidence of the Central Park South entrance that's been jiggling in my mind, she thought.

When she reached 116th Street, Regan pulled over and double-parked. Azzolino stopped their car at 115th Street and usurped the spot another driver was about to claim. They waited silently.

As more of the plot of Nora's book came back to her, Alvirah realized that in that story, the kidnapper had the wife driving back and forth from the East Side to the West Side. What he really had been doing, however, was maneuvering her farther and farther north, and nearer and nearer to the Harlem River, Alvirah remembered.

In the novel there was something about leaving the ransom money near the river. *Then what?* she wondered. She had read the book so long ago, it was difficult to remember the details. Alvirah frowned in concentration. I've got to put my thinking cap on. But first she thought she should at least say *something* about the similarity of what had happened in Nora Regan Reilly's novel and what was happening now.

"Don't the police have a boat unit on Randall's Island?" she asked.

"Yes, we have a Harbor Unit there," Jack said without turning his head. "Why?"

"Well, it's just that Randall's Island is right next to the Triborough Bridge. It would only take one of your boats a few minutes to travel across the river."

"That's right." There was a hint of impatience in his voice.

"You see, in one of Nora's books that I read a long time ago, the ransom drop was . . ."

At the same moment they heard, "Eagle base to all units. She's been instructed to continue north on Third."

"In Nora's book," Alvirah continued, "the victim's wife drove down a dock or a pier or something and put the money on a seawall. Somebody was waiting in a boat and reached up and grabbed it."

A trailer truck had been racing the light and was now caught in gridlock halfway across Third Avenue. Regan had just cleared the intersection before the truck crossed. Now they were blocked by the truck and could no longer see her. "Eagle one to all units," Jack snapped into the transmitter, "we're locked in. Don't lose her."

"Jack . . ."

"Alvirah, not now, please."

The trailer truck was moving slowly past. Azzolino floored the accelerator. Even running the light, they were now a full block behind Regan.

They were passing 123rd Street.

Somehow Alvirah was absolutely sure of what would happen next. Dollars to donuts, Regan would be instructed to drive on a lonely road along a dock on the Harlem River. They'll tell her to leave the money on a seawall.

"Jack, I know you'll think I'm crazy, but you've got to listen to me," she said. "Those kidnappers have read Nora's books, and they're following one of her plots. You've got to get some of your men over to the river around the Triborough Bridge right away. There's a boat there waiting to make the pickup."

We need this, Joe Azzolino thought.

"Eagle base to all units. She's been told to take a right on 127th Street."

Marginal Street, Alvirah thought. That's the road she'll be told to take.

"Jack, listen to me. You've got to get a boat on the river or you'll lose them."

"Alvirah, for God's sake—"

"Eagle base to all units. She's been told to drive east and take the exit . . ."

". . . to Marginal Street," Alvirah finished with him.

Marginal Street appeared to be not so much a road as a long, bumpy, desolate dock. Regan drove along it slowly, not sure how far to go.

The phone rang again. "Drive as far as the Triborough Bridge and stop." Again the connection was broken.

Wild with tension, C.B. phoned Petey. "She'll be there in thirty seconds!"

Petey squealed with delight, then lowered his voice until it seemed to be coming from somewhere deep in his toes. "Ready, partner."

He was proud of himself that, even in this moment of great stress, he remembered to disguise his voice.

Regan's eyes darted from one side to the other, but she saw no sign of anyone nearby. She reached the underspan of the bridge and stopped. Overhead she knew hundreds of cars were passing to and from the three boroughs, but this place felt so removed from all that activity that it might have been on another planet.

She looked to either side of her car, then in the rearview mirror. This road was so isolated that the appearance of any other vehicle would make it apparent to the kidnappers that she was being followed. *Don't come too close, Jack,* she thought, *you'll scare them off. I can handle myself.*

The cell phone rang and she grabbed it. "I'm here," she said.

"Get out of the car. Take the duffel bag to the seawall and put it down on the edge. Return to your car. Back up slowly. When all the money is safely in our hands, you will learn the whereabouts of your father and Rosita. If it is not . . ."

The phone went dead.

Regan got out of the car, walked around it, and opened the passenger door. Jack had told her the duffel bag weighed twenty-two pounds. She grabbed it by the handle, lifted it in her arms, and carried it to the seawall. As she leaned over to lay it down, she realized that there was a boat tied to the wall only a few feet away.

A boat, she thought with dismay. They're making the pickup in a boat! The mobile unit from the Major Case Squad would be useless.

But the duffel bag was bugged, and the overhead aircraft would follow it to its destination. Pray God that that was where they were keeping Dad and Rosita.

Wanting desperately to see anything that might later help her identify the kidnappers, Regan allowed herself a fleeting sideward glance toward the boat as she straightened up. The only thing she could discern was that whoever was on the vessel was wearing a wet suit.

Before she could get back in the car, she heard a voice from the boat call out, "Thank you very much, Regan."

"Eagle one to all units. Stay back. Pickup is probably by boat." They could see Regan's car roll to a halt nearly two blocks down the dock.

"She's been told to get out of the car and leave the money on the seawall," Eagle base reported.

"Hook me up to the Harbor Unit," Jack snapped.

Alvirah listened as in terse, urgent phrases, Jack told the commander there what he needed. "Follow the boat they're in . . . no running lights . . . do not apprehend . . ."

"Jack, Regan is backing up. She must have made the drop." Azzolino pointed to the BMW, which was slowly coming toward them.

Jack jumped out and was opening Regan's door before the wheels stopped rolling. "They were on a boat." It was not a question.

"There appeared to be just one of them. He was wearing a wet suit," Regan said, shaking her head. "I couldn't believe it. That weirdo called out to me by name to say thank you. It was chilling. He sounded almost like a little kid."

"He's a little kid who is very familiar with your mother's books," Jack said grimly. He looked out at the water. A Harbor Unit boat, its running lights off, could be seen heading down the river.

By now that guy's probably a mile away and ditching the boat, Jack thought. Our only hope now is the tracer in the duffel bag.

I should have listened to Alvirah.

Petey the Painter had never experienced such excitement. His head was pounding, his brain was throbbing, his ears were ringing, his hands were trembling. He had never been so deliriously happy in his life.

There was a million dollars at his feet! A million dollars for him and C.B. to have a good time with. He wished they were going to

Brazil tonight. He really deserved a vacation. The Copacabana, he thought. Beautiful girls! He heard that a lot of them went topless on the beaches down there. Woo-woo!

Inside his gloves his fingers were freezing. They'd warm up when he was counting the money.

The river's current was going north. But bucking against it didn't slow him down. The pier at 111th Street was right ahead. And so was the pedestrian bridge he would use to cross over the FDR Drive.

C.B. would be waiting there for him in the car. He would jump in with the money, and off they'd go.

He pulled up to the pier and quickly tied the boat to it. Now for the tricky part, he thought. He stood up, his feet parted, and braced himself to pick up the bag and hoist it to the pier. He reached down and cradled the bag lovingly in his arms. No mother had ever held her newborn with more tenderness.

It was time to go. Whenever God closes a door he opens a window, Petey thought sadly as he looked at his boat for the last time. Overwhelmed, he bent over to kiss the bow. As his lips touched the briny surface, a wind-whipped wave slapped against the boat. Petey felt himself toppling forward.

SPLASH!

As Petey belly-flopped into the water, his precious cargo went flying out of his hands, landing a few feet beyond his reach. The swirling current of the East River now claimed it as its own and began to whisk it northward.

Desperately, Petey began a furious dog-paddle in an effort to retrieve it but within seconds realized it was hopeless. The current was trying to suck him under. He managed to get back to the boat, which he no longer felt like kissing, and grabbed onto the side for dear life.

What can I do? What can I do?! he thought, his mind a jumble of confusion.

There was only one thing he could do, he thought, gasping for breath. Drag himself up to the pier, cross the pedestrian bridge, and meet C.B. He'll get over it, he kept telling himself. After all, it's only money, and I could have drowned.

Five minutes later, a soggy Petey was tapping on the window of C.B.'s rental car. "I've got good news and bad news," he began.

"You've done everything you can," Alvirah assured Regan as they drove from Marginal Street to the hospital. "And you said the guy in the boat sounded polite and even thanked you. That's a good sign."

"I hope so. Alvirah, I just can't believe these people got the idea for the location of the ransom drop from one of my mother's books. I read that book so long ago, I'd forgotten all about it."

"You'd have been just a kid when it came out."

Regan sighed. "My mother has written so many books, even she forgets the details of plots from twenty years ago. I'm trying to think how that one ended."

Alvirah knew. The kidnap victim had never been heard from again.

They exited the FDR Drive at Seventy-first Street and parked the car on First Avenue. Entering the hospital, they passed the gift shop on the way to the elevator. Inside they could see that Lucy was on duty. She and Regan exchanged glances, and Lucy waved.

"Still here," Lucy called out.

"She's the one you talked to this morning about the teddy bear, isn't she?" Alvirah asked.

"Yes."

In the elevator up to Nora's room, Alvirah made a mental note to drop in on Lucy on the way out. Sometimes you don't know how much you know, she told herself. Maybe if I talk to her, I can jiggle that girl's brain a bit. It's worth trying.

Regan opened the door of the room. Nora, Sister Cordelia, and Willy greeted her and Alvirah with expressions of stunned disbelief.

"What?" Regan asked through suddenly dry lips. "Did you hear something about Dad?"

"Jack just called here," Nora said. "He didn't

want to tie up your cell phone. He thinks there's a good chance you'll be getting another call very soon."

"About finding Dad and Rosita?" Regan asked, somehow knowing the answer.

"No." Nora paused. "The Harbor Police just plucked the duffel bag with the million dollars out of the East River."

"Oh my God," Regan gasped.

Nora's face was ashen. "Jack thinks it means one of two things. Either they dropped it by mistake—which would be good—or for some reason they panicked because they suspected there was a tracking device in it." Her voice rose sharply. "Regan, if we get a second chance with these people, there's going to be nothing but money in the bag."

"Mom, the only reason for using the tracking device was in the hope that they would take the money to where they're keeping Dad and Rosita. You know that."

They all knew that, but Regan could see the same fear on all the faces around her that she was sure was on her own. Whether it was a bungled ransom drop or a deliberate discarding of the money, it meant that her father and Rosita were in the hands of some very unhappy abductors.

"*You were kissing your boat good-bye?!*" C.B. howled as he drove up First Avenue. "You couldn't do it while you were waiting for Regan Reilly? You could have smothered it with kisses!"

"Would you turn up the heater? I think I caught a chill in that river." Petey sneezed. "See?"

C.B. punched the steering wheel. "You had the million dollars in your hands and you let it go."

"No use crying over spilled milk," Petey said. "I could have drowned, you know. Did you ever think about that?"

"Did you ever think about the fact we have no money, we have two hostages on our hands, and . . ."

"We should have set up a petty-cash fund for their food. I had to fork over six bucks for . . ."

"Petty-cash fund! You just lost us a million dollars!" C.B.'s throat was starting to hurt from the strain of shouting.

"We'll figure a way to get it back," Petey said optimistically.

"Just what do you suggest?" C.B. asked, his voice dropping to a dangerously low level.

"Good question."

"Do you think maybe we should call Regan Reilly and tell her what a bumbling idiot you are?"

"Uh-uh."

"Do you think we should get on that plane to Brazil with barely enough money for a week's vacation?"

"Uh-uh."

"Do you think we should release Reilly and Rosita, and then have a beer with them at Elsie's?"

"Uh-uh."

"Then what do you suggest?"

"It's hard to think when I'm cold." Petey leaned back and reached for the trash bag on the backseat. "Being that we don't need this anymore, I'm going to use it to try and get warm." He started ripping it at the seams.

"I had thought of everything," C.B. moaned. "I knew that they'd be able to come up with the million bucks. I knew that they'd probably call the cops. I knew that there'd almost certainly be a tracking device attached somewhere to the bag. I read a lot of mysteries, you know."

"Reading is important," Petey said approvingly.

". . . I would have dumped the money from the duffel bag into that trash bag, which I would now like to wrap around your neck. And that duffel bag should now be lying in the middle of 111th Street instead of floating around the East River."

Petey shifted in his seat, the trash bag crinkling around him. "Wait a minute. You think they called the cops?"

"Of course. They always call the cops."

"That irritates me. We asked her not to,

right?" Petey complained. "You should let her know that when you talk to her."

C.B. gave him a withering look, but then his eyes narrowed. The best defense is a good offense, he thought, as an idea began to form in his mind.

Shortly after 8:30, Jack Reilly joined Regan, Alvirah, Willy, and Cordelia in Nora's hospital room.

"I understand that I was a big help to my husband's kidnappers," Nora said.

"Apparently you were," Jack agreed. "I've got a little more information," he told them, "but not as much as I'd like. A boat was found tied to the pier at 111th Street. We're pretty sure it was abandoned by the kidnappers. It's on its way to the lab now. That was also probably the place where the bag with the money went into the water."

"How would you know that?" Sister Cordelia asked.

"It was at that point that the guys on the aircraft tracking the bag of money realized it had switched directions and started heading north."

"Did the boat have any markings?" Regan asked.

"None. And it's obviously a rebuilt motor, which means it probably can't be traced. We're hoping for fingerprints."

There was a moment of silence. Everyone understood that the next move was up to the kidnappers.

Sister Cordelia squeezed Nora's hand. "It's time we let you get some rest. We'll keep praying."

"I'm glad you were here," Nora said sincerely. She looked at Willy. "I can't believe you made me laugh."

He smiled at her. "I'm saving my best stories for when you feel better."

Alvirah turned to Regan. "Now keep me posted. Call at any hour. I'm going to do some homework with those tapes."

Jack had given her a cassette with all the calls from the kidnappers Eagle base had taped. "This might not be orthodox, but after what happened today, I don't care," he had said. "Alvirah, next time you try to tell me something, I swear I'll listen."

The doctor came in as Alvirah, Willy, and Cordelia were leaving. He obviously knew there was a personal problem of some kind but did not probe. "How's that leg feeling?" he asked.

"Not the best," Nora admitted, the weariness in her eyes clearly visible. Reluctantly she agreed to take a painkiller.

Regar was sure that if her mother were left alone, she'd fall asleep. "Mom, I'm going to run downstairs and get a cup of coffee. Iwon't be long. Can I bring you back anything?"

"No, but you should eat something."

Jack walked out with Regan. "Okay if I join you for that coffee?"

Once in the cafeteria, Jack prevailed on Regan to have a sandwich.

"We're certainly keeping you from enjoying the holidays," Regan said. "I can't believe tomorrow is Christmas Eve. You must have had plans."

"My family will still be there when I get home. My parents live in Bedford, and that's where the whole clan will be this week. There are so many of us, they won't even notice I haven't shown up yet."

Regan smiled. "Being an only child, if I don't show up it's noticeable."

Jack laughed. "If you were one of ten, it would be noticeable."

That remark would have snapped my mother awake, Regan thought, smiling. Kind of wakes me up too.

They talked about what the kidnappers might do next.

"My biggest fear is that absolutely nothing will happen next," Regan admitted.

"Regan, keep in mind that you talked to your father and Rosita less than three hours ago," Jack said.

"Those few words my father said keep running through my mind. He mentioned reading my favorite book to me when I was a little girl. I thought at the time he was just being nostalgic, like last night when my mother was remi-

niscing about when they were newlyweds."
She shook her head. "But now I'm not so sure.
I have a feeling he was trying to tell me some-
thing."

"What was your favorite book?" Jack
asked.

"For the life of me, I can't remember."
Restlessly Regan tapped her hands on the table.
"Maybe my father brought it up because my
mother and Imus talked about children's
books this morning."

"More than likely that's all it was. But you
know as well I do that kidnap victims often try
to pass messages if they possibly can."

"Oh, it's you two again!" The call came
from across the room.

They looked up to see Lucy from the gift
shop bearing down on them.

"Can't get enough of each other, huh?" Her
eyes darted around. "I always take a walk
through here before I go home. As usual, no
Dr. Kildares in sight." She shrugged. "What
are you going to do? Say, your mother must be
some stickler for writing thank-you notes. One

of her friends was just in the shop, asking about the guy who bought the teddy bear."

Regan and Jack looked at each other. "Alvirah," they said in unison.

Willy and Cordelia were waiting for Alvirah on a couch in the lobby when she emerged from the gift shop.

"Well, I did find something out," she reported.

"What did you learn, honey?" Willy asked.

"The man who sent that teddy bear with Luke Reilly's picture was carrying a Long's shopping bag."

"You knew that."

"Yes, but Lucy—that's the clerk's name—remembered something else. There was a red jacket or sweater, or at least some sort of red clothing, in the bag."

"So?" Cordelia asked.

"Oh, I know it's not much, but it's something," Alvirah said, sighing. "Maybe it will help jog the memory of the salesclerk at Long's when I talk to her tomorrow."

Cordelia was going home.

Alvirah and Willy put her in a cab, then hailed one for themselves. "Two-eleven Central Park South," Willy said.

Even though it was late and the temperature was steadily dropping, the streets were filled with people. When the cab reached the area of the Plaza Hotel, Alvirah remarked wistfully, "It always looks so festive around here during the holidays. ' 'Tis the season to be jolly,' and all that." She shook her head as she remembered the sadness in Nora's eyes.

When they got home, she changed into her favorite old robe, made a pot of tea, and settled at the dining room table. I began the day with this and I'll finish the day with this, she thought as she turned on her recorder.

She listened to all the tapes, playing them in the order they had been recorded. First, the original call from the kidnappers, then the conversation with Fred Torres at Rosita's home. She replayed that tape twice, each time stopping at one point. "Probably doesn't mean a thing, but it's worth asking him about," she said aloud as she jotted a phrase on her memo pad.

Willy joined her as she was playing the tapes of the kidnapper giving directions to Regan.

"What impression are you getting of that guy?" Alivrah asked.

"He's disguising his voice," Willy said. "He's smart enough to get off the phone fast, so his location can't be traced. He planned that ransom drop mighty carefully."

"He was smart enough to realize the plot Nora used could work for him, and it did to a point. Now listen to this one." She played the tape of the call in which Luke and Rosita spoke to Regan as she started driving into Central Park.

"Hear anything special?" she asked Willy.

"It's not as clear as the calls that came after it."

"That's right. The reception isn't as good. That's probably because of the location where they're being kept. You know, there can be a lot of interference in some areas." Alvirah played the tape again. "Did you notice any-thing about what Luke Reilly said?"

"Well, the poor guy's obviously reminiscing about his life. I did that when I was kidnapped. And . . ."

"And what?"

"He kind of puts a big emphasis on the word 'see.' It's almost like he's trying to tell her something."

"That's exactly what I was thinking,"

Willy glanced at the pad. "What's that mean?" He pointed to a notation she had made.

"It's something I want to run by Fred Torres tomorrow. Rosita told him that Luke Reilly always 'kept his cool.' I want to find out if Rosita talked about any specific situation where he had to 'keep his cool.' " She looked at her watch. "It's eleven o'clock, and still no word from Regan. That means she hasn't heard from the kidnappers."

"Maybe they're trying to figure out their next move," Willy suggested.

"Then they better figure it out soon. What worries me is that the longer Luke Reilly is missing, the more likely that word of his kidnapping will get out. If it ends up in the headlines, God knows what will happen."

C.B. did not attempt to hide the situation from Luke and Rosita. When he and Petey arrived back at the houseboat, he told them exactly what had happened.

"You can't make this stuff up," Rosita said, glaring at Petey as he went into the bedroom to change out of his wet suit.

"You actually used a scenario from my wife's book for the ransom drop?" Luke asked incredulously.

"It almost worked," Petey called from the bedroom. "Has she got any other kidnapping stories we could take a look at?" He poked his head out the door. "We can't miss our flight tomorrow night. The planes are overbooked."

"I've read all her novels," C.B. said shortly. "She doesn't have any other kidnappings."

Oh yes she does, Luke thought. The other

one had come to mind only a few weeks ago when he had business in Queens and took the wrong turn coming out of the Queens-Midtown Tunnel. He had found himself on the same route she'd used for a ransom drop in one of her early short stories. He remembered it because Nora had been pregnant with Regan when she wrote that story, and since she had been ordered to stay in bed, he had driven around and checked out the route she was planning for the kidnappers to use.

"What do you intend to do now?" he asked C.B.

"At some point I'm going to call your daughter and tell her she'd better be able to come up with another million dollars. Unless, of course, the cops have already recovered our money from the East River."

There was a note of desperation in his voice. They have to get out tomorrow night, Luke thought, and they can't go without the money. "When you put me on the phone again, I'll tell my daughter to be sure to get it for you."

"You bet you will. But first I've got to figure out a new place for her to leave it," C.B. blustered.

It's worth a shot, Luke thought. By now, Nora must have realized that they had used a ransom-drop location that was in one of her books. This time, would she think about that short story and talk to the cops about it?

It was probably crazy. A one-in-a-million shot, if not totally hopeless. But like his earlier effort to convey to Regan that they were in the vicinity of the GW Bridge and the lighthouse, it at least made him feel as if he was doing something to try and save their lives.

"You know, C.B." he began, his tone friendly, "a couple of weeks ago I had to pick up the remains of a client's grandmother from a small nursing home in Queens. When I came through the Midtown Tunnel and exited on Borden Avenue on the Queens side, I got lost. In only a few blocks, I found myself in a totally deserted area right underneath the Long Island Expressway. If I were planning a kidnapping, I think I'd use that area for a ransom drop. Check it out yourself and you'll see what I mean."

C.B.'s eyes narrowed. "Why are you being so helpful?"

"Because I want to get out of here. The sooner you have the money, the sooner you'll make the call telling them where to find us."

"I feel better," Petey announced as he emerged from the bedroom in a sweat suit. "Nothing like a dry change of clothes." He pulled a Mountain Dew out of the tiny refrigerator. "I heard what you were saying, Mr. Reilly. You're really using the old noodle. I know exactly where you're talking about. I got lost there, too, on my way to a job. I wasn't going to pick up a stiff though." He turned to C.B. "It's perfect. We'd be nice and near the airport. They get mad if you don't check in at least two hours before flight time. Sometimes they give your seat away. It happened to my cousin—"

"Petey!" C.B. shrieked.

"Oh, leave him alone," Rosita said. "I'd love to hear the rest of the story."

Luke could tell that C.B. was mulling the suggestion of the drop site over in his mind.

C.B. reached into his pocket and pulled out a

folded sheet of paper. On it he had printed the step-by-step directions he had given Regan earlier. He turned the paper over. "Okay, Mr. Reilly, fire away. Petey and I are going to take a drive tonight and see if you're as smart as your wife."

"Go back out in that cold?" Petey protested.

Luke gave C.B. the directions, then said, "Before you go, you'd better call my daughter and let her start arranging to get the money. And give her a break. She's got to be worried."

"Let her worry."

It was nearly midnight before C.B. and Petey returned to the houseboat. Rosita had dozed off, but Luke was wide awake. Over and over in his mind, he had been revising the few words he would be allowed to say to Regan when the next call was made.

When C.B. turned on the light, Rosita opened her eyes and sat up.

"Well?" Luke asked him.

"Not bad," C.B. said. "It might do."

"Scary around there!" Petey exclaimed. "I told C.B. to lock the car doors."

"I think your daughter should be plenty worried by now," C.B. said. "Do you think it's too late to call?"

"Somehow I doubt it," Luke said.

Regan was sitting by a sleeping Nora when the cell phone rang. Please let it be them, she prayed, her heart pounding. She picked it up. "Hello," she said quietly.

"Did you recover the money?"

Regan stiffened. "What do you mean?"

"I mean," C.B. said angrily, "we could tell there was a tracer in the duffel bag. Don't do that again. Have another million ready, or you'll regret it. I'll call you at four o'clock tomorrow afternoon. Here's Daddy."

"Regan, at this point, I'm seeing *red*. Do as he says and get us out of here."

The line went dead.

Saturday,

December 24th

Fred had heard from Regan shortly after midnight. She'd told him about the kidnappers' call, and how they had warned her not to have a tracking device in the next ransom delivery. She hadn't spoken to Rosita, but her father had said, "Get *us* out of here."

After the call, Fred had tossed and turned on the couch. If the next drop doesn't work, they'll give up, he thought. And they won't leave witnesses.

At 3:00 A.M., he had taken the blanket and pillow and stretched out on top of Rosita's bed. Before long, he was joined by two troubled little boys who curled up against him and fell back asleep.

"Mommy's sick, isn't she?" Bobby had asked quietly when they woke up.

"Maybe she got sick like Grandma did, and went to Puerto Rico without us," Chris suggested.

"All your mommy cares about is getting home and being with you guys," Fred said reassuringly. "But Mrs. Reilly really needs her now."

"She won't stay with Mrs. Reilly tomorrow, will she?" Bobby asked.

Tomorrow, Fred thought. Christmas Day. What could he possibly tell them if she wasn't back then? And what was he going to tell Rosita's mother when she phoned to wish them a merry Christmas, as she almost certainly would.

To help pass the time, he took the boys out to breakfast, but they turned down his offer of another trip to SportsWorld.

"We should be there in case Mommy gets home," Chris said solemnly.

Deck the Halls

Ernest Bumbles woke up on Christmas Eve
in what was for him a very grumpy mood.
He still hadn't been able to catch up with Luke
Reilly, even though he had stopped by Reilly's
Funeral Home twice yesterday—once in the
afternoon and again in the evening.

"A gift deferred is a gift denied," he told
Dolly as he packed his suitcase for their annual
trip to his mother-in-law's.

Dolly knew all about Ernest's passionate
nature. When he felt something, he felt it
with all his heart. When he wanted something, he let nothing stand in his way. That's
why, year after year, he had been unanimously reelected president of the Seed-Plant-
Bloom-and-Blossom Society. But he was also
a caring man. It was no wonder he never had
a plant die on him.

"Bumby," Dolly said gently. "We're not
leaving until late this afternoon. Why don't we
drive by Mr. Reilly's house and ring the bell on
our way out of town?"

"I don't want to seem like a pest."

"Oh, hush. You never could."

Nora had awakened to hear Regan talking to Luke's abductor. When the brief conversation was abruptly terminated, Regan told her, word for word, exactly what had been said.

The bedside phone rang almost immediately.

"They can't know there was a tracer in that bag," Jack said firmly. "They're bluffing. I wouldn't be surprised if the guy on the boat accidentally dropped it into the water."

"I wouldn't be surprised by that either," Regan said, "but my mother is adamant that there be no tracer in the bag this time."

"I understand," Jack said. "Regan, remind your mother that it's a good sign you talked to your father again. When he spoke to you, he said, 'I'm seeing red.' Is that an expression he uses when he's angry?"

"I've never heard him say that in my life," Regan said. "Neither has my mother."

"Then he's definitely trying to tell you something," Jack said. "See if you or your mother can make the connection."

Regan and Jack agreed to talk in the morning, then Regan had phoned Alvirah and Fred.

It was another near-sleepless night for her and Nora as they tried to make sense of what Luke had said and to remember what Regan's favorite book had been as a child.

Nora said, "Regan, when your father came home from work, you always ran to him with a book in your hand. I just can't remember what your favorite one would have been. Could it have been one of the fairy tales? 'Snow White,' or 'Sleeping Beauty,' or maybe 'Rumplestiltskin'?"

"No," Regan said. "It wasn't any one of them."

Around dawn, they both dropped off into a light, uneasy sleep.

Neither one of them had wanted breakfast. Then at eight o'clock, Nora was taken for X rays. When she returned to the room at 9:00, Regan went down to the cafeteria and brought back containers of hot coffee.

"Regan, while I was waiting to be x-rayed, something came to me that I think is important," Nora said after she took the first sip.

Regan waited.

"It is absolutely weird that a scenario from one of my early books was used for the ransom drop yesterday. That card with your father's picture was signed 'Your number-one fan.' If that person is the kidnapper, it's possible he's familiar with all my work."

"That's very possible," Regan agreed. "In which case we're dealing with an obsession. But what are you saying?"

"As I lay there, it came to me that I wrote another kidnapping story, a long time ago."

"You did? I never read it."

"I wrote it when I was pregnant with you," Nora recalled. "It was a short story, not a book, but it described in detail a ransom drop in Queens." She bit her lip. "My doctor had ordered bed rest when I was working on it, and I remember that Dad came up with the suggestion for the location of the drop. He drove out there, took pictures, and drew a map, even to the point of marking the best place to leave the suitcase of money. I was paid all of one hundred dollars for the story when it was published, and Dad joked that I should give him half."

Regan smiled briefly. "That sounds like Dad." Despite the stab of pain that hit her heart, she felt a surge of hope. "Mom, suppose you're right and the kidnapper *is* a pathological fan who's acting out your plots. It's very possible he's somehow gotten his hands on that story and will use that plot for the drop tomorrow. If we knew ahead of time the kind of directions he's likely to give me, the police can stake out the route beforehand without being visible. Where in Queens was the ransom drop?"

"God, Regan, it was so long ago, and as I said, Dad researched it for me. All I remember is that it was near the Midtown Tunnel."

"You must have a copy of the story."

"It's home somewhere in the attic."

"What about the magazine it was in?"

"It bit the dust a long time ago."

There was a tap at the door. The doctor breezed into the room, a holiday smile on his face, a batch of X rays under his arm. "Morning, ladies," he said. "How's my favorite patient?"

"Pretty good," Nora said.

"Good enough to go home?"

Nora looked at him, surprised. "You were pretty insistent on my staying for at least three days."

"You had a nasty fracture, but the swelling is going down nicely. The X rays look okay. You must be anxious to get out of here. Just be sure to keep that leg elevated." He turned to Regan. "Maybe next year, you and your parents will make it to Maui for Christmas."

"I hope so," Regan said. More than you can imagine, she thought.

When he left the room, Nora and Regan looked at each other.

"Regan," Nora said, "run and get the car. I'll get checked out of here. There are an awful lot of boxes in that attic."

At five of nine, Alvirah was in the fore-front of the throng of last-minute shop-pers waiting for Long's department store to open its doors. Unlike the others, she did not have a list of gifts to buy, most of which would probably be returned forty-eight hours later. She had already phoned Fred to ask about why Rosita had told him Luke "always kept his cool." He assured her that Rosita was only referring to humorous situations.

At 9:01, she was on the down escalator, headed for the basement. Fast as she was, there were already shoppers at the counter where the Christmas knickknacks had been further reduced to almost giveaway prices. They must have slept in the aisles last night, she thought, as with mounting impatience she waited to get the only salesgirl's attention.

The customer ahead of her, a thin, white-haired septuagenarian, was crossing names off her shopping list as she handed one picture frame after another to the clerk. "Let's see.

That takes care of Aggie and Margieand Kitty and May. Should I get one for Lillian? . . . Nah, she didn't give me anything lastyear." She picked up one of the "Jingle My Bells" frames. "Disgraceful," she proclaimed. "That'll be all."

"Are you Darlene Krinsky?" Alvirah asked the young saleswoman when she finally got her attention.

"Yes." Her voice was wary.

Alvirah knew she had to make it fast. She took out the frame she had purchased the day before. "My friend is in the hospital." That might get her sympathy, she thought. "Someone left one of these frames for her on Thursday night and didn't sign his name. We think he may have bought it when he was on the way to the hospital, because we know he was carrying a Long's shopping bag with some red clothing in it. He's a man of medium height, with thinning brown hair, and about fifty years old."

Krinsky shook her head. "I wish I could help you." With her eyes she indicated a group of teenagers who were waving the knickknacks they had selected, anxious to get her attention. "You can see how crazy it is around here."

"He was carrying an old wallet and may have counted the change out very carefully," Alvirah persisted.

"I'm sorry, I'd really like to help, but . . ." She trailed off. "I hope your friend feels better." She took a Santa Claus music box out of the hands of one of the teenagers.

It's hopeless, Alvirah thought dejectedly as she turned away from the counter.

"Wait a minute," the clerk said softly to herself as she started to ring up the music box.

As Alvirah reached the escalator, she felt a tap on her shoulder. "The clerk at that counter is calling you," a young man said.

Alvirah rushed back.

"You say he had a bag with red clothing in it? I know who it might be. One of the guys who plays Santa Claus was down here the other night. I'm sure that was the frame he bought. He tried to get an employee discount."

That's got to be him, Alvirah thought. "Can you tell me his name?"

"No. But he might even be upstairs now. The toy department is on the third floor."

"You must be talking about Alvin Luck," the manager of the toy department, a pinched-faced man in his late fifties, said to Alvirah. "He was working here Thursday evening, and no doubt was carrying his uniform home to press. We insist that our Santas set a good example for the children."

"Is he due in soon?"

"He doesn't work here anymore."

"He doesn't?" Alvirah asked, dismayed.

"No. He turned in his uniform yesterday. When we hired him, he made it very clear he couldn't work on Christmas Eve."

"Was he here last night?"

"No. He left at four o'clock."

"Would you have his address or phone number?"

The manager looked sternly at Alvirah.

"Madam, we have total respect for our employees' privacy. That information is strictly confidential."

Jack can get it in a minute, Alvirah thought, as she thanked the man and rushed to a telephone. And anyhow, he'll take over from here. If Alvin Luck *is* involved in the kidnapping, Jack will find out fast.

Alvin Luck and his mother handed their tickets to the usher at the door of Radio City Music Hall. Since he was a child, it had been their tradition to take in the Christmas Spectacular on Christmas Eve, and then treat themselves to a special lunch. In the old days they had dined at Schrafft's, and they both agreed that things weren't the same since that venerable purveyor of chicken à la king had closed its doors.

After lunch, weather permitting, they would take in the sights of Fifth Avenue.

Today they thoroughly enjoyed the show,

lingered over lunch, and then prevailed on a security guard to take their annual picture in front of the tree in Rockefeller Center. All the while they were blissfully unaware that half the police department in New York City was on the lookout for them.

It was nearly 11:30 when Regan, with Nora sitting sideways in the backseat of the car, her injured leg across the seat, pulled into their driveway in Summit, New Jersey. Alvirah and Willy were in a car right behind them.

Alvirah had phoned Regan as soon as she hung up with Jack and told her about Alvin Luck. "Jack will call you the minute they find him," she promised. Then, on learning about Nora's short story, she had instantly volunteered to help in the search through the boxes in the attic.

Leaning on her crutches, with Willy on one side and Regan on the other, Nora made her careful way along the walk and into the house.

"When I left here Wednesday evening, I never dreamed I'd come back this way. Or without Luke," she added, her tone flat.

The house seemed dark and somber. Regan quickly moved around, turning on lights. "Mom, where do you think you'd be most comfortable?" she asked.

"Oh, inside." She gestured toward the family room.

Alvirah took in every detail of the place as they followed Nora past the living room to the back of the house. The large kitchen spilled into the high-ceilinged family room, inviting with its generous couches, big windows, and open-hearth fireplace. "This is lovely," she said admiringly.

Nora hobbled over to the wing chair. Regan took her crutches, and when Nora was settled, helped lift the leg with its heavy cast onto the hassock. "Whew," Nora said with a sigh as she leaned back. "This is going to take some getting used to." The tiny beads of perspiration on her forehead were a testimony to the effort it had taken just to navigate the short distance from the car.

A few minutes later, after Willy and Regan had brought a half-dozen boxes down from the attic, they were all busy looking for the manuscript or magazine copy of the short story Nora remembered being titled "Deadline to Paradise."

"I thought I'd kept every piece of research, every version of every manuscript, every outline, even every rejection slip from the early days, " Nora commented. "So where is it?"

As the four of them sifted through the stacks of papers, Alvirah told them about tracking down Alvin Luck. "I can't believe that anyone who's been working as a department store Santa Claus could be part of all this," Nora said. Then they all fell silent. Half an hour later, Willy and Regan went back up to the attic to bring down more boxes. But it was a fruitless effort. At three o'clock, Nora said dispiritedly, "I may as well admit it. If a copy of that story still exists, it isn't in this house." Then she looked at Regan. "Why don't you call Rosita's and see how her boys are doing? I'm worried about them."

From Fred's tone, Regan could tell immediately that it was not going well. "They're worried that their mother is sick," he told her. "All I'm trying to do at this point is keep them distracted. I even opened the package of books your mother sent them for Christmas and read to them. Those, at least, they really enjoyed."

"I'm glad they liked the books," Nora said after Regan reported what Fred had told her. "I had Charlotte in the children's section of the bookstore put them together and send them over for me." She paused. "Wait a minute. She also sent me videos of some of the hot new movies for kids. I was going to give them to Mona." Nora gestured toward the neighboring house. "Her grandchildren are coming for a visit next week."

She looked at Regan. "Why don't you take them to Chris and Bobby? Then if you get a chance to talk to Rosita at four o'clock, you can tell her you just saw the boys."

Regan looked at her watch. She was supposed to receive the next phone call at four. It wasn't much more than a fifteen-minute drive to Rosita's. That gave her over an hour to get there and back. She knew her mother wanted her to be home when the next call from the kidnappers came. She said that just knowing her husband was on the other end of the phone made the nightmare seem a little less hopeless.

Alvin Luck and his mother could not have spent a better day together. That is, until they got home and found two detectives waiting for them.

"May we speak to you inside?" they asked.

"Sure, fellows, come on in," Alvin invited. With the security that comes from having led an absolutely blameless life, he was thrilled that real-life detectives had come to talk to him. Maybe something had happened at Long's, and they needed his help.

His mother did not share his excitement. When the detectives asked permission to look around the apartment, she glared at Alvin for granting it.

Sal Bonaventure, the detective who went into Alvin's bedroom, whistled softly when he saw the accumulation of crime literature that was stacked floor to ceiling. Piles of manuscripts crowded the shelves over the long table that served as a desk. In addition to a computer and printer, the table held dozens of books and magazines, most of them clearly very old. A stack of novels by Nora Regan Reilly, many of them lying open, was near the computer. Bonaventure saw that the pages were heavily annotated.

Sal and his partner had contacted Jack Reilly as soon as Alvin and his mother stepped into the entryway. He had told them to hold off on questioning until he got there.

Santa Claus may be the key to breaking this case wide open, Sal thought optimistically.

The snowstorm, predicted to hit earlier, finally had started—and with a vengeance—by the time Regan parked in front of Rosita's apartment. Fred Torres had been watching for her. "I told Chris and Bobby that you have some great new movies for them," he said heartily as he opened the door.

The boys were sitting on the floor, a dozen marbles scattered between them. They looked at Regan with some distrust. "When is your mommy going to be better so our mommy can come home?" Chris asked.

He's trying to be polite, poor kid, Regan thought, but he wants an answer. "Very soon," she told him as she held out the gaily wrapped package of tapes. "This is for both of you . . ."

Her voice trailed off; she did not notice when they took the present from her hands. She was staring down at the cover of one of the books lying on the coffee table. The title *The Little Red Lighthouse and the Great Gray Bridge* had caught her eye and evoked a flood of memories.

Daddy, read this one again, just once more, please.

The cover illustration was of a jaunty red lighthouse. She opened the book. The frontispiece depicted the unmistakable George Washington Bridge, with the tiny lighthouse tucked below it.

Your favorite book . . . I'm seeing red . . .

This was what Dad was trying to tell me, Regan realized with mounting excitement. From wherever he is, he can see the lighthouse.

"Regan, what is it?" Fred asked urgently.

Regan shook her head. "I hope you guys enjoy the movies. I'll see you later." She turned to Fred.

"I'll walk you outside," he said.

The tension emanating from C.B. had accelerated to an explosive level. Luke and Rosita silently observed his grim countenance as the time for making the phone call drew near. He knows this is it, Luke thought. He knows that if they don't get the money tonight, they never will. He could hear the winds building up outside. The boat was banging against the pier with ever-increasing force. If this storm keeps up, who knows when and if their flight will take off.

"Hey, C.B.," Petey said, "I gotta run home. I left my passport in the apartment."

No you didn't, Luke thought. I saw you looking at it a little while ago. What was Petey up to now? he wondered.

"You what?" C B. stared at him.

"I wanted to be sure it was in a nice safe place. I don't have much room here. You've been sleeping home these couple of nights, I notice. What's the difference? It's a five-minute walk. Pick me up at the apartment."

C.B. looked at his watch. "Be waiting outside at precisely ten minutes after four."

"Gotcha." Petey looked from Luke to Rosita. "We may not ever meet again, but I'd like to wish you all the luck in the world." With a snappy salute, he was gone.

Luke knew why his feet were feeling cold and damp. There was a trickle of water on the floor. The ice, he thought. This tub is beginning to leak.

Jack Reilly's immediate gut feeling was that Alvin Luck was no threat to mankind. He was a mystery buff, not a kidnapper. Nora Regan Reilly was just one of many writers he collected.

Any question he or the detectives asked Alvin was answered promptly and without hesitation. He acknowledged that he had taken the picture of Luke at a mystery-writers' dinner. He had bought the frame after he heard about Nora's accident.

"Didn't she like it?" he asked as they stood in his cluttered bedroom.

"I know why they're asking you all these questions," his mother butted in. "You didn't sign your name to the card." She shook her head vigorously. "They don't like that kind of stuff. They think it means you have something to hide."

"Mrs. Reilly was just surprised to receive an unsigned gift," Jack said soothingly. "You did buy the teddy bear in the gift shop yourself?"

"What teddy bear?" his mother asked. "Alvin, you didn't say word one about any teddy bear."

"I see you've written a lot of notes in the margins of Mrs. Reilly's books." Jack picked up one of them and flipped through the pages.

"Oh, yes," Alvin said excitedly. "I've studied hundreds of mystery writers to see how they plot. It's a great learning tool. I file my notes under categories like murder, arson, burglary, embezzlement. When I read about true cases in the newspapers, I clip them out for my files too."

"Is that why you have these notes on Nora Regan Reilly?"

"Of course."

"Any chance you ever read 'Deadline to Paradise?' "

"That was one of her earliest stories. I filed it under kidnapping." He walked around the bed to a file cabinet and pulled open the bottom drawer. "Here it is." He handed Jack a thirty-one-year-old magazine.

Regan drove as swiftly as she dared over roads that were rapidly becoming snow covered. *Dad and Rosita can see the little red lighthouse,* she thought with a glimmer of hope. They're somewhere around the George Washington Bridge. Jack had said that background sounds on the tapes indicated that they were near water.

She dialed Jack's number.

"I just spoke to your mother and told her that Alvin Luck has been eliminated as a suspect. But he might turn out to be a big help—he had a copy of her story."

"What?"

"He's a serious mystery collector. If by any wild chance the kidnappers follow the route used in the story, it'll be a lot easier to cover them."

"I have something to tell you too." Regan relayed to him what had just happened at Rosita's.

"Regan, this probably means they're being kept in New Jersey."

"Why?"

"Think about it," Jack said. "Your father left the hospital a little after ten. The car obviously was driven to New Jersey, because it came back across the George Washington Bridge into New York at 11:16. Then it crossed the Triborough Bridge into Queens at 11:45, which is just about how long it would normally take to travel that distance without stopping. If they didn't stop right after crossing the bridge into Manhattan, there's no way they could still see the lighthouse beyond that."

"For some reason, that makes me feel good," Regan said. The net is tightening, she thought.

Petey nursed a tequila sunrise at Elsie's Hideaway, where the annual Christmas Eve party was in full swing. The whole gang of regulars was there. I'll just have *one* of these, he promised himself. I've got to have my wits about me for the big night.

If C.B. knew I'd stopped in here, he'd kill me. But I couldn't leave the U.S. of A. forever without one last visit to this joint, where, like the song says, "everybody knows your name." I've gone fishing with some of these guys, he thought. Lotta laughs.

"Petey, you look down in the dumps." Matt, Elsie's longtime bartender, replaced his empty tequila glass. "Elsie says 'Merry Christmas.' "

"Aw, that's nice."

"I hear you're going away on vacation. Where to?"

"Going fishing."

"Where?"

"Down south," Petey said vaguely.

Matt was already with the next customer.

Petey checked his watch. It was time to go. He slid off the bar stool, looked at the free tequila sunrise, and with uncharacteristic resolve, left it untouched.

"Petey, do you feel all right?" Matt looked concerned as he poured cocktail peanuts into an empty dish.

"I feel great," Petey assured him. "Like a million bucks."

"Glad to hear it. Have a good time on your trip. Send us a postcard."

"Say, do you have any more of those Elsie's postcards?" Petey asked.

Matt reached under the bar. "We've got one left. Be my guest."

With a wave, Petey left Elsie's for the last time.

Regan had kept Austin Grady up to date with everything that had been happening. For the last two days, he had been fielding calls from friends of the Reillys who had heard about

Nora's accident and couldn't reach her or Luke.

When Nora phoned Austin at 3:15, he asked if he could stop by the house on his way home. Nora quickly responded, "I'd like to see you, Austin. You're the only one of our friends who knows what's going on."

Austin had been there only a few moments when Regan came in and told them about seeing the book about the red lighthouse.

"The Little Red Lighthouse and the Great Gray Bridge," Nora said. "Of course! You loved it."

"They've got to be in view of that lighthouse," Alvirah said emphatically. "There's no doubt that on those tapes he emphasized the words, 'I'm seeing red.' "

"Well, Jack thinks they're on the New Jersey side of the bridge," Regan said, and then explained why.

"If we only had some idea who did this," Nora said hopelessly. "But we have nothing else to go on, and they're calling in less than half an hour. Once they get the money, can we trust them to keep their end of the deal?" She gestured toward the window. "Look at the weather. If they did drop that bag by mistake yesterday, think of how much could go wrong today."

They all jumped when the doorbell rang.

"Regan, we can't have anyone else here. Say I'm sleeping . . ."

"I know, Mom." Regan hurried down the hall to the front door. Standing outside was the plant society president who had knocked on the window of Austin's office two nights ago. He was wearing a stocking cap, the top of which was slowly piling up with snow.

"Hi, Regan!" he chirped "Remember me? I met you the other night. Ernest Bumbles."

He was carrying a gift-wrapped package under his arm.

"Hello, Mr. Bumbles," Regan said hurriedly.

"Is your dad here?" he asked.

"I'm afraid not," Regan said. "He was delayed in New York."

"Oh, what a shame. My wife and I are on our way to visit her mother in Boston. Although with this weather, no one should be out driving! Anyway, I have this gift I have so been wanting to give to your dad. It breaks my heart that I keep missing him. But I want him to have it for Christmas."

"Let me take it then," Regan said, anxious to end the conversation and get back to the others.

"Could you do me a favor?" Ernest asked with a pleading look.

"What's that?"

"Could you please open my gift to your father now and let me take a picture of you with it?"

Regan felt like strangling him. She invited him to step inside, then quickly ripped off the ribbon and opened the box to find the framed proclamation.

"What's this for?" she asked as she read it.

Ernest beamed. "Your father has done so much for the Blossoms. He introduced Cuthbert Boniface Goodloe to our society. The poor man died just this week, but he left us a million dollars in his will. We can never thank your father enough."

"A million dollars?" Regan said.

Ernest looked misty eyed. "A million dollars. Virtually his entire estate! What a generous man. And it's *all* because of your father. We also have one of these citations to present to Mr. Goodloe's nephew, in honor of his wonderful uncle, but he's never home either! Now let me take your picture."

At Nora's request, Austin came down the hall from the family room to see what was going on. Oh my God, he said to himself when he spotted Bumbles. This guy never quits.

He caught Regan's eye but was stopped from brushing Bumbles off by the slight shake of her head.

Regan held up the citation. "Austin, look at this," she said with a forced bright smile. "My dad's the reason Mr. Bumbles' society received a million dollars this week from a Cuthbert Boniface Goodloe. Did you know my dad was directly responsible for that?"

Austin shook his head. "I had no idea."

"I was so sorry your dad had to miss our benefactor's funeral," Bumbles continued. "But the Blossoms showed up in full force."

"It's good you were there," Austin said.

Regan has the patience of a saint, he thought. "His nephew is his only family."

"He is?" Regan said. She looked at Ernest and asked jokingly, "How did he feel about his uncle leaving such a big gift to the Blossoms?"

Ernest put his finger to his cheek. "I couldn't say. But why wouldn't he be happy for us? We're a wonderful society. And he'll be thrilled to receive one of these citations, I'm sure. That is, if I can ever reach him."

"Where does he live?" Regan asked.

"Fort Lee."

Regan swallowed hard. The New Jersey side of the George Washington Bridge was in Fort Lee. Was it possible? "I know my father will love this."

"Well, I'm just glad you're home to receive it. I'm keeping the other one in the trunk of my car so I can drop it by when I reach that nephew."

"Give it to me," Regan said. "I mean, I'm going to be in the vicinity of Fort Lee tonight, and I'll drop it at his house so he'll have it for Christmas too."

"That would be wonderful!" Ernest cried. "But I don't have his address."

"I'll call the office," Austin said. "I'm sure we have it on file."

"I'll be right back," Ernest said as he turned, went outside, and half slid down the path to his car, where Dolly was patiently waiting. When he returned, he handed Austin the other gift. "Hold this, please." He turned to Regan as he readied his camera. "Now say cheese."

"Cheese."

"Got it."

"What's the nephew's name anyway?"

Austin and Ernest answered in unison. "C.B. Dingle."

"I win," Bobby said halfheartedly. "Now let's put in the tape."

"First we've got to collect all these marbles," Fred told him.

The three of them crawled on their hands and knees and gathered the marbles that were scattered all over the living room. "I think I saw one go under the couch," Fred said. He lifted the skirt of the slipcover and ran his hand around in the narrow space between the couch and the rug. His groping fingers closed over the marble, but he could tell that it was resting on a smooth paper surface, not the carpeting. Sliding the paper out, he realized that it was a postcard addressed to Rosita.

The scrawled message was surrounded by dabs of colorful paint. It read:

Hope we can have dinner here soon!!!!!!
                                        Petey

Chris was standing beside Fred. He looked at the postcard. "Mommy was so funny when she got that card. She said that guy's elevator doesn't go to the top."

Fred smiled. "Did you ever meet him?"

Chris looked at Fred as though surprised he would ask such a dumb question. "Noooo! Mommy met him at work."

"He works for Mr. Reilly?"

"Just once. He painted something there. They hated the color."

Fred turned the card over. ELSIE'S HIDEAWAY. EDGEWATER, NEW JERSEY. His heart skipped a beat. Flecks of paint in the abandoned limo. A guy who had worked for Luke Reilly and had been turned down by Rosita. A guy who obviously frequents a bar in the area of the George Washington Bridge.

"Start the tape," he told the boys. "I have to go in the bedroom to make a phone call."

Having bid farewell to Mr. Bumbles, Regan and Austin carried the gifts back to the family room.

"Well, this certainly supplies motive," Nora said as she read the proclamation. "But it could be another Alvin Luck situation."

"I wish we had more time," Regan said urgently. "I'd love to go up there and check him out. But the call is coming in ten minutes, and I probably will have to leave right away for

New York. Jack is going to meet me with the second batch of money."

The ring of the phone went through the room with the impact of a gunshot.

"They wouldn't call on this line, would they?" Regan asked as she ran to the phone.

It was Fred.

She listened. "Hold on, Fred." She turned to Austin. "Fred just found a postcard from a guy named Petey, who apparently did some painting at the funeral home. He had asked Rosita out. Do you know who I'm talking about?"

Austin nodded. "We only had him work there one day. He completely messed up the job." Austin paused for a moment and then exclaimed, "But wait a minute! He showed up the other night at the wake for Goodloe. He's a big buddy of C.B. Dingle."

Nora gasped. "He's a painter, and there were flecks of paint in the limo."

"And the postcard he sent Rosita is of a bar in Edgewater," Regan said. "That's just south of Fort Lee and still within view of the lighthouse."

Regan told Fred what they had learned about C.B. Dingle.

"What's Petey's last name?" Fred almost barked into the phone.

"Austin, do you know Petey's last name?"

He shook his head. "But hold on. I'll get it for you." He picked up his cell phone and called the office. "They're checking the files." A moment later he said, "His name is Peter Commet. He lives in Edgewater." Austin wrote down the address and handed it to Regan.

"Fred, here it is," she said and gave him the information. "They're calling me in two minutes. I'll get back to you as soon as I speak to them."

"Regan, I'm going looking for this guy," Fred said.

"I wish I could go with you."

At exactly four o'clock, her cell phone rang.

"Be at the Manhattan end of the Midtown Tunnel at 5:30."

"The Manhattan end of the Midtown Tunnel," she repeated, and looked at Nora.

"They're using my story," Nora breathed.

"I just brought my mother home from the hospital," Regan said rapidly. "I'm in New Jersey. I need more time than that."

"You can't have more time."

Austin put his hand on Regan's arm. "Let me go," he mouthed.

Regan nodded gratefully. "I'm not a good driver in this weather," she explained. "Is it okay if my father's associate, Austin Grady, delivers the money? He'll drive my car and use my phone. It won't do you any good if I have an accident."

There was a pause. Then she heard a reluctant, "All right. But for your father's and Rosita's sake, you better not be trying anything. Yell hello, you two."

For a brief instant she heard their voices in the background. *We're getting closer to you,* she wanted to shout. The phone clicked off.

She dialed Fred.

"I'm going up to Edgewater," Fred said.

"And Alvirah and I are going to Fort Lee."

"Can I drop the kids with your mother?"

Regan hesitated. "Don't they think . . ."

"I'll tell them Rosita's doing an errand with your dad. By tomorrow they're going to have to be told the truth anyhow."

Regan gave him directions to the house. "Give me your cell-phone number. Take down my mother's. It's the one I'll have with me. Austin will be using mine."

"We'll keep in touch," Fred said. "Be careful."

"Weather's pretty bad out there," C.B. told Luke as he clicked off the phone. "Your daughter's too nervous to drive in it, so she's sending that guy Grady."

Regan can drive in any weather, Luke thought. Is Nora all right? Is something else up?

There was an air of finality in the way C.B. looked around the cabin. He took the keys to their chains from his pocket and laid them on top of the stove, well beyond their reach.

"When we get the money, you get to go home. Once we're safely away, we'll let them know where you are."

"Unless you want to kill us, you'd better do it soon," Luke said, indicating the floor of the boat. The storm outside had intensified, and the boat was rocking with ever-increasing force. The thumping, scraping sound of ice chunks hitting its sides was becoming more frequent. The floor was completely wet.

"We'll call from the airport. As soon as we land."

"That's too long," Rosita cried. "You might not get out until tomorrow."

"You'll just have to pray that we do," C.B. said. The door slammed behind him.

At ten minutes of five, Regan and Alvirah parked in front of C.B's high-rise apartment building. "Here we go," Regan said as they got out.

The doorman rang to announce them.

Moments later he shook his head. "No answer. He must be out."

"His uncle died this week," Regan said.

"I heard."

"My father owns the funeral parlor that handled the arrangements and has to get in touch with Mr. Dingle. It's very important. Is there any way I could find out when he's expected?"

"The superintendent's wife cleans his apartment. I could call her," the doorman offered. "That's the best I can do."

"Thank you," Regan said. "That's very nice of you." She and Alvirah exchanged glances.

"Hey, happy to help," he said with a shrug. "It's Christmas."

A minute later he turned back to them. "Dolores said to go up to her place. She's in 2B."

Dolores's apartment was a cheerful reminder of the holiday season. The tree was lit, Christmas music was playing, the smell of roast chicken was in the air.

"We won't keep you," Regan said hurriedly, "but we do need to be in touch with Mr. Dingle."

Dolores, a woman in her late fifties, sounded sympathetic as she said, "Poor fellow. He told me he's taking a trip to make himself feel better. He was packing when I went up there this morning."

"You were up there this morning?" Alvirah asked.

"Not for long. I brought him some Christmas cookies. He invited me in for just a minute, but he seemed nervous and upset, like he was under a lot of stress. It'll do him good to get away."

"I'm sure it will," Regan said. Could they be hidden in a bedroom up there? she wondered.

"This building is lovely," Alvirah commented as she looked past her. "You have a wonderful view of the river. Is Mr. Dingle lucky enough to have one like this?"

"Oh no," Dolores said, smiling with a hint of superiority. "He has one of the small studios that face the street."

At quarter after five, snow swirling around him, Fred Torres was standing on the stoop of the shabby, two-family frame house in which Petey lived. Regan had called him after leaving C.B.'s building, saying that the only thing she had learned for sure was that he had left with his suitcases this morning, supposedly for a vacation. Luke and Rosita had almost certainly not been in his apartment.

Could they be here? Fred wondered as he rang the doorbell a second time. He had already tried the separate entrance to Petey's basement apartment, but it was dark inside, and no one answered.

Someone's upstairs, he thought. Lights were on, and he could hear the sound of a television.

The door was opened by a sleepy-looking man who appeared to be in his sixties. He was wearing rumpled jeans, an open flannel shirt, and bedroom slippers. He looked as though the bell had just awakened him. He did not seem pleased at the interruption.

"Are you the landlord of this building?" Fred asked.

"Yeah. Why?"

"I'm looking for Petey Commet."

"He left on vacation this morning."

"Do you know where he was going?"

"He didn't say, and it's none of my business." The landlord started to close the door.

Fred pulled out his police ID. "I need to talk to you about him."

The sleepy look vanished. "He in trouble?"

"I don't know yet," Fred replied. "How long has he been living here?"

"Three years."

"Ever had any problem with him?"

"Except for being late with the rent, not really. I know he'll come up with it eventually."

"Just a couple more questions and I'll let you go," Fred said. "Does he have any close friends around here?"

"If you count that gang at Elsie's Hideaway,

he's got lots of them. It's right around the corner. Hey, I'm getting cold."

"One more thing. Have you been down in his apartment in the last couple of days?"

"Yeah, I checked the thermostat after he left this morning. If he isn't going to be here, no use burning fuel—not at today's prices."

This time Fred did not stop him from closing the door. As he got in his car, Regan and Alvirah were pulling up alongside him.

"No luck here either. But follow me to Elsie's Hideaway."

Because time was tight, Jack Reilly made the transfer of money to Regan's car a few blocks from the Queens-Midtown Tunnel. "We'll be following you," he told Austin Grady, "but if he directs you the way we expect, our mobile unit will have to drop back. It's just too easy for them to be seen. We've got agents deployed in the buildings along the route. They'll track you. Good luck."

At 5:30 the call came in. "Drive through the tunnel. Stay to the right. Take the Borden Avenue exit immediately after the toll booth."

"That's what we wanted to hear," Jack said exultantly when Eagle base passed on the message.

His cell phone rang. It was Regan. "Both the nephew and the painter left with their suitcases today. They told people they were going on vacation."

Jack felt a rush of adrenaline. "Regan, I'll bet you anything that they're our guys. If they have suitcases with them, that means they're not going back to where they left your father and Rosita. After they pick up the money, they're probably headed to the airport."

"If they get away, we may never hear from them again."

"We'll keep them in sight, just in case they do go back to where they have your dad and Rosita, but the minute they hit either of the airports, we have no choice but to close in on them."

"Alvirah and I are heading to the bar in

Edgewater where the painter hangs out. Fred Torres is with us. Maybe somebody there will be able to tell us something."

"Regan," Jack said quietly. "Please be careful."

There was a crash followed by a startling lurch as the boat listed to a twenty-degree angle. Rosita and Luke were thrown to the side. Rosita cried out, and Luke winced as the manacles dug into his hands and ankles.

"Mr. Reilly, this boat is sinking! We're going to drown," Rosita sobbed.

"No we're not," Luke insisted. "I think one of the mooring lines gave way."

Less than a minute later, the boat was savagely hurled against the dock again.

Luke heard a gurgling sound, and water began to bubble from somewhere near the door. As the boat swayed once more, the ring of keys C.B. had left on the stove slid off and dropped to the floor. Desperately, Luke bent as far as the chains would allow and leaned forward. His finger touched the edge of one of the keys, but before he could attempt to grasp it, the boat pitched again, and the keys slid well beyond his reach.

Up until that moment, Luke had believed they had a chance, but not anymore. Even if C.B. made that call from wherever he was going, it would be too late. The water was rising steadily. Rosita was right—they were going to drown. Their bodies would be found chained like trapped animals, if they were found at all. This tub would be driftwood before much longer.

I had wanted a lot more years, he thought, as the faces and voices of Nora and Regan permeated his soul.

From across the cabin, he could hear Rosita whisper, "Hail Mary, full of grace . . ."

He finished the prayer with her. ". . . at the hour of our death, Amen."

Inside Elsie's Hideaway, things were hopping. Regan, Fred, and Alvirah took only a moment to orient themselves, then headed straight to the bar.

Matt the bartender came over to them. "What can I get for you?"

"A couple of answers." Fred pulled out his police ID. "You know Petey Commet?"

"Sure I do. He was sitting right where you are less than two hours ago."

"According to his landlord, he left with his suitcases this morning," Fred said.

"Maybe he did, but he was here this afternoon. He did say he was going on vacation."

"Do you know where? It's important."

"I'd like to help you, but to tell you the truth, he was kind of vague about it. Said he was going fishing down south." Matt paused. "I don't know if this means anything, but Petey didn't seem like Petey today. I asked him about it, but he said he felt like a million bucks."

Regan's blood ran cold. "Can you tell us

anyplace where he might have been hanging out between leaving his apartment this morning and coming in here a few hours ago?"

Matt shrugged. "He takes care of somebody's boat at the year-round marina in Weehawken. Maybe he decided to check it out before he takes off. He hangs out there sometimes."

"I know that place." Fred flipped open his cell phone. "Get me the number of Lincoln Harbor in Weehawken," he snapped.

A moment later he was speaking with the marina office. Regan could see the muscles in his face tighten. Whatever they're telling him, it isn't good news, she thought.

Fred finished the call and turned to Regan and Alvirah. "He took the houseboat out Wednesday afternoon and never came back. The woman I spoke to said he must be nuts. The ice is coming down the river. No boats should be out in these conditions, especially an old tub like that."

Alvirah put a comforting hand on Regan's arm as Fred put in a call to the Harbor Unit.

Matt, who had been busy making drinks, came back. "I've got an idea. Most of these people know Petey, and a lot of them work around here. Maybe they know something."

He jumped up on the bar and whistled. The crowd roared its approval. "Free drinks for everyone," someone yelled.

Matt waved his hands at them. "You already got free food tonight. Now this is important. Did anybody see Petey Commet around town today before he came in here?"

Please, God, Regan thought. She watched as people glanced at each other and shook their heads. Then someone called, "When I got off work, I drove straight here. I saw Petey coming up that path next to the Slocum Marina."

"That marina's closed for the winter. Why would he go there?" a customer near Regan mumbled.

Regan turned to him. "Where exactly is this marina?" she demanded.

"Go outside and make a left. It's a few blocks down on the right. You'll see the sign at the turn."

Fred, Regan, and Alvirah raced outside to Fred's car. He roared out of the parking lot, skidding on the snow-covered pavement.

"If they're on an old boat in this weather . . ." Regan didn't complete the thought.

"You just passed the turn!" Alvirah cried.

Fred did a U-turn and barreled down the steep, deserted road that led to the river. The wind-whipped snow reduced visibility to near zero. The road ended in a deserted parking lot. The headlights of the car penetrated the pall of snow enough for them to tell that the marina was empty. There was no boat in sight.

Fred grabbed a flashlight from the glove compartment and jumped out of the car. Followed by Regan and Alvirah, he hurried past the closed marina office. From somewhere off to the left they could hear a thumping, banging noise. Slipping and sliding in the wet snow, they rounded the corner and began to run. The powerful beam of the flashlight revealed a listing houseboat, slamming back and forth against the dock where it was moored. It looked as though it was about to sink.

"Oh my God," Regan screamed. "They're in there, I know it." She and Fred raced along the dock, Alvirah puffing behind them.

The line securing the boat to the dock was uncoiling from the cleat to which it was attached, and Fred grabbed and rewrapped it as best he could. "Alvirah, don't let this come loose."

"Dad!" Regan screamed as she made the dangerous jump onto the lopsided boat. "Rosita!" She began kicking the padlocked door.

At the sound of Regan's voice, Luke and Rosita thought they were dreaming. They were trying to keep their legs out of the icy water that was swirling along the floor. The bubbling leak had widened to a steady, gushing stream.

"Regan!" Luke shouted.

"Hurry!" Rosita screamed.

"We're coming," Fred shouted back. He was beside Regan.

Together they kicked the door repeatedly. The wood panel finally splintered, then separated. They tugged and yanked at the loose wood until they managed to make an opening big enough to step through.

Fred went inside first, shining the flashlight into the pitch-black cabin. Regan followed him, wading into the deepening water, horrified at the sight of her father and Rosita chained to the walls.

"The keys were on the floor under the stove," Luke said urgently.

Fred and Regan bent over, frantically feeling around in the freezing water, which continued to rise steadily.

Please, please, Regan prayed. *Please!* Near the refrigerator, something metallic hit her hand but then was gone. "I felt them," she said. "Right around here"

Fred directed the beam of the flashlight at the base of the refrigerator.

"There they are!" Regan screamed as she lunged for them. Now the water was up to her knees. She snapped open the key ring and gave one key to Fred. She waded to Luke and grabbed his wrist. The key did not fit.

Fred turned away from Rosita, and they made the switch.

This time the keys worked.

Within seconds, both sets of chains were dangling. Supported by Regan, Luke stood up. Fred lifted Rosita to her feet.

"This boat won't last another thirty seconds," Fred said. "Let's get out of here."

The four of them sloshed through the water and stumbled through the shattered door.

Outside on the dock, a fervently praying Alvirah was hanging on to a rope that could no longer bear the strain of a sinking houseboat. As the boat slammed against the dock one final time, she braced herself. Summoning the strength she had used to move pianos in her cleaning-woman days, Alvirah held the rope taut until all four were safely beside her.

Then beaming, she watched as Regan and her father embraced, and Fred wrapped Rosita in his arms.

I knew he liked her, Alvirah thought happily.

Austin Grady followed the kidnappers' instructions to continue east on Borden Avenue and then make a left turn on to Twenty-fifth Street.

"Then pull over and wait," he was told.

Austin drove slowly on the icy roads. The windshield wipers were barely able to keep up with the falling snow.

Twenty-fifth Street was dark and desolate, lined with old factory buildings that obviously had been closed for years. The phone rang again.

"Drive one block to Fifty-first Avenue and turn right. Go to the end of the street and pull over again. Leave the bag on the corner."

This is it, Austin thought. At the end of Fifty-first Avenue, he stopped the car, took out the bag with the million dollars, and placed it on the sidewalk. He got back in the car.

The cell phone rang again. "It's there," Austin said.

"Keep going. Make your left and get lost."

Jack was stationed four blocks away. His cell phone rang. It was Regan.

In a voice that was both tremulous and ecstatic, she said, *"We've got them!* We're on our way home."

Eagle base came on the radio. "Subjects picking up bag."

Jack keyed his transmitter. "Let's nail them."

Chris and Bobby were playing cards with Willy in the family room. Nora was sitting silently, staring into the fire. Numb with fear and anticipation, she jumped when the phone rang on the table next to her. She picked it up, terrified of what she might be about to hear.

"How's that leg of yours?" Luke asked.

Tears of relief coursed down her cheeks. "Oh, Luke," she whispered.

"We're all on our way." Luke's voice was husky with emotion. "See you in half an hour."

Nora hung up the phone. Chris and Bobby were looking at her expectantly. "Mommy's coming home," she managed to say.

C.B. and Petey, both of them handcuffed, were seated side by side in the back of the police car.

"It's not all my fault," Petey protested. "It was your uncle that died."

C.B. suddenly had the incongruous thought

that maybe jail was preferable to a lifetime in Brazil with Petey.

Jack Reilly was dropped off at his apartment in Tribeca. He went directly to his car; his suitcases and presents were still locked safely in the trunk. Home for Christmas, he thought. All's well that ends well.

On the snowy, nearly deserted streets of Manhattan, he resumed the drive he had begun two nights before. He headed east, toward the FDR Drive. Then, as though of its own volition, the car made a U-turn.

Fred and Rosita followed Regan, Luke, and Alvirah as they pulled into the driveway. The cars had not yet stopped when the door of the house was flung open and two little boys came racing out, wearing neither coats nor shoes.

"Mommy! Mommy!" they screamed, slipping and sliding as they ran down the walk.

Rosita threw off the blanket she'd been wrapped in, stumbled from the car, and scooped up in her arms the children she thought she would never see again.

"I *knew* you'd be home in time for Christmas," Chris whispered.

Bobby looked at her, his expression suddenly stricken. "Mommy, is it all right? We already decorated the Christmas tree. But we saved some of the ornaments for you to put on."

"We'll hang them on the tree together," Rosita assured him happily, as she hugged them to her.

Fred had stood back, but now he came over. "Which one of you guys do I get to carry inside?"

Luke and Regan and Alvirah opened their car doors. "Why isn't your mother running out to greet me?" Luke asked.

"Something about a rug I sent her."

They walked up the path together.

Willy was standing at the front door, waiting for Alvirah.

When Luke stepped inside his home, it was as though he were seeing it for the first time.

"Home sweet home," he said fervently, then hurried back to the family room where Nora was waiting, Alvirah close at his heels. Willy grabbed her arm. "Give them a minute alone, honey."

"You're right, Willy. It's just that I'm a hopeless romantic."

Forty minutes later, warmed by hot showers and changed into dry clothes, the captives and their rescuers were back in the family room.

The spread Nora ordered from the local gourmet deli had just arrived. Regan, Alvirah, and Willy began setting up a buffet. Austin had called, proud to have played a part in saving his friend's life.

"I'll drop by with the family tomorrow," he said.

Nora, a glass of wine in her hand, announced, "We're going to throw a big celebratory party next week—and I'm inviting Alvin Luck."

"Isn't he the guy who sent you a present when my back was turned?" Luke asked.

Rosita was sitting on the couch with Fred,

the boys at her feet. She turned to him. "Will you be back in time?"

He looked at her and smiled. "Do you really think that after tonight I want to get on another boat?"

Rosita's smile was brilliant as he said, "I'm not going anywhere, Cinderella."

The doorbell rang.

"I bet it's that Ernest Bumbles," Alvirah said jovially.

"I'm having a citation made especially for him!" Nora declared. "Put his name on the party list, Luke."

Regan walked slowly to answer the door, the sounds of laughter spilling from the room behind her. She felt overwhelmed with gratitude, peace, exhaustion . . . And something else in her heart.

She opened the door. The man she had met only two nights ago in her mother's hospital room was smiling down at her.

"Have you got room for another Reilly around here?" asked Jack.

POCKET BOOKS
PROUDLY PRESENTS

NO PLACE LIKE HOME
MARY HIGGINS CLARK

Now available in paperback
from Pocket Books

Please turn the page for a preview of
No Place Like Home. . . .

PROLOGUE

Ten-year-old Liza was dreaming her favorite dream, the one about the day when she was six years old, and she and Daddy were at the beach, in New Jersey, at Spring Lake. They'd been in the water, holding hands and jumping together whenever a wave broke near them. Then a much bigger wave suddenly rushed in and began to break right over them, and Daddy grabbed her. "Hang on, Liza," he yelled, and suddenly they were tumbling underwater and being thrown around by the wave. Liza had been very afraid.

She could still feel the sensation of her forehead slamming into the sand when the wave rolled them onto the shore. She had swallowed water and was coughing, and her eyes were stinging and she was crying when Daddy pulled her close and gathered her in his arms. "Now *that* was a wave," he said, as he brushed the sand from her face, "but we rode it out together, didn't we, Liza?"

That was the best part of the dream—having Daddy's arms around her and feeling so safe.

Before the next summer came around, Daddy had died. After that she'd never really felt safe again. Now she was always afraid, because Mom had made Ted, her stepfather, move out of the house. Ted didn't want a divorce, and he kept pestering Mom, wanting her to let him come back. Liza knew she wasn't the only one afraid; Mom was afraid, too.

Liza tried not to listen. She wanted to go back into the dream of being in Daddy's arms, but the voices kept waking her up.

Someone was crying and yelling. Did she hear Mom calling Daddy's name? What was she saying? Liza sat up and slid out of bed.

Mom always left the door to Liza's bedroom open just a little so that she could see the light in the hall. And until she married Ted last year, she had always told Liza that if she woke up and felt sad, she could come into her room and sleep with her. Once Ted moved in, she'd never gotten in bed with her mother again.

It was Ted's voice she heard now. He was yelling at Mom, and Mom was screaming. "Let go of me!" she cried.

Liza knew that Mom was so afraid of Ted, and that since he'd moved out she even kept Daddy's gun in the drawer of her night table. Liza rushed down the hall, her feet moving noiselessly along the padded carpet. The door of Mom's sitting room was open and inside she could see that Ted had Mom pinned against the wall and was shaking her. Liza ran past the sitting room and went directly into her mother's bedroom. She hurried around the bed and yanked open the night table drawer. Trembling, she grabbed the gun and ran back to the sitting room.

Standing in the doorway, she pointed the gun at Ted and screamed, "Let go of my mother!"

Ted spun around, still holding on to Mom, his eyes wide and angry. The veins in his forehead were sticking out and pulsing. Liza could see the tears streaming down her mother's cheeks.

"Sure," he yelled. With a violent thrust, he shoved Liza's mother at her. When she crashed into Liza, the gun went off. Then Liza heard a funny little gurgle and Mom crumpled to the floor. Liza looked down at her mother, then up at Ted. He began to lunge toward her, and Liza pointed the gun at him and pulled the trigger. She pulled it again and again, until he fell down and then began crawling across the room and tried to grab the gun from her. When it wouldn't fire anymore, she dropped the gun and got down on the floor and put her arms around her mother. There was no sound, and she knew her mother was dead.

After that Liza had only a hazy memory of what happened. She remembered Ted's voice on the phone, the police coming, someone pulling her arms from her mother's neck.

She was taken away, and she never saw her mother again.

1
—

TWENTY-FOUR YEARS LATER

I cannot believe I am standing in the exact spot where I was standing when I killed my mother. I ask myself if this is part of a nightmare, or if it is really happening. In the beginning, after that terrible night, I had nightmares all the time. I spent a good part of my childhood drawing pictures of them for Dr. Moran, a psychologist in California, where I went to live after the trial. This room figured in many of those drawings.

The mirror over the fireplace is the same one my father chose when he restored the house. It is part of the wall, recessed and framed. In it, I see my reflection. My face is deadly pale. My eyes are no longer dark blue, but black, reflecting all the terrible visions that are leaping through my mind.

The dark blue of my eyes is a heritage from my father. My mother's eyes were lighter, a cornflower blue, picture perfect with her golden hair. My hair would be dark blond if I left it natural. I have darkened it, though, ever since I came back to the East Coast sixteen years ago to attend the Fashion Institute of Technology in Manhattan. I am also taller than my mother was by five inches. Yet, as I grow older, I believe I am beginning to resemble my mother in many ways, and I try to distance myself from that resemblance. I have always lived in dread of someone saying to me, "You look familiar. . . ."

At the time, my mother's image was splashed all over the media, and still turns up periodically in stories that rehash the circumstances of her death, so if anyone says I look familiar, I know it's her they have in mind. I, Celia Foster Nolan, formerly Liza Barton, the child the tabloids dubbed "Little Lizzie Borden," am far less likely to be recognized as that chubby-faced little girl with golden curls who was acquitted—not exonerated—of deliberately killing her mother and trying to kill her stepfather.

My second husband, Alex Nolan, and I have been married for six months. Today I thought we were going to take my four-year-old son, Jack, to see a horse show in Peapack, an upscale town in northern New Jersey, when suddenly Alex detoured to Mendham, a neighboring town. It was only then that he told me he had a wonderful surprise for my birthday, and drove down the road to this house.

Jack is tugging at my hand, but I remain frozen to the spot. Energetic, as most four-year-olds are, he wants to explore. I let him go, and in a flash he is out of the room and running down the hall.

Alex is standing a little behind me. Without looking at him, I can feel his anxiety. He believes he has found a beautiful home for us to live in, and his generosity is such that the deed is solely in my name, his birthday gift to me. "I'll catch up with Jack, honey," he reassures me. "You look around and start figuring how you'll decorate."

As he leaves the room I hear him call, "Don't go down-stairs, Jack. We haven't finished showing Mommy her new house."

"Your husband tells me that you're an interior designer," Henry Paley, the real estate agent, is saying. "This house has been very well kept up, but, of course, every woman, especially one in your profession, wants to put her own signature on her home."

Not yet trusting myself to speak, I look at him. Paley is a small man of about sixty, with thinning gray hair, and neatly dressed in a dark blue pin-striped suit. I realize he is waiting expectantly for me to show enthusiasm for the wonderful birthday gift with which my husband has just presented me.

"As your husband may have told you, I was not the selling agent," Paley explains. "My boss, Georgette Grove, was showing your husband various properties nearby when he spotted the FOR SALE sign on the lawn. He apparently fell in love with it immediately. The house is quite simply an architectural treasure and it's situated on ten acres in the premier location in a premier town."

I know it is a treasure. My father was the architect who restored a crumbling eighteenth-century mansion, turning it into a charming and spacious home. I look past Paley and study the fireplace. Mother and Daddy found the mantel in France, in a chateau about to be demolished. Daddy told me the meanings of all the sculptured work on it, the cherubs and the pineapples and the grapes . . .

Ted pinning Mother against the wall . . .

Mother sobbing . . .

I am pointing the gun at him. Daddy's gun . . .

Let go of my mother . . .

Sure . . .

Ted spinning Mother around and shoving her at me . . .
Mother's terrified eyes looking at me . . .
The gun going off . . .
Lizzie Borden had an axe . . .

"Are you all right, Mrs. Nolan?" Henry Paley is asking me.

"Yes, of course," I manage, with some effort. My tongue feels too heavy to mouth the words. My mind is racing with the thought that I should not have let Larry, my fist husband, make me swear that I wouldn't tell the truth about myself to anyone. Not even to someone I married. In this moment I am fiercely angry at Larry for wringing that promise from me. He had been so kind when I told him about myself before our marriage, but in the end he failed me. He was ashamed of my past, afraid for the impact it might have on our son's future. That fear has brought us here, now.

Already the lie is a wedge driven between Alex and me. We both feel it. He talks about wanting to have children soon, and I wonder how he would feel if he knew that Little Lizzie Borden would be their mother.

It's been twenty-four years, but such memories die hard. Will anyone in town recognize me? I wonder. Probably not. But though I agreed to live in this area, I did not agree to live in this town, or in this house. I can't live here. I simply can't.

To avoid the curiosity in Paley's eyes, I walk over to the mantel and pretend to study it.

"Beautiful, isn't it?" Paley asks, the professional enthusiasm of the real estate agent ringing through his somewhat high-pitched voice.

"Yes, it is."

"The master bedroom is very large, and has two separate, wonderfully appointed baths." He opens the door to the bedroom and looks expectantly at me. Reluctantly, I follow him.

Memories flood my mind. Weekend mornings in this room, I used to get in bed with Mother and Daddy. Daddy would bring up coffee for Mother and hot chocolate for me.

Their king-size bed with the tufted headboard is gone, of course. The soft peach walls are now painted dark green. Looking out the back windows I can see that the Japanese maple tree Daddy planted so long ago is now mature and beautiful.

Tears are pressing against my eyelids. I want to run out of here. If necessary I will have to break my promise to Larry, and tell Alex the truth about myself. I am not Celia Foster, nee Kellogg, the daughter of Kathleen and Martin Kellogg of Santa Barbara, California. I am Liza Barton, born in this town and, as a child, reluctantly acquitted by a judge of murder and attempted murder.

"Mom, Mom!" I hear my son's voice as his footsteps clatter on the uncarpeted floorboards. He hurries into the room, energy encapsulated, small and sturdy, a bright quickness about him, a handsome little boy, the center of my heart. At night I steal into his room to listen to the sound of his even breathing. He is not interested in what happened years ago. He is satisfied if I am there to answer when he calls me.

As he reaches me, I bend down and catch him in my arms. Jack has Larry's light brown hair and high forehead. His cornflower blue eyes are my mother's, but then Larry had blue eyes, too. In those last moments of fading consciousness, Larry had whispered that when Jack attended his prep school, he didn't want him to ever have to deal with the tabloids printing stories about me, or digging up those old stories. I taste again the bitterness of knowing that his father was ashamed of me.

Ted Cartwright swears estranged wife begged for reconciliation . . .

State psychiatrist testifies ten-year-old Liza Barton mentally competent to commit crime . . .

Was Larry right to swear me to silence? At this moment, I can't be sure of anything. I kiss the top of Jack's head.

"I really, really, really like it here," he tells me excitedly.

Alex is coming into the bedroom. He planned this surprise for me with so much care. When we came up the driveway, it had been festooned with birthday balloons, swaying on this breezy August day—all painted with my name and the words "Happy Birthday." But the exuberant joy with which he handed me the key and the deed to the house is gone. He can read me too well. He knows I'm not happy. He is disappointed and hurt, and why wouldn't he be?

"When I told the people at the office what I'd done, a couple of the women said that no matter how beautiful a house might be, they'd want to have the chance to make the decision about buying it," he said, his voice forlorn.

They were right, I thought as I looked at him, his reddish brown hair and brown eyes. Tall, with wide shoulders, Alex has a look of strength about him that makes him enormously attractive. Jack adores him. Now Jack slides from my arms and puts his arm around Alex's leg.

My husband and my son.

And my house.

2
—

The Grove Real Estate Agency was on East Main Street in the attractive New Jersey town of Mendham. Georgette Grove parked in front of it and got out of the car. The August day was unusually cool, and the overhead clouds were threatening rain. Her short-sleeved linen suit was not warm enough for the weather, and she moved with a quick step up the path to the door of her office.

Sixty-two years old, Georgette was a handsome whippet-thin woman with short wavy hair the color of steel, hazel eyes, and a firm chin. At the moment, her emotions were conflicted. She was pleased at how smoothly the closing had gone on the house she had just helped sell. It was one of the smaller houses in town, it's selling price barely breaking the seven figure mark, but even though she split the commission with another broker, the check she was carrying was manna from heaven. It would give her a few months' reserve until she landed another sale.

So far it had been a disastrous year, saved only by her sale of the house on Old Mill Lane to Alex Nolan. That one had caught her up on overdue bills at the office. She had very much wanted to be present that morning when Nolan presented the house to his wife. I hope she likes surprises, Georgette thought for the hundredth time. She worried that what he was doing was risky. She had tried to warn him about the house, about its history, but Nolan didn't seem to care. Georgette worried also that since he'd put the house in his wife's name only, if she didn't like it, she might be wide open to a violation suit.

It was part of the real estate code of New Jersey that a prospective buyer had to be notified if a house was stigmatized property, meaning one that might be impacted by a factor that, on a psychological level, could cause apprehension or fears. Since some people would not want to live in a house in which a crime had been committed, or in which there had been a suicide, the real estate agent was obliged to make a prospective client aware of any such history. The statute even required the agent to reveal if a house had the reputation of being haunted.

I tried to tell Alex that there had been a tragedy in the house on Old Mill Lane, Georgette thought defensively as she opened the office door and stepped into the reception room. But he had cut her off, saying that his family used to rent a two-hundred-year-old house on Cape Cod, and the history of some of the people who lived in it would curl your hair. But this is different, Georgette thought. I should have told him that around here the house he bought is known as "Little Lizzie's Place."

She wondered if Nolan had become nervous about his surprise. At the last minute he had asked her to be at the house when they arrived, but it had been impossible to change the other closing. Instead, she had sent Henry Paley to greet Nolan and his wife, and to be there to answer any questions Mrs. Nolan might have. Henry had been reluctant to cover for her, and in the end she had been forced to remind him, rather sharply, not only to be there, but to be sure to emphasize the many desirable features of the house and property.

At Nolan's request, the driveway had been decorated with festive balloons, all painted with the words "Happy Birthday, Celia." The porch had been draped with festive papier-mâché, and he also had asked that champagne and a birthday cake and glasses and plates and silverware and birthday napkins be waiting inside.

When Georgette pointed out that there was absolutely no furniture in the house, and offered to bring over a folding table and chairs, Nolan had been appalled. He rushed to a nearby furniture store and ordered an expensive glass patio table and chairs, and instructed the salesman to have them placed in the dining room. "We'll switch them to the patio when we move in, or if Celia doesn't like them, we'll donate them to a charity and take a deduction," he had said.

Five thousand dollars for a patio set and he's talking about giving it away, Georgette had thought, but she knew he meant it. Yesterday afternoon he had phoned and asked her to be sure there were two dozen roses in every room on the main floor, as well as the master bedroom suite. "Roses are Celia's favorite flowers," he explained. "When we got married, I promised her that she'd never be without them."

He's rich. He's handsome. He's charming. And he's clearly devoted to his wife, Georgette thought as she stepped inside and automatically glanced around the reception room to see if any potential clients were waiting there. From half the marriages I've seen, she's a damn lucky woman.

But how will she react when she starts hearing the stories about the house?

Georgette tried to push the thought away. Born with a natural ability to sell, she had progressed rapidly from being a secretary and part-time real estate agent, to founding her own company. Her reception room was a matter of special pride to her. Robin Carpenter, her secretary-receptionist, was positioned at an antique mahogany desk to the right of the entrance. On the left, a brightly upholstered sectional couch and chairs were grouped around a coffee table.

There, while clients sipped coffee or soft drinks or a glass of wine in the early evening, Georgette or Henry would run tapes showing available properties. The tapes provided meticulous details of every aspect of the interior, the exterior, and the surrounding neighborhood.

"Those tapes take a lot of time to do properly," Georgette was fond of explaining to clients, "but they save you a lot of time, and by finding your likes and dislikes, we can get a very good idea of what you're really looking for."

Make them want it before they set foot in it—that was

Georgette's game plan. It had worked for nearly twenty years, but in the last five years it had gotten tougher, as more and more high-powered agencies had opened in the area, their young and vigorous brokers panting for every listing.

Robin was the only person in the reception area. "How did the closing go?" she asked Georgette.

"Smoothly, thank God. Is Henry back?"

"No, I guess he's still drinking champagne with the Nolans. I still can't believe it. A gorgeous guy buys a gorgeous house for his wife for her thirty-fourth birthday. That's exactly my age. She's so lucky. Did you ever find out if Alex Nolan has a brother?" Robin sighed. "But on the other hand, there can't be two men like that," she added.

"Let's all hope that after she gets over the surprise, and has heard the story of that house, Celia Nolan still considers herself lucky," Georgette snapped nervously. "Otherwise, we might have a real problem on our hands."

Robin knew exactly what she meant. Small, slender, and very pretty, with a heart-shaped face and a penchant for frilly clothes, the initial impression she gave was that of the air-headed blonde. And so Georgette had believed when she applied for the job a year ago. Five minutes of conversation, however, had led her not only to reversing that opinion but to hiring Robin on the spot and upping the salary she had intended to pay. Now, after a year, Robin was about to get her own real estate license, and Georgette welcomed the prospect of having her working as an agent. Henry simply wasn't pulling his weight anymore.

"You *did* try to warn the husband about the history of the house. I can back you up on that, Georgette."

"That's something," Georgette said, as she headed down the hall to her private office at the rear of the building. But then she turned abruptly and faced the younger woman. "I tried to speak to Alex Nolan about the background of the house one time only, Robin," she said emphatically. "And that was when I was alone in the car with him on our way to see the Murray house on Moselle Road. You couldn't have heard me discussing it with him."

"I'm sure I heard you bring it up one of the times Alex Nolan was in here," Robin insisted.

"I mentioned it to him once in the car. I never said anything about it to him here. Robin, you're not doing me or, in the long run, yourself any favors by lying to a client," Georgette snapped. "Keep that in mind, please."

The outside door opened. They both turned as Henry Paley came into the reception room. "How did it go?" Georgette asked, her anxiety apparent in the tone of her voice.

"I would say that Mrs. Nolan put up a very good act of seeming to be delighted by her husband's birthday surprise," Paley answered. "I believe she convinced him. However, she did not convince me."

"Why not?" Robin asked before Georgette could frame the words.

Henry Paley's expression was that of a man who had completed a mission he knew was doomed to failure. "I wish I could tell you," he said. "It may just be that she was overwhelmed." He looked at Georgette, obviously afraid that he might be giving the impression that he had somehow let her down. Henry was acutely aware that he had not managed to close a single sale in months. "Georgette," he said apologetically, "I swear, when I was showing Mrs. Nolan the master suite, all I could visualize was that kid shooting her mother and stepfather in the sitting room years ago. Isn't that weird?"

"Henry, this agency has sold that house three times in the last twenty-four years, and you were involved in at least two of those sales. I never heard you say that before," Georgette protested angrily.

"I never got that feeling before. Maybe it's because of all those damn flowers the husband ordered. It's the same scent that hits you in funeral homes. I got it full force in the master suite of Little Lizzie's Place today. And I have a feeling that Celia Nolan had a reaction like that, too."

Henry realized that unwittingly he had used the forbidden words in describing the house on Old Mill Lane. "Sorry, Georgette," he mumbled as he brushed past her.

"You should be," Georgette said bitterly. "I can just imagine the kind of vibes you were sending out to Mrs. Nolan."

"Maybe you'll take me up after all on my offer to back you up on what you told Alex Nolan about the house, Georgette," Robin suggested, a touch of malice in her voice.

3

"But Ceil, it's what we were *planning* to do. We're just doing it a little faster. It makes sense for Jack to start pre-K in Mendham. We've been cramped for these six months in your apartment, and you didn't want to move downtown to mine."

It was the day after my birthday, the day following the big surprise. We were having breakfast in my apartment, the one that five years ago I had been hired to decorate for Larry, who became my first husband. Jack had rushed through a glass of juice and a bowl of cornflakes, and hopefully was now getting dressed for day camp.

I don't think I closed my eyes all night. Instead I lay in bed, my shoulder brushing against Alex, staring into the dark, remembering, always remembering. Now, wrapped in a blue and white linen robe, and with my hair twisted into a bun, I was trying to appear calm and collected as I sipped my coffee. Across the table, impeccably dressed as always in a dark blue suit, white shirt, and figured blue and red tie, Alex was rushing through the slice of toast and mug of coffee that was his everyday breakfast.

My suggestion that, while the house was beautiful, I would want to be able to completely redecorate it before we moved in had met with resistance from Alex. "Ceil, I know it was probably insanity to buy the house without consulting you, but it was exactly the kind of place we both had in mind. You had agreed to the area. We talked about Peapack or Basking Ridge, and Mendham is only five or ten minutes from both of them. It's an upscale town, convenient to New York, and, besides the fact the firm is moving me to New Jersey, the added plus is that I can get in some early morning rides. Central Park just doesn't do it for me. And I want to teach you how to ride. You said you'd enjoy taking lessons."

I studied my husband. His expression was both contrite and pleading. He was right. This apartment really was too small for the three of us. Alex had given up so much when we married. His spacious apartment in SoHo had included a large study, with room for his splendid sound system and even a grand piano. The piano was now in storage. Alex had a natural gift for music, and thoroughly enjoyed playing. I know he misses that freedom. He's worked hard to accomplish all he has. Though a distant cousin of my late husband, who himself had come from wealth, Alex was decidedly a "poor relation." I knew how proud he was to be able to buy this new house.

"You've been saying that you want to get back to decorating," Alex reminded me. "Once you're settled, there'd be plenty of opportunity for that, especially in Mendham. There's a lot of money there, and plenty of big houses being built. Please give it a try, for me, Ceil. You have a standing offer from the people next door to purchase this apartment at a nice profit to you, you know that."

He came around the table and put his arms around me. "Please."

I hadn't heard Jack come into the dining room. "I like the house, too, Mom," he piped up. "Alex is going to buy me my own pony when we move there."

I looked at my husband and son. "It looks as though we have a new home," I said, trying to smile. Alex is desperate to have more space, I thought. He loves the idea of being near the riding club. Eventually I'll find a different house in one of the other towns. It won't be hard to persuade him to move. He *did* admit that it was a mistake to buy without consulting me, after all.

One month later the moving van was pulling away from 895 Fifth Avenue and heading for the Lincoln Tunnel. Its destination was One Old Mill Lane, Mendham, New Jersey.

The Winter Beach

freed from the trappings of vacationers, returns to its lonely grandeur. This is the story of Charles Ogburn's solitary exploration of that fascinating world. Beginning in October 1964 he journeyed from the rocky summit of Mount Desert Island in Maine to the disaster-haunted Outer Banks of North Carolina.

For his keen eyes and well-stocked mind, it was an exhilarating experience—identifying a soaring gull, a golden weed growing from a barren cliff, a rock carried south by an Ice Age Glacier, the wreckage of a once-proud sailing ship. For his philosophic spirit, it was a place for amplifying and unifying his concept of man and nature. As Orville Prescott of *The New York Times* observed, "Mr. Ogburn notices everything with the exact observation of an Audubon and poetic rapture of a Blake."

THE WINTER BEACH
was originally published by
William Morrow & Company, Inc.

Other books by Charlton Ogburn, Jr.

Big Caesar
The Bridge
The Gold of the River Sea
The Marauders
Shake-speare—The Man Behind the Name (co-author)
The White Falcon

 *Are there paperbound books you want
but cannot find in your retail stores?*

The
WINTER
BEACH

Charlton Ogburn, Jr.

PUBLISHED BY POCKET BOOKS NEW YORK

THE WINTER BEACH

William Morrow edition published October, 1966
Pocket Book edition published June, 1971

This *Pocket Book* edition includes every word
contained in the original, higher-priced edition. It is printed
from brand-new plates made from completely reset, clear, easy-to-read
type. *Pocket Book* editions are published by Pocket Books, a division
of Simon & Schuster, Inc., 630 Fifth Avenue, New York, N.Y. 10020.
Trademarks registered in the United States and other countries.

Standard Book Number: 671-78083-2.
Library of Congress Catalog Card Number: 66-23350.
Text copyright, ©, 1966, by Charlton Ogburn, Jr.
Illustrations copyright, ©, 1966, by William Morrow & Company, Inc.

Acknowledgments

I should like to express my appreciation of the help I received in the collection of material for this book from the following:

At Acadia National Park:
  Paul G. Favour, Jr.   Arthur Hathaway

At Parker River National Wildlife Refuge:
  William L. French   William R. Forward

At Cape Cod National Seashore:
  Robert F. Gibbs   Vernon C. Gilbert   Edison P. Lohr

At Fire Island National Seashore:
  Henry G. Schmidt   Gordon Noreau

At Chincoteague National Wildlife Refuge:
  Charles F. Noble   David L. Hall

At Cape Hatteras National Seashore:
  Karl T. Gilbert   Bruce W. Black   J. Fred Roush
  Clay C. Gifford

And elsewhere:
  Thomas F. Bates, Science Adviser to the Secretary of
  the Interior.
  Edward S. Peetz and Robert H. Rose of the National
  Park Service.

Rachel M. Barker, Gilbert Corwin and David M.
   Hopkins of the United States Geological Survey.

George P. Spinner of the United States Fish and Wildlife Service.

William C. Melson of the Smithsonian Institution.

Joseph Discenza, Lt.j.g., United States Coast Guard,
   and members of the crew of Coast Guard Cutter
   Cape Horn.

Eric Gregory Bragg, C.W.O., United States Coast
   Guard.

James D. Barton, Jr., Long Island University.

John M. Zeigler, Woods Hole Oceanographic Institution.

Kemble Widmer, State Geologist of New Jersey.

Richard Lee Armstrong, Yale University.

Finally, and most particularly, to the patient and ever-
helpful staff of the East Hampton, New York, Free
Library.

*To the granite and the kelp, the dunes
and the surf, the gulls, the pitch pines
and the sea-oats . . . and to Vera.*

Maps

1. MOUNT DESERT ISLAND AND
   COASTLINE NORTH OF BOSTON   12

2. CAPE COD AND NANTUCKET   84

3. LONG ISLAND   150-51

4. ASSATEAGUE, CHINCOTEAGUE AND
   MIDDLE ATLANTIC COAST   234

5. NORTH CAROLINA AND THE OUTER BEACH   270

The drawings which appear throughout the text are the work of Cape Cod artists, Edward and Marcia Norman

Contents

THE START   1

NORTH TO MOUNT DESERT   7

MORE OF MAINE AND SOUTH TO CAPE ANN   35

CAPE COD   77

NANTUCKET AND SOUTH TO NEWPORT   113

LONG ISLAND   143

LONG ISLAND AND THE CITY   191

DOWN THE COAST TO ASSATEAGUE   229

THE OUTER BANKS   265

AT THE END   305

INDEX   318

The Start

SEVERAL years ago a picture of a deserted beach fixed itself in my mind. There was an expanse of sand, a half-buried candy-wrapper that collected the drifting grains, a cottage boarded up against the weather and for all sound the crashing of the breakers. In my thoughts, the seas kept rolling in upon shores abandoned to the cold by the last of the vacationers and of the vendors who ministered to them. I began to have the feeling that this was what lay ahead of me. When I mentioned it to others—Vera, to begin with—I was impressed by the instant attractiveness the idea had for them. The very words seemed to be powerfully evocative: *the winter beach*. They knew at once what it was about it that drew me to it: the sweep of the horizons; the sense of timelessness induced by the procession of waves plunging upon the strand with elemental power from an inexhaustible store; the astringency of the clean, spume-edged winds; the emptiness and the vastness of the solitude it connoted.

The ocean, it is perhaps not too much to say, exemplifies the background against which, both at the start and at the finish, we see our lives as cast. A childhood excursion to the beach is an experience we never forget, I suspect because it is what first opens our eyes to the immensity of the potential that surrounds our lives—an impression only fortified by our subsequent reading of the adventures of mariners in the days of sail and of the voyages of exploration that in the course of centuries brought to our ken one by one the world's farflung, seagirt lands. With the years comes a transformation, or shift of emphasis, in what the ocean stands for in our minds. We see it not only in its extent, which Western man's cleverness with tools has so greatly reduced, but in its age

and agelessness. It comes to us how through unimaginable millions of years its tides have flowed and ebbed, its colliding waves peaked and quickly fallen, while lands of continental mass rose and sank beneath its waters and were again uplifted, and mountain ranges higher than the Alps and Rockies were thrust up only to yield to splitting frosts and the abrasion of gravel-laden streams and disappear and be succeeded by yet other ranges which in turn were worn away. As nearly as anything can be with which we share the earth's surface, the sea is unchanging and everlasting. The confrontation of the sea by the land is like life's confrontation with eternity —that eternity we all look on every moment, whether consciously or not, and, it is safe to say, with increasing consciousness as we grow older. High time I made myself accessible to whatever instruction might be gained on that momentous frontier, I thought. Moreover, for the past several years, with only brief intermissions, I had been tied to a desk and having to look within myself for the raw materials of the product by which I lived. I could think of nothing more tempting than to be out under the sky.

So, as a Bengali moneylender may in middle age feel the call to take up the begging-bowl or an innkeeper of Donegal to visit the Eternal City, I thought of devoting the next winter to the cold ocean beach. To transplant a family and totally change the routine of existence on the strength of a mere idea smacked of the irresponsible. However, a project like this, once the first steps are taken, generates its own momentum, and no insuperable obstacle to going through with what I had in mind arose. Thus it befell that in September— in order to be resettled by the beginning of the school term —we moved to East Hampton, a village we picked because of its situation and attractiveness. A resort of long standing on the south shore of Long Island, twenty miles from land's end at Montauk Point, East Hampton has a special character, epitomized, for me, by the sight I once had of an osprey coming in over the magnificent trees that make a park of the community, a large goldfish in its talons and a herring gull in pursuit. Flanked by some scores of estates to which affluence is clearly an old familiar, the town comes within reach of the nonaffluent at the end of the season, when rentals on its ordinary houses tumble 85 per cent.

East Hampton is also advantageously located between

upper Maine, where the first traces of the Arctic begin, and
the Outer Banks of North Carolina, where the coast approaches the Gulf Stream and winter as most of us know it
peters out—and I felt an urge to visit at least representative
parts of that portion of our Atlantic sea frontier that come
under the grip of the cold. This was more feasible than it
otherwise would have been because we owned, and had for
several years, a miniature bus fitted out for camping. In the
rear the bus had facing double seats with a table between
them, which collectively let down to form a bed. Extending
down the other side, across a narrow aisle from the seats,
was a counter which opened up to give access to a little sink
and a two-burner bottled-gas stove. Beneath the counter were
an icebox and cabinets. To enable you to stand upright—
which made all the difference while dressing and undressing
or washing dishes—the top had an erectable section. When
elevated, it made you think of a vistadome on a railroad car.
(The sides of the structure were hinged and lay flat when
it was depressed.) From the front, access to the living
quarters was over the motor, which was situated between the
driver's and the passenger's seats and level with them. Fully
three feet shorter than the conventional station-wagon, the
bus was yet remarkably roomy, and withal a quite cozy
little home.

By the last of October I was on my way to Maine. It was earlier in the autumn than I had meant to go on my first trip north, but I could not resist taking advantage of the last ferry of the year across the mouth of Long Island Sound, which saved a drive of two hundred miles.

North to Mount Desert

IF YOU have been spoiled by congenial companionship, the first consequence you notice of traveling alone, after the pang of separation, is a feeling of guilt. With every reward the miles brought; I thought how much Vera would have got out of it. But two girls under twelve cannot be left to forage for themselves, and convention discriminates cruelly against women. She had to remain behind.

You find also that traveling alone compares with traveling in company as voyaging under sail compares with voyaging by steamship. Bringing a lesser measure of circumstance with you, you are more the creature of circumstances around you. You miss much that an observant and reflective partner would point out but at the same time you are more possessed by the sensations the scene around you induces. You may sometimes at night (to be honest) feel yourself a deserted and lightless house through which the gusts of wind blow dolefully, but that is simply the price you pay for being more receptive to the atmosphere around you—in every way.

In Connecticut the temperature was an unexpected 70 degrees, higher than it had been in a fortnight. The dull-red barns north of Norwich were soaking up the autumn sunlight. Across the valleys the oak forests were a rusty brown and in spots, where a tree was late in turning, the color of chipped beef. Where there were maples, the woods were leafless and pale grey, almost as pale as the cloud-washed sky. A few little bands of robins took off over the treetops when disturbed, as if needing only slight provocation to go winging far away. . . . Indian summer, I thought, is like a last meeting between lovers when love has died out on her side and she is leaving, having granted the favor of this one-more-time.

7

In eastern Massachussetts groups of young white birches caught the sunlight with their spangling of browning yellow leaves. North of Boston the white pines, with their soft, misted-over foliage (as if they had been breathed on), began to challenge the sway of the hardwoods. Hemlocks appeared.

It is a very pleasant surprise to discover how extensive are the woods that remain almost on the outskirts of the most densely populated areas of the country, undersized though the trees are. The woods have, in fact, been returning, covering hills that were exhausted farmland fifty years ago. They help you forget for the time being the crunching counter-advance of the Atlantic super-city. To be on the open road in the autumn countryside, with summer's hordes departed, seems a wonderful privilege.

Maine and a darkening and cooling of the air came together. The withdrawn sun of late October was sinking behind a bank of cloud. The growing chill seemed to creep out of the low and tangled woods that stood now on both sides of the highway. Stiff, pointed spruces and firs, preceded by their forest mates, the talc-white canoe birches, made their appearance in the vicinity of Portland. They marked the beginning of the North Woods.

For a native of more southerly climes there is a peculiar excitement in coming to the home of these trees. Spruces and balsam firs mean to him remoteness, a cool purity of air, an intenser silence against which the wind sighs and a more solitary bird sings. They evoke, probably, stirring occasions, in my case a boyhood trip to the Adirondacks and excursions to the cloudland of the higher Smokies and Black Mountains of North Carolina. They recall also, to anyone inclined that way as a youngster, a sense of wonder that they should be distributed as they are, above 1,000 feet in the Adirondacks, above 4,500 in the southern Appalachians and above 8,000 in the southern tableland of Mexico. In the other direction, the North Woods—or, as they are called in scientific literature, the Canadian Zone, the Boreal Woods, or the Taiga—come down to sea-level in Maine and in Vancouver. In the old argument as to where in Maine the region called Down East begins, the neighborhood of Damariscotta would have my vote, for that is where the spruces and firs take over the coast.

In the morning, having left Portland, where I had spent

the night in a rather dismal outlying area, parked behind a boarded-up restaurant on the edge of a tidal flat, I got out beside the highway to have a closer look at the woods. There were white spruces and black spruces, and these, with the balsams, had foliage of the same blue-green color as the white pines but even more frosted. There were also red spruces with moss-green foliage more the color of the yellow-green foliage of the open, haphazardly-growing pitch pines, which were also common. With the spruces and balsam firs the upper branches extend stiffly from the trunk at an upward angle. The white pines, which are bigger, broader trees with long, fine, closely grouped needles (five to a cluster) producing a softer effect, have branches that issue more or less level from the trunk, then curve upward, making one think of arms held out to enfold a returning friend in a welcoming embrace. The branches of the hemlock, fuzzy with bristling needles no longer than the nail of your little finger (though the tree itself is among the most massive of the Eastern conifers), descend, then turn up at the ends almost to the vertical, like arms in flowing sleeves with hands raised in benediction. In a breeze they move up and down, in the gently admonitory gesture of an indulgent Druid—if there were such.

The highway was the Maine Pike. Beside it there was nothing to be heard but the quiet of the woods and the roar and yowl of cars shooting by at seventy miles an hour—nothing in between. This was only one way in which the new Interstate Highways resemble railroads. Like railroads, they are cut indiscriminately through the country pretty much on a compass bearing and have no communication with it except at established interchanges. Signs along the right-of-way are addressed to the man at the throttle in terse exposition and in large block letters that who runs may read; rivers and towns, prime movers in the nation's history, whisk by in the flash of a nameboard. You rocket along in your isolation until mealtime, when you discover that you are traveling as part of a large human community. But there is something, anyway, to be said for the Interstates, other than that they take you where you are going with expedition. They show you a fair cross section of the countryside, more so than the railroads, which seek out the hearts of the population-centers, and much more so than the conventional highways, along which commercial eruptions as unlovely as open sores are inevitable. If you were not prevented from taking in the landscape by the distance to which it has been plowed back from the pavement and by the relentless pressure of the traffic that looms up in your rearview mirror, you could look with more favor on them. Even as it is, you leave them with a certain reluctance, feeling that you are returning to the responsibilities and complexities of reality.

In Maine even off the Pike, from the old state highway running east from Augusta, you see mostly woods. These seem everywhere to be scrawny, however. There is little to remind you of the magnificent forest the first explorers found with belts of white pines of a size that astonished them. (Because these giants provided the British Navy with masts of a height, strength and lightness never before seen, the Crown declared reserved to its own use all specimens two feet or more through the butt, and the resentment this aroused helped bring on the American Revolution.) They are gone and the farms and villages that have succeeded the lumber-camps seem meager and of doubtful prospects. It is a land which the people have impoverished and which in turn has impoverished the people. I gave a ride to an elderly woman eighteen miles on the near side of Liberty, to which she was walking. At least I had thought she was elderly, but on closer view it was hard to tell. She seemed more worn and bent than years would have accounted for but had pinker cheeks and brighter, if slightly squinting, eyes than years would seem to have allowed. I realized that I was looking at the countrywoman of the backwoods as she has been through most of our history. The differences of intonation that made communication difficult for us were those of pre-electronics America. "Does it get very cold here in winter?" I asked. "I'm alone," she answered. "I board out."

The vista from a scenic turnoff on the approach to Belfast was of trees to the horizon. I had a cup of coffee there, looking out across an unmown meadow to the forest of marbled grey, brown and green that swept back over the worn-down hills. No autumn hue remained except at the bottom of the meadow where a belt of larches still retained their mustard-colored needles. There was the uneasy quiet of a mild day late in the season.

The coast is something else. Forests and furs paid New

England's bills in the beginning, but for the rest, the coast has always been, and still is, Maine's fortune. In the French and Indian wars, when the Abnakis repaid with torture and massacre what they had suffered from the greed and brutality of white invaders, the islands provided what refuge the settlers could find. So many thousands of them in that almost-century-long struggle were scalped or captured and marched at gunpoint over the long and bitter trail to Quebec that only four towns in the territory continued to exist. Long before then the wealth of Maine's cold, shallow coastal waters had been discovered—some say by the fishermen of Scandinavia, Brittany and Portugal many years before John Cabot appeared on the scene in 1498—and this is one resource that has not yet failed.

The protected waters of the bays that ran back into long estuaries fed by rivers reaching deep into the forests of pine and oak made the coast of Maine a natural shipbuilding area, probably one without peer. The first sailing vessel built in the English colonies—the thirty-ton pinnace *Virginia of Sagadahuc*—was launched at the short-lived settlement at Popham in 1607 and the largest wooden ship ever seen was built at Bath, once the most active shipbuilding port in the world. The men who fashioned the schooners, brigs, brigantines, barkentines and half-clippers went down to the sea in them too, often taking their wives and children with them, and there were many Maine families who saw nearly as much of one another in Shanghai and Canton as in Kennebunk or Searsport.

To take up the slack with the decline of shipbuilding and shipping, there was the allure for vacationers of a coast that, while only 250 miles long as the crow flies, has over 3,000 miles of shore. Catering to tourists may seem a comedown from an era when men and women rode out storms around the Horn and sailed the breadth of the Pacific under clouds of canvas in vessels they had seen take form from timbers hewn in their own back yards. We may as well recognize, however, that no great proportion of the population of Maine or any other state would willingly exchange the recompenses of the present for those of the past. *Vacationland* is what is printed on Maine's license-plates, and vacationland it is. *Hi Friend!* say official signs along the road, showing clasped hands. The highways are uncrowded in autumn and the out-

of-state cars in a small minority, but the succession of new
motels and manifold roadside marts along the route connecting the old ports give an idea of what it is like in summer.

On a map, the coast of Maine presents the appearance of a
frayed and tattered fabric. Between northward-reaching arms
of the sea, spattered with islands, are ragged, southward-
pendant peninsulas dripping with more islands. To a geologist
the origins of what the map shows are clear at a glance. A
striking example of the interpenetration of land and sea, it is
a textbook case of a "drowned" coast.

About 200 million years ago, a great uplift of the earth's
crust took place in what is now eastern North America. From
Newfoundland to Georgia the surface rocks were buckled and
heaved skyward to form the jagged peaks of a great mountain
range of which the remnants are known today as the northern and eastern Appalachians. It must have been a tremendous formation. Like all highlands great and small, however,
it was subject from the start to the processes of weathering
and erosion. In time, the young ranges of New England were

worn down to a plateau above which rose a few mountains of more resistant rock, most notably the higher White and Green Mountains and Mount Katahdin, standing a mile high today in north-central Maine. Over the plateau wound the streams that formerly, coursing down the slopes and ravines of the mountains, tumbling sand and gravel with them, had helped grind them down. Such was the landscape of 125 million years ago.

About 60 million years ago, when the continent had attained roughly its present shape, the land was tilted southward and eastward, possibly as part of the same crustal movement that slowly reared the Rocky Mountains at this time. The streams were reactivated, as the term is. Given new slope, they regained an impetus and a greater power in their concentrated and unremitting attack upon all that stood in the way of their shortest path to sea-level. New lowlands were excavated out of the softer rock, which increased the height above the valleys of the existing mountains and brought the underlying ridges of harder rock—the more resistant types of metamorphosed sedimentary rock and the higher granite formations—into relief as new, lower mountains. Among the monoliths thus exposed—if it had not been long before—was a ridge that was to become the most dramatic feature of the New England coast—dramatic both in the display it makes of the current contention of the earth-shaping forces and in the monumental record it presents of the work of those forces in the past. Some 75 million years before the raising of the Appalachians, a lake of light magma —liquid granite—had appeared far below the surface of the earth at the site of present-day Mount Desert Island. Above this hell's soup, as it pressed against them, the lower layers of the crustal rock were loosened. They gave way, collapsed and, being heavier, sank into the caldron below. The magma thereupon rose in the concavity thus created and there, at great depth, it slowly cooled to form a large-grained granite dome which was to emerge eons later with the wearing-away of the softer rock above it.

The tilting of the land also submerged the eastern margins of the continent, perhaps bringing the coastline of New England to somewhere near its present location. But then new sediments washed down from the highlands by the rivers were deposited off shore, to become resolidified. This new

ledge of sedimentary rock extending out from the shore (what
is now the edge of the Piedmont) became the coastal plain
when, after more millions of years, the ocean receded again.
It may be inferred that at this time New England had a
coastal plain as have the states today from New Jersey southward. Presumably its shoreline extended from outside of what
are now Long Island and Cape Cod across to a point beyond
Nova Scotia, standing as much as a hundred miles off the
present coast of Maine.

It is tempting to linger in the mind over the scenes of the
ancient past that have suffered all they can at time's hands
and now, existing only in retrospect, have a tranquillity about
them they can scarcely have possessed when they were real—
forested lowlands fissured by broad rivers lying beneath a
younger sun where the harsh seas now hold sway. But one
must return to the present. A million or a million and a half
years ago two forces were set in motion which were to have
catastrophic effects upon the earth and the life it supported.
One was human evolution. The other was the Ice Age, as it
is commonly called. Ice *Ages* would be more accurate, for
there were four of them, with long temperate periods between
them; one of these periods, it is thought today, may have been
more than 600,000 years long. Living at the present time, we
are far nearer an ice age than we should have been if we had
lived in the middle of any of the interglacial periods. The
ice, from its stronghold in the Arctic and its outposts in the
Sierras, the Rockies, the Alps and the Caucasus, could at any
time, so far as we know, commence a return. If it should, all
recorded human history could be regarded as having taken
place during a brief recession of the ice-sheet. Without being
one who delights in illustrations of man's puniness in the
limitless cosmos, a traveler may yet find it easier to bear the
spectacle of the monumental ugliness we have wrought from
the spoil of our country, the trash with which we have
defaced it, the suppurating encrustations that our cities have
become, by reflecting that the earth through its characteristic
processes can, and doubtless someday will, shrug it off in
favor of a fresh start.

An ice age began when for some reason it grew colder in
the earth's northern lands or, if a new theory is correct, when
incursions of warmer water opened the frozen Arctic Ocean,
which in turn released vastly more water vapor into the polar

atmosphere. In any event, at both the higher latitudes and the higher altitudes, in the mountains, more snow fell during the winter than melted in the summer. Century by century the snow accumulated and at depths of hundreds of feet, under its own weight, was compacted into ice. The masses grew higher and higher, heavier and heavier, until at length the ice of the bottom layers began to be pressed out, taking the pattern, it would seem, of a spreading lichen. The lobes pushed forward until they were halted by mountain barriers. Against these they piled up until in due course the passes were breached or the range outflanked. Pressing on through the valleys, the icesheet would meet and incorporate the glaciers descending from the mountainsides above. As it progressed it ground the forests to pulp, scalped the land of its topsoil and picked up rocks, and with these rocks, as with the teeth of a steel rasp, it scored and polished the mountainsides and gouged out valleys. The farther south it pushed, the more its rate of advance tended to be retarded by melting. When the ice melted as fast as it arrived, equilibrium was reached and the front stood still. But this did not occur—except temporarily—until, in the East, New England, New York and northern New Jersey had been buried. Along its forward edge the ice cannot have been very thick, perhaps a hundred feet or so, but over Canada it may have stood as deep as the Antarctic ice-sheet today, which covers the earth in places to a depth of two miles and totally conceals the presence of towering mountain ranges. In New England, it is certain, every summit was obliterated. For tens of thousands of years the land lay crushed in lifeless dark under the monstrous burden.

When, with a prolonged warming trend, the ice receded foot by foot to its present redoubts, enormous quantities of water were restored to the ocean, the level of which was raised. In addition, the land which had underlain the glacier had been pressed down beneath its stupendous weight. When New England was finally freed of ice, its coastal plain lay beneath the surface of the sea. Today, an elevated, outlying part of it about a hundred miles long, distant for the most part more than a hundred miles east and southeast of Cape Cod, its highest points only a few fathoms down, attracts boats from the world's fishing fleets. So, in addition to George's Bank, do other detached portions of the former coastal plain to the northeast, culminating in the Grand Banks, off Newfoundland.

When you come to the upper Maine coast, to the dark rock ledges extending out into the sea in promontories and islands with the prows of rams, tumbled about with the great boulders wrenched from them by the waves and wooded with dark conifers to the line of the storm-breakers' farthest reach, it comes to you in the light of what you have read that this is both a young coast and an old one. It is young in respect of the number of years it has been in existence; compared with the antiquity of the hills of which these rocks are the remaining pediments, the time of the last glacier's recession—about ten thousand years ago—seems so recent you almost feel that eyewitness accounts of it should have come down to us. It is ancient in that it represents the ancestral form of shores that today are very old indeed. Sand beaches are the work of time. Those that extend down the coast from New Jersey southward, long, flat, broad and nearly straight, have the form a coast takes in its maturity, when the effects of terrestrial disturbances are things of the past, have been outlived, and the beach is answerable only to the everlasting winds, waves and ocean currents and can endure indefinitely without change in character. All of them began with the pounding of ocean waves on the rocky headlands of a jagged coast.

If you have been primed for it, you see the work of the ice-sheet at Mount Desert even before you arrive, as soon as the island's humps lift into view between you and the ocean, where you would not expect to find mountains. They stand all by themselves. Originally, they were all part of a single broad ridge. The ridge ran east and west and thus lay athwart the path of the ice-sheet, which came out of the northwest moving southeast. The ice banked up against the ridge and then, rising to the height of its saddles, flowed over them, scooping out the stream valleys as it followed them down the other side. As its mass grew, it dug wider and deeper, gouging out troughs in the direction of its own flow and pouring out across the coastal plain beyond. And still it grew, higher and higher, overtopping the summits, finally standing a mile deep over them.

They are, today, mountains that patently have endured much. I think I have never seen mountains older looking. (Though the tallest of them is only 1,530 feet, one would not think of calling them hills.) The impression of antiquity they give may be owing in part to their resemblance to ancient pachyderms. Much of their expanse is bare. Like the backs of elephants, they are smooth, rounded and seamed, and the vegetation in the clefts and hollows and on the lower slopes recalls the hair that clings to hides of elephants, at least in their youth. In color they are even more mammalian, as pink as mountains could well be, or salmon. This is the color of the potash feldspar in their granite, but at first sight the color is startling. After a rain their steep sides, past which the glacier had ridden, glisten like marble. But the ice, while polishing the flanks and rounding off the forward faces, up which it had slid, plucked off blocks as it poured down the far sides, leaving these precipitous and piled at the base with chunks of granite of all sizes.

There are places that, however widely they have been extolled, you are persuaded have never been fully appreciated until you came to them, and you have from the beginning a feeling of proprietorship about them. Mount Desert is such a place to me. A newcomer finds it hard to know where to look first. There are the score of summits rising above the forest, which at the time of my arrival was still flecked with the gold of the birches as the ground beneath it might be flecked with sunshine in summer. There are the long, narrow lakes squeezed between the mountainsides in trenches plowed out by the glacier. There is the enveloping sea, blue as the sky or dark as a thunderhead, languidly licking or rising to smash in bomb-bursts of spray the ramparts of granite crowded with the bannered lances of the firs and spruces; every turn of the road opens a new vista of shimmering bays bounded by other islands or opening upon an empty ocean. The ocean's presence is everywhere on Mount Desert, even in the forest glades. You take it with you when once you look seaward between the capes and know that nothing has changed there since the redmen stared with astonished eyes upon the fierce-headed Viking boats riding low in the waves beneath their square sails. You are moved to hail it as Byron did: ". . . Thou deep and dark blue Ocean, roll!

"Ten thousand fleets sweep over thee in vain;
Man marks the earth with ruins, his control
Stops with the shore; upon the watery plains

The wrecks are all thy deed, nor doth remain
A shadow of man's ravage, save his own. . . ."

In Japan, Mount Desert would be a national shrine, a model for art and symbol of aspiration, the goal of pilgrimages and object of veneration through the ages, uniting the generations. Perhaps it will hold such a place with us in the future, together with the Grand Canyon, the Cascade Mountains, the redwood forests, the Great Smokies. If so, I venture to hope that its domes may have restored to them the names they once bore. It is enough to make one embarrassed for one's species to find such monumental relics of a past distant by tens of millions of years, such august majesties, tagged with the names of persons, of ephemeral human beings whose vanities and petty frailties are only too readily to be inferred from the fact that they *were* human: Cadillac and Champlain, and—whoever they may have been—MacFarland and Sargent. One may be grateful that some of the *monts deserts* at any rate have been allowed to retain names more in keeping with their character: Penobscot Mountain, Cedar Swamp Mountain, Pemetic Mountain, The Whitecap, Bald Peak.

The number of Mount Desert's devotees is already large. It has been growing ever since the island's beauties were discovered by Thomas Cole, founder of the Hudson River school of painting, in 1844. With the establishment of a steamship connection with Boston, Bar Harbor, on the northeastern shoulder of the island, became a summer resort for the well-to-do with few peers. It was never Newport's equal in the amount of wealth concentrated in the hands of its patrons—probably no other resort in the world has been—but the richest men in the country were Mount Desert regulars. J. P. Morgan's *Corsair,* Vincent Astor's *Nourmahal* and Joseph Pulitzer's *Liberty* were familiar sights, especially the last, for the blind publisher had a home here and from a soundproofed room in it ran his newspaper empire. Atwater Kent, fifty times over a millionaire, was famous for his dances in the last effulgence of the resort's great era, and it was at the same time—at the onset of the Great Depression—that the eighty-year-old E. T. Sprague disclosed in the Bar Harbor Club that he had achieved the ambition he had nursed since his struggling boyhood with the receipt of information that his fortune had now topped a hundred million dollars. But

Mount Desert was more than money. From the beginning to the present, it has attracted artistic and intellectual talent—from Thomas Cole and Louis Agassiz to Barrett Wendell (who declared the conversation at Bar Harbor to be the best in America) to Walter Damrosch and Walter Lippmann (both of whom married girls from here) to Samuel Eliot Morison, who is among the island's most distinguished present residents. If in the return to nature that was part of the tradition of Mount Desert there was something of the imitation of pastoral pursuits by Marie Antoinette and her ladies in waiting in the rustic setting of the Petit Trianon, there was much that was genuine too. (One Philadelphia beauty walked the twenty-two miles of the Ocean Drive in five and a half hours.) "Walks, talks and flirtations" were the distinctions of Mount Desert, according to Cleveland Amory (my authority in this field), who suggests that, in addition to the more material causes of the decline of the great resorts, it was the rise to popularity of faster-paced diversions that led to Bar Harbor's decline.

It is not that Mount Desert attracts fewer visitors today. Far from it. With the democratization of travel by the automobile (which was banned on the island until 1913), the influx has grown enormously. It has also become far more eclectic. Even the small minority whose ardor for the island is equal to the discomforts of tent-life on a coast often dripping with fog or drizzle is numerous enough to keep the two public campgrounds—located respectively at the southern edges of the island's two lobes—filled to capacity all summer long.

By rare good fortune, Mount Desert's popularity need not bring about its ruination. The major and grander parts of the island, to the extent of fifty square miles, are incorporated in Acadia National Park, which was established in 1919—the first east of the Mississippi. For the high-minded foresight that saved Mount Desert from commercial exploitation we cannot, however, give credit to our representatives in Washington, or to them primarily. Led by George Buckham Dorr, a seventy-year-old scholar of a noted Boston family whose favorite occupation was tramping the island, and by Charles Eliot, President of Harvard, a group of summer residents gave the land for the park, John D. Rockefeller being the donor of the largest tract. One wishes one could thank them. Their names deserve to be—but are not—inscribed in bronze at the park entrance.

Remembering how Vera and the girls and I had found not a tent-site free on our arrival in August two years before—the only other time I had been here—I moved curiously about the forested grounds at Blackwoods. The absence of mankind from a scene it once had frequented makes for a more freighted stillness and more pointed solitude. And there was not a soul about. The silence was total, like cotton batting in my ears, like a compress which drew out sound—the accumulation of traffic noises in my head—as a poultice draws out inflammation.

In the evening before dinner, when I could not see well enough to find my way anywhere else, I walked along Ocean Drive or on the path between it and the brink of the cliff above the sea, which the road skirted at a more respectful distance. The water was always very dark but the waves were discernible. They came hurrying in as if to an appointment, only to be thrown into a confusion of almost luminous foam on the rocks. A bell could be heard sounding from somewhere, incongruously to one whose memory responded with a picture of mountain valleys, for the halting rhythm and flat tone of its clanging were those of a cowbell's. But this bell was one that rode the swells in an iron scaffolding, its float anchored by a chain that plunged into the black depths, and it made you think of all the seamen who had drowned on this reef-toothed coast, their hands, as the chill got through to them, slipping from the floating timber to which they had clung.

As I walked on, I could hear faintly the calls of a flock of eiders, yipping or honking sounds, nasal but not unmusical, and there was a comfort in them, although the unmistakable disparity between the circumstances that afforded contentment to seaducks and human beings, respectively, left no doubt of the gulf between us. The promontory off which the flock had congregated, as was its habit, reached out very black into the sea, the conifers that formed a cockscomb along its crest standing back from its granite prow. There was nothing, I thought, like a forest of these northern evergreens to condense and hold the night. When the road cut through the woods at the base of the promontory, I found myself walking between pinnacled walls of total darkness. The road might never have known a vehicle, though it was a popular drive in summer, skirting the shore as it did and unfolding perhaps the most spectacularly beautiful scenery in the East. Recognizing what an unpleasant turn it might give a motorist to find a human figure in his headlights at such an hour and season as this with no car in sight to account for his presence (the campground was miles away by road though near enough by path), I was just as glad that none appeared; when you arouse an intense emotion in another person, you are likely to experience an echo of it in yourself.

Bar Harbor itself proved to be a not very cheerful place after dark. In this, other summer resorts after the season are not very different, as I was to learn. Hotels, restaurants and tabernacles of the seaside *vie sportive* were mostly shut down and like mausoleums bespoke the mortality of all things temporal. Leaves driven by the wind clattered down the streets from the deserted city park. The few inhabitants who were out on foot were in a hurry to be in their homes. Of those in cars—who could as well have been Martians—some drove down to the municipal dock, where I parked the bus and cooked and ate my dinner, but generally they left after circling it for the ostensible purpose of mystic if fleeting communion with the sea; in the case of the *jeunesse* it was perhaps because there was nowhere else to go. At seven o'clock a man in a pale green station-wagon ducked in and out of a cubicle at the end of the dock presumably to take a reading from a revolving drum on which a stylus imperceptibly extended a kind of sine curve of the rise and fall of the tide in obedience to a cord passing over several wheels into the black watery depths. At the campground, when I got back there, the darkness was Stygian and the battery-powered lamp I had with me threw too feeble a light to read by without strain. But if nothing else, the evening and those that followed (which in all respects were like the first) provided the satisfaction and stimulation one derives from a swim in water too cold for anyone to enter for fun. Besides, having been sent early to my sleeping bag, I was glad to be getting up when a sighting out of the window showed the branches of the trees silhouetted against the pallor of a grey, damp sky.

In the country, wild or pastoral, one's spirit responds to the dawn, when one is up for it, like a crowing cock. Not to lose any of the precious daylight, I shaved as fast as I could and hurried with breakfast. Comforting as were those boiled eggs with bread and jam and the hot coffee at that chilly hour, it did not do to linger over them anyway; they cooled too fast.

There were two golden-crowned kinglets at the edge of the woods when I set out the first morning. They were communicating in their invariable, beady, lisping voices, insectlike, and came almost within arm's length to see what I was about. The golden-crowned kinglet was one of the first bird-book birds I saw as a boy. It seemed to me then, as it seems to me now, that for creation to have produced this mite no larger in body than a joint of my finger yet able to come chirpily through the northern winter and to have adorned it gratuitously with a yellow cap (one having an orange center in the adult male) set off tidily between India-inked lines argued a profoundly consequential principle in nature almost, but not quite, to be grasped. The boy I had been would have gone numb with excitement before the day was half an hour old. The next few minutes brought a red crossbill singing, from the top of a conifer at the brink of a cliff above the sea, a rather nasal little song: *tsee-a, tsee-a, tsee-a,* it went. A finch on the way to becoming a diminutive parrot, in color a Victorian shade of dull red velour, the red crossbill was a Canadian Zone species (the very words would have been delicious to me) with a breeding range extending across the northern fringe of the country and, in the high islands of boreal forest on which the rain-clouds rested, to North Carolina and through Mexico to Guatemala. And there it was exactly as prescribed, and in a characteristically Canadian Zone tree, a red spruce.

The sun had by then burned, deep orange, through clouds that might have formed over a boiling sea. Across the cove, near the other shore, shrouded in the early mists, a fisherman solitary as a figure in a classical Chinese painting was slowly rowing a dory piled bow and stern with slatted lobster-traps. He must have been one of the last of his kind, to be using oars rather than an outboard motor.

The sun's rays flooded the earth horizontally, rich and glowing; there is no such light as that of morning when the sun breaks forth. It was as if all the objects on which it shone were breasting the tide of its radiance, as if one were standing before an ideal world. The weathered pink granite bulk of Eagle's Crag, bright as in a painting, against which the scattering of trees stood forth each above the pool of its own shadow; the bluffs formed of blocks of the same pink granite descending in steps to the sea; the conifers spreading their limbs as if in ritual celebration, their clean, fresh foliage stiff and motionless, jewel-sharp and jewel-bright in every needle: all was as if marshaled for a universal reveille, for inspection by the Most High. I could believe that the firs and spruces compressed in their bristling foliage the very burning-green essence of tree life. It was turgid with vitality, the needle-clustered twigs that composed the surface of the white spruces having the form of fingers of gloves inflated to distension and bunched. They are trees I am always stirred to see, as most of us must be, else we should not bring them so faithfully into our houses at Christmas, reaching back to a primitive past for a symbol of life's continuity through the nadir of winter. Even the infants of three or four years, only six or eight inches tall, stand erect and staunchly, as if it depended upon them no less than upon their elders to maintain the honor of the tribe that stands guard at timberline.

Beneath the outermost, wind-raked trees the sea was pouring over the pediments of the cliff, clear and cold. The water would swirl over and behind the rocks with a treacherous, caressing air, with concealed exultation, then wildly drain back, fanning out over the rock terrace and cascading into the face of the oncoming wave. The movement of the waves was hurrying and restless, but briefly the sea would seem to hesitate, as if meditating its next move. Sometimes a wave larger than its fellows would run up beneath an overhanging ledge, trapping a mass of air. There would be a dull clap then and foaming water would leap high to fall back with a drenching swish.

High over a grove of canoe birches still in full yellow leaf, against a field of snowy alto-cumulus cloud as seamed and fissured as the granite of the mountains, came a spearhead of Canada geese. When you have been watching ducks in flight, geese seem to fly in slow motion, heavy birds with great power in the downthrust of their big wings; you can feel it as the flock climbs. The passage of one of their formations is like the march-past of a phalanx with a mission on a remote frontier, their wild baying like the barbaric skirl of distant pipes. Why do they ceaselessly fill the air with their trumpeting, audible with ease a mile down wind? Whom are they seeking to signal? Unmusical it surely is; you could imagine that you were hearing the sounds of wheels turning under a heavy load on a cart's greaseless axles. Yet it is a summons that will rouse you from your sleep when it sounds from the night sky, and you wonder if an Indian may not have been recalled by the wild alarum from his commitment to eternity to watch the flock pass from a high rock in the moonlight or the ghost of a bison such as once roamed the vanished forests been caused to lift its shaggy head to listen. . . . So I reflected, my eyes on the bird at the apex of the V, an old gander, I supposed. He beat steadily on, composed and resolute, the leader of his clan (if I was right in my supposition), the conscious repository of responsibility for its welfare. Never mind that the wisdom of the canniest of wildfowl, and the one most faithful to its dependents, was no longer adequate, no match for the legions of gunners with high-powered, spray-shooting weapons, helpless against the filth that poisoned the waters, unable to bring back a fragment of the marshes buried under smoldering garbage dumps. His experience was all his charges had to look to and he would go on matching it against the odds until the end.

From the other direction, a raven swept in over the road, caught sight of me and banked sharply with a startled *crawk! crawk!* Twice the size of a crow, with a longer forward development of the head and neck and a bigger, wedge-shaped tail, he was near enough for me to hear the *swish-swoosh* of his spread pinions as he braked for the turn. He disappeared over the woods, from whence once more came that guttural call with its haunting timbre—*crrronk . . . crrronk!*—more resonant now. A somber bird, you would think, but in fact none is more given to high jinks. On a later excursion with a Park Ranger I saw two of them having sport with each other high over Green Mountain, grappling foot to foot to break apart just before their tumbling fall would have landed them in the treetops. "They're full of fun," the Ranger said. "I've seen them in a strong updraft doing barrel rolls." Green Mountain is what I call Mount Cadillac since that is the name it had before it was slicked up for the tourists and the old funicular railroad to the top replaced by a paved road.

In the cove, as in most other protected waters I saw along

the Maine coast, there was a flock of buffleheads—buffalo-heads as the little ducks were originally called by reason of the puffy feathering of the male's head. Among the smallest of ducks, they bobbed about like so many dumplings, the drakes very natty with their snowy bodies and black backs and heads, the latter with a white saddle. Among the diving ducks, which when not breeding spend much of their time at sea, the males usually combine black or near-black colors with white and shades of gray, as in fact do most adult seafowl. One reason for the sartorial vividness of male ducks may be (as James Fisher points out is the case with ptarmigans) that it causes them to attract predators away from the inconspicuously-colored, nesting female. It would be a form of gallantry of advantage to the species and scarcely less touching for being unpremeditated. (Regarding the plumages of birds, or the colors of flowers, I have to remind myself of the extreme unlikelihood that nature has as an objective the furnishing of aesthetic delight to a spectator with tastes like mine.) When one of the little buffleheads dived, it was with great suddenness, as if it had been yanked under water by a string attached to its beak. Its re-emergence was equally sudden. Simply, there one would be and you would not know it had been under except for the little toss it gave its head to flick off the drops of water.

From the apex of the cove came the cries of the gulls. One, which had been barking like a dog, broke into the well-known, rapid, clear, ringing *klee-a klee-a klee-a*, which has a break between the two syllables of about three full notes like yodeling. There is a similar break in the honking of geese, but where the goose breaks from a low note to a higher, the herring gull breaks from a high note to a lower. The effect in both is of invincible wildness. *Klee-a klee-a!* Even an imitation evokes for me a winter harbor with the fishing boats at their moorings, and the wind and the smell of the salt flats. . . . Then from one of the gulls came that cry of all cries of the timeless seacoast, one less frequently heard, which paralyzes me with the feeling of a spectral touch running along my nerve-ends—the loon cry of the herring gull, the yearning exultant *kaaaa-reeee!* that is half the voice of a sentient creature proclaiming its being, half the voice of the mindless wastes of water, the cry of a soul that is not yet a soul, weird, lost, doomed, and yet triumphant.

The coast of Maine has always attracted biologists for its almost museumlike display of the pattern by which the environment is parceled out among the plants and animals staking a claim on it. From the untroubled depths of the ocean up the shore to the land watered by rains alone, each step in the gradually changing conditions is optimum for some species, with the exception of an intermediate desert strip which is doused too little by the sea for marine species and too much for those of the land. The distribution of life by zones along the rocky shore is peculiarly satisfying to that part of the human mind that sets store by order. And to see things fall into place in accordance with a design is perhaps the next best thing to an affirmation of a universal purpose.

On Mount Desert, the pattern shows up very well at low tide at the Thunderhole, where the rackface is very steep and the zones are compressed. The hole is a cave at the end of a fifty-foot-long canyon in the granite, floored beneath the surface of the sea. Surging down this corridor, a wave slaps against the air in the dome of the cave as upon a drumhead. As the wave recoils the water in the passageway sways sullenly for a bit like some monster which has ineffectually assaulted an obstruction and stands shifting its weight and glowering about it. Then suddenly, with an effect as of the water gathering itself together, another wave hurtles into the cave, and once more there is a deep reverberating *boom*. This movement back and forth goes on even when the ocean appears quite tranquil. When one is scrambling about on the adjacent rocks, the waves keep up so continuous and conversational a chorus of wallowing, plopping and chuckling sounds that one has the feeling of being in human company.

The walls of the chasm are curtained in seaweed nearly to the upper reach of high tide. The topmost band is of bladder wrack, which somewhat resembles brown, flattened gloves and, to keep it upright when the tide is in, has air-sacs with tiny, pale blisters on them. Below it is a broader band of knotted wrack, which grows in bunches of olive-colored, noodlelike strands swollen at intervals with air-pockets. Wherever Mount Desert's rocky shores are protected from the full brunt of the breakers they are covered by these two wracks from the normal level of low tide almost through the intertidal zone, the green noodle mops of the knotted wrack covering acres of rocks in the coves where the slope is gentle. Hardy species, able to endure not only rough handling by the surf but exposure to hot sun for hours at a time, they belong to the brown algae, plants which have a leathery or rubbery texture and chlorophyl of greenish-brown pigmentation. Practically all the seaweeds are algae, which are among the simplest of plants. Some have "hold-fasts" resembling roots and many have what look like leaves and stems, but there is no differentiation in the cells composing these parts. Some algae, of only a single cell, are among the smallest of plants—though small as they are, the microscopic algae, free-floating in the surface waters of the world's oceans, account for 95 per cent by volume of all the plant life of the sea. Others are the longest of plants. One of the kelps of the Pacific Ocean is said to reach a fifth of a mile in length. The kelps, also brown algae, are represented on our northeast coast by the *Laminarias*, one of which is composed of a blade like a banana leaf up to twenty feet tall and three feet wide growing from a stalk up to ten feet tall with a hold-fast at its lower end like a many-toed hawk's talon. Parts of these formidable plants wash up on shore and help you imagine—if you have strong nerves—what it would be like to walk among their

beds six fathoms down, as through a forest of weirdly attenuated and sinuous trees swaying in macabre unison to the
passage of the waves.

Below the zone of wrack on the walls of the Thunderhole
are two red algae, each only a few inches long. Hanging on
the rock like flame-shaped tongues of deep-red jelly is the
dulse, which used to be widely eaten along the coast—just
as brown algae are today, in immense quantities, in the
Orient. Growing among the dulse, and much more rigid, is
the abundant and widely-distributed, crinkly *Chondrus*, mis-
named Irish moss, which resembles a brownish-purple or
purplish-green chicory lettuce. The red algae require the
minimum of light and grow at depths of the sea to which only
the blue portion of the sun's rays penetrates.

In the tidal pools around the Thunderhole, warmed by the
full sun, the rocks are seamed with the branched threads or
membranes of green algae. The third of the three groups of
algae of the sea, the greens are much more delicate than the
browns and many of the reds. The most striking algae of the
tidal pools, however, are the crustaceous algae, a form of the
red. One species coats the rocks at the bottom of the pools
with a hard film the color of pink liver-paste. Another gives
the rocks the appearance of having been painted with an
enamel the color of arterial blood, and one which dries to an
oxblood shade.

Competition, the quest for advantages, tends to push life
out in all directions from every habitat. What adds to the
interest of the shore is that it stands as the meeting-place, or
near meeting-place, of pioneer species from the two great
realms of sea and land, each advancing as far as it is able
toward or into the alien medium. In the long course of time,
to be sure, many have made the change-over completely. The
ancestors of all terrestrial plants and animals were forms
which made the crossing from sea to land, although, as
Marston Bates remarks, they "really never learned to leave the
sea. In going on land, they have learned how to take a bit of
the sea with them. In a sense, all land organisms are packages
of sea-water, variously wrapped and supported." Contrariwise,
eelgrass, sea-snakes, the few marine insects, sea-turtles, penguins, auks and their kin, dolphins, whales, manatees, seals
and sea-lions and walruses are descendants of species which
made the crossing back again, though most of the animals

which have gone back to the sea must return to land to lay
eggs or rear young and all must come to the surface to
breathe.

To exchange one medium of existence for the other makes
the most exorbitant demands upon the organism attempting
it. To enter the intertidal zone—the arena of opportunity and
trial—a marine species must subject itself to the brutal pounding and wrenching of the surf (though the surf, if it can be
withstood, is salubrious too, being richly oxygenated). The
farther it ascends that zone the less benefit it can draw from
the life-giving—but competitor-filled and predator-filled—
bath of the sea and the more exposed it becomes to the
death-dealing sun, the crystallizing cold of winter, the insipid,
lethally-leaching runnels of rain. The wracks, or rockweeds,
have made this inhospitable zone their own, not only surviving
its inclemency, but giving sanctuary to myriad marine animal-
cules, as one may discover (just as the gulls and shore birds
have discovered) by poking about under the fronds at low
tide.

I came very much a novice to the life of this rocky coast, as I did to the subject of geology, heavily dependent upon books for an understanding of them. I could well have wondered what justification there was for my nosing about along shores so distant from the locus of my obligations (largely unsatisfied) in the effort to improve myself in fields of knowledge in which I could never be more than a hopeless tyro. To give edge to the question and qualms to my conscience, moreover, there was the consideration that each morning I had only to consult my own whims in deciding how the day was to be spent, which was surely not the intention of the stern daughter of the voice of God. Somehow I managed to keep these misgivings at arm's length. For the most part I was nearly as absorbed in sorting out the denizens of the new world I awoke to in the mornings, as remote from other claims, as I should have been if I had expected to be led by observation of the roles in which they were cast to some new grasp of the universe. When I found a spot of brilliant green lichen, its goblets just the size to contain a pencil point, on the rocks *below* the highest little brackish pool (evidently it survived the dousings of salt spray it must have received by being in the overflow of a higher rain-water pool), the discovery was in my eyes meet for inclusion in the annals of science.

Among the creatures coping successfully with the rigors of intertidal existence, the mussels seemed to me especially attractive. Where the ebb tide left standing water in depressions and cracks in the rocks, and the wrack left room for them, they were packed solid. Anchored by coarse threads tough as silk, they appeared to be as tightly affixed as globules of the rock itself. The beds of smaller mussels resembled anthracite pea-coal. Beneath a blue-black epidermis, the shells of mussels are of a lovely, paler blue, the color of fountain-pen ink. In profile shaped like an elongated, rather pointed egg flat along most of one side, having exactly the right rotundity, delicately fluted in one species, a mussel seems to me artistically perfect, a tribute to nature's supreme sculptor, which is relentless adversity. From the moment when the free-swimming larva settles down, the mussel must endure continual pounding by the seas, and sometimes seas armed with rocks or cakes of ice. But the odds against a larva's achieving a secure lodgment to begin with are probably about as heavy as those against a particular American baby's becoming President of the United States. To maintain the mussel population, it is necessary for the females to produce millions of eggs each at a spawning. At such times, which appear to occur when chemicals secreted by a few spawning individuals trigger a like action on the part of the others, the sea may be milky with the spermatozoa of the males. At least the system works. Mussels are said to be the most abundant bivalves in the world.

Above the mussels, zonally speaking, were the rock barnacles, occupants of the more exposed rocks where the battering by the waves was too much for the wracks. There they formed a solid, khaki-colored encrustation, firm enough to be walked on. They also ascended the ever-damp crannies and fissures of the rock as forest ascends the creases of windswept mountains. Those along the edges of the bed were generally white—the native color of their plated shells—so that from a distance the rocks appeared rimed or as if salt had dried on them. The tenant and builder of these little ivory volcanoes was a small, shrimplike crustacean which stands permanently on its head and with its waving legs, protruded through the crater, extracts particles of food from the water the waves bring—an expedient ignoble and ignominious but no more so than some to which the necessity of earning a living drives representatives of a higher form of life.

The intertidal darling of the biologists (and, along with the mussel, of European diners) is the periwinkle. A compact little snail, it is highly instructive, for its several species on the New England coast are in various stages of emergence from the sea. The smooth periwinkle is still a marine snail and can endure only brief periods out of the water. The common periwinkle of European shores and tables, which is said to be a late immigrant to our coast and has in any case inched its way from Maine to New Jersey only in the past century, inhabits a zone reached only by high tides but is dependent upon the sea as a nursery for its eggs. The rough periwinkle is almost ready to join the ranks of the land snails, all of which originally worked their way up from the sea. Bearing its young alive and possessed of gills that serve almost as lungs, it can get along with a mere fortnightly wetting from the spring tides—indeed, even longer.

That something important is happening to the periwinkles

must be apparent from their abundance to any visitor to the
New England coast. I found the rocks, up to a level reached
by no other marine forms, pimpled with them, many of those
farthest from the water being no larger than cinders. In fact
the unavoidability of crushing them under foot detracted
from the pleasure of walking about.

Like slowly moving beads, sometimes clustered in strings
or mats, the periwinkles thronged the little pools left high up
among the rocks by the ebbing tide. They grazed on algae,
licking their way along. The mussels in the pools were also
feeding, their shells ajar to expose the slit opening of the two
siphons through which they draw in and expel the food-
bearing water. The barnacles, however, had everywhere drawn
the crater doors down tight over them, presumably for the
winter. In some pools, their beds were so compressed that the
colonists had been constrained to raise their usually cone-
shaped shelters into columns. One such cylinder which I
detached to examine it was three-quarters of an inch high
and looked like a tooth from a cow's jaw. When I dropped
it back into the pool it was immediately fallen upon by pale,
shrimplike creatures also about three-quarters of an inch long.
I surmised with distress that they were making a meal of
their still-living relative. Amphipods they were, I took it.
White-eyed and humpbacked, they moved as often as not on
their sides, as if maimed, and would jacknife their way along
energetically in a mere film of water. I wondered how much
cold such exposed little beings could stand, or the even frailer-
looking, threadlike worms that wriggled rapidly from one
covert to another. Even at that season, when most of their
denizens were dormant, the tidal pools had the fascination of
any complex world in microcosm into which one peers like
a giant or a god. They were as colorful as the autumn woods,
and in fact resembled a miniature, exotic landscape of cliffs
and savanna land, with here and there little trees of green
algae or a grove of curly *Chondrus* or, above a rust-colored
expanse, of knotted wrack scaled down by the biome (as I
suppose ecologists would call it) to tufts two inches tall.

The more you think about the conditions of marine existence, the harsher seem those which pertain on land. In the
sea, the annual range of temperature reaches 50 degrees in
only two places, it is said—the coastal waters for a short
distance below Kamchatka and those between Cape Cod and

Cape Hatteras—while nowhere can the diurnal range, except at the very surface, be more than negligible. Under water, winds are unknown, moisture cannot fail and gravity exerts only enough force on living creatures to make down distinguishable from up, if that. One might almost believe that quitting this salubrious medium for the stringencies of the atmosphere would have been for living organisms a traumatic experience leaving as deep an impress upon the nervous system as quitting the womb is said to.

Even more challenging, however, are the conditions faced by plants that, having become adapted to existence on land, have returned to the shore. There, to the searing effect of sun and wind, is added the burning salinity of the ocean's spray. Those that make their home in this zone appear to protect themselves in the same ways that desert plants and the marine plants of the intertidal rocks do, that is, by water-retaining succulence or by impermeable, generally hard surfaces. On the beaches of sorts that have formed at the head of the coves of Mount Desert, the plants that come nearest the water bear an extraordinary superficial resemblance to the wracks. The sprawling sea-rocket, an aberrant mustard, while light green instead of dark brown, also has leaves and stems that are pulpy and look alike in composition; it even has protuberances that resemble bladders, though actually they are the projectile-like seedheads that give the plant its name. Sea-milkwort is a plant of the same thick, rubbery texture and procumbent habit. It is a primrose, of all things. Those I saw still had a few tiny white flowers in their axils. Farther up the beach, protected by their sheer rankness, a few great burdocks still bore their purple shaving-brush flowers and there were small yellow flowers on the sowthistles, a plant so tough it occurs around the world. It was astonishing to find summer lingering so on this northern coast when a few miles inland even the autumn coloring had gone. There were more asters and goldenrod in bloom than I should have expected to find around my home in northern Virginia.

Fortunate are the inhabitants of islands and peninsulas! The ocean is a great reducer of the seasons, a radiator in winter, a refrigerator in summer. To warm up water requires three thousand times as much heat as it does to warm up the same amount of air to the same degree. During winter, the ocean slowly releases the heat it stored during the summer. Sea-water of between 35 degrees and 45 degrees feels icy indeed, but the breeze that comes off it is temperate compared with an air mass surging down out of Canada in January. In cold such as that brings, a winter ocean may be seen to steam. According to the National Park Service, the coast at Mount Desert, while 10 degrees cooler in summer than the adjacent mainland, is 10 degrees warmer in winter. Even so, the winter cold reaches lower latitudes along our northeastern coast than along any other coast in the world except the corresponding coast on the other side of the Pacific.

More of Maine and
South to Cape Ann

You could walk for a week on the trails of Mount Desert without retracing your steps, and in addition there are fifty-odd miles of old carriage-roads now closed to vehicular traffic. Built in the heyday of Bar Harbor society, these roads were beautifully and solidly engineered, or were if one may judge from the example that leads off from the former Rockefeller gate-house and circles a low mountain called The Triad. The gate-house, a small mansion of brick and stone now housing the Park Superintendent, is near the old rustic restaurant and stables at the end of Jordan Pond, on which the resort's highest-spirited surrey parties used to converge. Jordan Pond House, which still caters to the appreciative in season, seemed in its desuetude on a late autumn afternoon to be sunk in melancholy. Hope and youth might have fled forever from the world—though not without leaving a memento: at the far end of the pond itself may be seen two granite domes named by a young man with women's charms on his mind and now, with an "l" having been substituted for an "i," known incongruously as "The Bubbles."

I walked for several miles on the Rockefeller road, hoping to meet a deer around a curve but coming to wonder if in the failing light I might not be taken for one myself by one of the poachers with whom the Park Rangers were having trouble. In the west, behind some detached banks of sullen grey clouds, the rim of the sky was an intense apricot color. Against it the conifer-edged ridge across the valley stood out black and saw-toothed. It was a cold winter sunset, a northern sunset, as long-lasting as it was early. An hour after the sun had disappeared there was still red in the sky, like a stain of blood in deep-blue water.

Although I saw no deer on that walk (and was not mistaken for one) I came within twelve feet of a doe at another time on a headland below Blackwoods. She was browsing at the edge of the forest above the road, picking up her legs fastidiously as she took a step, from time to time flirting her tail. Her movements all had a winning abruptness, an adolescent girl's impulsiveness about them. I try not to be sentimental about animals but in this case tried without much avail. When she lifted her head to face me, not really anxiously but as if I were so extraneous to her scheme of things she was not quite sure I was there, the eyes she fixed upon me were of a liquid darkness quite impenetrable. She was the picture of guilelessness, so innocent, one would have thought, as not even to recognize the fear which her instincts must have been signaling to her. Her nose was black and around it the short, wax-smooth pelage was almost white, as was that on her underparts too, contrasting with the rich, tawny color of the rest of her coat; the pattern was precise. That entered very much into her charm: the neatness and precision of her design and her deportment. A fortnight before, on a Long Island beach, a dunlin, or red-backed sandpiper, had affected me similarly. Its eyes, too, were black and lustrous, its bill was black also and it had the same expression of sweetness, if I may be forgiven for calling it that, at the corners of its mouth. And I had thought how precisely figured it was, how mild in demeanor and how gently wondering to be all alone in the overbearing immensity of that setting.

The Rockefeller summer home, "The Eyrie," is about two miles south of the gatehouse, between two colonies of the affluent on the seaward, lower end of the island's eastern lobe. The houses of Seal Harbor and Northeast Harbor, expansive structures of frame construction, most of them three stories high and with wings and dormers, were in hibernation now, like the mansions of Bar Harbor. Many were grandly dark in hue, with trim as dark as the siding, and big trees grew close around them, further darkening them. Opulence seems to express itself naturally in somberness, which is suitable to those who carry weight in the world and do not require the induced cheerfulness of bright, airy colors. At least it did in the days when its possession set one apart, as only the services of a reliable household staff can set one part. But of course these houses were meant for occupancy during the time of year when light was in surfeit.

After the glare of the tennis-court, the twilight of the cavernous front hall was welcome. My eyes had barely become adjusted to it when she appeared in the doorway to the living room. "Ronald!" she exclaimed, advancing with her hand held out to me. "I—we thought you had quite deserted us!" Despite my attire of fresh white flannels and blue blazer with the yacht club insigne on the breast pocket, I was conscious that I cut a foolish figure as I stood with mouth agape. "Lucy, you're—you've grown up!" I could not at once extricate myself from this scene even after I had left the site of it behind, along with the huge summer hotel of carriage days that overlooked the bay at Seal Harbor, on the road to Somes Sound, and has since then been torn down.

Like Mount Desert's lakes, Somes Sound occupies a trench excavated by the glacier, but its bed was pushed clear through to that of the sea, which has filled it and created the only fiord in the eastern United States, unless you count the estuary of the Hudson River as one. I drew up beside the water at a spot across from and not very far above Fernald Point. This is said to be the site of the missions established on the island by the Jesuits in 1613 and wiped out a few weeks later by Samuel Argall of the Virginia Company, discoverer of the Gulf Stream, in the first action of the long contest between English and French for possession of North America. After a hike along the road skirting the sound I returned to the bus to warm myself with a cup of tea. Dark, misty clouds had come sailing in from the sea, obscuring the sun and bringing a chill with them. It takes only the sun's going under to dispel the Arcadian mood of Indian summer and replace it with one of foreboding, of time running out.

The approach of a cold front, bringing a foretaste of winter to the coast of Maine, was signalized by a rumble of thunder after I had turned in for the night, and presently another, both following well after the flash, which could have been cast by a light-house below the horizon. It was raining when I awoke, I saw to my regret. I had arranged the day before to go out that morning with a lobster fisherman—Bob Corson, he had told me his name was when, summoning up my nerve, I had accosted him on the Bar Harbor municipal dock. I was afraid the expedition would be canceled, but when I showed up at the dock at the appointed hour I found my skipper making ready to put out.

We cast off soon after I had clambered on board and headed out into Frenchman Bay, the launch settled low and seemingly happily in the water like a motherly duck; you still had the impression that she was enjoying her responsibilities even after the going became rather rough. The buoys marking our traps were painted black and white. (Lobster buoys, along with jockeys' shirts, seem to be among the last holdouts of heraldry.) I watched the procedures with the greatest of interest. Coming up alongside the buoy, Corson cut the motor to idling speed and snagged the mooring rope with a boat hook. Looping it over a pulley hung on a kind of davit, he quickly threw two turns of it around the shiny little brass drum of a winch worked by the launch's motor. Gathering in the rope off the drum as fast as the winch wound it on, he recovered first a bottle tied in the line to keep it off the bottom and finally the three-foot-long semicylindrical trap, made of laths, which he hauled up onto the bulwark by hand. One by one he snatched from the trap the seven or eight lobsters and crabs which were clattering about in it excitedly and belligerently. He was too quick for me to see how he managed to evade the armory of up-reared and gaping claws. The crabs—northern or Jonah crabs, the color of cooked salmon—all had carapaces too bumpy for the finicky tastes of the crab-buyer (it was explained to me) and were rejected. Only one of the lobsters had a thorax shown by the steel gauge to be of legally acceptable length. This one, when its captor had dipped into a box of stout red rubber bands with a pair of reverse pliers and snapped one over each of its claws, was dropped into a pail with a dozen others. The rest had to go over the side with the crabs. The penalty for being caught with undersized lobsters was five dollars on each count and loss of license for six months. And the warden, said Corson, was constantly on the job with an outboard motor reputedly capable of pushing his boat along at forty knots. He himself would not care to be one. The wardens risked being shot, at least in some places where the fishermen were tough.

The remains of the bait in the net bag—fore parts of herrings too long for sardine cans—were flung to the gulls which came to within a few feet of the boat to pounce upon them.

One went completely under in pursuit of a prize, but that
was exceptional. Herring gulls do not like to submerge, and
usually if a piece went a foot down, it was gone. I was
startled to see one of the birds put away a piece six inches
long at a gulp, but Corson said they could swallow foot-long
herrings whole, and they never seemed to be filled. They
looked hungry enough, with their rather gaunt faces dusky-
streaked for the winter and their eyes pale as a white Leg-
horn's.

The bait-sack replenished from a keg of fresher herring-
halves—the sweet-pungent smell of which was to cloy my
nasal passages all that day and the next—the trap was dropped
overboard and the motor gunned. You had to watch out for
the line paying over the side. That I had learned when Corson had clambered out aft to set the triangular sail you see at
the stern of most lobster-boats, the purpose of which is to
keep the craft headed into the wind, and the fisherman protected from it, while traps are being pulled. The vessel was
bucking in the choppy sea and the deck flowing water from
the rain and I had asked if he were not afraid of falling overboard. Falling was not the danger, he had replied. Pointing
out a boat at some distance, the only other one that seemed
to be out that morning, he said that just a few days before
its owner had got his leg caught in a loop of the line as it
was racing over the side and, having failed to throw himself
on the bottom of the boat—as he, Corson, had thought to do
once in a similar jam—had been whipped overboard. The lid
closed on him, as Corson put it. However, he had bobbed up
to the surface directly. The difficulty had been climbing on
board in his heavy, sodden clothes and with his boots full of
water. Corson had been at the dock when he had got back
and had given him the better part of a pint of whisky. He
had drained the bottle while stripping to his underwear—in
disregard and plain view of the public. He had had a bad
scare, said Corson, and declared that this was no sort of life—
had vowed never to go out again. But there he was, and on
a day like this, too.

It was not an inviting one. The wind was raw, the bay dark
and rough, the rain cascading out of clouds that coasted
across the sky trailing smoky vapors and appearing almost
too heavy to clear the water; the top of Champlain Mountain
was wholly fogged in. For me, who had no work to do and

could keep my hands in my pockets under my poncho, enjoying the bounce of the lively vessel as I braced myself against the side of the cabin, all this added zest to the experience. But even with the nips he took from a bottle he kept by the wheel, I did not see how Corson could stand it. His hands, in soaking-wet cotton gloves, must have been numb with cold. I knew from having plucked bits of marine life from the shallows how icy that sea-water was, and the fathoms of rope he had to handle every time he pulled in a trap were running with it. "In the winter," he said, "it's so rough sometimes you can't go out but a couple of times a week."

I am always interested in men who pursue a solitary livelihood without benefit of connection with the organizations that compose the framework of our society. What moves them to accept the uncertainty and inadequacy—usually—of income and the prospect of its cessation in illness and old age, recognizing that most of their catch will fail by the arbitrary standards of the steel gauge or be found too lumpy by the buyer? Is it, I wonder (having had some acquaintance myself with an occupation of that kind), a positive commitment to independence or is it negative, a diffidence or failure of nerve before the organization's impersonal demands? All I could tell about my host was that the life seemed to agree with him. Though he was old enough to have a son with his own fishing boat, his complexion was fullblooded, his blue eyes bright, his face, in which the nose was a trifle emphasized at the expense of the chin, cheerful. He had a laugh like Santa Claus's—"Oh-h'-h'-h'-h'-h'!"—and in his yellow oilskins suggested a less severe version of the Grand Banks fisherman immortalized in the statue on the Gloucester waterfront.

Under their bristling pelage of spruce and fir, the islands among which we were plying resembled hedgehogs crouching in the water up to their noses; the four are in fact known as the Porcupines. The snouts were the boulder-formed, seaward-looking southern points and the high foreheads the cliffs above them. On our other side, these cliffs were matched by the rocky promontories of the mainland, or what one thought of as the mainland; Mount Desert, though an island, is the second largest on our country's Atlantic coast.

"From the sea, the land looks dangerous and threatening, while from the land the sea does," I said, thinking how forbidding the sea appeared in the evenings from one of those headlands.

Corson agreed that it was so. "That washed her face off!" he declared. A small sea had slapped against the launch's windshield. The wind, setting in the northwest, had suddenly freshened. The rain soon stopped and whitecaps appeared. We had by then pulled a score of traps and Corson, vocally regretting the omission of long drawers from his day's attire, decided it was time to put back in. At the head of the bay the cloud roof had drawn back to open a crack along the horizon upon a cold, distant, light blue-green sky.

By the time we had stepped ashore and I had boiled a cup of water for coffee, the dark canopy of rain clouds had so far drawn back as to expose the northern half of the sky, blue and brilliant behind the procession of low strato-cumulus clouds following the main mass. All across Frenchman Bay the waves, running before the wind, were breaking into foam. Warmed by the coffee and a change into dry socks and shoes, I set off to drive up Green Mountain. The road, bearing in its studied accommodation to the character of the country the hallmark of the National Park Service (which builds harmoniously but too much), looped up the western flank. Below it lay the long, deep valley cradling Eagle Lake and farther to the west and south other rounded summits of *les Monts-deserts,* as Samuel de Champlain had called them in 1604.

Over a slope above me a little kestrel hovered, then dove to the ground. He rose when I rounded the next loop carrying a burden clearly about as large as he could manage. Delicate of movement even with his load, he put down in a bare tree ahead of me and I saw through my binocular that his victim was a vole. The poor dangling little creature, its neck awry in its captor's grip, was still kicking and squirming, but its struggles were mercifully brief. The kestrel—a dandy in his contrasting hues of rufous, slate and white, bearing on his head the shadow of the falcon's helmet—gave the vole not a glance, having none to spare from his continuing, nervous surveillance of his surroundings.

There were stands of beech and hemlock on the way up the mountain, and above them the more northerly conifers: spruce and balsam fir and, on a slope which it had pretty much to itself, northern white cedar. This last, also called arborvitae, was the winter staple of the deer and its condition a barometer of their numbers, a Park Ranger told me. A shoulder burned over by the disastrous forest fire of 1947, which had swept more than twenty-five square miles of the island, was occupied by scattered pitch pines, survivors of the blaze. As the road climbed, the height of the trees diminished with their exposure to the winds, the white cedar being gradually reduced to the proportions of a cushion. In a cut through which the road passes, the pink granite is severed by a vertical dark band several feet wide where basaltic magma was forced into a fracture of the granite to form a dike. Near the top is a free boulder apparently of granite porphyry (a granite mass in which large crystals called phenocrysts are embedded), which was deposited there by the ice-sheet after having been transported at least twenty miles. (Another such boulder, a monster, may be descried from Jordan Pond House precariously perched on the slope of one of the Bubbles, like a wart.)

When you ascend this highest of the desert mountains, your surroundings come into view progressively and piecemeal. If the panorama from the top were sprung on you all at once, you would be overpowered. You very nearly are anyway. There is no other point from which you can see so much of our country's Atlantic coast; you would find none other comparable on the coast to the south until you reached Rio de Janeiro. All around you, below the cloud of stone on which you stand, below the neighboring summits, lies the fragmented edge of the continent. On one side, as it advances seaward, it breaks up into islands of diminishing size and increasing separation. On the other it takes form gradually out of narrowing bays, gently rolling in contour, rising in a few places to the stubs of ancient eminences, as if there the blanket of the forest had been lifted by a round object placed beneath it, but the land is puddled with lakes and ponds as far as you can see, and farther—to the feet of Mount Katahdin and on into Canada.

The banks of strato-cumulus clouds, each like the ridge of lumpy snow left by the road-scraper, their flat bases grey in their own shadows, had come largely to cover the sky as they passed low overhead. Between some of their ridges glowed strips and patches of blue as intense as the blue of a stained-glass window, and there were corresponding zones of sunlight on the mottled grey and dark green of the forested earth and shadows on the sunlit sea as dark as the islands but vastly larger. From fifteen hundred feet up, the ocean looked entirely harmless, no more to be reckoned with than a painted floor, as it does from an airplane—until the craft lurches and restores your awareness of the nature of things. In its varying stains of green and blue—if a color could be assigned to its nameless dark where the clouds rode between it and the sun—the sea appeared static and immutable; its billows, distinguishable only in the blinding sheet of reflected light beneath the quarter of the sky in which the sun shone, resembled fixed corrugations, while elsewhere the whitecaps were like the accumulations of snowflakes in the lee of irregularities in the ground after the first light dusting; only by staring fixedly at them could you see them come and go. The two seemingly level expanses of cloud-furrowed sky and of intermingled land and water led the gaze between them off into infinite distance.

A near gale had risen. You could see why the vegetation mostly cowered in the hollows among the smoothed and rounded, fissured blocks forming the dome of the mountain. The trunks of the stalwart little firs and spruces that here and there grew erect stood firm against the blasts, but their foliage quivered like jelly. The voice of the wind in a grove they formed was as high-pitched as the swish of silk. The little bus rocked to the gusts. A few other cars appeared but did not tarry long.

Mount Desert was not entirely without pilgrims even at this season. Occasional out-of-state cars passed on the park roads and at midday there was likely to be a couple eating boxed lunches at Sand Beach or below the cliff of Newport (to give Champlain Mountain its earlier name). Schoodic Point, an outlying bit of park across Frenchman Bay, seemed to draw a light but steady traffic. It is a very exposed rocky promontory famous for the stupendous seas that crash upon it during storms. It is also well known for the sea-birds to be observed from it. All during the lunch I ate there little groups of eiders came winging in. On the water, the adult drake appears entirely white but for the rear two-thirds of his underparts and the top of his head. (The long, black-capped white head tapering to a beak put me in mind, I don't know exactly why, of pictures of scorchers from the early days of the bicycle craze.) Eiders, which breed on Arctic coasts, are big ducks, on the way to being thick-necked geese, with a deliberate flight. They were arriving about a dozen at a time and, with feet splayed in front of them, hitting with a splash and skidding to a stop. Now and again part of the growing raft of them off the point would skitter across the water, flailing the surface with their wings and whipping up a surf, all evidently in play.

In another car a girl was also watching the eiders, through a telescope. Looping my binocular conspicuously over my neck, I went over to exchange impressions with her. To dispel without delay any doubts of my bona fides, I remarked that as far as could be seen the male eiders in the vicinity outnumbered the females by a good four to one. We speculated why this might be so. She turned out to be well informed as well as attractive. She had, she said, seen two gannets and some American scoters (the least common of the three kinds) on her last trip to Schoodic. Her greatest find here had been a Kumlein's gull. Her eyes lighted up at the recollection. Had it been any farther away than at the end of the rocks, she declared, she would never have dared claim an identification. I asked if there were any chance of our picking up (I took care to keep within the idiom, since from the way she kept pulling her skirt down every time she squirmed around to get a better view of a bird I surmised she was not yet sure of my exclusive devotion to bird-watching) any alcids. (Alcids are what the fraternity call those northern-hemisphere equivalents of the penguins: the razor-billed auks, murres, guillemots, puffins and dovekies.) She explained that it took a storm to bring them close enough in to be seen and that if the storm were just a little bit too heavy the mist of the breakers obscured them; it was touch and go.

She was, I learned, a member of the Maine Audubon Society and had driven, all by herself, down from Bangor just for the birds of the Schoodic. She was distinctly an entry for the other side of the uneven balance sheet one draws up mentally as one travels about our country, she and the many thousands she stood for. "Whatever else America may be," said a friend of mine who had flown from New York to Washington after several years in Switzerland and been aghast at what he saw, "it is the land of the bulldozer." That is surely true. But there is another side. The national and state parks you see incorporate only a tenth part of the land they should—at least in the East—but for every acre of them men and women have sacrificed, have fought and bled in legislatures. Every living gull, meadowlark, raven, sandpiper, hawk, heron is testimony to other battles waged in its behalf —not for gain but for love; the self-servers all are on the other side, except for those sportsmen who contribute to protection to make sure of having something to kill in the future. The country is not all gas stations, outdoor movie theaters, roadhouses, wrecked-car lots, parking plazas, though it may seem to be so in places. Among them are trees, shrubs, flowers, planted and tended by people who had no other motive than a care for what is living and green.

I often wonder about the place of nature in the soul of Western man. Western literature from Shakespeare to the publications of the Sierra Club is eloquent in the responsiveness it reveals to woods, mountains and rivers, birds and four-footed animals, to the whole out-of-doors—clouds and sky and thundering sea. It leads to the belief that a feeling for nature and a sense of being integral with the natural world are deep-seated among us and have roots far back in the northern European past. Perhaps only in the art of China and Japan could one find comparable expression of such receptivity to nature. Yet (and this I can never fully fathom) we were led to adopt and at times have fanatically prosecuted a religion—that is to say, a view of what life is ultimately about—in which there is no fellowship whatever of man and nature. Christianity abstracts man from nature. Nature it at best relegates to subservience as man's handmaiden and for the rest stigmatizes as the source of impulses in man which he may scarcely obey without shame or even risk of perdition. So it is with all three of the monotheistic religions that arose in the eastern Mediterranean to sweep in time over five of the inhabited continents and part of the sixth. The God of Judah, Christianity and Islam created the animals solely to be of use to mankind. This is made explicit in *Genesis*. It is put unequivocally to Noah in a pronouncement that must have been meant as a blessing but reads like a curse:

> *And the fear of you and the dread of you shall be upon every beast of the earth, and upon every fowl of the air, upon all that moveth upon earth, and upon all fishes of the sea; into your hand are they delivered.*

Why this animosity to nature? Possibly the prophets of monotheism saw in paganism their mortal foe and in man's feeling of identity with nature the seedbed of paganism. Beyond that, nature meant the world of the present life, the satisfactions of which were an impediment to the realization of those of a postulated future life of eternal duration and were accordingly condemned. The consequences were to be immeasurable. Alienated from the world they lived in, the Judeo-Christian-Islamic believers were put on their mettle to prove themselves like invaders who owe the land no fealty and are denied the comfort of a sense of participation in its being, thrown upon their own to triumph or perish. The world around them had nothing of value to say to them; the tolerant, open-minded relativity of view we acquire from observation of the natural world was not for them. Theirs was the absolutism of revelation. There is no such incentive as the conviction that one possesses the single, preclusive, comprehensive and unalterable truth—as we have recently illustrated in the dynamics of Communism, that shaky amalgam of the Judeo-Christian social aim with the supposed lessons of science.

The disciples of the monotheistic, monopolistic, antinatural religions who set out to achieve the next world unquestionably won this one. Their God had given them the world as a fief of small and transitory worth for their use. He enjoined mercy toward their fellow men, and charity, and this surely was a teaching from which humanity could draw incalculable benefit, but of mercy toward their fellow creatures, of respect for the intricate and multiform family of plants and animals of which they were a part, nothing was said. In the writings to which the peoples of two-thirds of the civilized world have for centuries been taught to look for supreme guidance there is not a word making it immoral for man to stride across the earth with rapine and slaughter—provided only that he spare his own kind—and convert it into a desert lifeless but for himself. Perhaps there was less need when man's capacity for destruction was limited. But the march proceeds apace today and if there is thunder from the pulpit against the havoc we are wreaking on the lands we occupy and on their aboriginal inhabitants it is very muted thunder. The savage American Indian—even he—asked pardon of the spirit of the bear he killed out of necessity, but we may read today how communicants in good standing with church or chapel fly airplanes far out over the icepack to gun down the vanishing polar bears—for fun.

Indifferent to the natural world external to man and generally hostile to the nature that is in man, expressed in our spontaneous emotions and actions, our religious preceptors have left it to poets to sing of the wine that nature instills in our veins and of our kinship with the world around us in all its grandeur, its loveliness and its pathos. To the Greeks of the great age, religion and poetry were inseparable, but with us they have given rise to two distinct literatures with little overlapping between them. That this should be so seems to me symbolic of the cruel dichotomy of soul which is the price we have paid for our pre-eminence in the world; for Western man has been pulled in opposing directions by the governing forces of his existence.

Such being the pass he had reached, one can only give thanks for the birth of the scientific spirit among us. Science has shown us what we had been in danger of forgetting, how much we are a part of nature and how much nature is a part of us. In its exclusive concern with the apprehensible it has caused us to think more of making all we can of what this world has to offer instead of turning our backs upon it like the ungrateful dog in the parable who dropped irretrievably the bone he had been given in order to snatch at its shimmering reflection in the water. It has warned us in terms we have at last begun to heed of the consequences of impoverishing the earth. It has relieved us of much of the impossible load of guilt that an endemic puritanism had taught us to feel for being what by nature we are and must be. And its capacities for discovering us to ourselves and thus enabling us to live in greater harmony with ourselves and our surroundings may only have begun to be tapped.

At least one may hope so. But that is not to suggest that men can live by science alone. Science is only the method of rational analysis and what we have learned by it, nothing more. In all its findings there is less to warm the heart than in a single ration of rum issued on the wind-swept deck of a ship to the shivering hands. It offers no justification for or encouragement to those who in the fullness of their feeling would like to do homage to the Great Spirit in observances attuned to the gulls' cries and the sea's splash in a grove of balsams sacred to its worship. There are no shrines within its purlieus upon which we may unload the bittersweet burden that the experience of living lays upon our hearts. But if it does not enjoin reverence upon us it does not proscribe it either. And it wonderfully sharpens our observation and informs our comprehension of the Great Spirit's handiwork. Because that is its purpose, I would believe that comfortless though its uncompromising rationality may be (while being prodigiously productive of material comforts), science shows creation and hence the Creator the most genuine possible respect and deference. Those views of the universe that make creatures like ourselves its ultimate reason for being must necessarily be suspect. To see the universe as nearly as possible without regard to our own predispositions or desires, as science tries to, seems to me to approach the godly. Said Sir Thomas Browne three centuries ago:

> *The wisdome of God receives small honour from those vulgar heads that rudely stare about, and with a gross rusticity admire his workes; those highly magnifie him*

whose judicious enquiry into his acts, and deliberate research into his creatures, returne the duty of a devout and learned admiration.

Beside Schoodic Point lay Little Moose Island, described as a detached outpost of Labrador. It certainly looked like that: a flat, granite dome beset—as one could tell—by the fierce westerlies of winter from one side and from the other by seas whipped up by northeasterly gales. Its rock masses were as rounded as old haystacks, and its extensions, running out to sea, ended in worn protuberances resembling the paws of the Sphinx. Much of the island was covered by plants which long ago had spread southward out of the Arctic with the falling temperatures that preceded the ice sheet and when it retreated remained in situations too inhospitable for temperate-zone plants. The whole western side was carpeted with the most abundant of these, black crowberry, a small plant which puts out tiny leaves from all around its stems and somewhat resembles a large moss with black berries like huckleberries. On this side of the island few plants stood a foot high except some stunted white spruces. Moving east, you came upon a few mat junipers which irresistibly suggested enormous dried cow pats, then to patches of two other Arctic ground-covers—mountain cranberry, which resembles a tiny, red-berried, prostrate boxwood, and alpine bearberry, which looks quite similar but has longer, toothed leaves and black berries. Passing into the lee of the crest of the island you entered thickets of mountain alder—except that entering them was nearly impossible except on hands and knees along a deer path. With the alder was sheep laurel, which is a spindly, diminished cousin of mountain laurel with pale, lackluster leaves hanging dejectedly.

The mountain alder grew all over the region and, except on Little Moose, was still holding onto its nearly round, coarse, crepe-paper green leaves; it must be exceedingly hardy. The other plants of Little Moose—and of Schoodic Point—are among those you found on the tops of the mountains and in places growing in the thin soil on the cliffs above the sea. With them, but much more widespread, setting the slopes on fire, was a wild rose with leaves as dark and shiny a red as clotted blood, huckleberry scarlet in its autumn color and a little ground-creeper to which I was very partial. This last,

the wine-leaved cinquefoil, had inch-long leaves in the form
of a three-pronged V, like the broad arrow used to mark His
Britannic Majesty's official stores and once seen all through
Maine on the white pines claimed for the Crown. Trailing
over the gritty earth formed of decomposed granite and sending its runners up the cracks in the rocks to garland them
with Christmas red and green, it climbed all the way up
Gorham Mountain—as I did too, to do homage to the summit that reputedly was Samuel de Champlain's landfall. For
contrast with the lively little cinquefoil there were the two-inch-
high ghost forests of thorn lichen, pale relative of the reindeer
"moss" which brings the herds of caribou through the winter—
not to mention the lemmings. Lichens, which actually are two
entirely unrelated plants—an alga and a fungus—in a mutually
supporting union, will grow where nothing else will and there
were beds of thorn lichen on the poorest soil all over the
island. Each plant, nearly white when dry, pale pea-green
after a rain, resembled in miniature the skeleton of an oak,
though trunk and limbs were tubular, but they were packed
far tighter in their elfin forests than ever trees could be.

It is the rocks with which it all begins. Even the waters of
the sea, and consequently their offspring, the rains and the
streams, all of which unremittingly assail the rocks exposed
to them, were born of the minerals which formed the earth
and were only released to the atmosphere through volcanic
action. In the final analysis, the patient, undemanding rocks
are the universal providers. All plant life depends upon the
products of the rock— the plants of the sea upon the minerals
that had their source in the rocks, the land plants upon soil
that is only particles of rocks—like the sand of the beaches—
to which decayed material of plants and animals has been
added; and all animal life depends upon plant life.

You see the lichens spreading like paper-thin concentric
wafers upon the rocks, which their acid secretions slowly
break down, the herbaceous plants sending their roots into
the fissures of the rocks, the trees straddling the rocks with
their roots as starfish straddle the oysters they prise apart,
and you come to think of transitory living forms as in league
against that which is enduring, as dependent relatives will collect about the one self-sufficient member of the family to
sponge upon him. Water collecting in cracks in the bedrock
splits it asunder by its expansive action as it freezes and by

similar action scales granules from its surface. These granules
roll down the slopes to settle in hollows and give roothold to
plants or, carried by rivulets of rain or by the wind, scour
the mountainsides and produce silt or a finer abrasive.
Streams, dragging crystals of rock and fragments of massive
rocks dislodged by the frost and shattered in their fall, file
deep beds into which more rock, loosened by the weight of
the snow-pack and the melting and freezing beneath it, is
tumbled. At the mouths of the rivers, bars of sand are built
up, then beaches.

The waves, set in motion by the wind, build the beaches,
starting with rocks of the largest transportable size, torn from
the headlands. The sea never ceases its attack on the rocky
shores, never for a moment through untold centuries, through
millennia. It has two chief methods for cutting them back.
One is by the explosion force of the waves as they are
slammed against an air pocket in a crevice or under an overhanging ledge. The other is by using the rocks thus dislodged
to batter and grind one another and the exposed bedrock. On
such a coast as Maine's, if the sea is running, you can hear
the continual dull knocking and scraping of rocks on rocks—
an ominous sound if you have the interests of the land at
heart and of the trees at the edge of the ciiff. A visitor to a
mine extending under the sea in southwest England—J. W.
Henwood—left a striking account of what it is like to hear
the waves in action at close quarters within the afflicted earth:

> When standing beneath the base of the cliff, and in that
> part of the mine where but nine feet of rock stood between
> us and the ocean, the heavy roll of the larger boulders, the
> ceaseless grinding of the pebbles, the fierce thundering of
> the billows, with the cracking and coiling as they rebounded,
> placed a tempest in its most appalling form too vividly before
> me to be ever forgotten. More than once doubting the pro-
> tection of our rocky shield we retreated in affright; and it
> was only after repeated trials that we had confidence to
> pursue our investigations.

The agents of dramatic destruction are not the waves as
such but the breakers formed by the waves at the climax of
their lives. A wave meeting an obstruction, a seawall or jetty
of some kind, will merely rise up it and be reflected back.
No great force is exerted upon the obstruction because it is
the wave and not the water through which it moves that
rushes forward. Anyone who has seen a long line of troops
marking time to a band will have had an illustration of the
nature of waves. Sound takes an appreciable time to travel,
and accordingly the beat of the band reaches each soldier a
fraction of an instant before it reaches the soldier beyond
him, causing him to lift his foot slightly before the one beyond
lifts his. The effect is such that instead of all the feet in the
column rising and falling in unison, they do so in undulations,
in ripples that run down the line of men as they do down a
banner fluttering in the wind. What you see is the materializa-
tion of sound waves. The point to note is that while the
waves whip down the line of feet, each crest and trough
running the length of about 250 ranks of soldiers in a second,
the soldiers themselves do not move; their feet each time
come down at the spot from which they were lifted. Similarly,
each molecule of water is restored by a wave at sea virtually
to its starting place, although the path it follows is circular
rather than straight up and down as is the case with the feet
of the soldiers marking time.

Waves at sea, while they may cause a ship to roll or pitch
abominably as they heave it up their forward slopes and set
it down their rearward, normally do not endanger it—even
such terrifying monsters as those of between seventy and
ninety feet encountered in the North Atlantic by the *S.S.
Majestic* on December 29, 1922. It is the breakers, when tons

of water hurtle forward, that do the damage and may leave
a deck swept clear of movables and superstructure in wreckage. It is to prevent the formation of breakers that oil is
poured on troubled waters, the principle being apparently that
a very thin film of oil has a high tension and affects the
waves like a membrane on the surface of the water, elastic
but tight.

Waves become breakers when they reach a certain degree
of steepness. The degree is precisely known. If the angle between the forward and rearward slopes of a wave narrows to
less than 120 degrees the crest of the wave pitches forward.
Expressed in another way, the wave breaks when its height
exceeds one-seventh of the distance between it and the next
wave, called the wave-length. Size is immaterial. The wave
may be as big as an apartment house or as small as the
wind-chop that forms whitecaps at the critical stage. In the
open ocean, breakers result when the wind builds waves up
beyond the height they can sustain, or when waves from two
different systems intersect to form, momentarily, a super-
wave. Along the shore, the agency is shoaling water. As
waves "feel the bottom" they slow down and the distance
between them—the wave-length—contracts to less than one-
seventh of their height. At the same time the wave finds that
at the diminishing depth it cannot draw up sufficient water to
fill itself out. Its forward slope, deflated—dehydrated, actually—flattens out. The wave peaks as its rear closes upon its
depleted, retarded front, which begins to grow concave. The
water at the top, continuing the rolling motion of water in a
wave, finds nothing beneath it. A swimmer whom the wave
reaches at this stage may look up and see a barrel vault of
water over his head as the onlunging crest plunges forward
and down.

The power of breaking waves is almost incredible. According to a publication of the U. S. Navy Hydrographic Office,
twelve-foot breakers exert up to 1,755 pounds of pressure per
square foot, those of eighteen feet up to 2,370, while breakwaters in the Bay of Biscay have to be built to withstand
4,120 pounds per square foot. To top that, twenty-foot
breakers running onto the west coast of Scotland before a
strong gale registered over 6,000 pounds per square foot. A
mere babe six feet high would wallop a poor little
limpet with a blow of over four and a half pounds. Given

these fantastic forces, it is not too astonishing to read of waves throwing stones weighing up to nearly 7,000 pounds over a wall twenty feet high at Cherbourg, lifting a 40,000-pound concrete block twelve feet vertically and depositing it on the top of a pier almost five feet above high-water-mark in the harbor of Amsterdam, and wrenching loose from the Wick Breakwater in Scotland a mass of stones cemented and bound together and to the structure itself with iron bands, weighing a million pounds, or as much as three hundred motorcars.

Piled up by the strong and persistent westerlies of the northern hemisphere blowing over thousands of miles of open ocean, storm-breakers of an immense size pound the coasts of northern California, Oregon and Washington and of Ireland, Scotland and the Faroes. Those which damaged the Wick Breakwater ran to forty-two feet high while storm-breakers up to sixty feet high have been reported from the coast of our own Pacific Northwest. It is the easterlies that our Atlantic coast has to fear, and these strike less often in comparable force. This is especially true of summer—except for the few times a season when some part of the coast is struck by a cyclonic tropical storm known as a hurricane when its winds exceed seventy-five miles an hour. (A hurricane is very destructive because the low pressure of the atmosphere at its center causes the sea to be pushed up beneath it by the greater weight of the atmosphere surrounding it. Thus when it hits the coast the storm waves, high enough in themselves, ride in on top of a dome of water which alone is enough to cause disastrous floods.) The Hydrographic Office states that there is probably no better or safer cruising ground for small yachts anywhere in the world than the waters in summer between New York and Nova Scotia and that if this is less true of the waters south of New York it is only because safe anchorages are not as quickly available there.

Nevertheless, when our big blows come they create havoc. The original lighthouse on Minot's Ledge, off shore just below Boston, was carried away by breakers and the two keepers with it. During the fury of the storm horrified dwellers ashore heard the frantically pealing bell suddenly silenced. In the morning nothing was to be seen of the structure. Its replacement, a shaft ninety-seven feet high, has stood for a century although occasionally it is engulfed in white water. In fact a remarkable photograph exists of the lighthouse totally enveloped but for the light itself in a sheet of surf. The "spouting" of breakers, taking place when the plunging mass of water traps a pocket of air against an unyielding surface, compresses it and then is flung skyward by the air's explosive re-expansion, is what causes the highest surges of sea water.

Headlands are likely to take the worst beating from the waves, and for two reasons. First, the shore is apt to fall away more steeply from them than it does elsewhere, which can mean that waves will not break until the last minute, reserving for the headland their full destructive power. Secondly, waves tend to wrap themselves around a protruding shore as a whip will wrap itself around a body struck with it. It is an example of the phenomenon called refraction. For an understanding of it, recourse may be had again to a formation of troops. If you march such a formation from a smooth parade ground squarely onto rougher or muddy terrain, each rank will be slowed down when it reaches the line at which the going becomes harder and the interval between the ranks will be reduced. This is what happens to waves when, in approaching a shore, they reach shoaling water. However, if the marching troops come onto the impeding terrain at an angle to its edge, the column will be bent; its new direction will be more nearly perpendicular to that edge, the ranks more nearly parallel to it. This is because each soldier is slowed down a little sooner than the man beside him who reaches the impeding surface a trifle after he does. Again it is so with waves reaching a shoaling bottom. Approaching a shore at an angle, they tend to be brought into parallel with it by the retarding effect of the shallow water and to break upon it frontally. We might expect that the lee shore of an island would be protected from the waves crashing on its windward shore. Indeed, if the island shelves steeply into the sea it will be. However, if the slope is gentle, the drag on the leading edge of the waves, bringing them into near parallel with the shore, will cause them to curl right around and strike the island in the rear as well as in front.

Not only, therefore, is the tip of a promontory likely to be exposed to the heaviest onslaught of the waves but the flanks catch the waves as well. Because of the direction in which the waves strike, they tend to move the stones they dislodge toward the base of the promontory. Thus while the promontories are being reduced the bays between them are filling up. The indentations of the shores of Mount Desert may be seen to consist of beaches formed of rounded boulders up to the size of a football and larger, most of them laid neatly parallel to the water's edge—though actually the majority of these, instead of having been torn from the cliffs, were probably washed in from the offshore bottom where the glacier left them. The concave eastern shore of Little Moose is piled with boulders of up to two or three feet in diameter, the zone of the storm beach (as it is called) being from twenty-five to one hundred feet in width.

Barring movements of the earth's crust of a magnitude to undo the work of the waves, it is the fate of all irregular coastlines to be smoothed out in the course of time. But the time involved may be very long indeed. Willard Bascom, an oceanographic engineer, reports that old maps of Yorkshire show many villages where there are now only sandbanks far out at sea and that in some places the seacliff has been retreating at a rate of nineteen feet a year. On the other hand, as he also points out, the hard-rock coast of Cornwall has changed little in ten thousand years. The Maine coast is very different from that of Yorkshire and even from the coasts of Cape Breton Island and New Brunswick farther north, where the soft, sedimentary rocks forming the shore are giving way by as much as a foot a year, and in some places by more. It is more akin to that of Cornwall. The excellent pamphlet put out by the National Park Service paints a dismal future for Mount Desert: "Pounded by the sea, eroded from within, Acadia is slowly wearing away." But granite is hard, the process very slow. And while it is true that the sea's conquests may be hastened by the further submergence of the Maine coast as part of a process of continental tilt that is raising the West Coast, it is also possible that the land may be due to spring back even farther than it already has from the downpush it received from the ice sheet and that the sea may recede from Acadia and the shores to the north and south.

Several years ago I brought home from a trip to the upper Maine coast some quartz-veined cobbles to use as book-ends and was so taken by their powerful presences, their primeval immutability, that I have been coming home since then with other similar-sized rocks of different kinds. (This is a form of acquisitiveness one contracts at one's peril. A score of eight- or ten-pound rocks is not easy to take along when you are moving your quarters, and nothing in my experience indicates that a collection once started will stop with that number or with three times as many.) Trusting that the authorities would not mind, I took two bits of Acadia back with me when I left, a block of the pepper-and-salt-flecked pink granite from a pile of rubble stripped off Huguenot Head by the glacier and one of basalt, very heavy and of a sullen green slate color, like that of the winter sea under a dark sky, from a four-foot-wide dike in the granite of Schoodic Point. They form instructive companion-pieces, for they are the products, respectively, of the two principal varieties of magma—all aboriginal rock being magma which has cooled and hardened. Granite, a large-grained derivative of the lighter magma (lighter in both color and weight), in which the separate granules of feldspar, quartz and hornblende or mica are usually plainly distinguishable, chiefly constitutes the bedrock of the continents. The denser, finer-grained basalt, deriving from the darker, heavier magma, rich in iron-manganese compounds, forms the earth's crust beneath both continents and oceans. It makes an appearance at the surface through having, in its molten form, been forced up through fissures in the continental bedrock to harden into vertical dikes or horizontal sills or from having welled up and spread out over the crustal rocks in the form of volcanic lava. You cannot handle granite and basalt without feeling close to the origin of things.

With the two rocks from Acadia there is one that enchants Vera with its resemblance, as she observed, to a mountain in a landscape by the 15th Century Japanse artist Sesshu. Shaped roughly like an admiral's dress hat with a gnarled surface of deeply etched-out, vertical bedding-planes, it rises six inches from a bookshelf as from the sea, with all the authority of the Rock of Gibraltar. I picked it up near Port Clyde where the metamorphosed, sedimentary rocks forming the shore, conspicuously foliated and convoluted beyond any others I have ever seen, made one think of the twisted and misshaped stumps of trees wracked and done to death by gales on a mountainside. If ever there were rocks that had frozen under torture, these were they. Port Clyde is at the tip of a long peninsula halfway between Mount Desert and

Portland. I had lunch there on my way home, eating a can of Port Clyde sardines I had brought from Long Island while waiting to see if the ferry to Monhegan ran often enough for me to take it. Unfortunately it did not. Before the Ice Ages Monhegan was, like Mount Desert, a lonely mountain of the peneplain, as the geologists call it. Now it was a lonely island eleven miles off the mainland with a cliff a hundred feet high over which the spray of storm-breakers has been known to carry.

"Lonely" is to be understood in a geographical sense only. Monhegan is by no means overlooked in the summer influx into Maine and is in fact said to draw its share of the un-washed, unshaved and sandal-shod camp-followers of the arts. I often wondered about the confrontation of summer people and native stock. The Maine fishing villages, at least, seem so self-contained, so much what they are, that one would sup-pose them impenetrable by outsiders. There is an extra-ordinary consistency about them which helps set them apart, as if they were a separate species of human community, as I am sure they are. They have grown up beside inlets of the sea on the peninsulas below the port towns. The generally spare houses of the fishermen, many with lath lobster-traps and buoys brilliantly painted with the owner's colors in the yard, are scattered about on the slopes. A score of launches and often a light, orange hydroplane for spotting schools of fish ride at their moorings. On the muddy shores are a few lob-sterpens and, above them, the old wooden wharves. Red-and-black-plaid woolen jackets are uniform for the men, of whom a few, but never many, may be seen in consultation with one another or making deliberate progress along the road. If you have occasion to address one of them in a shop or gas station you receive your reply in a rather high and flat but elegant accent; the speech of coastal Maine is as attractive, to me, as any to be heard in the United States. Even the men who halt traffic where the road is undergoing repair sound like college professors and make you feel you ought to descend from the car to return their courtesy. Polite, respon-sive, even-mannered, self-possessed, untouchable, the tough survivors of generations of hardship, they would be with the amorphous, out-of-place summer invaders as oil with water, you would think, and Maine prove as impervious as the proverbial duck's back off which water flows. But money is the universal solvent. Even at Corea, the archetype of the remote, sea-pledged, Down East fishing-village way up on the Schoodic peninsula, the vacationers are making themselves at home. A subdivision is going in there. *Paul Bunyan Shores,* you may read on a sign: *By the Blue Atlantic.*

And: *Perry's Nut House. World Famous Nut Exhibits. . . . Authentic Indian Crafts. . . . Norsecraft. . . . Bob's Cut Rate Antiques Gifts.* By these signs you may know that you are entering Searsport, a town that once may well have sent more ships to sea for its size than any other in history in an equal period; at one time it was home to 150 shipmasters. Despite the inauspicious approach and the pre-emption of the main street by U. S. 1, the houses remaining from those days stand apparently much as they did in their prime, handsome, solid, patrician clapboard structures with massive eaves and cornices, some with column-formed corners, and dark, red brick houses, simple in form, often with stone lintels and sills and white-trimmed windows, in the Federal style. Some of the clapboard houses had barns behind them, attached by enclosed passageways. What a world there must have been here a century ago, and what a race of men and women to have had farms for back yards and beneath their front windows the searoads they sailed to Africa and the Spice Islands! To show them respect, I dismounted and made my way on foot along the streets they once had walked. It was a quiet Sunday. From the century-and-a-quarter-old Methodist church the iron clanging of a bell sounded without eliciting much response. It was like a Carolina coastal town on a winter day of crisp air and warm sun. There was even a grasshopper to bound out onto the road from some weeds, even a heron to pass importantly in stately flight overhead—a great blue. And Penobscot Bay, leading off from Searsport, was like a Carolina estuary, silent and empty. Only the fields of marsh grass were missing, and there were low hills dark with spruce and fir across the water in place of tall stands of pine.

The resemblance did not stop there. There was about Searsport, as about other once-proud towns of this coast, an air of depletion, and a stamp of ordinariness on the people one saw on the streets. Such towns had unmistakably been left behind, and what happened to them would be settled elsewhere. In a drugstore which served as a bus depot in Ellsworth, the town from which the road to Mount Desert turns off U. S. 1, there was the largest display I have ever seen of both hunting magazines (giant brown bear charging sportsman with rifle coolly at the ready) and romance-and-confession magazines (girl on bed with teary eyes pressing wadded handkerchief to mouth) and it hinted, surely, that there were deficiencies in the life these communities had to offer their inhabitants. All these things I had met before in small towns in Georgia and South Carolina.

Said the inscription on a modest-sized granite obelisk beside the main street of Searsport: *In tribute to our citizens who fought in defence of the Union, 1861–5*. The Civil War was terribly costly to Maine, I knew, both in the number of her young men killed in battle and in shipping destroyed by Confederate commerce-raiders. "Maine was annihilated," declares Robert P. Tristram Coffin, "a Maine that will never be again, a Maine on canvas wings." But it was not war that impoverished the towns of Maine or those of the South either. It was the skimming off, generation after generation, of the most enterprising sons and daughters of those towns by the lure of greater rewards elsewhere—ostensibly greater, anyhow—and the fate of small towns over the country as a whole has been no different. The ultimate determiner of our national life has been, and remains, the market place. The market place has devoured the resources on which the towns lived—the forests, the topsoil of the surrounding farmlands. It has spurned their crafts and simple manufactories. It has decreed centralization. And, Siren-Ceres, it has held out the promise of bounty unlimited to those who would leave the places of vanished opportunities and go where it has beckoned —to the metropolis.

If, as a result, there are fewer farms in Maine today than there were a hundred years ago and "the Kennebeck and Penobscot are empty, lonely rivers, where they used to be snowed with sails from all over the world," as Mr. Coffin reminds us, at least there has been money enough and affection enough to preserve the houses that stand as not unworthy monuments to Maine's glory and one of the great chapters in our history. It has been summer money, I suppose, and the affection of summer people, but at least the job has been done; and idling through Kennebunk and Kennebunkport on a brilliant sunny morning with the children collecting at the school bus-stops, I gave thanks for the chance that had brought me here at such a time to see those Roman homes, one after another, their rich white paint as bright and fresh in the bath of the sunshine—fuller for the lack of leaves—and as strikingly set off by the dark blinds as on the morning the first coat was applied.

But that was the next day—the day after Wiscasset. There is reserved for the traveler who crosses the long bridge over the Sheepscot going south (which is to say, on this coast, going west) a sight that at the gloomy end of a chill afternoon, with the light a wan yellow beneath the edge of a ceiling of cloud, must rock him as Bernardo and Marcellus were rocked by the apparition of the old king's ghost on the battlements of Elsinore. On a mud flat by a ruined wharf, no more than twenty paces from the Wiscasset waterfront, lie two schooners side by side, one a four-master, the other of a size but with masts gone. There they lie in their final berth, paintless and with every board distinguishable, as if they had been skinned, black below high-water-mark, enormous, gaunt, appalling, fixed in the mute, unanswerable appeal of the dead—the last of the ships that made Maine great. Even the mastless derelict has part of her rail remaining, some of her gear left on deck and chains extending out to the end of her bowsprit. The other, her name almost decipherable behind the not-quite-obliterated gilt of her filigree, still has what appears to be an almost full complement of ropes running to the tops of her tall masts. ("Arm'd, say you?"—"Arm'd, my lord."—"From top to toe?"—"My lord, from head to foot.") I wanted to go through the town laying hold of the citizens and crying, "Look! Look! Don't you see what's there? What are you going to do about it? Good God, you can't just let them lie there and rot!"

But what can be done? Raise them from the mud and move them to where they could be preserved? It would take a fortune, perhaps several times the $200,000 a celebrated actor and his celebrated actress wife recently received for a half-hour appearance on television. Douse them with oil and put a match to them, to give them a decent finish? I could not do it.

South of Portland, the Atlantic beaches begin. They are those which increasingly prevail as you go down the coast, evidencing the growing replacement of hard rocks by softer in the composition of the land. The one I came on first, south of Kennebunk, was a model of what was to come for hundreds of miles. There was a broad sandy beach curving like a scimitar around the sea with the height of the last spring tide marked by a line of the chicory *Chondrus,* whitened stems of *Laminaria,* some with holdfasts still fixed to lavender mussel shells, and leaves of sea-lettuce, an alga resembling the shiny green tissue-paper florists use. Back-stopping the beach, built by the wind-blown sand, was a zone of dunes and behind the dunes a marsh of salt grasses. The arrangement was typical and so was the plant community. The dunes were sparsely topped by beachgrass. If *America the Beautiful* were written out of a valid experience of our continent instead of contrived of a largely irrelevant sentimentality, our silkily rippling sea borders of *Ammophila breviligulata* would have a place in it. So would the national anthem if it were concerned with a more lasting siege of our coasts than that of Fort Henry, for where the rocks relinquish their guardianship of those coasts, the beachgrass takes it up. Sea-rocket will grow spottily on the margins of the beach as it did here, still retaining its flowers of four minute lavender petals and four minute lavender anthers. So will the well-known beach wormwood, or dusty miller *(Artemisia stelleriana),* a relative of sagebrush which came to our northeast coast from the Pacific coast of northern Asia where equal extremes of temperature occur; in a few places on the forward slope of the dunes there were cushions of its foliage, each leaf like a miniature, flat, bluish-grey suede glove, almost white, soft and dry to the touch. But in the pitiless, thankless environment of the shifting sands, no plant thrives and spreads as the beachgrass does. It is, in fact, the great sand-stabilizer, the trapper of blowing sand. In the lee of a tuft of its long, gracefully-bowed, needle-like leaves, the wind-driven grains collect—and a dune begins. The tough and venturesome roots reach out and send up another plant beside the first, and the base of the future dune is broadened. The beachgrass and the dune grow together, the dune burying the plants and new plants growing on top of it out of the old. And so the ramparts of the coast are erected and held and, when breached by storm waves crashing in on a flood, generally repaired. Without *Ammophila* (so gallantly streaming), the sand blowing in from the beach would doubtless be held somewhere, but certainly nowhere near so close to its source.

On the far side of the dunes were two stellar plants of the second echelon which wherever they occur (and they are widespread along the northeast coast) form thickets that are the outermost coverts for land birds—and the first into which, on migration, such birds may drop exhausted after fighting their way back in from the sea against an offshore wind. The more famous was bayberry, of twiggy, dense growth, tight clusters of waxy grey fruit as hard as BB shot and not much larger (though a good deal more decorative) and narrow, blunt, stiff, opposed leaves curving up like horns. The other, which I had once seen growing in magnificent clumps at almost the far extremity of the Maine coast, was another import from Asia which has gone native, the salt-spray rose (*Rosa rugosa*), a shrub of upright, thick stems hairy with spines, leaves coarse and shiny and so incised along the veins as to appear crinkly, and white or magenta flowers giving rise to hips like small tomatoes.

Of human life was no sign except a man and a girl who, on my appearance, disengaged from an embrace they could hardly have found very cozy, so bundled up they were, and retreated to their car, and, in the distance at the end of the curve of beach, the cottages of Wells, which in their close-packed profusion resembled an incrustation of barnacles.

The highway that led back to U. S. 1 passed through country in which I was again reminded of the Carolina and Georgia tidewater—flat, and with woods of white pines almost as tall as the longleaf pines. And as on a winter day in the deep South, the sun was too warm for the cold season and the stillness too complete for any other. The abandoned carnival trappings of the popular beach-resort of Wells could have been a painted backdrop on a stage.

At Ogunquit, the rock ledges came down to the sea again. In the coves the fishermen were back in their black-and-red plaids and knee boots with their boats, lobster-traps and buoys. The hilly road disclosed expensive and colorful summer houses on wooded slopes, farmhouses remodeled into studios and fashionable dress shops and taverns. There were the first of the rhododendrons that from here on to New York would distinguish homes of the comfortably off. South of York— Maine's oldest village, preserved and improved upon over the

years by the well-to-do of Boston, New York and Philadelphia
—the last of the spruce-fir forest vanished, replaced by the
oak-maple-hickory company, well laced with white pines and
hemlocks, of middle and lower New England, New York and
the Alleghenies. At Kittery, where one leaves Maine, roses
were in bloom and even portulaca, with its clear, pristine
colors.

In travel, as in everything else, overdoing it has its penalties.
Especially if you are improvising the amenities as you go
along and having no respites of either physical or mental
passivity you are apt to become impression-dulled. Although
I had spent the previous night in a motel (even in cold weather
the time comes when you have to have a bath) I had not
entirely escaped that. There was, however, Plum Island, off
Newburyport some thirty miles north of Boston. As the map
shows, it is the first of the barrier islands that fringe the coast
with few breaks from well out on Long Island all the way to
the Florida Keys, their origin being not entirely clear. The
island is also the site of the Parker River National Wildlife
Refuge. And it was now or not at all for Plum Island.

I crossed Plum River shortly before dusk and drove to the
headquarters of the Refuge, which occupies the southern
three-quarters of the island and much of the other shore of
the river separating it from the mainland. Shoreside resorts
can be the most sordid of all because of their want of trees,
the prevalence of bare, sandy areas, the insufficiency of
vegetation to conceal the drifting refuse, the overcrowding of
jerry-built cottages and—all attesting to the attraction water
has for the shiftless, possibly because of all human occupations fishing promises the most return for the least effort—
the trailer homes, rust-eaten automobiles, and untidy, down-
at-the-heels establishments selling bloodworms and pizza pies.
Much of the inhabited quarter of Plum Island is a case in
point, though the rest is respectable enough. Having seen the
supervisor of the Refuge and made an appointment for the
morrow, I returned to the mainland and put in a telephone
call to two of my closest friends, who, conveniently for me,
are married to each other. I had been expected in the vicinity
and been told to be sure to visit them, but I fear I left them
no choice as to the time. "I'm in an outdoor telephone-booth
beside a motorboat showroom without any lights," I said in
the voice of one at a loss and cold besides. "I think it's near

a place called Rowley." Thirty minutes later, indistinguishable from one of the water-bums of Plum Island I so deplored, I was at their marvelous house, set high on a cliff overlooking the sea with the harbor of Gloucester on the left and, somewhere around on the right, the reef of Norman's Woe.

It is the function of friends to listen while one recounts the wonders one has seen since having last enjoyed their company, and the signal injustices and instances of lack of appreciation that have been one's lot. Drawn out as I was by sureness of a sympathetic hearing as by the warmth of the open fire that muttered to itself on the hearth, it was some time before I gave anyone else a chance to speak. When I did, I heard from Phil of the excitement of sailing a catamaran: "like taking a horse over a jump for the first time." I had seen the contrivance in the yard, dismasted for the winter and having the air of sinister efficiency of one of those twin-nosed devilfishes. Under the enormous sail it carried, the thing evidently flew over the water, ruffling it rather less than it did the feelings of the orthodox sailing gentry: "She may be fast," the begrudging dictum seemed to be, "but I shouldn't care to be out with her in a blow." I learned that my hostess's great-grandfather had been Captain Joseph Brown Thomas, a Thomas of Thomaston, which is perhaps the most distinguished in character of all the former great ports of Maine. This was to me electrifying intelligence. I was shown an oil painting of a lean, black-hulled, four-masted topsail schooner —"five jibs flying"—named *Helen Thomas* for Anne's mother and a photograph of Captain Thomas which made entirely credible Anne's recollection of him as of so handsome and commanding a mien (he was six-foot-two to begin with) that children followed him in awe down the street. He had gone to sea at fourteen and when he had died at eighty-six had been owner or part-owner of thirty ships. I should give a great deal to have known him. Beguiled not only by the company but also by the comfort of a bedroom in which Greta Garbo had once slept—prematurely, some men in my position would have felt—I was late in getting back to Plum Island in the morning.

I like the naturalist Rangers of the Department of the Interior and am never let down by one. You do not feel called upon with them to explain why the minutiae of the wild scene should seem important and they evidently feel no need of any such explanation either. They are well-informed and ardent observers. The Ranger who drove me up Green Mountain did not have to be told that I should relish the sight of a Greenland sandwort in bloom or have my pleasure accounted for when he turned one up in a hollow on that frigid summit, its fragile flower of five notched white petals and yellow anthers (it is one of the pinks) borne on a wire-thin stem. It was so too with the Ranger who waded me out into the Parker River marsh to make sure that I grasped the succession of grasses on a representative tidal flat of the Northeast. There was first the high-tide grass, *Spartina patens,* which is short, reddish-brown or chestnut, fine, and tends to flatten out, lying like hair on a pelt; this is the grass that is mowed and harvested as salt hay. Next came the salt-meadow grass, *Distichlis spicata,* which also is short but is jointed with leaves issuing from the sides of the stem and is softer in appearance and buffy in color. At the third stage, where the water rises higher, there was a fine grass that stands two feet tall and is called switch grass, *Panicum virgatum.*

A pickup truck took us over the bumpy road that led to the end of the narrow island, six miles from the Refuge entrance, the dunes on one side, the broad flats on the other. As a special dispensation, I was driven also along the top of the earthen dike erected to impound fresh water. Flocks of geese, hundreds strong, were feeding on the greensward of winter rye planted for their pasture. Talkative assemblages, they waddled off with dignity and the onset of mild indignation, every eye upon us. On my calling attention to the large stature of one bird in a group of five, the Ranger ventured the opinion that he was a gander with his mate and surviving offspring. "The families tend to stay together," he said, then voiced an odd but expressive tribute to the species: "It would be hard to improve on the Canada goose." There were some five thousand geese on the reservation and generally they kept you aware of their presence. After a flock had been disturbed you would hear, long after you had left them behind, their scandalized vociferations, as varied in pitch as the voices of girls and boys on a school playground. Small bands were continually flying by, their muscular wings in weighty rhythm, like teams of athletes in training. *"R-r-r-r-ronk!"* they would cry explosively.

Ducks swam nervously off across the pond ahead of us or

took to the air—elegant pintails of the elongated, white-lined necks and satiny-smooth browns and green-winged teals, the smallest of our ducks, which sprang straight up from the water as if blasted off it and sped away on wings that whipped the air. (A hunter would speak not of pintails and teals but of pintail and teal. It is curious than an avicidal intent and the omission of the plural "s" should go together. A gunner who meant to shoot at them could be counted upon to speak of a "flock of robin.") Above all there were black ducks. This is the all-around duck of the East, the dark, dusky counterpart of the mallard of the rest of the northern hemisphere. It was largely to preserve the black duck ("without which there would be no duck-hunting in the Northeast worth speaking of") that the Parker River Refuge had been established. From two thousand in 1944, the Refuge has come to attract tens of thousands at a time.

The Department of the Interior has somewhat different aims in the National Wildlife Refuges from those it has in the National Parks. In the latter, the object is to preserve the natural scheme of things as far as feasible unaltered by man; even to hang up suet for the chickadees is *verboten*. Natural habitats are valued also in the Refuges but in these the primary purpose is to foster waterfowl to insure that game will not be wanting in the future, and to this end fields are flooded or plowed and planted to crops. For many of them, on parts of which hunting is allowed, "refuges" is a misnomer; "preserves" would be more accurate. Parker River is one of two score available to the ducks, geese and other birds that follow the Atlantic corridor of migration. (Four such corridors are recognized, the others being the Mississippi, the Great Plains and the Pacific.) The Atlantic corridor has the form of a funnel extending at the top almost across North America, from the upper left-hand corner of Greenland to the upper right-hand corner of Alaska, and encompassing Labrador, Hudson Bay and the northern Chesapeake Bay to the Antilles. Many waterfowl following it down through the interior of Canada reach the coast where the marshes of Essex County, Massachusetts, of which Parker River is a part, form a natural receiving area and way-station. I must say I find myself stirred to think of the small winged forms by the hundreds and thousands—hundreds *of* thousands it was in the past—beating steadily hour after hour through the night sky, each keeping even with its neighbors, the glint of moonlight in the myriad eyes, across the light-pricked farmland of Quebec and Ontario, over the dark mountains of New England, over the strewn jewelry of the cities, over the highway's trickling diamonds and rubies, to glimpse at dawn on the horizon the thin edge of the grey Atlantic and before it, severed by the silvered rivers, the dark mats of the marshes, and food and cover.

I was glad, being refreshed and restored, not to have missed Plum Island with its demonstration of the anatomy of a barrier beach. The dunes rose twenty-five feet from the beach; trudging through the loose sand between the first and second lines, you felt like the lone survivor of a patrol of Legionnaires. At the crest of the forward dunes, with only the beach-grass and wormwood in their van, were two other great plants of the sandy shores, as I had already discovered them to be from Long Island: beach pea and beach goldenrod, both like their conventional relatives but succulent in a rubbery way—tough customers, clearly. The second rank of dunes was invested by bayberry and also by beach plum, a shrub that shares bayberry's role and also its habit of growth. Many-branched, scraggly and dense, beach plums are witchlike little trees but the grape-sized plums they bear abundantly are relished by bird, beast and man, by the last raw or in jelly, jam or pie. Much of the slope of the dunes was transformed into moorland by the covering of beach heather, or *Hudsonia,* a little plant that carpets miles of Cape Cod and Long Island as with sprays of scale-leafed juniper. Among the dunes farther back from the sea were actual junipers and wild roses with hips like red candy-balls, pitch pines, poplars, smilax (nature's green, barbedwire entanglement) and stunted groves of choke cherry.

After the resort area, it seemed miraculous that there should be, right beside it, separated only by the width of a strand of fencing, a stretch of shore that looked as it might have to the Pilgrims. My guide, however, was not to be mollified by admiration. What he saw was the problem of keeping it from being obliterated under the feet of the quarter of a million visitors who surged over it every summer. In the competing interests which bore upon it, Plum Island was, I soon saw, illustrative of what must be increasingly in store for our steadily diminishing remnant of unspoiled shore under the pressures of a steadily multiplying and ever more mobile population. There were the waves of holiday-making families: motorists, picnickers, swimmers. There were the high-school and college-age crowds on their flings and forays. There were the beer-drinkers with cans to toss out of their cars. There were the beach-buggiers with their zeal to bring even this slight and fragile outpost of dunes and strands under the dominion of the automobile. (Where I had come from they had even formed a society—the Long Island Beach Buggy Association—as if some peculiar merit attached to the purchase of a four-wheel-drive vehicle with which to plow up the sand and save the exertion of walking.) There were the surf fishermen. There were the gunners: they lined up on the border of the Refuge and shot ducks down in it which they could not retrieve; they pressed for access to the Refuge itself—and are being given it in limited degree; and in some cases they sneaked in before dawn to take an illegal bag. (The warden, a one-man flying squad, pulled one in at daybreak the morning I was there and I thought was going to pull me in too.) There were the haymakers and the clam-diggers, both of whom retain the right to exercise their ancient callings in the reservation. There were the unfortunate victims of poliomyelitis for whom a summer camp is maintained on the Refuge grounds. There were the foraging housewives; we saw several whose surreptitious object was the collection of beach plums and sprays of winterberry—a deciduous holly that grew in clumps which might have been sprayed and beaded with red sealing wax.

And of course there were the bird-watchers, whose interest was in defending the Refuge against all encroachments that might damage it. Plum Island is one of the most bird-watched-over bits of land in the country. Wrote Edward Howe Forbush, the leading ornithologist of Massachusetts, many years ago: "Secure Plum Island and make it a bird sanctuary, for in my opinion it is the most important region on our coast." In the early 1930's, the Massachusetts Audubon Society, one of the very most effective and respected local organizations of ornithophiles in the western hemisphere, acquired 1,600 acres of it. This it contributed to the Parker River Refuge when it was set up in 1944, which gave it a total of 6,400 acres, or ten square miles. The Society keeps watch on the management with, I gathered, a cool and skeptical eye.

At the end of our tour we met an entourage of the Audubonites following a route often trod by the late, legendary Ludlow Griscom, dean and marvel of the field identifiers. There were six cars creeping along like a wagon train crossing the Great Plains, stopping at a flash of wings to discharge their binocular-carrying occupants, mostly very-pleasant-looking women of middle years, but two of them men, presumably retired. I joined the party while it had under observation a rough-legged hawk in the pale phase, identifiable by its black bellyband and black patches under the wing joints. (A bird of splendid form and carriage, it was soaring out over the ocean, demonstrating in this, as in the majestic spread of its wings, the aquiline direction of its evolution.) It developed that we had all seen the canvasback drake on the south pond and the buck deer running heavily, evidently winded, through the mud of the marsh, its antlers soon to put a price on its head by making it legal game. None of us had found the flamingo, blown up weeks before by a tropical storm. I had missed their avocet and they my snowy owl. (Probably just down from the Arctic, it had taken off in front of the truck, light as air it seemed on its broad wings, to fetch up on a mound of earth and stare at us over its shoulder with catlike intensity of disdain, as if we were the first of our noxious species to have intruded upon the realm it ruled over.) The party soon left to pursue a report of godwits on the flats of the Newburyport coalyards.

Sitting in the lighted bus all by itself in the night sometimes made me a little uncomfortable; an atavistic reluctance to be in conspicuous view when unable oneself to see one's surroundings may have been to blame. The evening at Plum Island was one of those times, for I was violating regulations in remaining overnight in the Refuge. I had scouted it for a hiding place, and though there were two bits of woodland into which lanes led off, these were inadequate to conceal the bus, which stood over seven feet tall. The night passed uneventfully, however, except that I was chilled and wakeful, though not quite wakeful enough to get more cover. Stiff and with a heavy, achy head when I got up, I may have missed something of the beauty of the brilliant morning—and beautiful it was I recognized as I walked down the island with the straw-colored beachgrass rippling soft as silvered fur, the waves breaking in ranks ten deep in froth like whipped cream on the ultramarine-dark sea, the little sanderlings, each above its reflection, probing the wet sand as frantically as if they were perishing of thirst. A northwester was blowing in gusts that went *whoooooooh* in one's ears, tiresomely. I felt estranged from the bittern in the salt marsh that kept its beak pointing skyward, absurdly pretending to be a tuft of reeds until it lost confidence in the act and sprang up, banking off into the wind . . . from the kestrel that launched out from a telephone pole where the empty cabins of the polio camp caught the drifting sands to attack a marsh harrier, diving repeatedly on the larger hawk, evidently for the simple purpose of relieving the tedium of the morning. The emptiness of the Arctic had taken possession of the land overnight, an emptiness without end.

But the bus had grown warm in the sun despite the cold wind and five minutes after I had climbed back into it I was nourishing myself with hot coffee and graham crackers. The treatment was definitely what was indicated. I could believe that there was a God after all. And it was only instant coffee at that.

I was on no account to pass Crane's Beach by, Phil had said. It was the next beach down from Plum Island, in the bight called Ipswich Bay, of which Cape Ann forms the southern and eastern shore. Why, I wondered when I had seen it, is it not more famous?

If one felt oneself in the sand hills of the Sahara among Plum Island's dunes, the higher reaches of Ipswich's recalled the scenery of the Alps—only with the pattern of light and dark reversed: the crests were vegetated and the valleys bare, and as blindingly white in the sun as snow-fields. What was soon apparent was that here was the arena of contest between antagonists of irreconcilable character. The struggle was proceeding in motion too slow to be perceptible, though by the standards of geological change, which it involved, it was progressing with dizzy speed. The dunes, under assault by the sea winds, which snatch sand off every surface from which they are able to lift it and whisk it on with them until an obstruction slows them down and forces them to drop it, tend inexorably to roll it in upon the land. At the same time, driven by a hunger as relentless as the wind's force, the plants press forward from the other direction against the dunes—the grass and herbs in the lead, then the shrubs, finally the trees and forest.

Most sand beaches are in a state of tenuous, ever-shifting equilibrium between these adversaries—except when storm waves smash in to make a clean sweep of both dunes and plants and set the battle back to scratch. It was all there at Ipswich—huge, naked, rogue dunes burying the stands of pitch pines and red maples in their advance; dunes brought to the first stage of stabilization by a triumphant topknot of beachgrass like a thin crop of hair on their pates; dunes immobilized under a thatch of beach heather, bayberry and beach plum; dunes well to the rear of the fighting front which yet had broken loose again after long submission and were pouring forward, inching up the trees in their path and killing them; dunes still farther to the rear transformed into wooded hills. As one walked toward the point at which the beach ended, laboring through the loose sand, one came upon high little valleys carpeted with the purple autumn foliage of cranberries. The dunes grew bigger. At length one reached summits standing not much less than eight stories above the sea, if my guess was right, and commanding a view out over the end of the peninsula of which the beach is part. On the left of the point was the bay, a line of breakers connecting its extremities as a string connects the ends of a bow and marking the position of the bar. On the right the great Essex marshes lay like fine-textured doormats of free-form design. Close by, just below the highest crest, on a slope wooded with aspen and birch, someone had once built a little house, but nothing remained of it except a chimney and a few planks and pieces of pipe. The top of the dune had been ruptured, was being hollowed out by the winds and perhaps by foot-traffic to form a crater, and spilled across the hearth. Once a dune starts to go, one hears, it is likely to go altogether.

While dunes may come and go on the shifting front of conflict, the duneland itself and the beach will be preserved, it seems safe to say; they remain today unbuilt upon except for some recreational structures at the roadhead. Through arrangements made by the late Richard T. Crane, the plumbing manufacturer and former owner of the peninsula whose great stone house, dominating the ridge that runs down to the base of the beach, is now the magnificent site of public concerts, they are in the safekeeping of trustees and may be enjoyed without apprehension as to what may befall them—a crucial consideration in connection with any surviving natural feature of our country.

It took me two hours to drive around Cape Ann. No one could do it in less who was susceptible to the disciplined humanness, the dignity and simplicity, of traditional New

England houses. In addition, I stopped to moon for a while over the edge of a stonefaced pier where a former lobster-packinghouse stood empty, held transfixed by the manner in which the little bushes of rockweed and leaves of bright green sea-lettuce just below the surface of the water swayed now forward, now back, and now stood hesitant, slightly rocking, in a syncopated rhythm to the passage of the waves—an exquisite and sensitive ballet, uniformly attuned to every slightest fluctuation of their medium, sinuous, never static, perfectly controlled.

While ledges of bedrock extend to salt water as far south as Long Island Sound and Manhattan, the last major abutments of granite upon the sea are at Cape Ann, which Rockport and Gloucester divide between them, and the much lesser cape to the south occupied by Marblehead. All three towns were settled in the 1620's by men of the sea; said a native of Marblehead: "Our ancestors came not here for religion. Their main end was to catch fish." Gloucester is still an important fishing port with big wharves at which the trawlers tie up to discharge their slithering cargoes by conveyor belt, in a fishy reek, while gulls swarm around like bats of the sea. But fishing by American vessels has been in a steady decline since World War II. "The American standard of living is too high," said Phil's son, a newspaperman like his father. "When people can afford steak, how many are going to buy fish—except on Friday? We can well be grateful for Fridays." Even with Fridays, the average American eats less than a pound of seafood a month. In addition, it would appear that American research and technology in the field have fallen behind. For the past two years the United States has imported 60 per cent of the fish and fish-products it has consumed, despite tariffs. Spokesmen for the industry maintain that more Federal funds are needed if the American fleet is to be able to compete successfully with subsidized foreign fleets which operate close to our shores.

Few of the descendants of those whom Kipling wrote about in *Captains Courageous* follow the sea today, and this caps with an echoing sadness the terrible and glorious story of Gloucester's long embroilment with the awful deep, which its marine museum tells. It was a story much on my mind as I lay that night, shamed by the ease of my existence, once more in the Greta Garbo room. A surface fog had

stolen in over the waters below the cliff and the groaner was
sounding its agony from a reef, a chilling dirge for those ten
thousand seamen of Gloucester who had put out in the
direction in which the statue of the oil-skinned helmsman
gazed from the waterfront and never been seen again.

Cape Cod

BETWEEN the drowned, hilly, rock-girt shore of northern New England and the flat coast south of the Bay of New York, formed of the decomposed rock of the coastal plain and that of the hills behind it, there is a coast of quite different character. This intervening coast, partly in Massachusetts and partly in New York with an islet in Rhode Island, is the creation of the Ice Age.

When the ice-sheets moved down out of the north, they brought with them quantities of mineral debris. They stripped away mountainsides, tearing off the rocks to which they had frozen or prying them loose by brute force. They scoured the lowlands, scraping away the soil and laying bare the bones of the land. Some of the soil was pushed ahead of the ice to be at times partly overridden and dragged along beneath it until eventually deposited. Some was carried along frozen in or along the sides of the lobe. Photographs of present-day glaciers remind one of a melting chocolate sundae, with the thick, white outflows of cream edged with dark syrup or streaked with it, as glaciers are which compound several glaciers of different sources. The ice-sheet doubtless had a similar appearance, and a frightful one. Mostly its movement must have been imperceptible, though thunderous cracking sounds, the dislodgment of a cliffside, the wrenching scream of a boulder scraped against bedrock, the splitting and sudden lurch of a tree and snapping of branches under the pressure of the ugly, debris-freighted forehead of the lobe must, in the case of the last ice-age, have made clear to the caveman and even to the giant bear and hairy mammoth that disputed with him for overlordship of the Pleistocene forests that something was afoot. In North America, ancestral Indians would have

been acquainted with the ice-sheet too; they were here at least 11,500, and possibly even 30,000, years ago, having been able to cross from Asia when, thanks to the immense quantity of water frozen in the icecap, the ocean stood between 150 and 300 feet below its present level and (as David M. Hopkins of the United States Geological Survey describes it) a level, treeless tundra hundreds of miles in breadth connected Siberia and Alaska. In relatively warm periods when the rate of the ice's melting exceeded the rate of its advance, the scene must have been as dismal as could well be imagined. Before the glacier would have stretched a vast barren ground of mud, gravel, and rocks of all sizes, puddled and running with the water that streamed off the ice. And where the higher temperatures were only local, the ice, grinding forward even as it was being melted back, would with ponderous slowness but with inexhaustible effect have continued to heap rubble upon the lifeless landscape which the rivers flowing down from it would have washed toward the shrunken ocean.

Four times in the past million and a half years or less the northern part of our country was subjected to this ravagement, ground down, dug out, plowed up by the ice, littered and stacked with the spoil. A new vocabulary has been required to identify the leavings as these have come to be recognized. Eskers is the name given to the long, sinuous ridges that show where a gravel-laden stream once coursed through a canyon in the ice. Kames are similar in composition; they are conical mounds formed by water pouring with its load through holes in the ice. The boulders transported by the ice and dropped at random are called erratics; New England is strewn with them in such multitudes that all the stone walls that have been built of them have made not a dent in their numbers. Where the glacier left icebergs embedded in the earth behind it in its retreat, some of them of enormous size, the ponds that came into being with the bergs' melting are called kettleholes.

The most peculiar products of the glacier are the long, narrow hills lying along the axis of its advance known as drumlins. These were formed when, for reasons not very clear, the ice acted as a kind of earth-moving machine and scooped up and carried along beneath it, then dropped, a mass of clay and gravel, elongating and smoothing it over in its passage. Drumlins form a prominent feature of the coast at Boston. Originally all were hills rising above *terra firma.*

Those that still do so include both Bunker and Breed's Hills. Others to the east were overtaken by the rising of the ocean as the glacier melted and if not entirely submerged became islands. There are many such drumlins in Boston Harbor, their seaward sides cut away by the waves and the material that composed them washed out and deployed by the littoral currents to create spits. In some cases the spits connect the drumlin with a neighbor or with the mainland.

Of all the ice-sheet's works of construction, however, the most imposing are those called moraines. These are ridges formed of the rubble the sheet pushed along before it in the manner of a bulldozer and left along the line of its farthest advance, supplementing it while its front stood still at that line (the rates of melting and of advance offsetting each other) by the debris it bore along like a conveyor belt. Cape Cod, Martha's Vineyard, Nantucket Island, Block Island, Fisher's Island, Long Island and in part Staten Island are remnants of the moraine—and monuments to the ice-sheet's stupendous power.

Of them all, Cape Cod is unquestionably the most remarkable. Indeed, it is surely the most arresting feature of our east coast—a hook thrust out like an arm and fist in the face of the implacable North Atlantic. One sets off to visit it feeling somewhat intimidated. One's apprehensions, however, are occasioned rather less by the distinctions the Cape owes to its geological origins than by others that have come to it more recently and from quite different sources. Even Maine is probably behind it in wealth of literary associations, and any outsider at all versed in New England anthropology may well anticipate finding himself shut out in some mysterious way by an invisible net woven of the intricate and involuted traditions of the high-caste Bostonians whose vacationland it has long been and the ancient, not much simpler, inward-turning tribal patterns of the Cape Codders themselves

No one likes to feel an intruder—but I need have had no misgivings. It being winter—a month after my return from Maine—the gentry had largely evacuated the ramparts and the natives, confirmed in the possession of their homeland in the ebb of the tourist tide, seemed relaxed and disposed to welcome the novelty of a stranger. There is much to be said for visiting such a preserve as the Cape in the off-season and for coming not with any idea of penetrating the human community but to absorb oneself in the natural scene, in comparison with which the oldest-timer and the squire of the most ancient lineage are parvenus. Beyond that, there is the fact that anyone who drives to the Cape by U. S. Highway 6 through New Bedford—and at that time there was no other route for anyone coming up from the south—will lose any diffidence with which he might have set forth. He will feel like turning around and going back. At least he will if to the defilement of the country before him is added a cold, relentless rain.

It was raining when I left home. It rained the length of Long Island, through the Bronx and from one end of Connecticut to the other, though there was compensation on the Connecticut Turnpike in the fresh, vigorous green of the laurel and hemlocks in the wet brown woods. With the last mile of the Turnpike, where it goes up a long incline to the Rhode Island border, the rain suddenly became freezing rain. In a matter of yards every treetrunk, twig and blade of grass was the core of a cylinder of ice. From then on there was no recompense except that the ice shortly vanished almost as abruptly as it had appeared. (Or it did from U. S. 6. Farther north it felled power lines supplying electricity to a population of 100,000.) The rain grew heavier and the commercial blight more predominant as Providence appeared and fell astern. After New Bedford, the lights began to come on— shopwindow lights, neon signs, the head lamps and tail lamps of the streams of motorcars, in front of you and behind, elongated by reflection in the swimming asphalt, compressed and multiplied in the drops and runnels of water on the car's windows and on the windshield beyond the reach of the wipers. A contrived assault on the nerves could not have been more effective. The country had been taken over by barkers. . . .

. . . *Bowling.* . . . *Cathay Temple.* . . . *Fred Hair Stylist.* . . . *Amanda's Antiques Bought and Sold.* . . . *Dorothy Malone Salon of Beauté.* . . . *Mr. Frosty's Kool Kone.* . . . *B. and B. Golf Range.* . . . *Tires. New Retreads Used.* . . . *Mel's Fine Food. Salt Water Taffy.* . . . *Grey Oak Barn Door. Gifts.* . . . *Austria Motel.* . . . *Martin's Mobile Homes.* . . . *The Lobster Bowl.* . . . *Bottled Liquors.* . . . *Whale Foodland.* . . . *Dairy Maid Ice Cream.* . . . *Palm-reading.*

*Open. . . . Gifts. . . . Lakeside Grove Trailer Park. . . .
Prince's Pizza Drive-in. . . . Gulf Gas. . . . Spiffy Paints. . . .
American Gas. . . . Schlitz. The Flamingo Cocktail
Lounge. . . . Cranberry House. . . . Budweiser. Cocktail
Lounge. . . . The White Rabbit. Good Food. . . . Benny's Dis-
count Prices. . . . Lighthouse Restaurant. . . . Ends 'n' Odds
Shop. . . . Beachcomber Gifts. . . . Minnick's Dairy Freeze.
4 Flavors. . . . Rosewood Motel. . . . China Maid. American
and Chinese Food. . . .*

There is a song in the style of a Negro spiritual in which
the singer is riding up to Paradise on horseback behind the
Lord with the Devil hard behind vowing he would catch them
on the Glory Road:

> *An' ah cried "Lawd save me!" An' de Lawd cried "Sho'!"
> An' da it was Heaben an' we shut de do'!*

There it was Cape Cod, and narrowly eluding the clutches
of the last, vast shopping-center, U. S. 6 was abruptly transformed into a limited-access parkway skimming along through
the dark, rainy, quiet night with woods on either side.

> *Oho, de Glory Road!*

After twenty-three soothing miles, with traffic sparse and
little but trees in the headlights, I turned off on a side-road
leading through the darkness to Dennis, which is on the north
shore about halfway out to the elbow of the Cape. Dennis,
one may learn from the W.P.A. Guide, has been a leader in
most of the characteristic ways Cape Codders have found for
making a living. Here, or hereabouts, in 1776 was built a vat
believed to be the first on Cape Cod for producing salt by the
solar evaporation of sea water, which became a prosperous
local industry. Dennis was an important port of the fishing
and coastwise cargo fleets when our young nation was flourishing on the seas but was more important as a supplier of captains to a larger merchant marine, 150 of its sons having been
in service as such at one time, in the year 1837. (Where
Maine's master mariners sailed generally from Maine ports,
those of Cape Cod, which lacked a hinterland, found greater
opportunities away from home.) In 1816, the first cultivation
of cranberries anywhere was undertaken in North Dennis.

Later, with the salt business killed by the salt mines discovered elsewhere and shipping long in a decline, summer people moved in to buy up and renovate old houses fallen into disrepair and build new ones. At the same time, Dennis became noted for its Cape Playhouse, the site of numerous tryouts of Broadway plays. And there you had it.

More immediately responsive to my needs were (1) a small, uncompleted, largely unoccupied shopping center, (2) a garage on one side of it with a young proprietor who seemed to live in and said I could go right ahead and pull up beside his place for the night, and, subsequently (3), a constable in a police car with whom I was able to clear the arrangement. (To avoid the risk of being routed out of bed in the middle of the night, it was always necessary to think of the police, whose interest was almost certain to be aroused by an odd-looking little bus with out-of-state plates parked with shades drawn. That was why pulling off to the side of a quiet road was never the answer to the problem of what to do about the night.) The constable, who made notes on my deposition, seemed a little puzzled when I told him I'd be leaving the bus for a while to take a walk around the town.

I could find no town. The Player Shopping Center, as it was called, seemed to be it. Nothing else was discoverable but dark, wet roads with occasional houses beside them. I suspect that I never did get to Dennis, that the place where I put up was East Dennis.

The night was not propitious. It rained steadily. At least I detected no intermission in the dripping of water into and outside the receptacles I had placed around me in the bus to catch it; the problems posed by an erectile roof had not been fully licked. The morning was not very propitious either. The northern sky over Cape Cod Bay was grey and sodden and a chill northeaster blew in over the sullen sea: a December day and no mistake. But for one in good health, footloose and free of responsibilities (or unable to do anything about them for the moment) the weather would have to be far worse than that to be bothersome. Driving out Cranberry Highway, which follows the north shore, though out of sight of the water, I was filled with enthusiasm, as it is easy to be on a Sunday morning in novel and beckoning surroundings before the world in general is out of bed. The character of the houses along the way was like a warrant for a cheerful

NATIONAL SEASHORE
AREAS TO BE ADDED IN THE FUTURE

assurance of spirit. One followed another, most of them in
the classic New England colonial style with two floors beneath
a steeply pitched, shingled roof, clapboard siding, blinds at
the windows and pillared corners. The variations on the pattern were as many as there were houses, but the basic theme
was the same. Every example was in harmony with itself and
with its setting, nestled into the landscape behind bushes of
lilac and mock-orange, beneath oaks and maples—all bare
now, of course, just as the houses themselves were mostly

closed for the winter. Always there was a compatibility of dwelling and site. You felt that these homesteads were protected and protective—a feeling one should like to have in all cases about the land that man inhabits—and that somehow they returned the love invested in them.

The response the houses called forth was sharpened, no doubt, by the complementary awareness one had of the sea's stern encompassment, which they offset, from which they offered harbor. That Cape Cod is a tenuous salient in the hostile domain of the waters was ever present in the mind. The land seemed to lie passive and defensive in this sphere of the sea's ranging winds. Certainly it appeared not to offer man an easy living. Occasionally in the flat lowlands the road passed square plots purple with cranberry—a native of the Cape's bogs and a relative of the blueberries—but for the rest instead of farms there were pinewoods, pitch pines everywhere, with black oaks and junipers far behind in second place and third.

From what I have learned since moving to Long Island, I am amazed that so little is heard of the pitch pine, that I was myself so little aware of it, for below Maine the pitch pine is an outstanding fact of life of the northeastern seaboard, as deserving of celebration as the white pine to the north and the long-leaved pines to the south. It has two notable capabilities. It will grow in soil that is nothing but sand and it will send up new growth from the stump when fire has razed a forest. (It is the only eastern conifer I know that will.) These attributes have made it supreme on Cape Cod. The Cape was not always the barren outrider of the continent it is today—barren, that is, in its outer section. Originally it apparently was largely covered by the same great forest as the adjacent mainland. Cutting and burning was begun by the Indians, who had a need of fuel and an interest in improving the forage of upland game-birds, and completed by the whites, who fired the woods to improve yields of blueberries and by inadvertence. Intensive farming depleted the soil. What nutrients the turnips, melons and asparagus left were finished by the cattle and the thousands of sheep turned loose upon the land. It was not the sea's proximity but man that debilitated the Cape. The compatibility of man and nature it exhibits in part today is not of ancient date.

It may be said that in the normal course of events you

cannot lose by being out in the open. If the weather is fair
and the air balmy, nothing else will afford quite the same
delight. On the other hand, if the elements are harsh and not
long to be endured, some psychic batteries within you are
recharged by the buffeting you take or the pelting from rain
and snow. And then, when you are finally driven indoors,
there is the sense of being altogether right with the world
that comes from getting dry and thawing out, from repose
after exertion, from a warm drink and a hot meal. So when I
say that the predominant impression I formed of Cape Cod
was one of grimness I am not complaining or voicing a
regret for any part of it. But, varied though the landscapes
were, the effect under the prevailingly grey skies was a grim
one. Or so it was on the Outer Cape, which was where I
spent my time, partly because that is where Cape Cod is most
distinctively itself, partly because this section is the site of the
National Seashore, established in 1961, which in time will
take in two-thirds of the forearm, including all on the ocean
side. Often there was a thin, driving rain or swirling snow.
The days were short. (The cold, which I had expected to be
the great drawback to travel on the coast in winter, turned
out to be not very troublesome. What did create a problem
was having the sun go down at four o'clock in the afternoon,
as it did on that far-eastern appendage to the continent, hours
before you were ready to quit for the day.) Finally, there were
the images I had brought to the Cape from what I had read.
I could not hear the waves running in without visualizing the
ships that had come to grief on the Cape's bars and shoals,
their crews found frozen to death when they could be reached.
My head was full of the geological processes that had shaped
and were reshaping the Cape, the remorseless processes of a
world to which mankind, with all the fine-spun conceptions
that form the psychological fabric of human life, is but an
incidental. On all sides there were reminders of those processes. The lower Cape was eaten out with kettleholes that
retained the outlines of the mountains of ice that had squatted
there—making, it must be said, though, beautiful ponds with
sandy rims at the bottom of the cup-shaped valleys. Often a
flock of gulls would be seen taking baths out in the middle,
washing off the brine in fresh water. I saw my first on the
drive out the Cranberry Highway, when I turned off into
Nickerson State Park, on the outskirts of Orleans, to see if it

offered a campsite. Cliff Pond lay in a declivity at the center of it. All around was a forest of pitch pines, some up to forty or fifty feet tall and eighteen inches through the trunk—big for the Outer Cape. The wind was in them and as if I had invaded the privacy of a retreat of sylvan nymphs the sound was of myriad spirits softly breathing a shocked "O-o-o-o-o-o-o-o-o-oh!"

In addition to being pitted with kettleholes, the Cape along most of its margins is bitten deep into by bays, which result from the intrusion of the rising sea into the lower-lying parts of a land unevenly assembled by the agency that created it and unevenly spread out by the waters that subsequently flooded down upon it.

If, as everyone does, you picture the Cape as an arm held out bent to display its muscle, fingers curled in an open fist around Provincetown harbor, then in terms of this analogy the hind arm (from shoulder to elbow) was formed by two lobes of the last ice-sheet. One, coming down through Cape Cod Bay (as it now is), deposited a moraine that remains today as Nantucket Island and Martha's Vineyard, then, withdrawing a stage, deposited another that forms the biceps muscle of the Cape. A second lobe, coming down on the left, from the northwest, and spreading toward the first, left a moraine that now constitutes the inland edge of the Cape's hanging sleeve and the Elizabeth Islands—that is, the eastern or outer rim of Buzzards Bay. The hind arm below the bicep, from Falmouth through Hyannis to Chatham, is an outwash plain composed of the rubble carried down from the moraine by the melt-water and precipitation, the finer material being carried farthest. The forearm of the Cape is also made up of outwash material, according to Barbara Blau Chamberlain in *These Fragile Outposts,* a geology of Cape Cod, Martha's Vineyard and Nantucket. It was built up as a plateau by sand, gravel and rocks, layer upon layer, washed down from two melting lobes of the ice-sheet. One of these was the lobe that came down through what is now Cape Cod Bay, the other a lobe that came down on the seaward side from Massachusetts Bay. The eastern edge of the former and the western edge of the latter faced each other—if the theory is correct—across a dreary waste that had been the bottom of the sea, and on this the plateau arose as the run-off of the two lobes deposited rubble between them. It must have been

twenty miles wide if the rate of its erosion by the sea has
been constant ever since the retreat of the ice-sheet, and it
may, moreover, have stood five hundred feet high or possibly
more. Today a high cliff of varying elevation, austere and extremely imposing, forms the outer shore of the forearm for
some seventeen miles. Walking away from its brink you start
going downhill at once; the inference is that when it stood
much farther out at sea it must have stood much higher too.
Continuing the bow-shaped line of the shore for ten miles
from the northern end of the cliff and for twenty-five miles
from the southern are sandy extensions created out of the
material washed from the front of the cliff and transported
by the littoral currents: Provincetown hook at one end,
Nauset Beach and Monomoy Island (a spit nine miles long
extending down from the elbow) at the other.

Walking along the beach below the lowering cliff brought
to a head my chronic feeling that somehow, as one might
come face to face with a living mammoth, I was about to
encounter the ice sheet itself; when you go long enough
without seeing other human beings the separation of past and
present seems to lessen. Once, for the tiniest fraction of a
second, I thought, "God Almighty! Here it comes!" It was
merely that a stone had been dislodged from high on the
face of the cliff, but it had done so without visible agency
and as it rolled down I could imagine that the cliff had been
given a nudge by the ice mass beginning to stir behind the
slope.

There can be nothing unusual in the falling-away of parts
of the cliff. The erosion of the eastern ramparts is continual.
I was shocked to find how casually it proceeds when I first
walked down to the beach. As it happened, I hit upon what
is probably, geologically speaking, the most strategic spot on
the Cape. This was the result of my pulling up at the first
established fragment of the National Seashore one comes to,
which lies between the head of Nauset Bay and the ocean and
includes a parking area as well as bathhouse and amphitheater; the temporary headquarters were in the old Nauset
Coast Guard station just up the hill. All the terrain features
come together here. You stand at the northeastern corner of
the moraine, at the southeastern corner of a zone of kames
(the deposits of glacial waterfalls) that extends across the
Cape just above it, at the northern end of Nauset Beach and

close by the southern end of the great cliff. The transition from moraine to beach could not be more abrupt: the sheared-off moraine, composed indiscriminately of clays of various shades of brown, packed sand and what looks like sandstone, gravel, rocks and occasional boulders, ends, and the loose, pale sand of the beach and the dunes begins at its foot. The surf runs right up to the steep end of the moraine, washing over the outlying parts of it and around the big chunks it has broken loose.

"When will it stop eating away the bank?" I asked of a rugged-looking man who had arrived at the spot with a younger, presumably his son, and stood digging at the soil with his toe. (It developed that Indian artifacts sometimes turned up here.) His complexion was of a mottled ruddiness and despite the cold he was lightly clad, in a camouflage jacket, and so was his companion.

"When it comes out the other side, I suppose," he replied in a voice that combined the light, discriminating accent of New England with a surprising cheerfulness. When you grow up with a process which has been going on for 10,000 years, I dare say you are not likely to ride off like Paul Revere to warn the villagers of its menace just because an anxious stranger points it out. Nonetheless, he confirmed what I had heard: that the old Nauset lighthouse, just a piece up the beach, had gone completely with nothing to show where it had been but the granite foundations and part of a brick wall sometimes poking up through the water at the ebb of a spring tide. The present lighthouse stands where you have your first chance to see the great escarpment and to look down upon the ocean from its brink. The wind was blowing strong in my face when I was there on my first morning and beneath the misty, heavy grey sky the sea, dull green, rolled in upon the land, bull-like in its soul, you felt. The breakers began a hundred yards offshore and from there to the beach spread a lace of foam.

The grim truth is that the face of the cliff with which the Cape fronts the ocean is receding at a rate of three feet a year. This is made very graphic at the site of the Marconi Station, where the grip of the bow formed by the shore would be. The National Park Service has an exhibit here including a model of the original installation, which was erected in 1901 to send and receive wireless transmissions across the ocean.

Of the masonry pediments of the four towers, standing to begin with at least 150 feet back from the edge of the cliff, the outer two have gone over the side and of these only one can be seen at all, 100 feet below, while the old powerhouse, formerly at the center of the four towers, clings to the face of the cliff on its way down. When Thoreau walked by the foot of the cliff here on October 11, 1849, in the course of his Cape Cod hike, and "put all America behind him," the Great Beach, as he called it, must have stood a good hundred yards off its present location.

The use of the area of the former wireless station by anti-aircraft batteries during World War II did nothing to improve it; the vista up and down the plateau is of sparsely brush-grown, exhausted, wind-swept fields. The vegetation here, however, is luxuriant compared with that of the former artillery range stretching away to the south which, though being replanted in beachgrass by the Park Service, presents a picture of soul-freezing barrenness hardly to be matched anywhere on the east coast. One of the two Rangers with whom I drove there, a rather small, reddish-haired youngster whose previous post had been in the lush Cascade Mountains, looked blankly up and down the plateau, still unable, after three months, to credit his being at such a place.

Yet within a short walk is the coziest, most verdant little
retreat on the Outer Cape. The trail to it, leading straight
back from the cliff, soon enters a Lilliputian forest, partly of
bear oaks. These are very much a feature of the Cape, as
they are also of Nantucket Island. They branch out from the
ground, like shrubs. And shrubs is about all they are, but one
grows very fond of them. Their choice of a life strikes one as
manful and their leaves, which are small and five-lobed,
resembling stretched animal skins or cutouts of little ghosts
with arms and legs extended, are of a creamy brown when
they have turned, a color that might be that of a dessert.
Their forest mates are pitch pines, which nearly everywhere
on the Outer Cape may be seen as an army advancing upon
the eastern rim, crouching lower and lower as they near it,
like Indians. On the trail through them you find yourself a
giant, your head on a level with the treetops. As you go
along, however, you shrink. The tops of the trees remain at
the same elevation but the ground falls away beneath them.
Soon you are of ordinary stature in a woods of pitch pines
and black oaks with the ground covered, as it is over most of
the Outer Cape, with bearberry, thorn lichen and broom
crowberry (a more attenuated little plant than the black
crowberry of Little Moose Island). Sheep laurel appears,
fresher and less sheepish than in Maine, and a bed of oval,
waxy green leaves of the scarce trailing arbutus, called Mayflower in Massachusetts, where it is the state flower. The
woods, acquiring an understory of inkberry holly *(Ilex glabra)*,
with privetlike foliage, grow greener. The goal is then at
hand: a swamp of Atlantic white cedar. It is for all the
world like a miniature cypress swamp of the deep South, grey
moss and all, standing in the same black water. The columnar
Chamaecyparis of course represents the cypress (from which
its name is derived), its foliage forming little fans like that
of the Northern white cedar but smaller and set at varying
angles to produce a frillier effect. The hanging Spanish moss is
replaced by the briefer, finer old-man's-beard *(Usnea)* and the
short, stiff mustache lichen *(Alectoria)*. As in the vast southern swamps the stillness, disturbed only by the nervous
departure of a few robins from one of the cedars, has a
primordial character and the gloom in which the vision is
swallowed up in a short distance a connotation of mystery.

You keep your voice low and tread quietly along the board-walk.

The builder of the walk was the young Park Naturalist who brought me here, a tall, gentle-spoken, unmistakably studious native of Gatlinburg, on the edge of the Great Smokies. The cedars, he said, all were doomed to give way to red maples, just as—if fires could be controlled—the bulk of the pitch pines on the Cape would eventually be replaced by hardwoods of the kind that had composed the original climax forest. (On Mount Desert the order is reversed; the hardwoods that came in after the disastrous fire are being replaced by conifers—spruce and fir.) In vain did I protest the sacrifice of the wonderful stand of cedars to the common-place red maples. His gentleness was that of a man unswerv-ingly devoted to first principles; in a National Park plant suc-cession, like other natural processes, must not be interfered with. "I'll come ring your bloody maples," I told him, but he only smiled. Perhaps after all the shade of these extraordinari-ly dense-growing conifers and the acid peat they lay down will be too much for their competitors.

Just as any visitor to Washington with a love of country should first pay homage to its father by a trip to Mount Vernon, so any partisan of the land itself who visits Cape Cod should go directly to a place that plays a stellar role in two classics of American nature-writing: Nauset Marsh. Tho-reau, though he did not write of it, must have had a glimpse of the marsh as he walked along through Eastham with his companion. (One has a vivid picture of the two figures as they passed: "We walked with our umbrellas behind us since it blowed hard as well as rained, with driving mists, as the day before, and the wind helped us over the sand at a rapid rate. Everything indicated that we had reached a strange shore. The road was a mere lane, winding over bare swells of bleak and barren-looking land.") For a more panoramic view than the one Thoreau had from the road, which is now U. S. 6, you may turn onto a secondary road a mile before Eastham —which New Englanders, I found, pronounce *East-ham,* giving the second "a" full value.

From the elevation to which the road leads—a protuberance of the moraine half encircled by water—you look far out over the marsh as over a great brown buckwheat cake. Gap-ing with waterholes, the cake is in greater part surrounded by open tidal channels and fissured by them as well. On the other side of it is Nauset Beach, a long, narrow spit crested with dunes beyond which the surf can be seen like a border of frosting. At the extreme left, a background to the marsh in the north, is the high land that ends at the old Nauset Coast Guard station. Across the marsh directly in front of you, just inside the dunes, is the site of "The Outermost House," in which Henry Beston spent a round of seasons forty years ago to write eloquently and poetically of what he had observed of the changing natural scene with an inexhaustible, scrupulous and ardent attention and what may only be called empathy. Solitude is to the powers of perception what the thorn was to the nightingale which pressed its breast upon the point to provoke its most moving song, and *The Outermost House,* which compels our absorbed interest by the depth of its veracity, could have been the work only of a man who had lived alone with what he wrote of. (While the house has been moved away, one is glad to know that it still exists.)

From the field running down to the channel bordering the marsh, meadowlarks put up on their seemingly inadequate, triangular wings. One can hear in the mind clear songs of four or five high, aspiring whistles, cutting the air like a knife, as Dr. Wyman Richardson used to hear them on an icy morning and be shamed into throwing off the warm covers. . . . There, in that robust individual, was a true New Englander, a leading Boston physician who yet never ceased to be a boy on the Cape, in fiber no less sensitive than tough, one would judge, who knew as home and studied with affection the marsh, river and woodland for which his gusto never flagged. The Old Farmhouse—*The House on Nauset Marsh*—lies just over the ridge on the left, and if no one is around you may go up to it as I did, a burning feeling in my throat from thinking of the death, only a few years before, of the man whose home this was and who had become so real to me from what he had written. I could not remember whether he had ever remarked on the junipers around his house which were sprinkled with fruit like bayberries but of a most strikingly bright pale blue, creating an effect, as some Christmas trees do, of a frosty, starlit northern night.

As Dr. Richardson demonstrated, the way to see Nauset Marsh (or any other) is by boat. I did the best I could by walking out in it from the parking area by the National Park

amphitheater. Mussels grew in the salt meadow grass and so
did a noted plant of the tidal flats, glasswort, which made me
think of an earthworm that has stood up and branched out in
the process of becoming an herb. Two months earlier the
whole marsh would have been astir with flocks of shorebirds
pausing on their way south. Even now there was a late-linger-
ing flock of "peeps"—the collective term applied by desperate
ornithophiles to the three species of small, brown-streaked
sandpipers that are difficult to tell apart. These, by the look
of their comparatively large, droop-tipped bills, were Western
sandpipers—which would mean that the little creatures had
flown here all the way from the far side of Alaska. There
were several hundred, all hurriedly probing the mud, as
anxious as travelers at a lunch-counter in a railroad station
with the train on the point of departure. And indeed the
analogy is probably valid; if something startled the flock every
bird in it would be instantly and irresistibly snatched away
even if a succulent worm were between its mandibles. As I
drew nearer I could hear their continuous cheeping, sounding
as if fingers of the wind were plucking the highest strings of
a harp.

On Nauset Beach a day or two later a light snow was
blowing like sand. Two groups of gannets came by well out
beyond the breakers. Sailing along the green front of the
waves, as white as the whitecaps, then beating with an easy,
shallow stroke of their long, narrow, black-tipped wings, they
made a grand sight. Larger, more aerial birds, they overtook
the gulls without effort. "Sophisticated" would be the word
today for the gannet's rakish design. Slim, tapered, with setback wings, the gannet reminds you of a bow and arrow, and
like an arrow it dives from on high—like a judgment hurled
earthward from Jove's down-flung arm. . . . Some of the
female eiders I had missed in Maine were here. Two were
close in among the breakers off the end of the moraine, a
most unusual situation for ducks to let themselves get into.
But clearly they knew what they were about. I watched
enchanted as they would let a wave lift them up its front,
then, just before it crashed upon them, would dive with a
mighty kick under the toppling crest to shoot up on the other
side as sleek and serene as mannequins. It was difficult to believe that the exercise had any other object than sport.

There were extraordinary things on Nauset Beach. I kept

stopping as I walked to gaze down with what must have seemed a drunkenness of astonishment at the piles of washed-up seaweed with which the beach was fringed, of the kind I thought of as fried-bacon kelp; every pile of it was a mass of foam bubbles, large and small, seemingly blown out of gems, of magic purples, blues and greens, and some of true, unbelievable gold. At night there was an even more miraculous phenomenon. At every step I took pinpoints of white light shone and expired in the sand around my feet. I took it to be, like the firefly's illumination, a case of bioluminescence, as scientists call it, the product of some minute organism's agitation. But I felt like a god striding across the firmament and creating ephemeral constellations with every pace.

The perennial problem of where I was going to put up at night had presented itself at the start, of course. It was not going to be on any of the three large tracts (in addition to the small one by Nauset Marsh) so far incorporated in the National Seashore; that was made clear in official accents mild but brooking no discussion: "There is no provision for camping in any of these areas." Ah, but there was the Massachusetts Audubon Society's Sanctuary, which I knew did include a campground, not to mention guest cottages! The Sanctuary was on Cape Cod Bay, at the mouth of the subsidiary bay called Wellfleet Harbor, which is where the forearm muscle being displayed by the Cape would be had it not been—to judge by appearances—eaten away. I repaired to it.

There was a well-lived-in old house on high ground and a nature trail descending from it. The trail made a highly worthwhile circuit of marsh, shore and hillside and by means of numbered markers referring to a mimeographed booklet on sale at the headquarters gave you an introduction to the flora of the Cape such as would take you days to equal by working with books alone. The superintendent proved to be no less helpful than the book, and patient too. But the camp-ground, he said, was closed for the winter. "Member Audu-bon Society Central Atlantic States," I had managed to insert mumblingly into the conversation. And: "Traveling alone, small self-contained bus." But it was no go. The campground was closed. *Fermé. Geschlossen.*

The liquor dealer in the big shopping center at Orleans was quite willing to let me park overnight in the alley beside his store. The arrangement was not quite the kind I had in mind in setting off for winter's wild littoral but I thought it would have to do until I could make some other. However, when I called at the police station for official sanction (what a pass of complexity we have reached when the State has to be squared before we can spend a night outside our own or some-one else's four walls!) I raised the question of whether I could not stay in Nickerson Park, closed for the season though it was. The man in uniform at the desk, grey-haired but of unlined countenance, turned out to be an understanding and considerate gentleman. He undertook to intercede with the manager of the park and put in call after call on the tele-phone until he ran him down. The required permission being forthcoming, I was quartered like a landowner on his estates that night and subsequent nights. The park was entirely mine and I felt it so from my roost in the woods above Cliff Pond.

Wherever I happened to be at six o'clock in the evening I had dinner. Twice it was at Wellfleet, a small port in a deep recess of Wellfleet Harbor called The Cove. From the water-side, the picture of the town's casually clustered little white houses, brooded over like so many chicks in a brush-growth of trees by a solid white hen of a church with steeple alertly erect, must be fixed in the mind of every devotee of the Cape. Eight or ten boats lay side by side at the municipal wharf where I ate; the fishing fleet that reputedly was once second only to Gloucester's has not entirely melted away. About 35 feet over-all, I guessed, the boats had stout wooden hulls, heavy winches, cordage bestrewing masts, derricks and deck, and an eclectic assortment of names: *Huckleberry Finn, Navigator, Lilian C., Magellan, Hero, Old Glory, Squid.* Two hardy-looking Yankees in plaid jackets were working on *Florence and John* in the cold white light of the garish wharf-lamps. While I had no compunction about eavesdropping on their talk, which had a pleasantly didactic Cape Cod accent, I was over my depth. They were discussing the idiosyncrasies of an ammeter, if I got it right. "You mean to say the poles are reversed? Well, how will you know which is which?"

On occasion before returning to the park I walked around the streets of Orleans, past the big lighted houses, beneath the tall elms, which seemed a world's distance from the moorland, sea and barren sands I had quitted at the darker end of that hour known as "twixt dog and wolf." It was always black night when I rolled up to the campsite. Yet much of the evening remained. With the shades drawn to deny any chance wayfarer the advantage of me, I would sit sunk in comfort with a book beside the old-fashioned gas-mantle lamp which —incomparably superior to the up-to-date anemic electric lantern—emitted a brilliant, bus-filling light, a very welcome warmth and a steady, companionable hissing.

In a drizzle there was a penalty for camping in the woods; the trees caught and amalgamated the droplets and let fall great dollops on the aluminum roof. Lying sleepless beneath it you could believe that solid pellets were being bounced on it. However, grey though the skies habitually were, it was usually not raining. One morning it was even clear. Since the air had been aswirl with a light snow when I had turned in, the two stars I glimpsed when I pulled the shade aside were a joyful sight. With the first light I heard the clangor of a passing flock of geese. The lake, behind the black bars of the pines' trunks, was a mirror of the yellow light that presently filled the eastern sky. . . . There was, after all, much to be said for a Polar Canadian air-mass if it moved in without much wind, even if it dropped the temperature to the low twenties. While the color began to flood back into a landscape which for days had largely lacked it, so that one had almost forgotten what it was, I thought: here I sit, answerable to nobody, having ahead of me more of this new world to discover, with this fresh, unlived day before me and these warm boiled eggs, this hot coffee and toasty honey sandwich!

I knew I was as happily disposed, even, as I should recognize myself in retrospect to have been.

All told, I spent many hours tramping the Great Beach. The cliff that rears up behind it is of even-textured, coarse sand the color of a lion, sparsely embedded with stones, and rises to remarkable heights—175 feet in one place. It appears very steep. On the strength of the impression it leaves, one might well guess, looking back on it, that the angle of its face is as much as 70 degrees. Studying it at the time, I guessed 45. But 35 is what it is, the Park Service tells us. All the same, it towers overawingly, and because its angle of declination is constant, it has, if very faintly, an air of the deliberately constructed, as if it were a breastwork erected by giants or a monument built by contemporaries of the Pharaohs to outstare Time from beneath its slightly overhanging brow of sod. The illusion is possible only because the bowlike bend of the beach, though slight, prevents your seeing more than a short stretch of the cliff at any one place.

I had the benefit`of a full initiation on my first go at the Great Beach, heading into a driving northeaster which was armed with needles of rain. The wind sent the billows rolling massively in to break in a curl of plunging water the color of deep aquamarine or of dilute lime juice and with the sound of a great throaty rumble. Amid the roar on roar you felt your-self in the presence of enormous goings on. A few herring gulls rode along the edge of the cliff on the updraft caused by the slope's deflection of the wind. Six or eight others, evidently attracted by something in the water, held a position for a long time low over the sea, beating hard to hold their own in the teeth of the punishing wind, dropping to the surface and rising again to keep from being buried beneath a breaker. Not another soul was to be glimpsed from start to finish, even where cottages crowned the cliff. It was a mono-tone vista, harsh and unrelenting, with nothing in it to suggest that there was any ingredient of the universe to indulge the softer side of human nature. It did not matter. I felt tireless, as if, like the gulls borne on the upshot current of the wind, I tapped the forces of the boisterous elements, as if the very thunder of the surf were transmuted into an intoxicant in my veins.

The beach, though nearly devoid of shells, was littered with kelp, both the fried-bacon and the green-noodle kinds, and with it what could have been the wrack of a demolished civilization: timbers, planks, glass bottles and plastic bottles, bits of polyethylene toys, a tennis ball, a red rubber ball, a cheap gavel I pounced on and carried until I asked myself what I thought I was going to do with it, an orange balloon (collapsed), a piece of yacht's teak hatch-cover, contra-ceptives, pieces of styrofoam floats from fishnets, a fluorescent orange lobster-trap buoy also of styrofoam, electric light bulbs, a milk carton, a jar half full of jam, a wine bottle with rope around its neck (probably from a lobster-trap line) and an-other with barnacles on it (probably ditto), a plastic bottlecap marked Cape Ann Liquor Chest which had come a long way —not trash, these things, but objects to engage the archaeolo-gist.

The Cape is a substantial body of land. Even the forearm is as much as five miles across (at Wellfleet). When you see it as it is, not so exclusively in terms of the abstractions you brought with you, you cease to think of it as altogether secondary to the sea, or as existing on the sea's sufferance. It has mass and ruggedness and grandeur of its own, especially in those somber cliffs.

For a taste of its atmosphere away from the sea I took a hike at the forearm's widest part, into the hills at the head-

waters of the Herring River. One of the detailed maps the Park
Service had lent me promised "Beech woods (rare) with
maple and pine on ridge; good trail." I never found the beech
woods, but the trail, which set off from a swamp-edged pond
in the woods, was indeed a good one (though I think the
wrong one) until it petered out and I got briefly lost. The
walk left a peculiar impress on me, associated with an in-
definable and inexplicable gladness and liberation of spirit.

From the last human habitation, a big, putty-colored
Victorian house blending with the woods, which I could easily
have coveted, the trail went up and over steep-flanked,
forested ridges. Pitch pines are not the aristocrats of their
tribe; there is a hint of scrubbiness and of twisted grain about
the best of them. If in the early days of the industrial revolution their wood was preferred to any other as fuel for loco-
motives and foundries, it has never been held especially
qualified for any loftier employment. Those along the trail
seemed too to have rather a lot of trunk and limb for the
amount of foliage. But personality they do not want for. With
the rain on them, their bark was nearly black and the tufted
needles a radiant yellow-green almost as if sunlit against the
soft, rich browns of the foliage of the black oaks and bear
oaks. The paler green wafers of lichen on the boles and the
deep-pile mats of sea-green thorn lichen covering the tops of
the ridges were brought to life by the rain, chill as it was;
you could taste the vegetative freshness in the air, like cool
cucumber. I walked on and on, up hill and down, as through
the setting of a story heard in childhood vividly, if incom-
pletely, remembered. There was no reminder of the sea's
presence, no whisper of the surf, no sound of any kind, for
that matter, except once the startled shrieks of a blue jay one
would have thought was being murdered—the hue and cry
that exasperates hunters by putting every creature on guard
for a quarter of a mile around. "The Outer Cape *has* an
interior," I said to myself. And yet I had the feeling too of
being near the end of something, at a remote extremity, such
as one has on a mountaintop. It was as if one were at a brink
beyond which lay only the undiscoverable. When presently
the drizzle became a damp, quiet snow the feeling was intensified, as if even that which I could not grasp were being
veiled.

At the wrist of the Cape you come to the end of the glacial deposits and to the end of the Cape itself as it presumably was at the time of the last ice-sheet's withdrawal. Here begins the duneland created out of the sand washed from the cliffs and carried north by the littoral current—and still being augmented. Here also you come to the beginning of the permanent English settlement of New England. The Pilgrims, after making a landfall midway on the forearm of Cape Cod (as Bartholomew Gosnold had named it eighteen years earlier), steered south in an attempt to sail around the elbow. Turned back by the "deangerous shoulds and roring breakers" (as many a stout ship since then has, or has wished it had, been), they rounded the Cape in the other direction and dropped anchor off what is now Provincetown, which occupies the palm of the half-closed fist. This remained their base for five weeks.

A 1,700-acre "Pilgrim Heights Area," a state park before it was made over to the National Seashore, incorporates nearly all the wrist and with it a spring believed to be the one from which the Pilgrims drank their "first New England water with as much delight as we ever drank in all our lives." (They had brought with them Captain John Smith's term for the region as well as his superior maps.) From the Park Service's "Interpretative Shelter" you can walk down to fresh-water marshes walled by dunes and a boggy, woodsy hollow where, among the beach-plums, huckleberries and Juneberries, the purple canes of black raspberry with their lavender bloom and the reddish, twisted twigs of the highbush blueberry add color to the winter scene, just as a little flock of myrtle warblers with yellow rumps and yellow chest patches adds animation to it. But from above you look out on an open, shelterless, wind-swept hilly terrain with bearberry moors stretching westward from the dunes along the shore.

You realize how fortunate it is that the area was long ago given protection as a park, for, as you see demonstrated a little farther on, an exposed prostrate landscape is extremely vulnerable; one nondescript building can dominate two or three square miles of it and with its quality of the sordid impose upon its surroundings the mood of a city's blasted, treeless outskirts. And yet, curiously, a lighthouse in such a setting will give the whole a character of nobility. It would seem to follow that what primarily affects us is not the aspect of the natural scene alone but what account man gives of himself in his intrusion upon it. You cannot visit the winter beach and be spared the sight, rendered more stark by the drabness of the season, of glum and anomalous structures of cement blocks, crowded and tasteless cottages, billboards and gas stations that set your teeth on edge with their neon lights, and the conglomeration sickens you because it portrays human existence as squalid, a mean scramble among gross persons for material advantage. If the compensations of your travels outweigh the drawbacks, as they do, greatly, one of the reasons is the sight of lighthouses, of the columnar beacons at Nauset, Race Point, Sankaty Head, Montauk and Hatteras, for these symbolize the best in our species—a warm and unflagging concern for our fellows in peril of their lonely lives on the treacherous deep and a dauntless idealism that looks afar over the seas, beyond the horizon, to what we do not know—and they only gain in splendor from the wintry harshness of the headlands they crown.

Above the wrist, where the Cape widens again, the pitch-pine forest resumes its sway, but before you get there you pass a stretch where the sand is on the move. Rogue dunes forty feet tall are burying the forest alongside the highway and spilling over onto the pavement itself, which can be kept clear for traffic only with earth-moving machines. They are even in process of filling in the upper end of Pilgrim Lake. This body of water, which extends about half the width of the wrist, used to be open on the bay—*Mayflower*, in fact, sailed into it—but it has since been sealed off by a spit of land, which is the usual ultimate fate of indentations in a sandy coast. The rows of identical little box-cottages that cut off the view of the bay all along the spit, as monotonous as freight cars on a siding, unfortunately appear to be in no danger from the advancing dunes. They tell you all you need to know of the fate that was in store for the area until the Cape Cod National Seashore was created. Most regrettably, the legislation that saved the Outer Cape in the nick of time so far sacrificed the general interest to that of individual property-owners that the houses now standing on National Seashore lands may be retained permanently in private owner-ship but at least no others may be built on such lands.

Long before Congress was moved to preserve the Outer Cape,

however, the people of Massachusetts had taken action to save its extremity. In addition to Pilgrim Heights, the "Province Lands," incorporating all the fist apart from Provincetown itself and its environs, was a state park, and one seven square miles in extent. What is almost incredible is that these lands were set aside as a reservation as early as 1670. Not everyone would agree with Samuel Eliot Morison's claim that the Pilgrims were the "spiritual ancestors" of all Americans, but one could wish that in their foresight as conservationists they had been.

As you go on toward Race Point, than which there is no going farther, it becomes easy to believe that this is land built out into the sea within the period of human history. The Cape slopes down from dunes encrusted with the black patches of huddled pines—as if the land had scabs, it seemed at day's end—to dunes clothed in beachgrass orange in the setting sun, to the last dunes of all, on which the beachgrass stands as fine and sparse as the hair on a blonde girl's arm, and as golden above the pale sand; after them there is only the long slope of the empty beach.

I think I have never seen the ocean as green as I saw it on a cloudy day from the Race Point Coast Guard Station, on a high ridge of dunes on the outer curve of the fist. Above the horizon was reared a black rectangle; one of our newer class of submarines was rounding the Cape, outward bound. Throwing up white foam at her bow and stern, her deck awash, she appeared a malevolent object and a sight in keeping with that cold and white-flecked sea. I could imagine her watch officer looking back upon the land, which would have appeared as unfeeling to him as his sinister vessel did to me, and I wondered if he had a thought of the hundreds of seamen who from their storm-wracked vessels had looked with terror on that indifferent shore, destined to be the last on which they would ever look. Very possibly he had; rammed by a Coast Guard vessel, the submarine S-4 went down in twenty fathoms just off shore around the Point in December 1927, taking with her forty men, who slowly died of suffocation.

On his way to Cape Cod, Thoreau had arrived at Cohasset while bodies were still being recovered from the wreck of the brig *St. John,* laden with immigrants from Galway. He wrote:

They were within a mile of its shores; but, before they could reach it, they emigrated to a newer world than ever Columbus dreamed of, yet one of whose existence we believe that there is far more universal and convincing evidence— though it has not yet been discovered by science—than Columbus had of his. . . . No doubt, we have reason to thank God that they have not been "shipwrecked into life again."

If ever I were capable of Thoreau's confidence and equanimity in the face of death, it would not be amid such scenes as he had witnessed, I thought, or at Race Point either. Less than a mile from where I was standing the British man-of-war that in Boston harbor, on the night of April 18, 1775 ("A phantom ship . . . a huge black hulk"), had embarked the Grenadiers for Concord had been wrecked three years later with the loss of all on board. *H.M.S. Somerset* was a victim of Peaked Hill Shoals, on which in a single day in 1802 three vessels from Salem had broken up. Much nearer on my other side the remains of the steamer *Portland,* which had vanished mysteriously in 1898 with more than two hundred aboard, had been found only twenty years ago with the bow of another vanished ship—a granite schooner from Maine—embedded in her side. Heaven alone knew when the first European lives were lost on this shore. Early in their stay here the Pilgrims found a skeleton with blond hair. Before Henry Hudson and John Smith, before Gosnold and Champlain, before even Verrazano and Cabot—all of whom sailed by here—the Cape, like the coast of Maine, may have been visited by Basque, Portuguese and Breton fishermen and earlier still by the Vikings, whose "wonder strands" some historians believed to have been the Great Beach.

There was little left of sunset when I came into Provincetown, and that little was on the wrong side. Provincetown is very disconcerting about directions. It seems impossible to bear in mind that Race Point faces not north but west, back toward the continent, and that in rounding the Cape from the Great Beach you describe not merely half but three-quarters of a circle so that from where you are on the bay side of the Cape you look out not across the bay, to the west, but back across the forearm of the Cape, to the southeast; Provincetown remains the place from which the sun rises in the west and sets in the east.

It consists mostly of two streets paralleling the waterfront for several miles. You come prepared to resent it as you would any town so long and so notoriously swarmed over by charm-seekers and you are not mollified by the knowledge that many of the seekers have been writers and artists, and good ones; "artists' colony" itself has unattractive connotations. It may be that in the summer your apprehensions would be justified. But the truth is that with the crowds gone, and in comparison with the run of impersonal American communities, in which it would seem that only automobiles and construction-machinery could feel at home, Provincetown is captivating. It is disarmingly small-scale to begin with. The waterfront side of Commercial Street is occupied mostly by businesses but along the other engaging little frame houses press close together, as if for mutual comfort, creating an atmosphere of coziness and sociability. Some have little plots of grass, and probably beds of flowers in the summer, protected by picket fences or hedges; others are crowded right out to the sidewalk. Alleys lead off to the side bordered by little dwellings that seem to have been built on happy impulse and pleasant second thoughts.

The windows of most of the houses were dark, though in some of these a telltale patch of blue light was visible, and

Commercial Street was nearly deserted. Cape Cod loses three-quarters of its population in the winter, and the Outer Cape must lose much more. I felt a little as if I had strayed into, and been reduced to a size commensurate with, a toy-train village which the owner had lost interest in and forsaken. *The Mexican Shop* was boarded up. *Gale Leah (Galerie et Boutique)* was dark. *Hoot Mon, Fair and Foul Weather Clothing,* was dark and empty. *Ciro and Sal's Italian Restaurant* was dark. There was a raw wind and I stepped into a puddle in the dark. A boy came by with a dog on a leash and then two girls, brunette and stocky, talking in tones of repressed excitement. *Joe's Soda Shop* was dark. *(Sorry, We've Closed.) Phyllis Jewelry* was dark. *Casa Gernika Motel Tourist Home (Winter Rates. Vacancy Heated)* must have been open but no one was in view. A few cars passed. There was no sign of life at *Inn at the Mews (Waterfront Accommodations. Open All Year. Private Beach Area. Galleries).* The Chrysler Art Museum in a towering old white church would be open in the morning, admission one dollar. It was planted with recumbent juniper and displayed a few pieces of statuary that in the dim but naked light of the street-lamps looked as if they had been pulled out of taffy. I stepped in another puddle. The Madeira Club of the Pilgrim House was closed but the Fo'castle was doing a bit of business; in its dark bowels the shadowy figures of a few youths and girls could be discerned before the bar, the thumping of a jukebox be heard.

Then, out of Adams Pharmacy *(Established 1875),* up and across the street from a warehouse promising ART IN ACTION (which manifestly Art was not at the time), up from the Church of the Redeemer (promising ANTICIPATION OF GOD), poured the youth of Provincetown, some 20 strong, lads and lasses. Their coats were unbuttoned to the chill night, doubtless to set them apart from their staid elders. They appeared—but it is difficult to say how they appeared without sounding a bit above oneself, in fact a snob. The girls tended to a certain dumpiness, reminding one that the permanent population of Provincetown is predominantly of Portuguese descent. In the wake of the straggling procession, three young girls rather short of stature and also of skirt were taking running jumps at, and trying to touch, a shoe-store sign swinging out above the sidewalk. They were surprised at this by a young policeman, who come from around the corner.

"You can either get out of here or come to the station!" he bawled at them. He was quite ferocious. But then for eight months of the year there can be very little excitement in Provincetown, and for a substitute the nearest movie theater is twenty-seven miles away, in Orleans, and open only on weekends.

If I ever saw a ghost I should doubtless faint with astonishment. Yet there are occasions when I am almost astonished that none appears. Provincetown provided one such. Its past could never be deciphered from its present. It had its start over three centuries ago as a hangout of a "wild, undisciplined and unprincipled crew of traders and fishermen from nearly all parts of Europe," whose "drinking, gambling and bacchanalian carousals, were continued sometimes for weeks with unrestrained license," an impressionable historian tells us. The Provincetowners who, with the men of Truro, ten miles to the south, took to the pursuit of whales off shore in longboats in the late 1600's commenced a chapter of American history perhaps unsurpassed in the demands it made on the stamina of its authors—a chapter which (though Provincetown continued to send out whalers down to the present century) was carried to its apogee by the ships of Nantucket and New Bedford in the decades before the Civil War. Before that, Provincetown had twice been what is called a ghost-town. Pitilessly exposed to hostile navies, it had been abandoned by its inhabitants at the outset of the French and Indian War and again during the Revolution. (Having twice been licked, it more or less joined the enemy in 1812.) But it is in no sense a ghost-town today. Of its barbarous and two-fisted past, nothing remains discernible to a casual visitor. To one alone on its streets it may come as more chilling than the wind from across the Cape to have it borne upon him that a past supremely defiant of death in its day will be expunged without a trace by time. The specter one might think to encounter at the corner of one of those tidy, pert little houses gazing in puzzlement at the motorcars is not there, and if one hurries by, a little shamefaced in one's modern softness beneath its stern, imagined stare, it is only because of what one has found in books.

For the night, I had all to myself a very fine private campground in the pinewoods at the entrance to the Province Lands Area. (The owner, whom I managed to reach in town by telephone, refused to accept any payment from so unlikely a customer.) In the morning, long before daylight, on a sudden, horrid suspicion, I pulled back the shade and found a heavy snow falling. Instantly deciding that I had better get the somewhat unwieldy little bus down out of the hilly campgrounds without delay, I pulled on my clothes without taking time to light the alcohol heater, climbed into the front seat and took off for Provincetown. The darkness was still pitch-black when I rolled onto the municipal dock. The sticky flakes of snow were driving at the car windows from the northeast, I observed to my disquiet; I had no wish to be snowbound. Then I recalled that directions are very nearly reversed in Provincetown and quickly confirmed with a compass, with an upsurge of gaiety, that it was as I had deduced: the wind was coming from just a little south of west.

The first light turned the sky a deep blue. Against it, the dead glare of the mercury-vapor lamps was chartreuse. They were bright enough for me to cook breakfast by them. By the time I had eaten and was ready for a walk, daylight had come and the lamps were off. It was still snowing, though.

A long pier named after Commander Donald B. MacMillan, the Arctic explorer whose home this was, extended out from the dock. From the end of it, I found, Provincetown could be seen as in a painting. Under the snowfall, the pattern of light and dark characteristic of ground and sky was inverted, giving you the sense, as a familiar scene will when viewed in extraordinary circumstances, of exciting mystery beneath the commonplace. Apart from the shaft of the Pilgrims Monument (closed for the season) rising over 250 feet from the top of a steep hill—a former dune—in the immediate background, one might have been looking at an illustration for a northern fairy tale.

Off the end of an adjacent pier half-a-dozen great black-backed gulls were in a state of excitement highly unwonted with these magnificent creatures, which fear neither God nor bird—or so one would judge from their proud and lofty bearing and rapacious ways. I had never heard them so vocal. The deep, hollow, inarticulate *k'hawk, k'hawk, k'hawk* was like the cry of a mammal or of a herring gull in a cardboard box, or one hoarse from barking. *Awrrrrrrrk!* one of them threatened; I could have believed it was human. (Great black-backed gulls are significantly larger and, on our shores, generally much less numerous than the herrings. They have the commanding presence of eagles. They look like eagles, too, whether standing on an eminence, dark of wing and back, white-headed and white-tailed, or in the air, soaring or flying with slow, majestic wing-beats, the head advanced like an eagle's. They are at their most superb, I think, with the forest-topped cliffs of Mount Desert for a background.) On the seaweed-covered beach, herring gulls squabbling among them-selves over a mess of offal (they would hardly have squabbled with the black-backs) were protesting in their piercing, petulant squeal, high as a mouse's squeak. Then while I listened, one gave voice to the loon cry, the long-drawn, wild, weird, yearning *kraaaaa-eeeeeeeeeek!* Heard through the fall-ing snow in the chill, damp air, against the vista of a grey sea that merged with the blur of the snow-hazy sky, it all but drew my soul out of my body.

Cape Horn, a Coast Guard patrol boat, was moored along-side, its wheelhouse on a level with the pier, for the tide was out. I wanted badly to go aboard but with no one about there seemed to be no way of contriving it. When my feet had suf-ficiently frozen from strolling around the neighborhood, where early-rising workmen were setting off on the day's round, I went back to the bus to thaw them out over the alcohol burner and have that second cup of coffee.

On my next try at the patrol boat, I caught a young seaman on the bridge. He was coatless and perhaps hefty enough not to suffer for it, but as I kept plying him with questions he must have despaired of cutting me off and getting away. (*Cape Horn* was ninety feet over-all. All of her class were named after capes. She was powered by four diesels. They developed six hundred horsepower each. They operated two to a shaft. Her complement was thirteen men. . . .) There was nothing for it but to invite me aboard. I scrambled down the ladder and was soon seated in the mess-cabin with two or three of the crew drinking coffee from a cup like a shaving-mug and hearing about *Cape Horn*'s day in the limelight. Comman-deered by an admiral to take him out to his aircraft carrier one gusty night after a party ashore, WPB 95322 was caught by a sea under the carrier's fantail and heaved up into it and her superstructure crushed. A magazine article delightedly retailing the misadventure was produced for me. "It was really

too rough to be trying a maneuver like that," my host avowed.
I asked if they couldn't have begged off, at least until morning.
"Well, the admiral had been having a pretty good time," he
replied, "and he was Navy—and we're Coast Guard.'

Cape Horn's quarters were clean, snug and warm. Every
inch of space was made the most of, all the neatly stowed
gear had its purpose. In recesses adjacent to the mess-table,
inscrutable and omnicompetent mechanical and electronic
devices were to be seen. The machine age, so domineering and
soul-crushing when it fills the landscape, is altogether different in microcosm in a setting of bleak and forbidding wildness. In that cold, wet harbor, lapped by the waters of the
North Atlantic, veiled in the still-falling snow, being below
decks in the patrol boat made one feel a little as a boy does
when enclosed and absorbed in some contrivance—ship or
other—created in his imagination to pass sore-tried but
victorious through the manifold perils of the vasty deep. . . .
Did they have to go out in very rough weather? I was told
that recently they had met seas running thirty-five feet high.
(That would be midway between the fourth and fifth floors of
a building.) The commanding officer, who had just come
board, told me that the vessel had heeled over so far that one
of her sea-chests—scoops for bringing in sea water to cool the
motors, located only two feet from the keel—had been visible.
He thought her list must have been nearly seventy degrees.
Up on the bridge, he had had to hug the radarscope with
both arms and brace his feet against an upright to stay put.

Most of *Cape Horn*'s work, I learned, was in replying to
distress calls that came in by radio from fishing craft which
had got their propellers fouled in a net, lost their rudders or
run out of fuel or got water in it. Carrying enough oil was a
problem for the fishing boats. Some of them might well be
suspected of deliberately allowing their fuel to run out when
they saw a chance to fill their holds by keeping after the fish
and relying on the Coast Guard to tow them in; to get help
from a commercial organization would cost far more than the
fishermen had any intention of paying. The boats from
Provincetown went out chiefly for cod and haddock. They
were owned almost entirely by Portuguese—who, one of the
sailors put in, had more pride in their boats and took better
care of them than the fishermen of some other ports he could
name. The big operators were mostly from New Bedford.

They went out to Georges Bank and dragged for scallops in addition to trawling for fish. Another of *Cape Horn*'s tasks was keeping in touch with the Russians, who sometimes had as many as twenty fishing vessels off the New England coast. Occasionally they ran into port from storms and recently two of their ships had come in after colliding with each other. Relations between the seamen on the two sides were good, I was told. The Russians, a surprising number of whom spoke English, had even had the Americans to a dance on board one of their ships, in which there are women as nurses, librarians, cooks, and so forth. But the Russian officers were distant and would not allow their men to receive periodicals from the Americans. (While New England fishermen have often complained of the methods of the Soviet fishing fleet in waters they regard as practically their own, the U.S.S.R. has recently shown itself disposed to cooperate. Soviet officials, pointing out that their ships are chiefly interested in herring and whiting, not greatly sought after by the Americans, have offered emergency medical aid in their mother ships to American seamen in need of it and have accepted joint inspection teams to insure compliance with international conventions.)

"Do you ever say to yourself, 'This is the life!'?" I asked the commanding officer, a lieutenant junior grade with an Italian name.

"Yes, in the summer," he answered without hesitation. "It's wonderful then." In his narrow overseas cap he had the appearance of a soldier in the Spanish civil war. And Barcelona, it came out, was to be his next assignment—at a Loran station. He was naturally cheerful at the prospect. Loran (an acronym for long-range navigation) enables a vessel to determine its precise position by comparing the times that radio signals arrive from three transmitters. I was astonished to learn that we maintain Loran stations along the coasts of Europe, western Greenland and northern Canada and on the other side of the Pacific.

In the course of demonstrating for me how Long Point, the tip of the Cape's hook, across the harbor, looked on the radarscope (it looked like phosphorescent scrambled eggs), the lieutenant produced a chart of the Cape which had marked on it the sunken vessels that constituted a threat to navigation. They were far fewer than I surmised they would once have been. The lieutenant observed that since the Cape Cod Canal had been dug, coastwise shipping had been spared the journey around the great promontory. (Opened in 1907, the 17.4-mile-long ditch severs the Cape at its narrow shoulder-joint and is used by 15,000 vessels yearly.) The toll taken by the Cape's vast shoals is largely a thing of the past.

It had stopped snowing. The clearing wind, however, proved to be a cold one. That night at South Yarmouth was dark and bitter, but I was snug and clean again in a motel. The floodlighted façade of the white Methodist Church, which I passed on a walk, looked like the month of December in a pictorial calendar. I remember it for the curious text posted in front of it, which succeeded in sounding at once servile and presumptuous: *Thy Will Be Done Through Me.*

Nantucket and
South to Newport

To BE an initiate of Nantucket is even more of a distinction than to be an initiate of Cape Cod. It is easy to see why. To begin with, of course, Nantucket is harder to reach. Between it and Woods Hole, at the tip of the Cape's drooping sleeve, where it hangs lowest, there is a three-hour trip (including a call at Martha's Vineyard) by seagoing ferry.

Who makes the trip in early winter? Not a great number. Those of whom I was one kept mostly to a kind of waiting room that occupied the main deck. Fitted with curved, leather-covered settles around the sides and with tables and chairs at the after end, it also had a snack-bar amidships. A young woman was asleep on one of the settles, an Air Force noncom on another. A young husband and wife, pale and thin, were proving unable to deal with a screaming infant; they looked as if they were haunted by chronic inadequacy. A middle-aged woman, dressed for a bridge party, was executing a design of roses in needle-point with decisive stitches. A man to be recognized anywhere as a New Englander, though he resembled George Catlett Marshall, was reading a book. He was the only soul on board to be so employed, though a lean, baldish man in a crisp business suit with a Tattersall vest was lost in a brochure—a diagrammed prospectus for Membrane Weather-Proofing, I managed to see. Also lost in the written word were a young man in a rough sweater, a Cockney type from a British film, who was scribbling on the top of a folded newspaper—working out the odds?—and a ten-year-old boy who was deep in some comics. A female contemporary of the boy's was kneeling on a settle beside him looking out the port. "I love to watch the white water come out," she

113

said. She was eating coughdrops. "Jerry, have you opened your Vicks yet?" But Jerry only grunted.

There was also a party of hunters, a very-ordinary-looking crew, though superior to their loutish follows on the return trip who—one in his undershirt—paraded a four- or five-day dirty stubble of beard. While shooting animals in the United States today seems to me to make about as much sense as it would to go after Indians on a reservation with a machine gun, it appears that some millions of Americans feel a need every year to go afield and act out fantasies of maleness with a gun. Deer-hunting week had begun while I was on Cape Cod. I had kept running into Natty Bumppos made up as clowns in caps, jackets and/or vests of fluorescent red or orange, for it seems to be characteristic of these hawk-eyed woodsmen that they cannot be trusted not to blaze away at anything that stirs unless it looks like an animated cartoon in neon lights. Later, when I was out on the uncovered upper deck, one of the party of gunners came up to me—a large-faced, stocky, red-haired Irishman.

"I saw you watching a sea gull when we were leaving Woods Hole," he said. "Was it some special kind?"

One up for him. He had noticed and had cared enough to ask. It was an Iceland gull, I explained, down from the Arctic.

The adults are nearly white even on the wings but this had been a young one with a brownish wash on its plumage. With its short, dark beak it had looked hawklike. Seeing it as it tailed the ferry for a time at a distance, a creature to which these icy waters were as a tropical winter resort, was a great satisfaction. The Irishman spoke of the albatrosses that had followed his ship in the Pacific when he had been in the Navy, putting down on the water at night and overhauling the vessel in the morning. Scanning the sky, he said he was going to have to go back on the next ferry if it began to snow for he made a living—"that's all, just a living"—clearing highways under contract with the state. I asked him if he enjoyed killing deer.

"I don't know," he said. "I've been going out for four or five years, mostly to Maine and New Hampshire, but I've never hit one. For me it's just an excuse to get out to the woods—to get away from it all."

Yes, one recognizes the need—to have an objective for expeditions to the distant hills, the lonely shores, something concrete to bring back. Merely to receive impressions is seldom enough, for most of us. If men are ever to live at peace with the remnants of a disappearing wildlife, a psychological equivalent of hunting will probably have to be found. Photography, often suggested, hardly fills the bill. The trophies are secondhand, mere shadows of reality, and almost always prove anticlimactic. Perhaps mineralogy comes closer to it than anything so far. It can take you to the nearest stream or farthest continent in quest of specimens and as deep into science as you care to go.

In mid-course there were few birds but scattered white-winged scoters and occasional loons. The latter would dive as we approached, giving a brief glimpse of a pale form beneath the waves. I have been growing fonder of loons and more admiring. You find them off shore all winter long and as far north as Nova Scotia, generally solitary birds. What occupies their minds, you wonder. Light and mettlesome on the water, they have sleek lines and their heads, sloping trimly up from the long, sharp bill—the two in perfect proportion—are finely carried, with serpentine grace. They fly with heads slightly lowered on outthrust necks, warlike, it would seem, and because their bodies are flattish, along the lines of rafts, they look thin from the side view they usually present as they speed by, like javelins. . . . One, evidently of the more lightly-built red-throated species, must have been prevented by an injury from either diving or flying, for it went flapping pathetically over the surface before us, uttering a hoarse *aaaaaaaak! aaaaaaaak!* Sea birds at best have a difficult time getting off the water and few will attempt it except against the wind. The scoters, black, chunky ducks built to withstand the buffeting their sea life subjects them to, pattered strenuously over the waves away from us, like fat commuters running for a bus, before their flailing wings would take the load, even with their feet spread out horizontally behind them to give them another planing surface.

As we neared Nantucket the birds increased to nearly tropical numbers; one felt as if one were moving through a museum habitat group come to life. Scoters were hurrying by on all sides and eiders pouring in toward the island by the hundreds. In the distance could be seen a sprinkling of phalaropes, those strange little sandpipers that breed on Arctic shores and winter at sea in the grey wastes of the far South Atlantic. White at such a range, they rode high in the water and with their long, erected necks resembled decoys. Most stirring were the long-tailed ducks. These lissome waterfowl, looking from afar like chocolate-and-white parakeets with high-browed heads, the drakes with tapering, pointed tails as long as their bodies, flew with the fluidity and style of shore-birds. Other ducks fly because their business requires it, but the longtails fly for fun, spontaneously and fast, the flock executing aerial evolutions as it goes, zigzagging and wheeling. They can dive from the air and, it is said, re-emerging, shoot clean out of the water from the side of a wave.

The moraine of which Nantucket is formed, running east and west where the island is widest, rises in one place to over a hundred feet, but as you beat up to its concave, landward coast the shore that half encircles you seems as fine as a pencil line and you feel that the island is the merest accident; if the ocean were a few feet higher—as there is no apparent reason why it should not be—almost all of what you see would vanish. But Martha's Vineyard and the southern shore of Cape Cod give the same impression, and the truth must be that if the ocean were higher the shores would be too, though they would come out less far. It is the sea that disposes the sand that forms the beaches. This is demonstrated by the spits with which the waves and currents have partially sealed off

bays all along these coasts—or wholly sealed them off, as on
the ocean side of Martha's Vineyard, where fingerlike coves
have been converted into lakes. The harbor of Nantucket is
formed by a spit extending from the northern corner of the
island to the middle of its landward coast; you can think of
a crab defending itself by holding a claw before its face. It is
a very odd spit, fluted on the inside, illustrating the propensity
of waves and currents to form hooks at the ends of the spits
they create by swirling around them to deposit more sand.
In this case, it appears that every time a hook started to form
the spit was extended, and that it happened five times. The
same phenomenon occurred twice at the most famous and
strategically situated formation of this kind in the country—
Sandy Hook, at the entrance to the Bay of New York.

Sailing up to the harbor's mouth, which is formed of a
pair of breakwaters like a tweezer's prongs, I noticed the
skeletal remains of three wooden vessels at the end of the
spit. That is about all that remains of the great days of
Nantucket shipping; back in the 1820's and 1830's, one reads,
as many as three hundred vessels might be seen in its harbor.
But the town itself—Sherbourne, as it was once attractively
and sensibly called, to distinguish it from the island—has lost

nothing in the past century. At your first sight of the wonderful jumble of grey, white-trimmed houses pressing upon the harbor, seemingly as content in one another's company as a throng of uniformed schoolgirls, or as if there to meet the new arrival and take him to their hearts (I say that because they went straight to mine), you feel, as you do in Williamsburg, that it is too good to be true. And of course Williamsburg *is* too good to be true. But in hard fact, so is this. Nantucket town is a relic preserved by accident of circumstance and restored to life by persons of means and taste—not that I think the less of it for that. In its heyday it had two or three times the present number of its permanent residents and, treeless and newly raw, as much of it was after the fire of 1846, which destroyed 360 houses, could not have been nearly so attractive. It was a one-industry town, a whaling port, and disasters struck that one industry. New Bedford's natural advantages as a port were too great for the island to compete with, and more and more whaling moved to the mainland. In the Civil War, *C.S.S. Shenandoah* played the same kind of havoc with the Arctic whaling fleet that *C.S.S. Alabama* played with the North's cargo shipping. Meanwhile, a method of producing an illuminating fuel from "rock oil" superior to and cheaper than spermaceti was found. Nantucket fell into a kind of trance, like a Sleeping Beauty. But if life, so to speak, passed her by, so also did the age of the factory that, while it spread wealth across the New England seaboard, spread also a baneful ugliness.

Houses of shingled siding weathered grey, narrow of eaves, of white-framed doors and windows—these predominate. The style seems appropriate to Nantucket's Quaker background. Yet the houses are not as straitened as their appearance leads you at first to suppose (in which too they may have something in common with Quakers). Most of them are very ample. And there is more variety of architecture than you take in from the ferry. Among the grey-shingled majority are many of the traditional white-clapboard construction of the mainland and a few handsome, red-brick Georgian edifices and white-pillared mansions of the Greco-Roman revival built by whaler captains at the height of Nantucket's prosperity. Snuggled together as most of them are, room has yet been found for little gardens beside or behind many of them. All the streets but two—Main and Broad—are narrow and most of them are angled. Vistas, accordingly, are limited, generally to a block or two in the side streets.

No town in the East is more remote from my origins than Nantucket. Moreover, if I settled here with my family, even my children would be considered off-islanders to the end of their lives. Yet, walking up Broad Street from Steamboat Wharf, an Army field bag over my shoulder (to have brought the bus across would have cost twenty dollars), I had an extraordinary sense of home-coming, as powerful and sweet as if homesickness were being allayed. I doubt that I should have had it if this had been summer, when (according to the landlady of the rooming house at Broad and Centre where I put up) the island's population leaps from 3,500 to 16,000 and streets are clogged with cars, the nighttime quiet rent by fusillades from the exhausts of motorscooters. But I had it now, almost as if by a trick of time I had changed places with a seaman just off a ship returned after years from the other side of the world. And I knew without having to speculate long why this should be. It was the past that Nantucket preserved that was home—a past that was of human scale, for which, indeed, perhaps most of us are in one way or another homesick. The industrialists and the big-time panderers to human weakness and greed—the advertisers, the entertainment-mongers, the commercial land-developers and their like —have not found Nantucket a fruitful field or have been restrained by law. Nantucket is of a time before we were dwarfed and denigrated by the hugeness of a machine-built civilization having for its standards the common denominators of a mass market. Its character is of the days when it was the natural world that was vast and overpowering, when the communities into which men and women drew together in their common interests, out of necessity, had, it is evident, some of the intimate quality of a gathering around a campfire. One need not be enamored of the past as such to feel the appeal of an order of things that was essentially human, in which a person's relationships were primarily human, not institutionalized and mechanical, when even material objects, being the product of human hands, had a warmth and life.

Nantucket's particular past would certainly, I must confess, have been uncongenial to me. One to whom asceticism, whether accepted as a condition of rewards in the next life or as a condition of rewards in this one, is chilling, a denial of life, like a foretaste of the grave, must be struck with dismay by the voyages that supported the town. Minuscule, floating monasteries, cramped, comfortless, imperiled, the whaling ships were exiled from the human community for ever-longer terms as the chase took them from the coastal waters to Brazil and the South Atlantic, then around the Horn into the Pacific, to Japan and finally to the Arctic. From months, the voyages lengthened to two, three and four years in duration.

"Did you notice that shingled frame house across the street from the Pacific Club?" asked my neighbor at the counter of Allen's Diner that night. (The diner was a refurbished, polished-up railroad car, the only piece of rolling stock left on the island of the railroad to Siasconset, built in the 1880's and shipped bodily to France in World War I.) "Back in the old days the lower floor was a saloon. They sold blackstrap rum there and the customers who drank too much woke up next morning in a whaler. It got so the only way you could get a crew for a whaler was to shanghai it." But the speaker, a weathered-looking sixty-five-year-old with a full jaw and somewhat close-set, candid eyes, was not, he explained, an islander, though he had lived here two-thirds of his life; he was a native of Provincetown. "There was good money in whaling, but it was the captains who made it, the ones who built the grand homes up at the top of Main Street. They'd sit in the Pacific Club and talk profits." Formed by the captains in 1854, the Pacific Club occupied a fine brick building just up the street, one erected in 1772 by the owner of the three vessels that had tea dumped off them three years later by Bostonians made up as Indians. On my way to the diner I had seen through the window, seated around a big stove, ten or a dozen veteran fishermen, or so they appeared to be—lifelong cronies, at any rate: of that one could be sure.

The Provincetowner, a boatyard-owner, drove me along the waterfront to the American Legion Hall, once a warehouse used for storing the oil unloaded by the newly-arrived whalers at the nearby docks. (I spent a while the next day contemplating, with that ghost-filled vacancy of mind known to all who gaze on ruins, the L-shaped stone foundations of one of those same docks, against which the waves spilled loosely.) In the side of the building the outlines of a wide doorway, long since bricked up, were distinguishable. Through it had been rolled the hogsheads of oil—2,000 from a single ship,

on the average. "When I first came here in 1922," my guide
said, "the smell from the oil-soaked dirt floor was still so
strong you could hardly pass the building without retching."

That brought to mind what I had trouble forgetting, that to
create this enchanting town the seas had been incarnadined.
No more brutality may be involved in killing a whale than
in killing a heifer or a rabbit. All I can say is that to me it is
worse, and that I cannot imagine a God one could revere
whose wrath would not be provoked by the near annihilation
of the right whale for the satisfaction of human avarice.
Neither can I see how the slaughter of hundreds of thousands
of the great beasts is made less abhorrent by the manner in
which they were done to death, driven to exhaustion with
the fanged harpoon tearing at their vitals and the steam
issuing from their blowholes red with blood. After leaving the
Provincetowner and returning to my room I read with the
greatest satisfaction an article by Charles E. Hinkson in a
magazine I found there telling how Captain James I. Waddell,
commanding *C.S.S. Shenandoah,* destroyed twenty-one Northern vessels, the majority whalers, after the end of the war—
news of which he dismissed as preposterous. (The crews were
sent home in three others which he had spared for ransom.)
Would there were a modern *Shenandoah* to fall upon the
great, powerful factory-ships that are today's whalers and
scuttle the lot of them! The blue whale, largest creature ever
seen on earth, and one too big for man to tangle with until
the gun-fired harpoon with explosive head was invented—
since when a third of a million have been butchered—might
even now be saved from extermination. The sperm whale,
battler of the giant squid in the ocean's depths, upon which
the whalers fell when they had largely wiped out the right
whale, would have a better chance. Perhaps they and other
whales can be saved anyway if Japan, Norway and the Soviet
Union—the only nations left in the deep-sea whaling business*
—will respect the sanctuaries and catch limits established by
international agreement and if these protective measures can
be expanded and offshore whaling brought under control. But
that is a big *if.* And the slaughter that Nantucket first made a
business goes on.

Yet there is Nantucket today.

---

* And the Norwegians have now announced that because the falling-
off in catches makes whaling uneconomic they are getting out.

Like Provincetown, Orleans and Wellfleet, it gains in appeal through contrast with what lies about it. I should, I was told, have come two months earlier, at a time when the color of the mainland's woods is rivaled by that of Nantucket's ground-cover, or in summer when the heaths are in bloom. In December, the island's garb is at least as skimpy and austere as the Outer Cape's. After finding a room, I lost no time in renting a bicycle from a dealer who advertised "See Nantucket the cycle-logical way" and had six hundred in stock (all of which, he told me, would be out on a big weekend in summer) and pedaling the three miles south across the island's waist to Surfside. The scattering of low houses there stood out starkly on the treeless plain, above the fields of beachgrass running down to a near-silent sea. On the way back, the stunted pitch-pine woods with their understory of bayberry in open parts, giving place occasionally to fields of tall, tufted oakleaf-brown broom sedge *(Andropogon)*, began to be drained of color with the approach of dusk. It was a comfort and, with my Nantucket citizenship all of three hours old, felt very natural to be back in the confines of the narrow streets, where a sprinkling of lights was now coming on in the sheer fronts of the houses. To be out of danger of being shot was gratifying too. I had been warned that deer-hunters might be misled by my sand-colored storm-coat and let me have it, but I could not see myself shelling out $1.85 for one of those orange vests, as I was advised to do, let alone wearing the infamous rig.

The commercial quarter of most towns seems to have been contrived to be harassing, as indeed it has been. Nantucket's Main Street was an exception. Planted with shade trees at a time when trees of any kind were few on the island, it was paved in 1837 with cobblestones brought from Gloucester. These, moreover, were the real rounded ones, not the brick-shaped Belgian blocks often called cobblestones. Under iron-rimmed wagon-wheels they must nearly have jolted a driver's teeth out. What was more to the point, they now enforced a certain discipline even on motorcars—which, one may hope, the Nantucketers may someday discover they would be better off without and ban. (The Nantucket Historical Trust is installing gas street lamps in the old town and is planning to bury all telephone and electric wiring in the section now established by law as "The Historic District.") The shops lining Main Street have been kept largely unobtrusive, like those of Williamsburg's Duke of Gloucester Street. Finally, the people one met there seemed often to have a distinction and quality of cultivation not conspicuous in many of the winter residents of the other summer resorts I had seen, and—what was most unexpected and agreeable—they met one's eye in a friendly way, acknowledging one's existence. Perhaps an insular habitat has had its effect and, like the birds of Galápagos, they view the interloper without alarm.

While trying to brew a warming decoction from a tea-bag and a cup of tepid water at a soda fountain, I fell into conversation with a woman beside me of blonde and ruddy complexion and of about my own age, it turned out, whose sparkling grey eyes and youthful animation made me think less dismally of the stage of life we had jointly arrived at. A mainlander, she was married to a Nantucketer, a fisherman. In the summer, while her husband operated a charter boat for sports-fishermen, she took tourists around the island in a Volkswagen bus. During the scalloping season, which was now, they went out together in a smaller second boat. While her husband hauled in the drags—iron scoops with nets made of steel rings attached to their hind edge, somewhat like half of a woman's chain-mail handbag—she did the culling. It could be uncomfortable work in an eighteen-foot boat unprotected from the raw wind, but they managed to gain a fair return from it. Scalloping was an important local occupation; the scallops were the small, sweet, bay kind. The islanders could not afford to neglect any source of income, she said; it was not easy to make a living in Nantucket. By January or February, before the spring work on the summer people's houses began, many were on relief. I asked if she had not found that the hardships of scalloping were made a little easier to bear, anyhow, by the knowledge of how much a scalloper contributed to the picturesqueness of the local scene. She replied that it had helped in the beginning though not much thereafter. But, she went on, everything in life was relative, and being out in the open boat in the sleet surely made you appreciate the small comforts when you came in—the warm, dry clothes, the hot drink. One thing was evident: she thrived on it.

In the morning, I rode to the outermost, seaward bulge of the island, due east. That is where the village of Siasconset is located, the one that, as I afterward learned, the inhabitants mean when they speak of Sconset. From Nantucket town, it is the most distant point on the island accessible by road— about eight miles. The country going east struck me as being as lonely in character as it had when I went south, as lonely as only open, undulating country, permitting distant views to a bare horizon, can be. Pine barrens gave way to barrens of bear oaks, the tallest only twice my height, and these to fields where the narrowly-plumed seedstalks of the broom sedge vibrated in the breeze. The wonder was that the land should have had even this clothing of vegetation. Small white pines planted along the highway two miles from the shore were sered from salt spray, which is said to blow clear across the island. (That it does so is easy to believe. Even a four-mile-an-hour zephyr has been found to carry microscopic droplets half a mile while salt spray driven by hurricane winds will completely destroy foliage as far as ten miles inland.) There was nothing particular in the natural scene to induce cheer, or in the occasional passing cars, some bearing parties of the idiotically-attired deer-hunters, but I pedaled along in a state

of extreme contentment. On that island out in the Atlantic—
Nanticut, the "Far Away Land" of the Indians—I was beyond
reach of all long-neglected tasks and, except for the contents
of the Army field bag, without possessions. Even the bicycle
was someone else's. It was a sense of freedom that made my
heart light. What we own, I reflected, owns us. Yet we devote
ourselves to acquiring things. We go through life like the
tortoise that carries the elephant that bears the world on its
back, and such energy as we have to spare from staggering
beneath the load is devoted to adding to it. Heigh-ho! Would
I remember the lesson, or, remembering it, be guided accordingly in the future? Almost certainly not.

Between the sweep of the grey and brown landscape and
the belt of champagne-colored beachgrass leading to the sands
of the shore, Siasconset was a ghost of a village. It was
ghostlike in its near emptiness; for all sound there was the
distant knocking of a hammer and the stridulations of a
starling trying, in the immemorial manner of its kind, to find
its singing voice. It was ghostly in the uniform grey of its
houses, nearly all of them closed for the winter, a few with
herring gulls perched along the rooftree like ornaments on a
bedstead. And to anyone who knew the American stage half
a century and more ago it would have been inhabited by
ghosts. As a summer colony of actors, Siasconset before
World War I had no rival. One reads that in its heyday it
numbered fifty members of the Lambs, the great theatrical
club of New York. But time passes. Their names stir only
vague echoes in my memory, and to a party of carpenters I
fell in with the past seemed to speak even more faintly,
though several were older than I. They did know, however,
that the house they were reshingling—one of the larger ones
along the bluff north of the village—had been built for Bertha
Galland, who they explained was an old-time actress, and they
presented me with one of the old shingles as a souvenir.

Actually, it was because of the shingles that I had stopped
to talk to them. I had wanted to be sure I had got it right,
that the shingles that gave Nantucket houses—and many on
Cape Cod and eastern Long Island—their characteristic color
were of white cedar, which without requiring stain or paint
weathers to a soft grey. I was told they were and that they
were good for from twenty-five to thirty years without any
treatment. I also learned that the dark-brown shingles in which

many houses were sheathed were of weathered red cedar—juniper. Later we met again around a table in a little grocery store which to my surprise I found open and serving hot coffee. They told me what they knew about the actors' colony but seemed to associate it with the stars of the silent films. "Mary Pickford had one of the little houses," said the senior of the party.

The antique dwellings were small even for cottages. Descended from the fishermen's shanties that had constituted the original settlement, they snuggled close to the ground, some under a mantle of creepers, hardly a line in absolute plumb, modest to the point of self-effacement and altogether irresistible. On a rail fence in front of one of them, a climbing rose bore a flower still retaining life and color at its center. . . . Below the village the beach was strewn with the bleached remains of a red algae resembling the frayed ends of hemp rope and with skates' egg-sacs, those small, rectangular black purses with stringlike projections from the corners which make one think, somehow, that the Devil has passed that way. The sun shone with a wan light, but bravely, through the washed-out overcast the southeast breeze had brought, and the sea beneath it, wearing a silken sheen, was as dead still as if it lay under a spell. Where the road ended in the sand, the vanished human race had tossed out the inevitable testimony to its visitation—bottles, crushed cigarette packages, flattened cardboard cups—but it had also left, freshly lettered in the sand, a legend that, as its final word of parting, made one think better of it and like a beam of sunlight cleaving the clouds transfigured the somewhat forlorn scene it had quitted: I LOVE YOU.

Behind the older part of the village was the Casino, what we today in our pretentious way would call the cultural center, a sprawling structure of the prevailing driftwood grey, built in 1900. Passing it, I was brought up short. "Hello," I said, "what are *you* doing here?" On the bough of a tree was a mockingbird. It was hunched up and silent, hardly to be recognized as the swashbuckler of the bold white eye I knew at home but indubitably a mocker. I was touched by sentiment. But love of nature is a one-way affair and can be frustrating. The errant bird could throw no light on how it got here or whether it was alone, and it hardly would have if it could have. It recognized no bond between us and flew off indifferently just before I could take its picture.

A mile and a half to the north the bluff rises to a cliff like that of Cape Cod. This is Sankaty Head and it is crowned by a white lighthouse with a broad red cummerbund. It is also the end of the moraine. Signs warn the public back from the brink, and the drop is beyond doubt a dizzy one, a sheer eighty-five feet.

Bicycling farther, along a sandy lane, past more deserted summer houses, I found a way down to the beach where the embankment was lower, through a gutted ravine. Embedded in the side of it was a grapefruit-sized rock of pink granite exactly like that of Mount Desert. I wondered if the ice-sheet could have brought it from there. I picked up one of pepper-and-salt granite for the collection.

The face of the cliff presented a picture of the disorderly mixture of sand, clays and rocks typical of glacial till, as the geologists call it. As well as being undermined by the sea, it was being eroded by rains. One so far personified the great ice-age relic as to be affected with a slight uneasiness by its brute insensibleness of the injuries it was enduring, which were wasting it away. While I watched, a stone dislodged by the thawing of the night's frost rolled down the slope, as one had at Cape Cod. It was like the ticking-off of a second of geological time.

A granite rock, a fistful of sand in a candy-wrapper, photographs that I should puzzle over in later years, half-a-dozen bear-oak acorns it took me a mile of searching to find (and that subsequently refused to germinate)—I was more trophy-bent than any deer-hunter. But Nantucket was hard to leave behind.

Woods Hole, where I spent the night in a parking lot by the ferry-slip, is located at the end of the snout-shaped Falmouth peninsula. It is almost surrounded by the waters of Buzzards Bay and Vineyard Sound. Nearby, directly across from the tip of the peninsula, is the low, forested shore of the first of the Elizabeth Islands, formed—like the shore of Cape Cod to the north—of the moraine left by the Buzzards Bay lobe of the ice-sheet. The Woods Hole Oceanographic Institution, an independent research organization owing 90 per cent of its support to the Federal Government, is like a college with a campus bounded by yacht basins. For biologists, physical scientists, chemists, geologists and meteorologists working in the now booming field of oceanography, on our last terrestrial frontier, it must offer almost ideal conditions. I strolled around the grounds in the dark, impressed by the bookstore (not a feature of every American town) and by the intelligent-looking couples, women two-by-two, and single men entering one of the buildings as if for a concert but presumably for a lecture. I loitered in the foyers with my nose pressed against the glass of cases containing diverse exhibits: a huge bas-relief model of the east coast of North America with the continental shelf sloping to its sudden drop into the abyss, its edge cut by mysterious canyons; photographs of the institution's four seagoing vessels; containers used in taking samples of sea-water at various levels; nets for capturing marine specimens; pictures taken at depths of miles. By an exit door, two clocklike instruments with gently vacillating hands indicated the speed and direction of the wind outside. Oh happy breed, I thought, the highly-evolved men and women who worked with these instruments, in these laboratories, in these ships on distant seas, who dealt with ascertainable fact, who knew what they were doing and were doing it with system and precision, who knew what they were seeking and would recognize it when they found it, who were extending the province of knowledge! I had a chat with an expert on sharks, who, surrounded by specimens in formaldehyde, was still in his office, waiting to give a talk to a busload of high-school students delayed en route. He had sharkdom at his finger tips, I could tell; he was on top of his specialty. He had a good chance of being someday king of the world, sharkwise. What confidence and serenity must be his!

I was dismayed by the contrast between life as it would seem to be lived in Woods Hole and life as I lived it. For the sake of my peace of mind, I undertook to persuade myself that scientists despite appearances might not be immune to the plagues of the human condition or beyond reach of human frailties. Maybe they too became upset over trifles, chafed over stringencies imposed by insufficiency of means, were sometimes distracted from the selfless pursuit of truth by thoughts of personal preferment or the inclination to take it easy. Could I believe that? . . .

By misadventure I had arrived on a Friday night and the expectation I had had of instructive interviews faded with

the discovery that the institution would be closed for the next
two days. The question on which I had most hoped for
enlightenment was what was happening to the shellfish of the
east coast—the lobsters, clams and oysters. When I had
managed to obtain the name of the expert in the field I tele-
phoned him at his home. Stating what was on my mind and
adding that one heard alarming reports on the subject, I
asked him if he could possibly spare a few minutes on the
morrow.

"Well, now," he exclaimed heartily, "Saturday is bath night,
you know. Anyhow, nothing is happening to the shellfish.
Every generation thinks the one preceding it had things a lot
better, that's all."

I thanked him in a just-before-hanging-up voice, at which
he spoke up quickly again.

"There's a book on *The Marine Fisheries of North Carolina*
—that's the title. While it's concerned with North Carolina
particularly, it has a lot of general information."

It was by no means altogether true that nothing is happening to the shellfish, but to find out just what is happening was
to prove a great deal more difficult than one would have
expected.

I was awakened at four in the morning by the sound of a
fine rain whipping against the aluminum roof and of a slow
dripping on the counter beside me. It rained all that day,
most of which I spent en route to Newport. The weather did
not, however, conceal the attractiveness of the country bordering Buzzards Bay to the north of Woods Hole. Steeply
hilly and grown up in vigorous forest, it was a good deal like
Westchester County or western Connecticut except that in
place of outcroppings of bedrock there were the great boulders of the moraine everywhere protruding through the soil.
I thought that if it were a matter of spending the rest of
one's life on the Cape, one could do worse than to live here,
preferably in one of the mansions overlooking the bay from
half their fifty windows and their splendid grounds from the
other half. A moisture-laden air-mass with a temperature of
50 degrees had rolled in from the direction of Bermuda with
consequences easily foreseeable when it reached New England
waters. These were just ten degrees colder than the air according to a chart with daily entries maintained on the wall beside
the anemometer at the Oceanographic Institution. The mois-

ture in the air condensed; all the inlets visible from the highway were overlaid with mist. The harbor of New Bedford was clear when I pulled into the small, bare park at the head of it, but before I had finished lunch a fog had stolen inland and erased it. However, feeling it would be wrong to pass through this great fishing port without even a glimpse of what went on there, I had already marked the location of the dock around which the most boats seemed to be and I had no trouble finding it.

It was a very big dock indeed with perhaps thirty vessels tied up two and three deep along its three outer sides. They were steel-hulled vessels ninety feet long and broad of beam with a great deal of deck, sturdy masts and derricks, and coils of net inside the bulwarks. One of them was being made ready for departure. Four of the crew were working on the deck and a fifth—a big brawny Scandinavian—was on the dock attending to the hawsers. It was not just a matter of casting off and pulling away; *N—* had to be eased out from between the dock and another vessel moored to her off side and the latter maneuvered into the place she was vacating. I found out from the Scandinavian that they were going out to Georges Bank and would be gone for nine days. The fog evidently posed no problem; like all her sisters, *N—* had a radar antenna atop her bridge. I was astonished that fishing craft would be so equipped, but the Scandinavian said that in the foggy waters of the New England coast you couldn't stay in business nowadays without radar. *N—* herself was a new vessel, having been brought down from Maine, where she had been built, only the month before. She had cost $175,000 and her owner had two others, I was told. I asked if he went out in one of them. There was laughter on all sides at this. *"Him* go out? He sits in the office and counts the money!"

At the suggestion of a well-dressed bystander with whom I started talking when *N—* had pulled out, I dropped in at a beer joint across the street, being assured that it was patronized by men from the fishing boats and that I should hear some "rare talk" there. I may have at that. The trouble was I could not understand a quarter of what I heard.

The saloon (and that is what it was) was dimly lighted. It had a bar along one side and tables and chairs occupying the remainder. After getting out of my wet raincoat I sat down

at the near end of the bar beside a small, downbeaten-seem-
ing man in his fifties with a round face and a chin mashed
up into it. He looked like a secondary character on the stage
of the Abbey Theatre. He also sounded like one except that,
being groggy with drink, he was even less comprehensible. It
cost me two bottles of beer to find that out—one for him
and one for me. When he started trying to cadge a sandwich
on the grounds that his stomach was burning something
terrible—which I did not doubt but considered he should have
thought of before putting in for the beer—I moved off to the
other end of the bar. There I was welcomed by, and promptly
installed between, two other seamen in a state of volubility
and of readiness for a listener. I congratulated myself on
being now about to get the New Bedford fishing story, with
full authentic detail—but prematurely. I was little better off
than Alice sitting between the Mad Hatter and the March
Hare. The Mad Hatter, on my left, who put one in mind of
a debauched matinee idol, was only somewhat less drunk than
the Dormouse I had just left to his empty beer bottle. The
March Hare—and he looked a little like that, too—was a
Norwegian with an affectionate and gentle demeanor which I
doubted any quantity of drink would affect; the difficulty
here was that he had a purring accent that was all but un-
intelligible. I did understand him to say, with a sweep of his
hand around the room, in which a dozen other seamen were
sitting and drinking or reading newspapers, that his friend here
was the best skipper of the lot of them. The friend demurred.
He wasn't a skipper, he said. "But I'm damned good—except
that this stuff's got a hold on me. But I'm breaking myself
of it." I looked to see if he were speaking ironically, but
evidently he was not.

On the wall behind the bar hung a small blackboard with
two columns of ships' names on it, one headed DRAGGERS
and the other SCALLOPERS, and with each name followed
by a figure in the thousands. After struggling for a while to
follow the talk of the two men I pointed to the blackboard
and expressed surprise at the size of the cargoes the ships had
brought in, as I took the figures to signify—correctly, it
appeared. Some ran over forty thousand pounds. But the
matinee idol said they were nothing. "Those ships can carry
a hundred thousand pounds." "Draggers," I learned, meant
fishing boats. I said it seemed an odd thing to call them

since dragging was just what scallopers did. He agreed that it was. I asked what kind of fish they were bringing in. He said to read out the names of the boats and he'd tell me. So I did, and his answer in each case was "Yellowtail" (a kind of flounder) until I came to *Skipjack*. "Ah, that's different," he said. But we were interrupted then and I never heard what *Skipjack*'s cargo was.

The Norwegian had been over here for twenty-five years. Speaking with very little movement of the lips (that was part of the trouble), he said he had begun in boats as an engineman. There had been a lot of work to do on the diesels when they first came in but since then they had been so improved that now they practically took care of themselves and there wasn't much for an engineman to do. He took any job that was open now, on the deck or even as a cook. So much I understood. But when he started talking about recently having brought a fishing boat up from Florida, I missed what he said of the circumstances. They had come around Cape Hatteras, he said, and it was just like Cape Cod: storms came up without warning and there you were. He said they lost a couple of boats every year out of New Bedford. On my asking how, he made a motion with his hands of a wave breaking over a boat. He was going out himself in an hour or two, for a week or more.

An affable gent with thin grey hair, bearing a resemblance —superficial, to be sure—to a banker, presented himself at the bar and was immediately addressed by the seaman on my left. "What are you doing these days, Pop?" Pop, in a modest but straightforward manner, cited the endeavor that preoccupied him as, he indicated, it always had. There was outspoken skepticism all around as to his ability to succeed in it at his age but he was visibly unbothered by the raillery. An unfrocked banker enjoying his freedom: that was what he was.

Most of the patrons seemed to have money on the horses. At least I was told that it was the race returns one of them was trying to get on a radio behind the bar while the others stood around waiting. My dissipated neighbor had crossed the room behind me and, most surprisingly, had the jukebox in an embrace and seemed to be struggling to maneuver it out into the open. The proprietor, who was serving at the bar, asked dispassionately what the hell he thought he was trying to do. Bald and smooth-faced, he looked Jewish and seemed a not unkind person but a realist, probably. Yes, I thought with a second look at his inexpressive eyes, definitely a realist. "I'm trying to find the wire to unplug the goddamn thing so we can hear," the seaman replied. "You couldn't find your ass," the proprietor stated matter-of-factly, and went over and silenced the Stentor.

Said the Norwegian, with a nod at his friend, "You wouldn't know him at sea. He's entirely different. There's no better man there. With him in the powerhouse, I always say to myself I've got nothing to worry about. Yes, with him in the powerhouse, I always know I've got nothing to worry about." He wanted to pay for my second bottle of beer, but I would not let him. He waved a two-dollar bill. "It's no good out there," he said. But I was firm.

Driving off through New Bedford's dripping, ugly streets, I thought with commiseration of the men who endured so much on the cold and sometimes terrifying North Atlantic only to spend so drearily and so emptily the time and money they gained. The Norwegian had spoken at length of his American wife and of the trip back to Norway they had made together. Yet this was how he chose to spend his last hours —killing time and wasting money—before another week or ten days of deprivation and travail. The saloon was not essentially different, I suspected—though tamer, very likely—from others of fifty, a hundred or two hundred years ago. I wondered if this was what the sea did to men or whether it was that the sea, repelling by its harsh terms those who could earn a livelihood serving any other master, became the province of those who, defeated by a bent toward self-destruction, took to it as a last resort.

The outstanding fact of the state of Rhode Island and Providence Plantations (the divine law of compensation having seen to it that the smallest state should have the longest name) is the deep recess of the coast which it encompasses, to which, in fact, it is an adjunct. Narragansett Bay, which may also be considered a notable feature of the east coast as a whole, extends nearly thirty miles inland and, like the great bays of Maine, contains some considerable islands—three, to be precise—and a few small ones. At its upper extremity is Providence, at its easternmost Fall River, Massachusetts, and at its entrance, exactly in the middle, occupying the southern end of Rhode Island itself (now called Aquidneck Island), Newport. The bay was scooped by the ice-sheet out of the young sedimentary rock that, in contrast with the harder, igneous and metamorphic rock underlying most of New England, forms Narragansett basin— geologically a "down-folded trough." Rhode Island and Conanicut Island, its neighbor to the west, owe their existence to the hardness of their bedrock, which held fast as the ice dug deep on either side of them; there is granite at the seaward tips of both.

At Newport, as if someone had forgotten to turn it off, the drizzle persisted desultorily. However, arriving in a city you have never seen before, and which confronts you with the question of what it is all about, is stimulating regardless of the weather. What Newport was all about was abundantly evident in the multiplicity of inconsiderable shops, the number of sailors to be seen in the downtown area, the dark bars along the dark street by the waterfront with more sailors lounging inside with their girls or playing table-shuffleboard, the dock where destroyers were crowded side by side like cows in a barn, the miles of barracks and of servicemen's housing. Newport was a purveyor to a naval base.

But what of that other Newport, the onetime multimillionaires' preserve protected by invisible but nearly unscalable barriers to the more *nouveaux venus* of the *parvenus*, manned by implacable matrons armed with snub-machine guns? "The Oldest Resort in America," say signs leading into the city. And it is an old one. By the middle of the eighteenth century numerous aristocratic Southern families, mostly from Georgia, South Carolina and Baltimore, were coming here for the summer, drawn by the pleasant climate and the elegance of the town's society, noted even in Europe, for which its lucrative sea-borne commerce (including slaving and privateering) paid the bills. After the Civil War, Newport became the Bath of wealthy Northerners, though it was a Savannahian, Ward McAllister, coiner of the phrase "The Four Hundred," who reigned as king (like Beau Nash in Bath a century before) over the gay post-war generation at the resort and a Baltimorean, Harry Lehr, who, seconded by Mrs.

William Astor, did so in the era of unrestrained opulence that began about 1890. . . . As I drove around and about and saw nothing but a blend of Navy and small commerce, I wondered where on earth the legendary Newport was. Then I found myself driving out of town on a road called Ocean Drive. . . .

I am not sure what I expected or whether I should have been much moved one way or another had I made the excursion on an ordinary sunny afternoon. As it was, the landscape of which I found myself an insignificant and awestruck detail was like none I could have anticipated. Shakespearean was the only term adequate to the power of its mood. In the failing light, in the mist of rain, I drove along a shore formed of rock ledges up to thirty feet high jutting out into the sea. Along the shore or set back far apart on what appeared in the gathering dusk to be a wild and lonely heath were the mansions—no, not mansions, merely—the castles of the rich. Dark but for a very few lights in the scores of windows where presumably the caretakers lived, they lifted the line of the horizon as if they formed part of the earth, like craggy eminences of the living rock. I turned off onto a dirt lane that ran out onto one of the promontories to brew up some tea while I came to terms with this extraordinary scene. Judging by the quantity of beer cans around me, the spot was very much in the public domain, but the only car sharing it with me stood some way off, a low-slung sedan containing an even-lower-slung couple.

I might have been back in the heroic gloom of the Middle Ages. "Brooding" was the term given to such somber edifices as those summer palaces, I thought, and, in their more than human grandeur, brooding they seemed to be—brooding on the secrets of time and destiny. I could have thought myself on the desert heath near Forres about to hear Macbeth hailed Thane of Cawdor. Best at this juncture, I reflected, to serve science, and I got out to examine the rock ledge that led, as down an irregular stairway, to the water. The seas were washing in over the lower shelves out of a fog-shrouded spirit-realm, with sounds of gurgling, plopping and cascading much more varied than those of waves on a beach of sand. From out of the mists came the repeated blurt of a horn-buoy and, half beseeching, half menacing, the foghorn of a ship inching her way anxiously, blindly, out into the night. . . .

The ledge was of an extremely dense and heavy slatelike rock that split both along the bedding-planes and across them at an angle to form rhomboidal blocks with ax-sharp edges. Only where it lay within reach of the waves were its corners rounded and smooth. I collected a block of it and some of the faintly greenish-lavender grey sand of a little beach which had formed in a cove. From overhead, out of the heavy sky —from whence Harper might have cried " 'Tis time, 'tis time!"—came the piteous, lost *deeah, deeah, dee-dee-dee-deeah!* of a killdeer.

Where was I going to spend the night? I tried to screw up my nerve to apply at one of the great houses for permission to lay over on the grounds somewhere, but the proposal sounded so like the first step in a transparent scheme to case the estate for a burglary that I could not bring myself to go through with it. Having tentatively decided to utilize the parking lot of a large, modern school incorporating what looked like a glass roundhouse, I was waiting at an intersection, uncertain which road led back to town, when a car with a man and a woman in the front seat stopped to ask if I needed help. The upshot was an invitation to park overnight in their driveway and to drop in for refreshments before I turned in. So on my return, after having dinner in a little park where some of the chaste abodes of Newport's merchant princes of two centuries ago still stand, I did so. The Mac-Auliffes turned out to be a most hospitable couple. I sat for a long time with them over milk and massive slices of layer cake talking of Newport's golden half-century, era of the New York financiers, of Lorillards, Stuyvesants, Tiffanys, Rhinelanders, Van Rensselaers, Belmonts, Astors, Vanderbilts, Millses, Morgans, of liveried footmen in knee breeches and powdered hair, gold bathroom fixtures, parties costing in the six figures, of incredible splendor and ostentation. What had finished it was probably not so much the graduated income-tax as the Crash of 1929 and the drying-up of the pool of servants in the classless society. As I knew, most of the great houses were closed up today or were in the possession of schools. Here, as in other wealthy resorts, Capitalism's loss had been Catholicism's gain. (The problem of how tax bills are to be met on elephantine properties can be solved in a trice by removing the properties from the tax rolls for the benefit of the Church.) "The Breakers," the Italian Renaissance palace built by Cornelius Vanderbilt in 1895, had been leased to the Newport Preservation Society for a dollar and opened to the public as a museum. "Marble House," built by the William K. Vanderbilts at a cost of $11,000,000, was sold in 1932 for $100,000, and "Seaview Terrace," which had cost $2,000,000, for $8,000 in 1949. That very evening a Christmas party for eight hundred guests was being given in the Berwinds' mansion, "The Elms"—leased for the occasion by an electronics corporation. . . . And there the great piles were as I had seen them, ornate beyond description, shadowy forms under low-hanging clouds ghost-lighted by reflection from the nearby demopolis, relics of a day that had gone over the same horizon as the ice-sheet that created the moraines. Newport in its prime would have been hard to take, I have no doubt, its glitter hard as steel, the whole edifice built undisguisedly on money, hostesses clawing at one another's backs to get on top and elsewhere millions working at starvation wages to make it possible. Yet in its passing something important was to be regretted, and I was still wondering, half consciously, what it was when I fell asleep.

A clear sky after rain! The heart takes wing at the very thought of it. Mine leapt up when a star in a black sky met my first look out of the window in the morning. Before sunrise I had shaved, dressed, had breakfast and driven to "The Breakers," which the MacAuliffes had urged me not to miss and where, they said, I could pick up the famous Cliff Walk, which wound along the shore. It was one of those dawns of a freshness that partakes of the first creation when the earth has the quality of a novel and untried idea. Where puddles had stood in the road there now was ice and the air was frosty, but the beatific purpose that had triumphed in the universe took the edge from the cold and the windless morning felt mild. I was transported. A convert to the True Faith shrived of his sins and beholding before him the literal image of salvation might feel so. The world had come through the nighttime of the spirit, been purified and emerged into the dawn of immortality.

A lingering stratum of cloud dissolved the division of sea and sky, as if they had been sponged out along their juncture. Above it, all the way around, an orange-pink flush melted into the blue. The castles of the great were hazy shapes on the sky line—except "The Breakers," which reposed in its might behind me, magnificent and lonely in the emptiness of the seventy rooms behind the storied loggias. While I stood there, looking out beyond the black abutments of rock, jagged and formidable, and as if of martial purpose, an orange sliver of sun appeared above the band of cloud and rapidly swelled to a disc, slightly flattened. Wherever one looked, the earth appeared touched with surprise and delight, charmed by its deliverance from the powers of darkness. One could conceive of the cosmos as a translucent sea shell and creation its precious contents. Close above the blue sea that rippled in silver with the light of the morning flew V's of cormorants, responsive to their cue in the master score. (The cormorant is a bird that seems to stand midway between a goose and a raven.) On the reefs of rock the gulls stood about amid the golden filigree of the wrack as if dazed with wonder, their whiteness crystallizing the purity of the day. One had a sense of being free at last in a world of boundless potential, a world weightless in space. Beside me, a song sparrow had come out of the bed of admirable salt-spray rose that bordered the walk and, plump and fussy, was picking for seeds at a desiccated beach goldenrod. The midget, I could almost believe, was overwhelmed by the sublime spectacle and, like a person present at a greatly moving occasion to which he knows himself unable to rise, took refuge in an elaborate busyness.

When, later, I drove away, past the wrought-iron gates of "The Breakers"—themselves as big as the façade of an ordinary house—I met two nuns coming down the street, a little distance apart, one on either side. In the neighborhood of Salveregina College (successor to the Goelets in the 100-room mansion of "Ochre Court") the presence of these conical figures of black was not unaccountable, but they struck me with amazement. Something in me was left breathless by this display of the colors of death in the face of the consuming glory around us. It seemed to me impious—no, not quite that, but as if the Almighty were being reproved or reprimanded, called to task for so letting himself go in this abandon of loveliness. And perhaps to the Church there would be something reprehensible in such a heavenly indulgence of the senses—a backsliding into the Deity's old pagan ways. It had already occured to me that on such a morn as this—allowing for climatic differences between Cyprus and Aquidneck—Aphrodite arose from the foam, and Aphrodite would be no very welcome guest in any presbytery I knew of.

And lo! I had not driven thirty seconds before, in a manner of speaking, she made her presence known. In front of Vernon Junior College were two chicks in short skirts bearing an urn—probably of coffee. It was impossible to believe that the Most High did not rejoice in them. The Greeks of the great age would certainly have had no doubts on that score. "Thy Will Be Done Through Me": the words were spoken in my mind before I could suppress them.

I used to reason that the automobile had made one positive contribution to our civilization: it afforded, when you were alone in it, a place where you could sing with the full power of your lungs in perfect security. And the time was when, driving along on a morning like this one, I should have put my all into Walter's "Prize Song." But those days were gone. The world had been too much with me for too long; I had been too much concerned with filling each unforgiving minute with sixty seconds' worth of distance run—or, rather, too much concerned over how infrequently I managed to put sixty seconds' worth of distance run in a solid hour. So, in enforced emulation of the song sparrow, I pulled over to the side of the street for coffee and graham crackers, thinking what a mercy it was that neither the black-garbed priesthood of a later age nor the eternally-reckoning, minute-pinching, self-abashed kind of Puritanism I was heir to had descended upon Attica before that miraculous and portentous dawn for mankind had led to Phidias and Praxiteles.

But then, under way again, and on my way home, I thought, Why not?

> *Morgen-lich leuch-tend,*
> *I-im ro-o-sigen Schein. . . .*

It seemed to be as feasible as it had been in the past.

More and more I fall under the spell of rocks. But as my susceptibility grows, so does my frustration when I am unable to tell anything about those I encounter, which is to say when there is no one to tell me. The cross sections of rock in the cuts through which the Connecticut Turnpike passes as it skirts the coast made me chafe at my ignorance, so dramatic and varied were the juxtapositions of formations they revealed. Inquiries after I had returned home led to a *Preliminary Geological Map of Connecticut*, put out by the state Geological and Natural History Survey, and from this, though it was small in scale, I learned that I had seen a fair sampling of the pre-Triassic metamorphic rock of which Connecticut is chiefly composed—mostly gneisses, some running out into the Sound in rounded ledges. (Gneiss is a highly metamorphosed rock, one which has been drastically recrystallized under intense heat or pressure. It is very varied, streaked or banded and granitelike—and sometimes granitic in origin.) Near New Haven, where the terrain is very hilly, you come to sedimentary Triassic rocks formed mainly of alluvial deposits (thousands of feet thick in central Connecticut) and consisting "largely of pink to red arkosic sandstone, silt stone, and conglomerate." Between Norfolk and Darien you cross an outlying section of a field of "granite bodies" in "mica quartzite [metamorphosed sandstone] and mica shist [a grainy, silky, much metamorphosed rock]." . . .

But this knowledge, Olympian at best, came too late to help and I could only wish as I drove along that state agencies or universities could put out guidebooks identifying the rock of specific cuts through which main highways pass and explaining its significance.*

Abend-lich däm-mernd. . . .

---

* There are, I subsequently discovered, already a number of such guidebooks, notably for the Pennsylvania Turnpike, U. S. 40 in Ohio, and especially interesting roads in Oregon.

Long Island

ON THE night of December 23-24, 1811, which had begun mild and calm, ships on Long Island Sound suddenly found themselves in a snowstorm driven by a gale which sent the temperature down almost to zero and blew without respite for twenty-four hours. Before it fell, between fifty and sixty sailing craft had gone down or been driven onto the northern shore of the island, where the bodies of the drowned were found covered with an inch of ice in which the physiognomies of the victims "appeared in all the ghastliness of death."

In the face of such witness of the Sound's exposure to the weather it may seem hardly justified to characterize Long Island proper as surrounded by sheltered waters except for the eastern, or outer, end and some thirty-five miles of the southern shore leading back from it. All is relative, however, and mean as the waves can be that a blast whips up in the Sound, they are scarcely comparable with, say, the terrible seas that took 40 lives and destroyed many substantial houses on the beaches of the Hamptons during the equinoctial hurricane of 1938.

My small daughters preferred the shores of the sheltered waters to those of the outer beach. Until the cold set in, there were tiny crabs, baby fish and baby eels, two inches long, to be netted in the shallows and kept for a time in a jar and the shells were of a more eye-catching kind than those along the ocean. Of these, none so arouses an acquisitive mania in the newcomer as the jingle-shells. Those you find are the domed upper valves (the flattish, lower ones generally remain fixed to—and fitted to—the stone or larger shell to which the little mollusk attaches itself) and these, from half an inch to two inches in diameter, and varying in color from a silvery

lemon-white, like sherbet, to lemon-yellow and tangerine, and semitranslucent besides, are like flower-petals fashioned by a lapidarist. The colors are so citric that the sight of a bowl of them causes the glands beneath the jaw to salivate painfully. Occasionally a gun-metal-colored one is found. To see them, for the first time, sprinkled along the shore is like finding money scattered in the street. You fall upon them, filling your pockets and baffled by their abundance: you cannot collect them all; neither can you be resigned to leaving them lying there.

As beautiful, but less glittering, were the scallop-shells, works of art, these, with shades ranging from porcelain-white to carnelian—almost red, you tell yourself—and iron grey, a near-slate grey, the colors often in bands that arc across the ridges like the bands on a folding fan or that sometimes are fragmented to give a calico effect. Scallops are not only decorative; they are the only free-swimming bivalves (*Time* once described the panicky flight of a school of them from a starfish as like a stampede of agitated dentures) and they have eyes, a row of them that stare through the slit between the valves, spookily, I should think.

The most abundant of all were the boatshells or slipper shells, which resemble lifeboats an inch and a half long, decked at one end. Scientists have named the boatshell *Crepidula fornicata*, obviously because of the way it affixes itself to the backs of scallops or other shells or of its own kind, but whether they have done so with solemn literal-mindedness or puckishly, probably only a taxonomist could tell us.

With the scallops and boatshells you could count on finding whelks, the pear-shaped marine snails, resembling conches, which are the largest mollusks of the northern shores. I had found the three together at Brant Point, in the harbor of Nantucket, and wherever there were quantities of one there seemed always to be the other two. At Accabonac Harbor, near the spot on the shore of Gardiner's Bay at which visitors to the manor of Gardiner's Island used to light a fire to signal a boat to come get them, empty boatshells formed windrows at high-water-mark and whelks must have been unusually common, for their broken shells littered the asphalt road along the spit that formed the harbor. Elsewhere gulls dropped bivalves on paved surfaces to crack their shells but here they dropped knobbed whelks. In so doing they were paying back some of their debt to the bivalves, for knobbed whelks are great destroyers of oysters and clams. They drill through the shells of their prey with their rasplike tongues and extract the meat through the hole or, it is said, seizing a clam in their fleshy "foot," fracture its shell by hammering it with the rim of their own.

The total helplessness of a clam or oyster singled out by a whelk, moon-snail or starfish, the inexorability with which it is slowly ingested in the embrace of the predator, is not too pleasant to think about. It is futile to impose human terms upon nature and irrational to choose sides in nature's conflicts, especially on the basis of innocent victim and heartless killer. Such logic would require the condemnation of mankind itself as the first order of business. Still, it is difficult not to take some satisfaction in the knowledge that whelks as they flow forward, alert to the current of water from its outlet siphon by which a clam's presence beneath the sand is betrayed, are sometimes intercepted by that doughty customer, the blue crab. Of course there is little to commend itself to the squeamish in the fate that then befalls the whelks: its captor breaks its shell away with its powerful claws and consumes it. As for the blue crab itself, colorful *boulevardier* of the coast from Cape Cod southward, with green carapace and bright blue legs sometimes marked with scarlet, it is—ominous words!—"the common crab of commerce," even, it is said, "our most important sea-food product, next to the lobster." Annually, millions are dropped alive, fighting to the last, into boiling water. . . . If the way of transgressors is hard, the way of moralists is not much less so.

Along the sheltered shores and even among the rocks at Montauk Point were quantities of a green sea plant that grew attached to stones. Rather fleshy, it put out fingerlike branches, up to a foot long, from a short trunk, rather like the finger sponges *(Chalina* and *Desmacidon)* that wash up all along the Atlantic coast. It puzzled me greatly, for I found it impossible to track down in any book. Finally I learned from a marine biologist that it was a *Codium,* one of the green algae, which I had eliminated as a possibility because Long Island was well north of the range ascribed to it. Apparently (like the green crab and mantis shrimp, which in recent years have ascended the coast of New England) it has

been moving northward. On Long Island its habits tend to be
suicidal. As the plants grow they present more and more
surface to the waves, like ships hoisting sail, until ultimately
those affixed to the smaller stones drag their anchors and are
washed up on shore, there to shrivel and whiten. The doom
of such attractive plants—they make you think of diminutive
barrel cactus—is sad to contemplate, and while recognizing
the silliness of what I was up to I could not help picking
them up as I walked along the shore and heaving them back
in the water. The beltlike brown algae—*Laminarias*—which
grow off Montauk Point are constantly meeting their death
in the same way, only these, instead of dragging an inanimate
stone with them, are likely to come clutching the shell of a
luckless and innocent mussel, which expires with its abductor.

I made a point of visiting a number of the inner beaches.
One was Sunken Meadows State Park, on the Sound, to which
the parkway descends steeply from the wooded hills of the
moraine. The main attraction there at the time was a flock of
several hundred herring gulls feeding in the mussel beds on
the stony flats exposed by the ebbing tide and demonstrating
that getting a meal was not simply a matter of flying up with
a mussel and letting it fall; the process often had to be
repeated several times before the victim's shell would break
and the dropper, while always following close behind, would
even so sometimes lose the prize to an evidently higher-
ranking gull. There was Long Beach, on Shelter Island Sound,
which I remember for the scoters. The scoters are the draft
horses of the duck world. Rather large-headed and very
chunky on the wing, they drop heavily into the water with
a *ker-plunk* and a high splash. The white-winged scoters have
eyes set in a slanted white slash-mark, which gives them a
cruel, sinister, oriental appearance. The surf scoters, on the
other hand, with white patches on the nape of the neck and
forehead and a beak like an inflated artificial, orange-pink
nose, look as if they were turned out for a comic masquerade.
And there was Northwest Harbor, east of Sag Harbor. There
the eelgrass—one of the few marine members of the class of
flowering plants—had washed up on shore in such masses that
for a mile you might have been walking on a mattress of
dusky-brown packing material. (In fact, collecting it for
mattress-stuffing used to be a business.) A ridge of flake-ice
edged the shore, slipperier than soap-flakes. In the desiccating

northwest wind the blue water had a gemlike hardness and nothing alive was abroad but some gulls which seemed the last of their kind.

There was always something of interest; and for a biologist, indeed, the inner tidal flats are likely to be much more rewarding than the outer beaches, where even in summer most of the animal life is hidden in the sand. Yet I always felt a letdown on the backwaters. The wind blew and the tasseled fishing-poles of the reeds, edging the shore in close-packed stands, bent to it resistantly. A myrtle warbler, flushed from the now leafless bayberry, was snatched away and fluttered into cover a hundred feet to leeward. You picked your way among the flotsam of the shore in which, now and again, like a half-buried German helmet on a battlefield, was the cara-pace of a horseshoe crab, one of nature's outstanding suc-cesses, a marine creature at home in the tropic waters of the Caribbean and the frigid Labrador current off Nova Scotia, in bays and in the ocean, a relative of the spiders whose near ancestors dominated the seas in the long ago when the first coherent fossil record was being written. But the flat shield of the water and its wintry margins seem desolate and forsaken. You feel yourself a straggler in this world. You come to the point when you can hold off no longer from crossing the spit or the island to the open ocean side. And what a differ-ence is there! Perhaps it is the sheer scope of the sea, which frees you from the particular, throwing open doors within you to other shores, to other lands and other times to which the changeless sea-road leads, setting you at large in the limitless. Or perhaps it is the character of the sea itself, its ceaseless, rhythmical movement, the reiterated and soothing gush of its surf, its attributes of a living force commanding an awe undiminished by your knowledge that any significance in its solemn and sonorous pulse lies far outside the terms of human thought. You can walk for hours on the beach with no sense of loneliness, as a dog may walk with its master, whose company is an end in itself.

From East Hampton, a number of roads run out to the ocean. The most popular is a projection of Main Street that terminates in a parking apron between a quite superior public bathhouse and a well-known and expensive hostelry, the Sea Spray Inn, both closed during the winter. From town, the distance to Main Beach, as it is called, is a mile and a half.

Pedaling between our house and the ocean accounted for most of the eleven hundred miles I put on the odometer of my bicycle—which did not include the nearly daily trips by car when I had Vera's company for a walk on the beach. Except on weekends, when some of those who came up from New York City might be out for a stroll, the beach was deserted. From Montauk Point, twenty miles to the east, to the end of Fire Island, sixty miles to the west, it was probably almost equally deserted. Yet all day long people drove to the beach from town. The turnover was rapid, but at Main Beach there was generally a car or two, or one on its way. The procession might begin with a police-car not long after dawn and continue with mechanics and plumbers in panel trucks, retired businessmen and their wives, elderly widows (for whom East Hampton seems to be a gathering place), fashion-plate girls in sports cars, mothers with children, high-school gallants with their steadies in two-color, underslung sedans with amplified exhausts. It was the same phenomenon I had seen at Bar Harbor and, for that matter, Cape Cod. Few of the visitors so much as opened the door of their cars, unless to let a dog out for a run. But they came. And they sat and looked. Whatever the ocean was doing that day they then knew.

When in a period of nine months you have seldom missed a day's hegira to the sea's edge, you wonder how you are ever going to live away from it. The pull of the sea is like the pull of gravity. It is not a matter of whether you "like" the sea. Those who know it can have no illusions about it, among them being Joseph Conrad, who in one of his prefaces grimly recalled to our minds Shakespeare's "More fell than hunger, anguish or the sea." The sea lays siege to the imagination as the palace of an all-powerful monarch must have enthralled the least subjects of the realm in the days when kings ruled by God's mandate and the question of whether the Throne was to be approved of or disapproved of could scarcely have entered anyone's head. The sea is infinite. The continents are bounded; you come to their end. But to the sea there is no end. True, beyond the sea there is space, beside which the sea's vastness is as nothing. Yet the sea has for us somewhat the character of space, as if it were the expression on earth of those inconceivable distances at which lie the other galaxies, as much of infinity as the human mind can en-

compass—if not more. And while we may hurl a new breed
of explorers to other planets, it is on earth that human des-
tinies will be worked out, and few can doubt that when the
last man-made satellite with loss of altitude plunges into the
atmosphere to be incinerated, the ocean will be there to
receive its ashes—and in the long hereafter also to bear upon
the fringes of its bays and estuaries the timid barks of the
untutored tribesmen who may follow us, beginning the cycle
again.

> *So gladly, from the songs of modern speech*
> *Men turn, and see the stars, and feel the free*
> *Shrill wind beyond the close of heavy flowers;*
> *And, through the music of the languid hours,*
> *They hear like ocean on a western beach*
> *The surge and thunder of the Odyssey.*

You hear that, on our shores, on a southerly wind.

In winter, the wind is prevailingly from the northwest. The
westerlies pile up waves on the other side of the ocean, having
had hundreds of miles in which to roll them forward, but on

our side, blowing against them from off the land, they iron them out. Under a strong northwester the sea off the beach is ruffled by the wind but at the same time flattened beneath its weight. The low waves seem to slink upon the land, becoming noticeable only at the last minute—and I have never seen a day at the beach with no surf whatever—and they break, a mere foot high, with a sudden, exhausted plop, their crests swept back by the breeze in a white veil of mist.

In the wake of the northwester comes the day of faultless blue. The road you are traveling approaches the shore, and then there it is, matching like the two halves of a clamshell, the sky of unfathomable blue, the bluest imaginable blue, and its mirror image, the serene blue sea sparkling in the path of the sun as if myriad lights were flashing on and off on its surface. If you are one of those born with the love of blue you drink it in, as if you were drawing clean, fresh air to the bottom of your lungs. Against such a sky the gulls overhead glow with a luminous intensity of white; you catch your breath at their beauty. When the breeze is stiff, their evident exultation in it seems also of a piece with the quality of the day. Turning their backs to it, they tack across it, shooting out to sea in a grand sweep, down to the surface of the water, there to wheel into the wind, flapping shallowly and easily, and, light as leaves, be whisked aloft. Or, turning after the long glide, they may hang motionless in the face of the blow and, ever so slowly, allow themselves to be deposited, without so much as a drop of splash, upon the surface. Uncomfortable in heavy seas, they find the flat ocean in the lull of a north-wester to their liking. In such a lull, too, when the sun has warmed the earth, a whole flock may soar high on a rising column of air over the land, interweaving among one another on outstretched wings.

In the northern, continental weather that the northwester brings, the ocean leads in the mind's eye to the Arctic and the dazzling wall of the glaciers from which icebergs are calved. The air is pure, as sterile as the ether of space, and you feel yourself in an everlasting openness. Poseidon is in another, distant reach of his empire. In the extreme of such conditions, in midwinter when the wind is cruel, the outer beach may be entirely lifeless. You may walk for an hour and see not a gull. Yet there are rewards. You feel better for enduring the knife-edge of winter, and you are privileged to esteem yourself no mere fair-weather communicant of the august vastness.

Perhaps you can tell something about yourself from your meteorological preferences. The day of the Polar Canadian air-mass, when from Montauk Point the shores of Block Island, Connecticut and Rhode Island are in clear view, is for those whose favorite season is autumn with its days of cloud-less sky, of spaciousness and clean, far-ranging panoramas—those who view nature with detachment, for whom nature's appeal is primarily pictorial, classicists as opposed to roman-ticists, perhaps. On such a day one is visually excited, physi-cally exhilarated, mentally stimulated. Only not much is left for the imagination.

The direct antithesis—a kind of day for the moody, for those who respond most strongly to the suggestive, who find a kindred voice more in, let us say, Wagner's or Prokofiev's questing, eerie tonalities than in Haydn's or Mozart's con-fident, radiant, cleanly defined and perfectly balanced har-monies—is less common at the shore. I associate the type with Accabonac Harbor, for that is where we were one after-noon in mid-November when a tide of damp, temperate air from off the southern coast had settled in upon us and had come to rest, windless, unstirring. A fog had arisen, as I suppose it had above other protected, shallow waters which had become chilled by the cold nights. On all sides the quiet water faded into the mist. The spit could have been an island out of dim memory, in seas beyond time. The air was soft and mild and felt touched with the breath of invisible presences. From out of the fog, not loud but resonant, came a *clonk* . . . *clonk*. . . . (When the fog thinned, it turned out to come from a scallop dredge which resembled a group of structures picked up from a shantytown and deposited on a wooden hull.)

At the edge of the shore was a bird the size of a bustard, one manifestly quite beyond the resources of the native avifauna to produce. This did not astonish me as it ordinarily would have done. But its size turned out to be a trick of the mist; it was much closer than I had realized. It was a black-bellied plover tarrying on its southward flight, pale grey at this time of year but with its characteristic short black bill. It flew off as I approached with a melodious *ker-loo-ee*, the middle note lower in pitch than the other two. Where it put down again I saw that it had joined another of its kind and three greater yellowlegs—rather large, attenuated sandpipers with a habit of rocking stiffly forward, like bowing marionettes. They all took alarm together when I drew too near and vanished into the fog, the yellowlegs sending back a sad, longing *klew-klew-klew*. Had this been the shore of the Aegean two thousand years ago I should have returned home to tell how I had encountered three lovely maidens transformed into shorebirds whose cries of lamentation over their fate had touched my heart.

On our coast it is the east wind that rouses the ocean. Such a wind is likely to set in a day or two after the westerly has spent itself and you have been able to tramp the beach in the calm of an interregnum. An off-sea breeze springs up and whitecaps appear; the waters are choppy. The sun goes. The sea turns from blue to a dark opacity of shade such as you obtained as a child by mixing all your water-colors together. Waves run before the wind, growing larger.

Within four or five hours of the beginning the build-up is complete.

The world around you on the beach is possessed by a wild and tempestuous vitality. Surf and wind create an uproar that is almost continuous. Inshore of the zone of breakers the sea is of boiling milk. Stampeding under the lash of the bouncing, speeding gusts, the great waves come in crowded ranks, each pressing harder on its forerunner as it comes. As they reach shoaling water they seem to draw themselves up to their full height, as if taking a deep breath. Foam-crested, they present fleetingly a picture of dark, snow-capped mountain ridges. Gaunter the wave grows, unable to lift sufficient water from the shallows to fill out its forward slope, and hollow-chested as, its pace slowed, it leans into its split-instant, suspenseful climax. The top, unslackened in its speed, pitches forward and, unsupported, curls over in a downward, cataclysmic plunge, foam streaming back from its lip. Momentarily there is a rolling cylinder of olive-green water, like silk thread on a spool. With an explosion of thunder it strikes. The foaming turbulence rebounds, leaps skyward, as the rest of the wave follows the course of the tumbling summit. A self-perpetuating avalanche of pouring, bouncing, foaming water charges shoreward. Already another sea has upreared behind it and, diving, has come crashing; the waves break almost upon one another's backs. Up and down the beach as far as you can see there are lines of cataracts surging in upon it. The hastening clouds, scudding overhead, are low in the sky. Out over the horizon from whence the waves roll in they form a confusion of mountains, darkest where their masses are thickest. The rain on the wind strikes almost horizontally. The pellets in your face make you wince and resound like gravel on the hood of your poncho. Around the edge of the hood the roar of the wind is such that you can scarcely hear above it.

You cannot think of the sea as inanimate. How can it be other than impelled by an insatiable, uncontainable living force? The breaking of the waves is like the gnashing of the sea's teeth. To behold the charge of the inexhaustible ranks of rolling, breaking, tumultuous, boiling, frothing water is to share in the universal exultation—as you cannot doubt that it is. Every action produces an equal and opposite reaction; life rises in you to meet the buffeting of the billows of wind that rush by you like invisible living hosts. The easterly awakens the Viking in you. You want to match it blow for blow, pound your chest in the teeth of it like a gorilla, outshout it.

The breakers spend themselves in a mad rush of foaming waters up the beach. Where the wash strikes at an angle the foot-high bluff left by a previous storm, its leading edge rushes down the face of it like an express train. But another wave is shooting straight up the beach. There is a collision and an upshot sheet of spray and foam.

Watching from just beyond reach of the waves' wash, you are troubled by your ignominy. It is too much like standing before a caged tiger, relying on those iron bars to afford you the protection you could not provide for yourself. You feel you ought to stride into the surf, breasting the breakers and taking your chances as you roar defiance into the tumult. . . . The wind catches a wave that has broken higher and closer in shore than the others and flings the spray over you, and the lunging wash, outdistancing its fellows, chases you up the beach like a dog on the heels of a tramp. Good for it!

A gull is out beyond the surf, dipping into the troughs of the seas and just clearing the crests as the billows roll under it. In the tide-rip of the forces of gravity and of fluctuating wind, it is in full control, entirely self-possessed. Several other gulls take off from the shelter of the stone groin ahead of you. They beat hard and steadfastly into the wind and let it bear them aloft. But flying against such a blow is work, and, veering off, they sweep away to the west. So does a flock of six pounding their way up toward the beach from the landward side. Off across the wind they go in a grand, descending aerial skid. Hooray for the gulls! They disappear behind the yellowish mist that hangs over the beach in the distance. The mist is perhaps actually a trick of the light. There is always this aura over the beach when you look down it. When there is snow on the ground it is white.

On the waves accompanying a stiff easterly there are always patches of ochre foam. I am not certain of the explanation of this phenomenon either. It seems likely, however, that the larger breakers, with their deeper troughs, stir up silt from the bottom which normally lies undisturbed. Much of the suds that come in on the wash is of the ochre-colored sort. The sheets of water shoot it up the beach and there the wind catches it and blows it free, whisking it over the sand to join it to a bed of similar suds, a shivering accumulation a foot or more deep in a slight depression in the beach. The wrinkled, discolored mass of lather resembles the contents of an old dirty mattress. Under the wind it shakes and shudders like palsied prune whip.

The south wind is the wind of Odysseus. Knot for knot, it pounds the Long Island shore with a surf as formidable as the easterly brings. But the mood is different. The south wind brings heavy, misty clouds hung with greyish sheets which may be their shadows or squalls of tepid rain. Through them the sun makes brief and rayless appearances as they sail by in response to a summons that, soundlessly adrift on the breeze, causes some spirit within you to prick up its ears, like a dog on the hearth to something passing in the darkness outside.

When the southerly comes up in the night you awake to a fecund mildness in the air and to the sound as of a distant railroad train rumbling endlessly by, which is the voice of the ocean. Upon arriving at the beach, you have first an impression of a general whiteness. The scene might be one done in silverpoint. The stampeding seas are leaden-hued, but over all there is a bloom of white. Perhaps it is the faint mist of rain and spume in the air. The ocean on the horizon is alive with waves as with schools of leviathans that breach and submerge; waves of two systems differing in origin are intersecting, alternately reinforcing and counteracting one another. The seas cannot contain the forces that possess them. The incoming rollers begin to spill over while they are still far off shore. The foaming turbulence pours down the upper slope of the charging monster like a surfboard rider, cascading but borne ever back as fast as it tumbles until, already breaking, the roller rears in a wall of water, arcs over and with stupendous abandon crashes in a cataclysm of exploding spray and foam.

In the growling roar that is the voice of the sea as far as the shore extends you seem to hear the surf as it was heard at the beginning on all the empty beaches of this once boundless world by the first voyagers of our kind to set foot upon them. It is in these breakers that the Odyssey surges and thunders. The air of the southerly wind is soft and tangy with the salt sea's breath. Gusty it may be, but its touch is caressive and it brings with it an insinuation of the tropics. On it fly the spirits of all the seafarers who ever sailed in answer to the south wind's promise of siren isles, and the call comes as alluringly as it ever did to the youth that has not yet died within you—the call of far places, the call of the over and beyond, the call that reaches back in us to we know not where.

Perhaps the call comes with most authority when the wind has died and the sea is calm but for the swells that follow in a storm's aftermath. (To the oceanographer, the undulations of the water created by the wind are waves so long as they are receiving energy from the wind and swells thereafter, when they are carried forward on their momentum.) Then the sea is at its most regal. The pandemonium has been quieted and the swells come in singly—the bigger they are, the farther apart—as deliberate and portentous as judgments pronounced by a supreme ruler. Each as it drains the beach of water in its path and collects itself for that ripping, curling dive brings into epochal climax the drama of the ocean; you hold your breath. Then, too, is when the phenomenon of geysering occurs. A volume of air trapped beneath the roiling, tumbling, seething mountain of foaming water is compressed to the exploding point and bursts, sending spray like a fountain shooting twenty or thirty feet into the air. Terrific!

More often than not in winter, the southerly or easterly will be succeeded with little lapse by a northwester. Gone then will be the breath of the lagoon and the memory of enchanted voyages. You are back on a northern beach and on the sharp edge of the present moment. From that point of vantage, however, there is a grand sight to be beheld—the plunging and breaking of the swells against the wind. That is when you see the famous white horses of the sea. In run the combers like Neptune's mounts, in a soft, drowned thudding of hooves, fifty white steeds abreast, their lathery haunches awash in the blue sea, their necks arched, their misty manes flying out behind them. And if you have a low winter sun at your back you will see the rainbows in their manes.

When, in the full blast of a wind from the sea, you watch the successive lines of breakers surging in, likened in your mind to knuckles of foam, you perceive the scene suddenly with a sense of the uncanny. What happens to the waves? It is as if you were watching ranks of charging troops that vanished at the high point of their advance, melting into nothing. It is like an optical illusion, akin to the impression you had as a child of spirally striped barber-poles, up which, as they rotated, the stripes seemed to flow off into space. The long, cascading waves, one after another without end, pour

upon the shore and fade away before your eyes. You see the
wash of an expended wave flow back with gathering force
into the sea and check the onrush of the succeeding wave,
which the turncoat takes by surprise. Yet even so the in-come
seems far greater than the out-go. So much violent passion
appears to be in continuous process of mysterious dissipation.
The breakers assault the shore with earth-shaking force and
fling themselves in rapine-bent sheets of water up the beach.
But then from the line of farthest advance the wash slants
back off in a curiously abstracted, uninterested manner. It
makes you think of a member of a rampaging mob who, finding that he has overrun the scene of violence and is all by
himself, veers off casually on private business.

What is so difficult to comprehend is that there is no
emotion in the impetuosity of the waves. That such tremendous, lifelike movement could be without volition, purpose or
consciousness is almost beyond our grasp. The sea is not
angry or furious. In the "raging" storm there is no malice, no
intent, no feeling. The drowning man must be driven to a near
insanity of horror by the indifference, as he sees it, of the
element which is taking his life, but the actuality is beyond
what he imagines, or is capable of imagining. The sea is not
even indifferent, which implies a capacity for concern. What
would there be if the universe had never been created? If you
can answer that, you know what lies at the sea's heart.

And yet. . . . And yet, having acknowledged that, I come
back to where I started. The sea's presence to me is sovereign.
I cannot be in its vicinity and remain long away from it.
Apart from it, I am aware, in a subtle sense, of deprivation.
Being beside it, I am in some part of me, and in an inexplic-
able way, completed.

One Sunday morning in April I was startled upon bicycling
to Main Beach before breakfast to find fifty cars already there.
I could not imagine what could have brought them out at
such an hour. Then I discovered a small crowd of men and
women huddled together on the porch of the bathhouse. And
I remembered: it was Easter; this presumably was a sunrise
service. My surmise was confirmed by the women's finery.
Investing in a costly and frivolous new hat has its odd aspect
as a means of affirming the Risen Christ, but if one thinks
of it as decking the hair with flowers in celebration of
the springtime awakening of the earth it seems very reason-

able. What is extraordinary is that the chief Christian feast should be designated by the name of the pagan goddess whose festival was held at the time of the vernal equinox and be dated in accordance with a formula harking back to its ancient origins, based upon the date of the first full moon coming on or after the day of the equinox. However, there was in any event little of the pagan spirit in this decorous assemblage. At the conclusion of the hymn or recitation—I could not tell which it was above the crash of the surf—it dissolved and the chilled parishioners hurried to their cars. Only four, one a child with its reluctant mother in train, came down to the ocean's edge, and to tarry only briefly.

I was brought back again to the curious divorcement of man and nature in Christian beliefs. From the time I had first begun to think of such things, I could never see how God and nature could be considered twain. The apparition of the two nuns on that radiant morning in Newport led me at length to see what I had never fully taken in before. Their black raiment, in such a setting, brought home to me that the Church is in perpetual mourning for Christ. This in turn suggested to me the significance of the choice of the cross as the supreme symbol of Christianity. In the figure of Christ nailed to the cross, his bared body and his pose irresistibly connoting sacrifice and helplessness, one may see the figure of Prometheus chained in similar fashion to the Caucasian rock, there to have his liver torn out by a bird descended from the skies. Prometheus was doomed because he provided man with fire and with the arts or—depending upon the legend you accept —because he created man in the first place. Christ was doomed because he was the Messiah who had come to bring man eternal life. In the case of the one it was Zeus himself who decreed the punishment. In the case of the other, Jehovah merely permitted it. He had no part in it but, omnipotent, he did nothing to prevent it. The temporal authority, responsive to the scribes and pharisees, imposed the sentence, but Christ's fate was inevitable from the start. He was born to martyrdom—as are we all whose term of life on earth is limited. Christ was our champion. We form behind the cross in black vestments as the followers of a hero fallen in the people's cause parade in mourning in his funeral procession under the eyes of the Sovereign Power to which his death is chargeable.

I began to see Christianity as a protest movement, man's rebellion against the fate God has visited upon him. This made more understandable Christianity's extraordinary homocentrism, exemplified in its inveterate concern with organization *(Onward, Christian soldiers, marching as to war)*, the enormous importance of written texts in its rituals, its communicants' predilection for congregating among themselves, their practice of worshiping under a roof and within four walls, the infrequency with which they seem to feel a need to go out in solitude into the woods or by the shore to receive directly, away from human influences and distractions, an intimation, if possible, of the divine will. In Christianity, the divorcement of man and nature is a reflection of the divorcement of man and God. To the Christian, man's life on earth as part of the world of nature is not an instance of God's bounty but is a condition of the exile man is enduring because of his fall from grace; it is not without significance that the awareness of nature that informs the Old Testament is absent from the New. That man at the very outset became alienated from God is the explicit premise of Christianity. Christ was crucified to redeem mankind from the conditions God himself had imposed upon it. Indeed, his sufferings, including his crucifixion, were necessary, we are told, to satisfy God for man's sins. And we will never let his martyrdom be forgotten. We raise the cross on high. To the believer in immortal life, a man's release from this world, or a god's, would scarcely seem an event to be grievously mourned, certainly over the space of two millennia. But in the crucifixion we see not only Christ's death, we see the fate upon which we ourselves enter at birth. *Man that is born of woman is of few days, and full of trouble.* In the figure of Christ on the cross, as in that of Prometheus on the rock, we see man himself, the son of God, bound, spread-eagled, hand and foot, a prey to torment under the eye of Heaven. The image is burned in our minds. The moment in the Christian story when, as it were, the wraps are off and, I think, we see to the heart of the matter comes with Christ's final despairing cry, "My God, my God, why hast thou forsaken me?"

Man has, by all that is holy, reason for feeling forsaken and in need of an interceder with the Almighty. He cannot let his thoughts range across the reaches of space, past the millions or billions of galaxies with their billions of suns, or even through the realm of nature on our own planet without dismay. If God takes note of a sparrow's fall, it can only be with indifference; otherwise he would go mad at the carnage of the world, wherein every moment sees sparrows and their kind fall by countless myriads. Rending and being rent: that is the incessant business of life. To a being whom nothing escapes a single, unremitting scream of agony would, it would seem, din in his ears as the voice of the living world. And of this order of things, man, so long as he is upon earth, is inseparably a part. If he is decreasingly likely to be torn asunder by stronger beasts or consumed from within by liver-flukes and tapeworms, and if his years are increasingly extended, he meets his end inevitably as microbes multiply in his tissues, ravenous as sharks; only now he is apt to be deprived of the quick finish he could once have expected at nature's hands and, it may be, to pay for his longer life by lingering on through interminable months of physical pain and mental anguish. The terms of existence apply finally to him no less than to his fellow creatures: *One event happeneth to them all.*

> *Who sees with equal eye, as God of all,*
> *A hero perish or a sparrow fall,*
> *Atoms or systems into ruin hurl'd,*
> *And now a bubble burst, and now a world.*

The affirmative and unfailingly appreciative eye with which Henry David Thoreau looked insatiably at nature is, I am afraid, beyond my attaining to. His reply when at the end his aunt asked if he did not think the time had come to make his peace with God expressed the tenor of his life and mind: "I did not know that we had ever quarreled." Happy man! I have quarreled with God every day of my life and have little doubt that I shall go on doing so, to my detriment. My thoughts turn black with revolt when I hear of children asphyxiated in flaming houses; when I reflect upon the millions of my contemporaries who fell in the terror of battle, deprived of the chance ever to realize what was in them; when I see those I love grow old and die; even when I recognize in myself the toll my mortality is taking. I feel a chill of nausea when I observe mud-dauber wasps stocking their nest-tubes with paralyzed, still-living spiders for their larvae to consume at leisure; when I read of small birds fluttering helplessly in the webs of tropical super-spiders, awaiting the thrust of the envenomed fangs; when I think of a lion gnawing off the haunch of a not-yet-dead zebra. The cheeping of a junco I saw borne off by a sharp-shinned hawk last winter still sounds in my ears.

So fell are the impressions nature is capable of making that before moving to the shore I had times of wondering whether I should be capable of enjoying it. If the struggle for survival as I witnessed it on land gave me bad moments, I reasoned that I should be far worse affected by the reminders of the slaughter that takes place on a more lavish scale in the sea, where life is more abundant and the death-dealing seems more pitiless and ghoulish for being enacted by slithery assassins of a cold-blooded and mindless character and in a medium fatal to man and filled for him with the dread of the shadowy unknown. How could Rachel Carson write of a tidal pool as "that enchanted place," a far-worse-than-Roman arena that it is, wherein every flowerlike *Tubularia* she found so exquisite had tentacles for petals with which it reached out to ensnare the infant larvae of mollusks and crustaceans, her elfin starfish had a protrudable stomach in which it could digest its victims in their own shells, the little wriggling worms were dragons in miniature, merciless on the trail of their quarry? What horror was there not in the sea? The little wriggling worms—*Nemertea*—grew to monsters (a species in British waters up to ninety feet long) and yanked their victims into their mouths in the coils of a whiplike appendage shot from a sheath. One pictures the unspeakable: slimy, snout-faced moray eels ten feet long lunging from their underwater grottoes to snatch a diving bird and swallow it in convulsive shudders; octopuses holding their prey in writhing limbs while ripping out its vitals with their beaks; the floating *Physalia,* or Portuguese man-of-war, trailing beneath it tentacles up to fifty feet long studded with capsules that eject poisoned darts at a touch; sea-anemones drawing whole into their body cavities the fish they have paralyzed with venom from their stinging cells; packs of killer whales falling upon a school of dolphins in a welter of bloody froth—everywhere the thrashing of predator and captured prey.

And the scale of it! The diatoms, the minute, one-celled algae encased in intricately-fashioned silica shells that constitute 99 per cent of the plant life of the sea, exist in inconceivable numbers at the ocean's surface, up to several million in a single quart, and when mineral-rich waters from the ocean's depths well up to the top may double their numbers in a day. Like the other one-celled organisms—animal, or intermediate between plant and animal—which feed upon them, they may stain the sea with their colors, though individually invisible to the human eye. (The grim "red tide," in which fish perish wholesale, is composed of one of the microscopic plant-animals called dinoflagellates.) Yet as fast as they multiply they are devoured by the protozoa and the other organisms of the plankton (the "drift")—copepods (the barely visible, basic protein-providers of the sea), the young of crustaceans and mollusks and the like. And so, as fast as their ravagers reproduce, are they in turn ravaged by the somewhat larger carnivores—the half-inch-long, voracious arrow-worms; the gooseberry-like comb-jellies that flail the water with sticky tentacles; the jellyfishes and the infants of the bony fish—and these by yet larger, in a pyramiding of massacre that stuns the mind. The blue whale, whose slaughter at man's hands I have raged over, consumes at a single meal a ton of the two-inch-long shrimplike krill, which it harvests by swimming openmouthed through the plankton, straining the water through the rake of whalebone jutting from its upper gums. And the requirements of a krill—of which over one billion billion are spawned in a single year, an expert of the National Science Foundation tells us—are proportionately no less than a whale's upon the smaller carnivores of the plankton (the crustaceans, worms and baby fishes), as are theirs upon the copepods, which in turn may eat their own weight in diatoms every day.

Yet from the beach itself the total impression is far from the nightmare one could well anticipate from the books— about as far from it as is the total impression of the earth one has from a meadow. I had fallen under the sway of that which is more terrible than any monster of the ocean's depths (and more enchanting than any seraph of Elysium): the imagination. To the creatures of the sea it cannot be as we picture it. The brief, horror-beset existence we ascribe to them would surely be unrecognizable to them, to whom life must seem quite ordinary—far more so than it does to us, who can conjure up the direst calamities to make the future frighten-

ing. Only the highest animals can have much conception of
death or any understanding that it must come to them. And
there is this mitigating if not saving grace: that it can come
to each of us but once. A trillion deaths have perhaps no
more meaning than one death. The panorama of an infinity
of bloody encounters exists only in human minds, not in those
of the organisms which people the battlefield, which see only
what is before them, remembering little if any of what
preceded, unwitting of what must come. To suffer vicariously
is given to man alone—perhaps also in a lesser and more
restricted way to other warm-blooded creatures. It is the price
we pay for our privileges. *He that increaseth knowledge increaseth sorrow.*

It helps to bear the thought of nature's seeming savagery if
we recognize our community with all living, the predators no
less than the preyed-upon. The deadly killers of the hillside
and of the sea may look malevolent, but in fact malevolence
possesses no living creature, unless it be man himself. Spiders,
sharp-shinned hawks, moray eels, sharks did not choose their
way of life. To speak of animals as vicious or cruel is as
wrong-headed as to ascribe anger to the storm. The passion
to live is nothing that any living creature devised or asked
for. The relentless electric current that charges us all derives
from a source outside ourselves. We are equally the victims
of hungers that were implanted in us at birth to gnaw at us
from then on with but brief interludes of respite. Mole crabs,
sea-leopards and men have about as much to contend with as
they can manage, and in the end more.

To feel a fellowship with all other creatures in all circumstances is clearly impossible. Even a Jain, who wears a cloth
over his face to keep from accidentally breathing an insect in
to its doom, would hardly look with benevolence upon a
giant squid plunging with him to the submarine darkness. But
to feel no kinship at all with the animals with which we have
a common abode, a common origin and in salient aspects a
common predicament seems to me to be less than human.

To recognize that the faculties of the lower animals do not
encompass what ours do is not—that is to say—to deny their
possessors the capacity for suffering. Once when I was working in a downstairs room in our house in Virginia I heard the
baying of a couple of dogs nearby and looked up in time to
see a young grey fox trot the length of my window sill,

which was at ground level. He was gone in a trice, but not before I had heard his whimper and taken in that he was tired, uncertain and afraid. The picture he left remains fresh in my mind, for he was what all creatures are a good part of the time, we may be sure, including our own kind. And sooner or later the dogs of one variety or another would pull him down and he would die in pain and terror, as most living things do within the limits of their capacities. While persons whose faith leads them to spurn this world seem to me to have chosen a strange way to celebrate its Maker and theirs, I sometimes feel capable of going them one better. If it were possible to bring about the instant and total dissipation of our planet by throwing a switch, would not mercy call for doing so? Can one not at least conceive of reaching for the fatal handle?

If one has harbored such thoughts, how would one answer for them to the Creator of that which one could have imagined effacing, in the event that one should have to? One could of course truthfully deny that one could ever have been so vainglorious as actually to have taken such a decision upon oneself. For the rest, one could at least disavow having been one of those whose professed love of God is the idealizing love that adolescents pine with, which in fact rejects the reality of the loved one in favor of an image answering the lover's own need of comfort and security, of assurance of his importance, and of fulfillment. To that, it is not difficult to guess what the Creator's retort might be: "You tell me what your regard for me was not. Let me hear now what it was!"

"Almighty Father!" I should reply. "I took to heart the command of Alexander Pope, which I construed to be the ultimate in wisdom: 'Presume not God to scan!' "

"You lie. You were not like my good servant Henry David Thoreau. You were a faultfinder from the word Go, as you have admitted."

"Only against my better judgment, and when exercised. And if I was easily exercised it was because, Great Zeus, you instilled in my veins, more than in Henry's, the stuff that makes one a carrier of life's processes rather than a reflective observer of them. I could not have been content with solitude in an isolated cabin in the woods, at least with that alone or for very long. Of an evening I should have dreamed of sneaking in to a cabaret and dancing the flamenco on a tabletop. I, as you know, married and had children. I was too much at the mercy of the day-to-day or even moment-to-moment emotions of a member of the cast to see the action as a whole."

"And now that you have been released from involvement and can view the cosmos with disinterest, what say you?"

"Immortal one! That the terms of existence, in all probability, could hardly be greatly different from what they are, even if you in your omnipotence desired to have them so. A different set of rules would be hard to imagine. If there were much give in one place, there would doubtless have to be some take in another. If life were much harsher—and here I speak as a human being—we could not live it and would succumb and thus be freed of its travails. If it were much happier, the anticipation of losing it would breed such anguish in us as would counteract the added pleasure. 'O world! But that thy strange mutations make us hate thee, life would not yield to age.' But yield it must. There could be no other way."

"So you see the creation I have wrought as a place of balanced diet. You make it sound a dreary fare. I begin to think the gift of life was wasted on you. Instead of you, I might perhaps better have made provision for another thousand krill."

"Ah, but, Mighty Thunderer, I have not spoken of the elements that I thought were in balance. The landscape of existence seemed to me no mere peneplain on which the hills scarcely rose above the valleys but a terrain of abysses and mountaintops. The depths were bloodcurdling, of a gloom and horror to unseat the mind. But what a glory was on the heights, with the blue above and the green meadows below studded with flowers and a golden light over all! The heart was ready to burst with love of it. Life at its best so far beggared description as did life at its worst, and what more could be said of its sublimity than that?"

But my interrogation, if it is to come, is still, I trust, some time off. Meanwhile—

> *I stand amid the roar*
> *Of a surf-tormented shore*
> *And I hold within my hand*
> *Grains of the golden sand—*

How few! yet how they creep
Through my fingers to the deep,
While I weep—while I weep!
O God! can I not grasp
Them with a tighter clasp?
O God! can I not save
One from the pitiless wave? . . .

I have certainly been trying. My desk is full of sand, sand in little bottles, sand from Race Point, Nauset Beach, Siasconset, Rocky Neck, Montauk Point and beaches southward. Science is my excuse.

Sand, like so many minutiae over which the eye ordinarily passes unseeing, turns out when examined closely to disclose vistas one could imagine exploring indefinitely with unabating interest. Except for that which is made up of the granulated shells of marine organisms, all sand is the product of the fragmentation and abrasion of rock. There is no upward limit to the size of the grains. Between a cobble beach and one of sand, as we generally think of it, there is a complete gradation. Indeed, the cobblestones are on their way to becoming ordinary sand. Given continued exposure to the ocean's waves, that is what they must become. On the lower side, if the grains become light enough to remain for any length of time in suspension in water, currents will carry them seaward; the ocean keeps beach sand clean, which is to say free of silt and clay. The grains of sand themselves do not necessarily grow smaller and smaller, however. On reaching a certain degree of fineness, the experts say, they become practically immortal as a result of being shielded from contact with other grains by a film of water which envelops them; the particles of sand that compose a hard-packed beach are not touching. On the other hand, the sand that reaches the dry upper beach where the wind can move it must be subject to further abrasion. The quantities of sand on our east coast, insofar as they can be imagined, give an idea of the mass of mountains that had to be ground down to produce them.

Like the rock crystals of which it is formed, sand varies in shade from the starchlike, pure white quartz of the beaches of Florida's Gulf Coast panhandle, so fine and tight-packed it squeaks underfoot, to the brown of rutile, the near-black of tourmaline and the coal-black of ilmenite, magnetite, augite and hornblende;* all these are said to be present in the sands of the northeast coast. Blues, greens, yellows, reds are represented in various shades and amounts. Grains of sapphire and ruby have been found in sand from Martha's Vineyard. On the west coast, as in Hawaii, there are beaches of grey-green sand, produced by the weathering of basalt. Quartz, however, because it is one of the most abundant minerals of the continental crust and particularly durable, is the commonest component of sand, at least in the east. Above southern Florida's coral beaches the sand, formed largely by the weathering of granite, seems to consist of at least 50 per cent quartz.† In the common sand-colored sands, you can see under a lens that the proportion of the glassy quartz granules, mostly colorless or shaded toward yellow and running up to about $\frac{1}{32}$nd of an inch in diameter, is much higher, with most of the other grains being of opaque, orange-tan feldspar. The sand I brought back from the cove in the rock ledges of Newport is finer and looks grey but under a glass is seen to be composed of colorless quartz grains, some that are pale lavender or aquamarine (from slate or similar rock), and tinier grains that are nearly black. Darker grey and finer still is the sand from Atlantic City; in it the minute, shiny black particles (composed more of hornblende than of anything else) almost equal the quartz in volume. The Hatteras sand, as is characteristic of sand from North Carolina southward, contains shell fragments, mostly resembling feldspar granules.

All sand is beautiful under a lens, but the most beautiful I know is garnet sand. I saw it as far north as Ipswich and on Cape Cod and have found it from one end of Long Island to the other, a stain on the beach that looks as if black-raspberry juice had been spilled and washed over by a retreating wave. The most unobservant are struck by it. At closer range you see that it is made up of pink grains and black. The latter are of magnetite and ilmenite; clusters of the former cling to my young daughter's magnet. Under a lens the clear crystals of

---

* Rutile is an oxide of titanium, ilmenite an oxide of titanium and iron, and magnetite an oxide of iron, while augite and hornblende are both compounds of silica, magnesia and lime, augite also containing iron.

† Granite is composed of quartz (about 30 per cent) and potash feldspar (about 60 per cent) and is liberally sprinkled with granules of mica or hornblende. Potash feldspar may be white, grey, or glassy as well as salmon-colored.

garnet, enhanced in their richness by their jet-black associates, are seen to be of all shades of rose. On one side they fade off toward the colorlessness of clear quartz. On the other, tiny though they are—minute, rounded pellets which lie three abreast within the ½nd-of-an-inch division of my ruler—they deepen almost to the tawny-port shade of full-sized garnets. Some are clear, brilliant amber. What the lens reveals is a heap of uncut gems of a rajah's prodigal store—a king's ransom; you can lose yourself in it, gazing at it. Though there are tons of it on the beaches and a lotion-bottle full of it stands at my elbow, I take care not to spill any of the pinch of it I have at the moment in a fold of paper, as if it were irreplaceable.

Not the least wonderful thing about the garnet sand is that we should be unaware of its existence but for the propensity of the sea to segregate it. You find it in patches, in a veneer on the ordinary sand usually only a few grains deep, though in places on Fire Island I have come upon bands of it half-an-inch deep and several feet wide and a hundred or more long. There it is, all together, where the wash of the waves has carefully laid it, always at about their upper reach, always like a stain running toward the sea. It is as if a conscious mind had arranged the display.

The proclivity of the sea to sort out the materials of the beach is quite uncanny. Doubtless it is all a matter of masses and specific gravities plotted against the energies of waves with allowance made for current-deflecting terrain-contours, but it gives you an impression of the sea as an old recluse with a fetish for order in the arrangement of her ancient, mulled-over possessions. At Montauk Point, where the shore-line is irregular, it seems more understandable that there should be a pattern, though the consistency with which it is carried out is startling. On the northern side of the point, facing Block Island Sound, the intertidal zone is of cobbles and larger rocks, which in the warm months swarm with periwinkles. (With its abundance of mussels and crabs, the lee of the point is the site of a permanent garrison of gulls.) Above it is a zone of sand and gravel and above that another of smaller cobbles. If you continue on around away from the point you come to a cove in which high-water-mark is bordered by a wide, deep belt of rotting organic debris which the old lady, the sea, has here methodically disposed of, including

rockweed; whitened, stone-clutching kelp (the *Laminarias* grow
on the boulder-strewn bottom here as they do on Maine's rock
ledges); sea-lettuce; Irish moss; the green, spongelike *Codium* and mussel-shells; the salmon-pink carapaces of northern crabs; boatshells; shark-eyes (the shells of moon snails);
and perhaps even a lobster-claw (though thought of as a
New England species, *Homarus americana* extends southward
to North Carolina.) In the other direction, working your way
around the lighthouse to the seaward side, you come to the
end first of the sand beach and then of the shells and have
before you nothing but stones—and stones sorted by size.
There will be expanses of pebbles and expanses of egg-sized
stones, then a beach of stones the size of footballs or larger.
The coves will be piled high with stones along the shore, the
average of cobble size and of a chalky cream color.

On the familiar, smooth, straight sand beach, one part of
which looks to the human eye very like another, the sea is
apt nonetheless to find some basis for discrimination. On
Long Island's outer shores there are few shells in winter: the
remains of a few shark-eyes as large as apples and more of
the shells of surf-clams, which come five inches long and are
stout and heavy to withstand the pounding of the waves. But
what shells you find are likely to occur in fields. Pebbles,
which you might expect to find distributed in a parallel relationship with the edge of the sea, turn out to be organized
perpendicularly to it too, also in patches. At times you can
look down the beach and see pools of pebbles at regular
intervals. And not only that; you may find that they are
grouped by size, those in some accumulations averaging larger
or smaller than those in others.

It is these pebbles that make it difficult to come home with
empty pockets from a walk on a Long Island beach. They
are the fruit of the moraine, the berrylike fruit, one might
say. In their variety they are more absorbing than the displays
in the windows of Fifth Avenue jewelers and, in the subtlety
of their colors and designs and muted luminosity when still
wet from the brine, more beautiful. Worn smooth, those on
the outer beach are likely to be flat as well, but the more
protected the location or the more recently they have emerged
from the glacial till, the larger and more irregular they are
likely to be. (An exception are those from recently exposed
beds of gravel. They received their rubbing-down and polish-

ing from the action of freshets of the melting glacier many millennia ago.) There is an unbroken gradation in size from the grains of sand through the pebbles with which the outer beaches are strewn, and which entirely compose the shore along parts of the Sound, through the cobble-sized stones, randomly varied in color, texture and composition, under the weight of which (five or six in one's hands and field-bag) one staggers back to the car at Montauk Point, to monster playthings of the ice-sheet up to eight feet on a side and of complicated structure—most of them probably gneisses from the bedrock of Connecticut—which have only recently been unearthed by the erosion of the cliffs and come tumbling down to the sea.

On the quiet reaches of the bays are stones that would receive short shrift from the surf if they reached the outer beach. Among them are discs and lumps of sandstones and mudstones in earthen colors, the solidified sediment of ancient waters, which are soft enough to leave the fingers feeling chalky if you rub them. Others are the conglomerates, which resemble handfuls of pebbles and sand or earth squeezed together. A remarkable one we brought back is like a small reptile's head irregularly bumpy with slick, wartlike bumps of brick-colored jasper. Also in this category are the schists— wafers of grey biotite schist, light in the hand, that glisten like silk in the light and ovals of muscovite schist sparkly as brooches of solid rhinestones with insect-bite scabs on them which are garnets. One I have that I should never have recognized as belonging to this group, its composition is so uniform, is a dull-grey graphite schist—it leaves a mark on a piece of paper—the size and shape of my thumb unevenly encircled by white lines down to a hair's fineness which appear to have been executed by the most sensitive draftsman but are in fact veins of quartz that cleave the stone.

The garnet sand is the product of the decomposition of garnet schists and garnet gneisses. One of the latter I picked up at Montauk, a solid, hefty stone around which the hand closes with satisfaction, has a woven appearance—as gneiss often has—because of its grain, the grey and yellow-white stitches being quartz and feldspar crystals. The garnet crystals that measle it are indented rather than protruding; evidently they break off faster than the highly metamorphosed, granite-hard gneiss weathers.

Those of which one clasps all too many in a firmer grasp are the quartzites. They are probably the commonest pebbles and stones of the outer beaches, and among them are numbered the most beautiful. The majority are of a slighty trans-lucent white or intermediate between white and colorless, and more translucent, with internal fractures or crystal-faces. Hardly to be distinguished from these are the moonstones, buttons of the white sodium feldspar called albite, which is common in granitic rocks; in the wake of the waves they have the slightly bluish transparency of ice formed of partially melted snow refrozen and seem to have an inner glow. Some of the quartzites are of soft, semitranslucent greys wonder-fully shadowed and lined within. Some of the whites are veined or stained with deep flesh tones, and specimens can be found of a pure, lovely, complexion pink. There is also a strong trend to yellow among the quartzites. You find stones that resemble lemon-drops or even orange-drops. But the range goes far beyond that. There are quartzites resembling apricot-colored laundry soap, lumps of maple sugar, chunks of muscle combining meat and fat, and small kidneys. One in the collection we made, totally unlike any other, looks as if it were coated with a pitted celadon glaze; the opaque greenish cast comes from chlorite. Several could be crystallized golden wine and one a lump of golden sugar half soaked with blood of a royal purple. A large chunk I broke off a quartzite the size of my head makes you think of a magnified section of watermelon-meat when you look at its juicily-glistening frac-tured end; its giant-grain crystals shade from a thin yellow (actually citrine in one spot) through clear white to pale pink and finally a near-red.

Unless you have been prepared for the phenomenon, perhaps by Thoreau's mention of it in his Cape Cod journal, you will be in for a disillusionment when you bring home the stones from the sea's wash. When dry, though still attractive and no less interesting, they lose their luster. In contrast with what they were, they appear dead. I was struck by a thought in this connection one January day on a walk around the inner tip of Fire Island, a beach notable for the number of huge, creosoted timbers that wash up there. Such, in fact, was the amount of human booty on the beach—an inch-thick hawser (more than I could carry), an expensive bronze plastic pail marked *Deck Use Only* (Man proposes, God disposes)—that I was in danger of forgetting the naturalist's quest I conceived should occupy me. Suddenly I had a picture of the Creator so charmed by the human beings he had produced that he decided they should be immortal and commenced gathering their souls to him, only to find that removed to paradise from the vital medium in which they had captured his fancy they suffered the same change as the stones one brings home from the sea. I saw him seated disenchanted among the glowless and apathetic relics.

In the case of the stones, the dimming of their light has a probably prosaic enough explanation—and the process can be reversed by restoring them to water. Evidently abrasion by the sand leaves their surface frosted, like ground glass. When they are dry, this disperses the light, which makes for opacity. A film of water, however, fills the microscopic pitting as varnish would, producing a smooth surface through which the light rays pass directly. Even the opaque stones are affected. And the variety of these surpasses even that of the quartzites.

There are pure potash feldspars the color of a sunburned complexion which when turned this way and that respond with a flash of sheen as of a sheet of satin. Other feldspars resemble potted salmon with quartz bodies representing gristle. Still others will in addition sparkle with embedded flakes of biotite (black mica) and of muscovite (common mica) like flecks of fresh solder. The most arresting I have is a feldspar-quartz gneiss with a mottled surface of caramel and grey-blue (which when wet is a startling true blue) cut by veins of pistachio-green epidote. Epidote adds greatly to the interest of stone-collecting, forming fascinating lineations in the pale feldspar-quartz gneisses. One I have is a little, faintly yellow-stained mound of grey-threaded gneiss on a quarter-inch-thick base of epidote, another a small, heart-shaped stone of creamy gneiss bisected vertically and horizontally by epidote veins. A hornblende granite resembles a chunk of rock-sugar with a quarter of the crystals being of anthracite coal. Another granite has the flesh tone of feldspar with glossy flecks of biotite as well as the deader-black bits of hornblende. In a third, the grains are as fine as salt and pepper granules. A fourth granite with hornblende is like a yellow-tinted sea bird's egg with black markings. There are stones you could believe have a human history. One is like an eye from an effigy, a conical grey gneiss with a white ring around the apex. Then there is a flattish, four-sided stone of concentric, alternating dark and light rings, a metamorphic stone, this, of interbedded sandstone and shale, looking as if it had some optical purpose. One I can scarcely put down is a somewhat-arrowhead-shaped piece of greenstone (usually a metamorphosed basalt) which I think of as a talisman worn butter-smooth in the hands of generations of its protégés. The stones work a necromancy on you. With the treasure of the beach at my feet, I could see myself becoming a dealer in them, infatuated with the ever-swelling contents of my shop and caring not at all whether I ever made a sale.

Given nature's characteristically orderly processes, by which rocks of one kind are created in one place, of another in another, the thought strikes you at first that a deviation comparable to a suspension of the law of averages must have taken place for such an electric assortment of minerals to have accumulated here. The explanation gives you an even livelier appreciation of the glacier's thoroughness. Long Island's rocks represent the scourings of a swath of New York and New England well over 100 miles broad and how many deep I have never seen estimated. That sector of the ice-sheet to which Long Island owes its existence could have brought spoil all the way from Canada in the process of pushing and scraping its way down from the north.

A million or two years ago, before the ice ages, when the northeastern coast stood higher in relation to the ocean than it does now, Long Island was part of the coastal plain of the mainland, but the island would not exist today had it not been built up with material dumped by the fourth, or Wisconsin, ice-sheet. At least it would probably not have amounted to much. (There is a kind of clay on Long Island, Gardiner's Clay, dating back to the period between the third and fourth ice-sheets.) Until recently, it was believed that it contained till from the second and third ice-sheets, but the oldest discovered now turns out to date back no farther than the fourth. (It is astonishing that ice-sheets separated by scores or hundreds of thousands of years should over long distances have reached lines no more than twenty miles apart.) The fourth twice pushed across the site of Long Island Sound, and of the two moraines it left, Long Island is the remnant.

Both times the ice reached a line extending from the western nose of Long Island (from which the Verrazano-Narrows Bridge takes off to Staten Island) northeastward through Flushing to Manhasset. Its first advance took it to a line extending from thence roughly down the middle of the island through Lake Ronkonkoma to the vicinity of Riverhead, where the island forks. From here, the line curves around the south shore of Peconic Bay (which divides the prongs) to Sag Harbor, then takes a fairly direct course on out to Montauk Point (with which the south prong ends) and Block Island. The morainal ridge left by this advance reaches its maximum elevation at High Hill, south of Huntington, which, standing 410 feet above sea level, is the highest point on Long Island. After retreating, the ice-sheet returned but this time did not, for the most part, advance quite so far. The line it reached extends past the heads of the bays along the shore of the Sound out the northern prong, which ends at Orient Point, through Plum Island and the Gull Islands to Fisher's Island, only two miles off the coast of Connecticut. Harbor Hill, just east of Roslyn, with an altitude of 384 feet, is the highest point on the moraine left by the second advance. As the ice-sheet melted northward for good, an Arctic flora grew up in its wake. Leslie Sirkin, who has driven tubes down through the sediment of a number of Long Island's bogs to a depth of as much as thirty-three feet, has found pollen grains of willow, birch, sedge and grasses—vegetation typical of the tundra—at the bottom. These were laid down, he estimates, 17,000 years ago. Remains of spruce forests he has encountered at a higher level have been shown by measurement of radioactive carbon decay to be 11,000 years old. Pines, he reports, became dominant 8,500 years ago, with oaks succeeding as recently as 500 B.C.

The main body of Long Island is comparable to the inner arm of Cape Cod in that in both there are morainal hills in the northern part and outwash plains to the south. Both are well supplied with kettle ponds, but Long Island (with Lake Ronkonkoma as its largest) not so copiously as the Cape, which on the map is as shot full of holes as the hardest-hit battle-flag. Both incorporate plateaus left by the third ice-sheet which fall off in sheer slopes, but where the Cape's most imposing cliffs front the ocean, along the outer arm, Long Island's are on the inner shore, along the Sound. Hence, where the Cape's have been worn back to an even face by millennnia of heavy surf, Long Island's are still carved out by deep bays, which look out between headlands shaped like plowshares that make you think of ships putting boldly out to sea.

The ocean shore of Long Island, its southern shore, consists altogether of broad sand beaches backed by dunes except at Montauk Point. There the southern moraine reaches the shore and, cut back by the waves, forms bluffs up to seventy feet high facing the ocean. Lower than the Cape's, these are in every way more uneven: their front, following the wavy shoreline, is irregular, as is their slope, which is often gentle at the foot, sometimes rising to a near vertical; and the material that composes them is an untidy conglomeration of clays, sand, gravel and boulders.

The face of a moraine which has been cut away is, it must be admitted, as ugly as an embankment thrown up by man's own indiscriminate, earth-moving excesses. Because it looks so inhospitable to life we were doubly astonished one day early in spring—March 17th, which is still winter where the wind blows in from across the cold sea—to find growing out of the lower slope of the bluff at Montauk a patch, a small bed, of flowers resembling frilly golden asters. So wildly out-of-keeping a display seemed explicable only as a bunch of store-

bought chrysanthemums dropped off the cliff by a Coast
Guardsman at the lighthouse above. The blooms were, however, growing there, on short stems devoid of foliage, pushing
up through the caked, sandy clay on thick, pinkish shoots
akin to small asparagus tips. (It must be these that give the
plant—an immigrant from Europe— its name of coltsfoot.)
The burst of golden blossoms against the sordid, gullied front
of the wintry moraine was like a witness of a happy propensity in life in which fairy tales would have us believe.

Montauk Point is the *Ultima Thule* of Long Island. If you
start from Brooklyn or Manhattan you are two-thirds of the
way to Martha's Vineyard when you arrive there, halfway to
the farthest point of Cape Cod. When I saw it in September
of last year, it was for the first time since shortly after I had
been graduated from college. The place I remembered from
the earlier, midwinter visit had felt as remote as a promontory
of the Orkneys. The one to which I returned was an adjunct
of New York City. Holidaymakers of all ages and in all the
metropolis's variety of physical types and costumes filled the
picnic tables on the heights; trailed up and down the worn
paths to the shore cut through the waist-high mattress of
beach-plum, bayberry, wild rose and Virginia creeper covering
the slope; sat or milled about the sand-and-cobble beach; or,
in some cases and at some remove, stood hip-deep and rubber-
booted on the rocky bottom and cast for striped bass. A
regatta of sports-fishing boats stretched as far as the eye could
reach, trolling for tuna and swordfish. It seemed to me that
Montauk of thirty years back than that one had been
from the Montauk of three hundred years before, when the
Indians whose tribal name it bears kept watch from the
cliffs for their dreaded enemies of the mainland or rubbed
down and drilled bits of the shells of periwinkles and quahogs
to make wampum for the payment of tribute.

From the Midtown Tunnel that takes you under the East
River from Manhattan to Long Island, the distance to Montauk Point by car is about 125 miles. For the first 85 there
is nothing exceptional in the natural scene which is, in fact,
fast disappearing where it has not already disappeared. Then,
after crossing a gap in the moraine through which the Shinnecock Canal has been cut, you look out over Shinnecock
Bay on your right and Peconic Bay on your left, the two
bodies of water almost meeting here to nip the southern prong

of the island off at its base. Thereafter, like a lobster's claw above the basal joint, the peninsula widens out and for twenty miles, past Southampton and East Hampton, you traverse a countryside of wide, flat fields bordered by woods, which sometimes close in on the highway, and of unusually attractive, tree-shaded towns settled three centuries ago and still retaining some of the character of their antiquity. In the vicinity of Amagansett there is a drastic change. The highway rejoins the morainal hills, which since Southampton have been to the north of it (mostly wooded in a starved-looking second-growth of pitch pines and black oaks), but it does so only to descend from them. The moraine, in fact, peters out as the peninsula abruptly narrows: the lobster's claw with a finger missing. With the sea in sight for the first time, you come out upon a low isthmus of sand plains and dunes. It is a maritime landscape and there are the seaside plants one has grown familiar with: beachgrass and beach-goldenrod on the outer rim; tight skeins of the box-leaved bearberry covering the flats, rugs of beach heather (*Hudsonia*) on the dunes, as grey and lifeless-looking in winter as old, dirt-soaked cotton mops; pitch pines, scraggly and yellowed but scrappy; and bear oaks. After six miles there is another outcropping of the moraine, almost two hundred feet high and covered by scrub-growth and a low, dense, spindly oak forest. This is Hither Hills and a state park, and it provides a welcome break in the scattering of billboards, cabins, motels and restaurants. After another gap in the moraine, a mile wide, in which the village of Montauk is to be passed as rapidly as possible, the highway ascends abruptly again and within another three miles comes to a high point at which a turnoff is provided for the wonder-struck. The view from it, though requiring one to overlook radar and radio-transmitting installations, is hardly to be surpassed on the east coast south of Maine. Beyond the rolling hills of brush-growth and grassy moorland of the peninsula, itself deeply hollowed out by the bay called Montauk Lake, there is the ocean on one side and on the other Block Island Sound and Gardiner's Island, and beyond them Orient Point and Plum Island, and farther still the mainland. Clean and open and blue to infinity, the world suddenly appears. The serenity of the distant capes seems deep enough to absorb all the troubles of our frenzied race. The panorama of the sea conveys what it always conveys to one who has been away from it for long: the illimitability of time and space, of which there is so little in the existences most of us lead. Freedom is our birthright, the sea tells us, and we may wonder at that moment how much of all we purchase with it—and it is our sole currency—is worth the cost.

The last two miles of the highway are bordered by a forest of oak with a green understory of holly and mountain-laurel; this is Montauk Point State Park. In the autumn, these seaward extrusions of the land are like beds of burning coals with the scarlets, carmines and burgundies of oak, sumac, tupelo, huckleberry, blueberry, Virginia creeper and beach-plum; between the blue sea and sky they make you gasp. At that season the birds pour through Montauk. Evidently there is a populous, off-shore route of migration that runs through Block Island—where on some days there may be more land birds of more species than in any other area of comparable size in the country—and down the coast of Long Island. One day in mid-October I watched tree swallows streaming into Montauk Point by the hour from the direction of Block Island. They collected above the grass-covered dunes like gnats, hovering and seeming always about to alight but never doing so, sometimes all being moved in unison to rise high in the air, though only to descend again. Near the end of the season there are scoters by the thousands in rafts off shore, with others winging by in small strands holding their positions relative to one another as if they were strung on invisible cords. Songbirds, shorebirds, terns, gulls, cormorants, loons, grebes—Montauk is a funnel for them all, the strait through which the tide surges.

As the most forward part of Long Island, Montauk Point bears the brunt of the seas. The easterlies that beat broadside upon Cape Cod's Great Beach Long Island takes end-on. There is no mistaking the damage; you can see at the end of the moraine that landslips and stonefalls are routine, though human beings scrambling about on the slopes probably reduce them faster than the sea does. Montauk lighthouse—the oldest still in service today—stood 390 feet from high water when it went into operation (burning whale oil) in 1797. It is said that President Washington himself sited it where it is after computing that at the going rate of erosion of the cliff it would be good for two hundred years. As usual, the calculations of that methodical visionary were sound. In June 1965 the edge of the cliff came within 45 feet 10 inches of a watchtower built 60 feet in front of the lighthouse. Should the erosion continue at its rate up to now the edge would be about 50 feet from the base of the lighthouse on its bicentennial—mighty close for comfort. In fact, the rate seemed to have been lessened by a defense-works of enormous boulders brought from a quarry on the mainland and heaped around the base of the cliff. Measurements taken every month show an average loss of one inch with each reading, according to a slim, serious-minded young Coast Guardsman from Mississippi who showed me the pegs from which the measurements are made. He told me that regulations had called for a standing watch at the light ever since 1951, when a grossly overloaded excursion boat called *Pelican* had capsized in heavy seas off the point, unobserved, with forty-five lives lost. He also pointed out the black buoy marking the pinnacle of rock twenty-four feet down known as the Great Eastern Rock in honor of its discovery by the fabulous vessel of that name—the largest to be built for forty-five years from the time of her launching in 1858—when it opened a huge rent in her outer hull in 1862. (The novelty of a double hull saved her from sinking then and there. As it was, the damage was not discovered until later when she developed a list.)

One estimate has it that Montauk Point has so far been worn back four miles, and the U. S. Geological Survey considers that as much as half of Long Island has been washed away since the ice-sheet deposited it. At that rate—and presumably the rate is and has been diminishing—nothing would be left fifteen or twenty thousand years hence. Even if that were the prospect, Long Island's life-expectancy would be triple that of the Outer Cape's. Long Island not only benefits from its angle to the sea, but the bottom off Montauk Point is covered with rocks and has a gentle gradient, in both respects exerting a drag on the waves. The bottom falls off sharply from Cape Cod's Great Beach, and the products of the cliff's erosion, instead of widening the beach, are carried away, mostly to the south to extend Nauset Beach and Monomoy Island and to add to the vast, wreck-strewn shoals that extend all the way to Nantucket and as far again below it. On Long Island, away from Montauk, one has not the sense one has on the Outer Cape of the fearful progress of the sea's assault, although its encroachment is imperiling some of the mansions built thirty or more years ago along the outer dunes at East Hampton and doubtless others elsewhere.

When waves strike the beach at an angle, the sand they pick up on breaking is deposited farther along the beach on their recession. In addition, there is a southward drift of water on our Atlantic coast. These two agencies in combination move sand prevailingly down the coast. (The mystery of what ultimately happens to it is being investigated by the Geological

Survey.) The glacial till at Montauk Point has probably supplied much of the sand from which the broad, straight beaches
along the ocean side of Long Island have been built, and the
westerly movement of sand continues. For more than thirty
miles west of Montauk Point the beach fringes the mainland
of the island; the former bays across which it has formed,
sealing them off, are now fresh-water lakes, similar in origin
to the finger-lakes pointing inland from the southern shores
of Nantucket and Martha's Vineyard. From Southampton on,
however, the beaches are detached as long spits seldom more
than half a mile in width (nowhere more than a mile) and
generally much less. Extending for almost ninety miles, they
enclose a succession of large bays—Shinnecock, Moriches,
Great South and Jamaica—which communicate with the
ocean through narrow inlets. The last of the beaches, which is
set back from the line of the others and looks as if it formed
a runner or skid for that most westerly, lumpy projection of
Long Island called Brooklyn, is Coney Island.

The sculpturing of the beaches never ceases. The littoral
current is invisible, but it is plain to see that the churning waters
of the breakers as they come frothing up the beach are the
color of a wheat cereal with the sand they bring tumbling
in with them, while as they wash back into the sea the lower
beach itself seems to be sliding back with them. A third
agency engaged in the reworking of the beach is the wind,
which carries off a mist of sand whenever it blows hard
enough over the dry upper beach. Throughout its length, the
beach is everywhere being enlarged or diminished or maintained roughly as it is by a balance of accruals and losses.

> . . . I have seen the hungry ocean gain
> Advantage on the kingdom of the shore,
> And the firm soil win of the watery main,
> Increasing store with loss, and loss with store. . . .

One would perhaps expect the beach to be washed away
entirely and the sea steadily to encroach upon the land. After
all, sand is heavier than water and physics would seem to
ordain that when dislodged it would slip down and away
from shore. And indeed to anyone who keeps the beach
under observation during the winter it is very apparent that
something of the sort is taking place. The beach grows pro-

gressively narrower and steeper. If you did not know that the coastline remains in nearly the same location year after year, and if you had not read that in summer the process is reversed, you might wonder if the erosion were ever going to stop anywhere.

It is the magnitude and frequency of the waves piled up by winter winds that cause the beach to be cut back while they are blowing. When one huge breaker is charging in on the rear of another, there is a great inflow of water on the surface which has to be balanced by an equal and opposite outflow. And it is—by an equally powerful outflow below which carries seaward the sand stirred up by the churning waters. Grains of sand are so small that they readily remain in suspension in turbulent water just as dust remains in suspension in turbulent air. (The smaller an object, the larger its surface in proportion to its mass.) When the turbulence is quieted, as it will be at a certain depth, the sand sinks to the bottom. Along the line at which it tends to sink a sandbar is formed. The normal thing for a beach is to have a bar standing off shore. Indeed, if the tide-range is more than five feet, there will be two bars—a high-tide bar and a low-tide bar. Because the water over the bar is relatively shallow, large waves will break when they reach it, sending more water coursing in over the surface; in fact the position of the bar is likely to be revealed by a line of breakers. The action of big waves on a beach is a little like that of a dog digging at an embankment: as it excavates in front of it, it piles up dirt at its rear.

To understand the effect of summer's lower waves, we must recall that waves move objects in a circular path. In the upper half of the orbit objects are being moved forward, so that if anything impedes their movement in the lower half of the orbit their net displacement is ahead. With the shallow waves of a gentle sea, the drag of the bottom has just this effect. Moreover, even when the movement of an object in its orbit is not interfered with, the wave will leave it a little in advance of the position at which it picked it up; the orbit is not quite a closed circuit. The sand of the bar is gradually moved forward. The breakers stir up sand and the inrushing wash carries it up the beach, leaving part of it behind as the water at the maximum reach of the wash sinks into the sand of the slope. You can see the evidence of this in the "swash marks" that remain; every wave leaves its ghost behind in the thread of tiny pebbles or sand grains coarser than the average that trace the line it reached upon expiring. In winter, the waves are likely to follow so hard upon one another that the slope of the beach remains saturated and little water sinks into the sand except at the top. There is also comparatively little evaporation from the beach at that season so that it is waterlogged to begin with. Moreover, the cutting-back of the beach in winter necessarily creates a much steeper slope, down which the reverse wash rushes with accumulating momentum, dragging with it the sand of the lower slope and the gravel that (on Long Island, at least) forms the bottom of the beach.

The energy of eight thousand waves—the average number striking the shore in a day—is far from negligible. In the season when they are running high, mountains of sand are moved. Even on Long Island Sound, where waves cannot compare with those of the ocean, the transport may be prodigious. Dr. Rhodes W. Fairbridge of Columbia University has calculated that two hundred thousand cubic yards of gravel and boulders are carried every year around Lloyd's Point, at the end of the promontory forming one side of Cold Spring Harbor. One storm alone can drastically alter the profile of the ocean beach. The heavy seas following Hurricane Isbell removed so much sand from the beach at East Hampton that a sheer little cliff two feet high was left running its length—a phenomenon new to me. The cliff was in time undermined and washed away, but subsequent storms left evidence of their depredations in further temporary cliffs. What creates the cliffs are high waves that strike the beach at an angle and send their wash laterally along it; it is that sidewise rip that does the job. Often a channel will be scoured out behind the forepart of the beach, which will then be cut off for a distance like a sand bar. The wash of the higher waves flows over the hump and down the other side into the channel. The water pours through the channel like a river, parallel to the beach, until it reaches a depression in the bar (or hump) separating it from the sea. There, colliding with a similar flow of water from the other direction, it turns and races through the opening back into the surf. As in a brook running over an irregular bottom, there are standing waves in the water coursing through the channel. I have seen them reach a foot in height when the wash of exceptionally heavy seas kept the channel in flood. (On the ocean or on a lake, the waves move while the water stays put, whereas in a stream the waves stay put while the water moves.) The standing waves are both the cause and the consequence of the rippled configuration that the bottom of these channels always acquires, just as the bouncing of motorcars on an unpaved road is both the cause and the consequence of the inevitable corrugating of the road's surface. For a channel to form, the forepart of the beach must stand higher at its crest than the part behind it, as a slight ridge. What builds it up to this height seems to be the deposit of sand by the waves at the summit of their reach.

In contrast with the broad, gently sloping beach of summer (which will be the gentler in its slope the finer the sand of which it is composed), the winter beach is likely to be stepped. On the analogy of a staircase, there is a slanting riser, then a tread which often slopes slightly to the rear (causing a channel to form when the seas are high), followed by another slanting riser, which waves reach only during storms or spring tides, finally a second, uphill tread of dry beach ending at the dunes. Spring tides (the term "spring" having of course nothing to do with the season but referring to the act of rising) occur every fortnight at the times of the new moon and full moon when earth, moon and sun are roughly in line and the gravitational effects of the two heavenly bodies reinforce each other and create exceptionally high and exceptionally low tides as they pull the ocean first this way, then the other. At intermediate stages, when the waning or waxing moon is half full and with the earth and sun forms a right-angle triangle, the two gravitational pulls on the ocean—of which the moon's is about twice that of the sun's, owing to its much greater proximity—work against each other to produce tides of minimal range, called neap tides.

By the time summer's rebuilding of the beach begins, the angle of the foreslope will be so great as to change the character of the breakers. The swells from an April storm far out in the Atlantic, seeming to rise out of nowhere—like the waves in a bay that follow long after the passage of a ship well off shore—curl over and plunge only at the last moment, very close to anyone standing at the brink of the wash. It is extremely impressive, not only because of the big breakers' nearness, but because they crash upon the steeply-sloping beach almost perpendicularly. The concussion from the toppling wall of water is terrific. It is as if the beach were being bombed by the waves, which in fact do blast a small gully out of the gravelly lower beach. The foam leaps high. There may even be a double breaker as the air trapped in the first plunge explodes to create a second upsurge of foaming water.

Waves carry sand higher up the beach above sea-level than their own height (their height at sea, that is), in fact, almost one-third again higher, it has been found. From there on the transportation of sand depends on the wind. The net effect of the wind is to carry the sand farther from the water. This is not because the wind is prevailingly from the sea but because it strikes a surface tilted up toward it with much more force than one tilted down away from it. The beach presents a windward, exposed face to the sea, a leeward, sheltered face to the land. Then, when the sand has been air-lifted beyond the ordinary reach of the waves of spring tides and storms, it is subject to stabilization by vegetation, around which dunes form. The trend is toward the aggrandizement of the dunes—up to a point. The higher the dunes grow, the stronger the winds they have to withstand, including rampaging westerlies, and the more vulnerable to a breach in their vegetative cover. Then, too, no part of our east coast is secure from hurricanes, and the storm waves that ride in on the dome of water that forms at the center of a hurricane can lay waste the shore—dunes, man-made structures and all. And at beaches where the littoral currents generated by waves coming in at an angle are moving sand away faster than it is being replenished, the dunes will inevitably be undermined as the shore is cut back.

Before the days of extensive seaside developments the retreat of a section of shoreline received scant attention. Today, where substantial investments are being carried away, it is a different matter. Various kinds of constructions have come into use to stay the depletion of the shore. Along with sea-walls of one sort or another there has been much building of groins of rocks or pilings. Jutting out into the sea, these are designed to trap behind them the sand being moved along by the currents. In some places where groins have been found ineffective (as they often are) resort is actually being had to the transport of sand from areas of accumulation to areas of deficit by truck. Following experiments in Denmark, a novel application is being made at Brighton, England, and on the coast of New Jersey of the principle of the retardation of shore erosion by seaweed, which acts in the water as beach-grass acts in the wind. A seaweed substitute consisting of long strands of plastic is being anchored at intervals on the bottom. It strikes one as almost too perfectly in character to be true for our society to counter the sea's depredations by the employment of motor vehicles and plastic substitutes for plants.

On the contest between man and the sea for dominion over the shore, perhaps the final word has been spoken by Willard Bascom, an oceanographic engineer and author of the fascinating book *Waves and Beaches:*

> *The ocean is huge, powerful and eternal. Puny man can scarcely expect to win by overwhelming it, and anyone who counters its attack with brute-force solutions is doomed to expensive disappointment. Rather, the engineer must try to understand how the sea acts and learn to take advantage of the geographic and oceanographic conditions so that everything possible is in his favor. Then, on a battleground of his choosing, for the short span of human interest, he may be able to hold his own.*

At one time I should not have believed how much satisfaction was to be had from observing along the beach what marks the wind and waves had left, what alterations they had wrought since the day before. Copious, varied and frequently novel fare seemed to me the diet of the good life. The prodigality, variety and exuberance of nature were what excited me (not that they do not do so still). Birds appealed to me especially because they exemplified those propensities in their multiplicity of forms and plumages, their movements, their vitality, the changeableness of their populations as they came and went; and it was the chance of seeing those that were out of season or out of place or otherwise new to me that got me up early in the morning. But now when I raise my binocular to the gull that looks as large as a blackback and as pale as an Iceland I am not greatly disappointed if it is not, after all, a glaucous gull down from Labrador or Baffin Island. A common herring gull is not less expressive of the artistry and balance of nature's processes than its rarer cousin. Perhaps as one grows older one comes to discover more in less. One comes to see the whole universe implicit in a quartzite and to take a delight one would find difficult to account for in nature's most incidental designs: the circles transcribed in the sand around it by a blade of beachgrass swirled in the wind; the swash marks of the waves like the outlines of overlapping hills in a drawing; the draperies of pebbles spread on the beach; the little craters or inverse nipples in the sand where it was dry when the wash of the waves poured over it and air bubbled up through it; the ripples left on the beach by a steady wind or flowing water in a channel which are at once mathematically even and ever-varying in pattern; the scalloping of the shoreline on a thirty- or forty-foot interval through some trick of currents or of intersecting wave systems: the plaques of white jade up to two feet or more in length smoothly sculptured in abstract forms that are left along high-tide mark when the waves have wetted down and compacted a deep blanket of snow, then returned to carve out the translucent white slabs into which it had frozen.

The most casual and minor handiworks of the elements—attestations all of nature's internal order—acquire prominence from the spareness of the winter beach, and its spareness is one of its attractions. Oriental artists discovered a thousand years ago that wealth of detail, especially of conflicting detail, dissipates the observer's attention and that if most of it is dispensed with the evocative power of the remainder is enhanced. Empty space, they learned, enlists the observer's imagination in the artist's behalf. By sparing his mind the multifarious claims upon it that a crowded canvas presents, it also—as their instincts must have told them—frees him of the sense of time's pressure and induces tranquillity and serenity.

Principles that are the antitheses of these govern our civilization. While we are deprived of the openness of space and time we are loaded with a surfeit of almost everything else. We may not—almost certainly do not—possess all the goods we think we should like to own, but we must have remarkable detachment, or perhaps be wonderfully wanting in nerves, to escape feeling besieged by the plethora of material things around us that demand that we heed them, trivial though they be, that accost us from shopwindows and periodicals. Whatever the hardships and perils of the past, it is certain that never before has man been so hounded by distractions. Perhaps the appeal of the winter beach, where, as in a work of art, a little counts for a great deal, lies in part in its conducing to the reassembly of one's scattered powers.

Long Island and the City

FROM East Hampton you would have to travel a considerable distance to the west before you could distinguish the lights of New York City in the night sky. By day, however, the shadow of the metropolis is cast over the entire island. And it is cast not over the island alone. Driving in toward Manhattan, you see progressively what is in store for the entire northeastern seaboard, barring a reversal of present trends as revolutionary as those trends themselves have proved to be. Long Island's future will be no more an outgrowth of its past than if the island were to be buried beneath the lava and pumice of a volcano.

In its historical background, human as well as geological, Long Island is next of kin with Cape Cod, Martha's Vineyard and Nantucket. Like them, it was formed of soil from the continent to the north. Except for its inner end, its original settlement was, like theirs, also from that source, and it took place about the same time as theirs, in the 1640's. The Dutch, of course, had already arrived. Henry Hudson, seeking the elusive northwest passage, landed on Coney Island in 1609. By 1624, the Colony of New Netherland had been planted, and soon thereafter the colonists had crossed the East River from Manhattan to establish Breuckelen. Though the English arrived later, they had taken possession of four-fifths of the island before a dividing line was drawn at Oyster Bay. Those who settled East Hampton were from Kent—the village was originally named for the Kentish town of Maidstone, and ties with the parent town are still maintained—but the others were largely from Connecticut and the Massachusetts Bay Colony. Though the entire island was made part of the Province of New York with the capture of the

Dutch holdings by the British in 1664, its affinities remained
with the lands to the north and northeast, and it shared fully
in the great saga of New England seafaring. Whaling began
about as early on Long Island as it did at Truro and Provincetown, and in the same way, with the pursuit of the quarry
off the beach in longboats. (It was the same technique that
was employed on Washington's Birthday, 1907, by the veteran
harpooners who rowed out of East Hampton and Amagansett
to bring in the fifty-seven-foot-long right whale whose features
are known to more persons than those of any other whale that
ever lived, for her bones were carted off by Roy Chapman
Andrews to form the framework of the replica that hangs
in the American Museum of Natural History.) Sag Harbor,
which is situated on the lower shore of the bay between the
prongs, halfway out, was once the home of one of the
country's great whaling fleets, as well as the first Port of
Entry for New York. The Whalers' Church, the Greek
Revival mansion housing the Whaling Museum, the Broken
Mast Monument to those townsmen who lost their lives "in
actual encounter with the monsters of the deep," and the
many whaling captains' houses give the town even today a
facet making it unique outside New England. Greenport, the
still-active fishing port facing Sag Harbor across Shelter Island,
which almost spans the bay, was only a little behind it in
renown. In the days of sail, Long Island's great stands of
white oak helped make it a shipbuilding center as well. Before
the industry's heyday ended in the 1880's, 179 vessels had
gone down the ways at Northport alone. The brig *Daisy,* in
which Robert Cushman Murphy sailed from New Bedford to
the Antarctic in 1912 to write what is surely the most engaging narrative ever to come out of a whaling voyage—*Logbook
for Grace*—was launched in 1872 near the author's home in
Setauket, on the Sound.

Robert Cushman Murphy is a distinguished ornithologist. In
Fish-Shape Paumanok—the title taken from a poem by Walt
Whitman, who was born on Paumanok, in Brooklyn—he has
written a brief reminiscence of Long Island, recalling what
has been lost. In the beginning it must have seemed to offer
nearly everything. Its promise was made known to the early
voyagers even before they could discern its shores, for according to the writer who in 1670 published the first description of Long Island in English, its wildflowers caused "the

Countrey itself to send forth such a fragrant smell, that it may be perceived at Sea before they make the Land." They do so no more. The "innumerable multitude of seals" off shore of which he wrote are gone too, and gone likewise are the herds of whales that could be seen spouting and breaching from the land; in 1700 a woman walking along the ocean from East Hampton to Bridgehampton counted thirteen stranded on the six-mile stretch of beach, so abundant were they. Already, by then, the ax had been swung to such effect that the villages stood on treeless plains. In the post-Civil-War period the movable steam-powered sawmills ate through the last of the great forest of hardwoods that covered the hills of the island's northern spine. With the forest went most of the streams that led Walt Whitman to speak of Paumanok as "Isle of sweet brooks of drinking-water"; mostly the dry beds alone are left.

Of Long Island's original endowments, much remains, of course: protected waters on both sides of the island and in the deep cleft of its eastern end that are unmatched in extent in the environs of any great city of the world; a relatively moderate climate; hundreds of miles of beaches, many still uncrowded; great tracts of woods, even if the woods are mostly of the bristly, cutover kind; easily worked topsoil on well-drained gravel that makes for superior farmland. But the portents can hardly be misread. Between 1940 and 1950 the population of Long Island outside Brooklyn and Queens (which are governed as part of New York City) increased over 60 per cent. Between 1950 and 1960 it increased more than 100 per cent, reaching nearly two million. There is nothing to indicate that the rate of increase (which itself has been increasing) is slowing down. No end is in sight. The superhighways that carry traffic at a steady sixty miles an hour are advancing down the island with the flying panzer columns behind them. There is even agitation for a bridge from Orient Point across the mouth of the Sound to make Long Island a main thoroughfare of interstate coastal traffic and open it up to crowds from New England. Says a local businessman, "The development of the region requires it." Unanswerable argument!

The New York Times reports in a story entitled *"In Multi-Faceted Montauk":* "An energetic tourism and resort program has been instituted to fully utilize the abundance and variety

of the natural assets and activities of this sun-bathed tip of
Long Island. . . . These are not new ideas for Montauk.
Similar visions were held in the 1920's by the late Carl G.
Fisher, who sparked the development of Miami Beach out of
a tangled mass of swamp forestland. However, fulfillment of
the original goals, although on a less grandiose scale, is more
possible now than at any time since Mr. Fisher's plans were
halted by the stock-market crash. . . . The new president of
the Chamber of Commerce has been a prime mover in the
ambitious program. All resort factions and most individual
businessmen are cooperating with her vigorous drive."

A monument to the Miami developer's vision in the form
of a narrow, eight-story, crenelated onetime hotel architec-
turally inspired by a roadside ice-cream stand towers incongruously over the village of Montauk, on which it is hard to
believe that a cent has ever been spent except for the purpose
of making two others. But clearly it is more than a monument; it is an augury. And it is the auguries, multiplying with
every westward mile from Montauk, that take away most of
the pleasure in traveling on Long Island.

One has seen the auguries everywhere from Richmond to
Boston, heaven knows, but here the drive to get what is to be
had while the getting is good seems to have even more pressure behind it than elsewhere. It takes all the well-known
forms: cottages cropping up on every waterside and every
road through the woods, once-proud old houses converted into
inns and restaurants and real-estate agencies, neon and
chromium hamburger-and-ice-cream hawkeries, diners, grills,
"pancake houses," model-home displays, soft-drink bottling
plants, life-insurance agencies, builders-roofers, concrete-block
manufacturers, construction-machinery pools, motorboat sales-
rooms, the ubiquitous accomplices of the automotive age—
those that sell new cars, that sell used cars, that collect the
corpses, that fuel cars, that repair cars, that paint cars, that
wash cars, that park cars. The subdivisions jostle one another,
and with them come the shopping centers, the supermarkets,
the discount houses. Like an invading army paced by armored
juggernauts, the city is pushing forward behind the bull-
dozers, the front-end loaders, the earth-movers, the draglines,
the demolition crews. As shore and countryside fall to the
new resorts, the older ones like the Moriches and Bellport,
with their somehow integrated atmosphere of leisure and

dignity, are yielding to the atomization and confusion of new suburbia, while in the old suburbs of Long Beach and Rockaway the next wave of invasion is erecting the blockhouses of the urban mass—apartment buildings. Rockaway, the last of the barrier beaches before Coney Island, is on the New York subway. In Rockaway you are in the City.

Fissured by Newark Bay, New York Bay, the intricate bays at the narrowing end of Long Island Sound, and by the spectacular estuary of the Hudson River, the metropolis spreads over 200 or 250 or maybe even 300 square miles. Such is the extent of the honeycomb of steel, masonry, glass and asphalt in which the hum and throb of the human swarm it contains never ceases. You cannot approach its distant towers that rise like rods of mineral extruded through apertures in the earth's crust or the bridges that span its waterways—webs of blast-furnace spiders hung against the clouds —without recognizing New York as an indisputable pinnacle of the human adventure and, for what it is, supreme on earth, supreme in all time. You cannot give a thought to all that must be entailed in the daily supply of food, water, light and power to the population of a city which, beneath the pall of its exhalations, fills the field of vision of a viewer at the top of any of its peerless eminences without a new and incredulous realization of what is possible to human organization; and if you have any capacity for marveling left over, a moment's reflection on the problem of disposing of the city's wastes (enough refuse is collected daily to fill a train seven miles long) should take care of it. The more your acquaintance with it grows, the more assured your knowledge that the total accomplishment of the human race since the glacier left its grooves on the rocks in Central Park has been drawn upon in the creation of this ultimate of cities. In Manhattan you are in the Mecca of the world, that point on the earth's surface to which all its inhabitants bow one way or another, if not six times a day, at least many times during their lives —the spot to which all will repair, if their means permit, at least once, to be swept along in never-ceasing streams of people indifferent to the visitor's place of origin, traditions, habits of mind and fate in this world or the next.

If the human race can produce it, New York will provide it—for those who can pay what it costs. You have no doubt of this as you walk along mid-town Fifth Avenue, where treasures as mankind construes them are commonplace just as the earth's commonplaces—trees, shrubs and flowers—are, side by side with them, fostered as treasures. On either side, behind the plate-glass windows, are the displays of shops which together could satisfy the appetites of all the luxury-addicted courts of antiquity and never feel the loss. Around you, moreover, or above, up the sheer-walled buildings, is the greatest concentration anywhere of the arbiters of human culture: the publishers of great newspapers, books and magazines; theatrical and television producers; the eastern offices of the motion-picture satrapies; the leading art galleries, private museums and concert halls; the national advertising agencies; the determiners of all that is known as fashion; the wealthiest churches and most cathedral-like banks; the up-town offices of investment and brokerage houses; the alumni clubs of the great eastern universities; buildings bearing the names and housing the offices of the nation's biggest indus-trialists; the eating-places of the pre-eminently successful and the homes (no farther away than Park Avenue) of those who more than any others dispose of the world's hard cash. One would have to be a decrier of vanities of more than Old Testa-ment severity not to pick up some of the charge that is in the air or walk more smartly and with a quickened pulse for the knowledge that if the city disappeared tomorrow it would be talked of as it had been at this moment as long as men were alive to talk of it. You are—and everything you see confirms it—at the growing tip of human civilization. Beyond New York there is no precedent; there is only what New York itself may in the future evolve into.

A disposition to conceive that whatever New York offers must excel or at least equal the best that other communities can show had led me to look forward to seeing the Jamaica Bay wildlife refuge, which local ornithophiles have made famous. During the preceding autumn, some snow geese, a blue goose, a white pelican and a flamingo had been observed there among many less sensational transients, as *The New York Times* had reported. (Another instance of New York's quality is the adult, informed and enlightening coverage its press gives news in the world of natural history.) It had even in recent years become the site of a summer breeding-colony of glossy ibises, as little likely to have been expected there in times past as marabou storks from Africa.

If you picture Long Island as a whale butting into Manhattan and nosing Staten Island, Jamaica Bay is its high-arched mouth, with the long spit of Rockaway forming the lower jaw. At its widest, the bay is four miles from shore to shore, and it is along this dimension that an avenue crosses it, taking advantage of a narrow island that covers three-quarters of the distance. The island's bare, sandy soil supports shafty clumps of broom sedge and hummocks of little low trees and bayberry. The land slopes down on one side of the avenue to fields of salt meadow and on the other to marshes of reeds through which openings have been mowed to permit views of the water and of further salt-meadow islands with which Long Island's western bays are typically crowded. When I walked down through one of the clearings, black ducks put up from the shore and hundreds of lesser scaup ducks edged away. These latter are prominent winter ducks of Long Island's bays; grey and white with deep-purple heads, they are so beautifully proportioned, so like sculptures of soapstone in their solid forms and waxy smoothness, that you cannot see one nearby without mentally handling and stroking it. Still farther out, buffleheads were bobbing chirpily about, as always adding sparkle to grey winter waters.

I was filled with admiration that these islands and waters, from which the two clusters of Manhattan's skyscrapers, the downtown and the mid-town, stood high on the horizon, could be dedicated to a wildlife sanctuary, one protected by a warden well equipped to put the point across with several

powerboats and even an amphibious tracked vehicle from
Army stock. I was also appalled by the realization that came
upon me of how far metropolitan civilization had gone, that
a place like this should rank high as an oasis, that the hunger
that leads to the pursuit of birds had to be satisfied by the
sight of them in such a setting. On the northeast, on tracks
laid over causeways and other islands, black subway trains
rumbled continually by, bound to or from Rockaway. Beyond
the subway line, forming the eastern shore, was Idlewild—
now Kennedy—International Airport, and jet-powered air-
liners were constantly surging overhead with the roar of city-
eating lions. For good measure, on the opposite side of the
bay, there was another field, the Navy's Floyd Bennett air
station. As bad as the airplanes were the streams of cars
and trucks immediately at hand—four lanes of them. The
boulevard was greatly improved by a line of plane trees
down each side and another down the middle, but these were
clearly to be kept subordinate to the telephone wires that
passed above them.

Worse, if possible, than the noise was the trash. For a
hundred feet on either side of the roadway the refuge had the
character of a city dump. Among the preponderant litter of
papers were bottles, boxes, the sheddings of automobiles—
inner tubes, exhaust pipes, mufflers, hub-caps, chromium
strips—part of a refrigerator, filters from air-conditioners, a
mildewed upholstered chair, anything you could think of that
human beings might no longer want. On the sidewalks the
crunch of broken glass underfoot from bottles tossed out of
passing cars made it sound as if you were walking on gravel.
Experiences provoking anger at one's fellow men are always
disintegrating. And a walk down the Cross Bay Boulevard
reminds you, as you are only too often reminded in going
about our country, of the unmentionable skeleton in the closet
of democracy: the fact that a large portion of the human
race is made up of defilers and despoilers who, in D. H. Lawrence's phrase, "pull life down and devour it like vermin" and
are a scourge and a menace to the rest of us.

From experience of both, I am not sure of the adage about
the relative merits of New York as a place to visit and as
one in which to live. If you live there you at least learn to
exploit its advantages with the minimum of fruitless circulat-
ing about, while familiarity to some extent dulls your percep-

tion of its monstrosity. One who comes new to it, unless he has the money to bring it to heel, is overwhelmed by the enormity, by the unending Saharas of drabness skirting the sky-aspiring palaces of empire as its core, by the unnerving concomitants of so vast a mass of humanity: the filth of the streets; the grime that rains down from above; the din of roaring trucks, buses screaming in labor, motorcar horns, wailing ambulances and clanging fire-engines, power-shovels, pneumatic drills and riveters, policemen's and doormen's whistles, banging car-doors and trash-cans; the disturbing quality of the people in the crowds, made exhibitionist in dress and manner by the need to assert an individual existence and made unresponsive in expression and unseeing of others by the need to insulate themselves against the abrasion of ten-thousand-fold daily contact with their fellows. Overweighing everything else, even the physical immensity of the city, are the rivers of automobiles that, six abreast, clog the streets and hour after hour, morning and evening, crawl and stop and crawl again on the superhighways leading to the suburbs, bumper to bumper for twenty-five miles. The press is only a little less between commuting-times. "Already in a city like New York," says August Heckscher, looking to an even more desperate future, "one is impressed by the degree to which traffic remains heavy far into the night and the early morning; there is no rest for the great city of modernity." For fifty miles around, at all hours, there are cars, cars, cars, cars, cars. You have the feeling that human life, the human past and the resources of the future are being crammed into a meat-grinder that extrudes motorcars, multiple streams of motorcars, like link sausages, and that the process has become ungovernable, is running away with mankind.

When I get back to East Hampton from a trip to the city I am in a kind of repressed frenzy from hours-long subjection to the inescapability of man and his aggressively ugly works. I marvel then that the New Yorkers can suffer so patiently the penalties they pay for their advantages. As much, almost, as by the magnitude of the columns of creeping commuters' cars on the access highways am I impressed by the orderliness and relative silence of the twice-daily processions. Here, even the horns are stilled; perhaps there is a general consciousness that an untoward noise could provoke instant hysteria and a stampede. No one leaps from his vehicle to scream that he

has had enough; there are no butting contests between mad-
dened drivers. The cars simply move as they can and stop
as they must. Yet it is an illusion to suppose that only the
outsider is aware of what New Yorkers must put up with.
The newspapers emit continual outcries of concern and alarm
over the pollution of the atmosphere; the chronic shortage
of potable water; the choking of the streets by traffic; the
destruction of the city's past at the hands of the wrecking
crews; the mushrooming of office buildings like immense,
glass-paneled cages at the city's heart; the tensions generated
by compression of population that break out in crime and
violence; the ever-rising costs of social services; the spreading
destruction of the natural environment. "The countryside is
crowded, so that it becomes more and more difficult to reach
open land," says August Heckscher. "We flee to the seashore,
only to discover that the old silence of the sea is broken by
noisy motorboats which are becoming almost as hard to dock
as it is to park cars." In winter one can guess that from the
size of the marinas and from the stacking of boats—too
numerous to be stored except one above another—in those
near the city. In summer, the bays, like the highways, must
be overhung with a pall of hydrocarbons.

For the greatness of New York a price has inevitably to be
paid. Whether the greatness has been worth the price is a
point impossible to settle and not worth debate. But no one in
his right mind, I should think, would wish New York any larger.
No sane person could possibly imagine that the quality of the
life it offers would be improved to anything like the extent
that its ills would be multiplied and exacerbated by its continuing growth. Whatever in New York needs amelioration
and improvement will be made more difficult to ameliorate
and improve as more people crowd into the city and as it
grows to accommodate them. Yet the population of the metropolitan area continues to swell. The highways gouged straight
and wide through homes and hills to give the city's masses
an escape become the avenues of its further advance, the
extenders of the congestion from which additional escape-
routes become required, the breeders of more cars which
demand more highways. So it is everywhere, of course. *Distance is less of a locational handicap in the age of the automobile, and new highways have added to the number of potential sites,* the National Association of Real Estate Boards

exclaims. *Today intensive land use is under way in areas considered remote only five years ago. Construction is consuming thousands of acres strategically located around and within urban complexes.* And the Department of Commerce estimates that the nation's spending on construction this year will be 3 per cent more than last, when it came to nearly sixty-six billion dollars.

The question of where New York's spread is to end is not even raised. The city grows because its inhabitants reproduce faster than they die and because it attracts immigrants. Nothing foreshadows a time when the birth rate in the city will decline to near the death rate or a time when the city will cease to pull surplus population from the overcrowded cities and overworked farms of Greece and Italy, the slums of Puerto Rico and the decaying villages and increasingly mechanized farms of the American hinterland. To the world's population, the equivalent of another Great Britain and another Netherlands is added annually, to that of the United States, another Chicago, and no slowdown is in sight; on the contrary, our annual increment of three million is expected to reach five million in the next few decades. Barring revolutionary changes in human affairs, New York will presumably continue to grow, *ad infinitum,* and with it the other cities of the seaboard. To speak of a future Gloucester-to-Norfolk megalopolis has become commonplace, but nothing I have read indicates that even when that nightmare becomes a reality an end will have been reached or that even a pause may be expected. Travel where you will on Long Island or anywhere else on the northeast coast and you may anticipate that, in default of some unpredictable and certainly hitherto unplanned intervention, every bit of woodland you come upon, every quiet shore, will be invaded by the metropolis. Either it will be put to the bulldozer or—should it, against all the odds, be made into a park and protected from direct destruction—be overwhelmed by human numbers.

Such is the age we have entered upon. But I have come to wonder if perhaps the trouble is not altogether with the age but equally with a failure on our part to understand what it means to have entered upon it.

Mankind seems quite evidently to be taking one of the momentous strides of its history. One would judge the present to be comparable to those periods in the past that brought transformations in the human way of life: from stone age to bronze age to iron age to age of steel; from man-power to animal-power to wind- and water-power to combustion-power; from hunting to agriculture to handcrafts to industry. Each of these leaps forward gave us more control over our physical environment—and the cost in each case was a more far-reaching organization of society and the diminution of the sphere in which the individual was self-sufficient. As the individual became increasingly independent of nature he became increasingly dependent upon society, and correspondingly society progressively replaced nature as the source of restraints upon his freedom. Thomas Jefferson spoke enviously of the social organization, or lack of it, of the American aborigines, who enjoyed a degree of manly independence that even the colonists could not claim. Most of us, however, probably including Jefferson, would doubtless hold that our gains through civilization have more than offset our losses. (But of course we are the offspring of that civilization. The Iroquois and Sioux, the Vikings and the Franks might well disagree and despise us for having bartered our manhood for pusillanimous security and women's fripperies.) In any case, it would seem reasonable that as the power of each of us to affect the lives of our fellows grows, the power of the whole, the collective power, to prevent our exercising it inimically would have to grow whether we like it or not. Despots who have arrogated this power and wielded it arbitrarily may be overthrown, but the mass of laws and regulations and the apparatus required to administer them tend always to expand and to gain in ascendancy; in a highly industrialized society, no room is left for privileged classes above the law.

That we are now in a second Industrial Revolution as portentous as the first seems generally to be acknowledged. The pace of scientific advance has been so swift that it is almost as if some kind of fetters had been thrown off. In the mere space of the past quarter-century our reach, our power over our environment, has been growing by almost unimaginable bounds. Those of us who capitalize on the new technologies have the means of making their presence felt by their fellows as never before. One way in which they are making their presence felt—and in varying ways and degrees we are all implicated—is by threatening to render our common environment unfit for habitation. The racket of machines (now capable of shattering our windows at three thousand paces) grows louder and the clamor of the hucksters more insistent and pervasive. The atmosphere is poisoned: 350,000 tons of noxious gases are poured into it daily by automobiles, the numbers of which increase even faster than the number of people available to buy them. (The birth-rate of the one is currently just twice that of the other.) Citing an analysis by a special committee of the City Council, *The New York Times* reports: "Those who breathe New York City air may inhale in a day as much of a suspected cancer-causing substance as they would get from smoking a half-dozen or more cigarettes. They are subjected to a steady rain of sooty dust that sometimes exceeds one hundred tons a square mile. Sulfuric acid mist, a by-product of the city's smokestacks, eats at their lungs, corrodes the city's monuments, renders illegible hieroglyphics on Cleopatra's Needle, the obelisk in Central Park." Of our rivers, six hundred are listed as dangerously polluted. An expert with the Fish and Wildlife Service, George P. Skinner, reports that of the 2,000,000 acres of habitat along our Atlantic coast suitable for shellfish* 3 per cent has been destroyed and 20 per cent, or 400,000 acres, closed to harvesting because of pollution. (According to Dr. Harold Haskin of Rutgers University, a "terrible fight" will be needed if the oyster is to be saved as an article of commerce. In addition to the damage from pollution and reckless mismanagement at the hands of the industry, the drought in the Middle Atlantic states in recent years has, by increasing the salinity of the bays and estuaries, favored the spread of the oysters' natural enemies—starfishes, the carnivorous snails known as oyster-drills and, infinitely worse, the protozoan that causes the dread MSX disease—and these have laid waste the beds. While the drought is a natural and presumably temporary phenomenon it can be followed by a man-made one, the director of the Oyster Institute has pointed out, as the northern cities take more and more of the flow of the Susquehanna and Potomac Rivers.)

Ugliness expressed in the garish, the malproportioned, the

---

* This includes acreage variously suitable for oysters and hard clams (also known as quahogs, littleneck clams or, when immature, cherry stones) or for soft-shell clams (also known as long-necks or steamers) or for bay scallops.

shoddy, the spurious daily extends its conquests—and, as Heckscher declares, "The mind of man reflects and repeats the forms which it finds in the exterior world; the soul is colored by the colors of the objective landscape." With increased human mobility and prosperity, the littering of the landscape grows, while the genius of our age, which overlooks no detail, sees to it that the litter will be increasingly of materials resistant to decomposition—glass, aluminum and plastics. The physical plant of civilization becomes ever more pre-emptive, its demands growing by what it consumes. Accustomed scenes that give us a feeling of belonging and of sharing in the continuity of that which is greater than we are now go by the board in wholesale lots. We are left to feel alien in a world in which we are encompassed by overbearing buildings, car-filled highways and pander-temples of commercialism. Not only are the human millions better and better equipped to devastate and befoul their surroundings but medical science, preserving the lives of children who once would have died, insures that there shall be ever more millions of them to do so.

But the evils of a runaway population do not stop with the physical effects. Human inflation must have the consequences of every other kind of inflation. It must depreciate the value of the article inflated. Says James Reston, "If there has been a decline of decency in the modern world and a revolt against law and fair dealing, it is precisely because of the decline in the belief in each man as something precious." But how could we expect such a belief to be sustained when four-fifths of the human race live where a plethora of people is a major problem? And the epidemic of human numbers gives every promise of raging on. We should ask ourselves not only what demands the future hordes will make upon resources but what psychological climate will prevail when seething multitudes of people overwhelm the land in Coney Island infestations. It is already evident that the overcrowding of the planet can in the end lead only to the renewed onslaught of mankind's ancient scourges—war, famine and pestilence. Who in the light of such an outlook would bank heavily on the survival of whatever in our way of life rests upon an exalted valuation of the human individual?

If the past is any example, the cause of civilization would seem to depend upon an abridgement of the latitude allowed the individual commensurate with the enhancement we are witnessing of his means of extending himself at the expense of others. Men in general, as has only too often been shown, cannot be relied upon to repress their own propensities toward aggression and self-aggrandizement. If we are given high-powered motorcars, traffic laws must be enacted and police provided to enforce them such as were unnecessary when our capacity for injuring others was limited to the horse-power of a horse. The curbs that nature has in the past applied to human beings having been further and drastically weakened by the new technology, it would follow that society must take up the slack if there is not to be more or less of anarchy. This would mean the curtailment of rights we are accustomed to viewing as inalienable but which cannot much longer be indiscriminately indulged without intolerable cost to society. I am thinking of rights which amount to license to abuse our common environment and thus to deny others their equity in it—in short, to rob them. And crucial among these, I should think, is the right to reproduce to one's heart's content. It is true that even the strongest advocates of governmental action to combat the population explosion usually disavow any intention to seek legal limitations on the size of families; for the state to intervene in this intimate personal domain would be "unthinkable," it is claimed. There was a time when it was also unthinkable for the state to take over the administration of justice and outlaw the private righting of wrongs by sword and battle-ax. Yet it had to become thinkable if order and civilization were to prevail over chaos.

"Life is good in America," the Secretary of the Interior has observed, "but the good life still eludes us. Our standard of living is admittedly high, but measured by those things that truly distinguish a civilization, our living standards are hardly high at all. We have, I fear, confused power with greatness." The United States—to follow him further—has led the world "in pollution and blight and despoliation." What is called for, he urges, is "an American Renaissance," including "the building of handsome and balanced cities, the reclaiming of the rivers of America, the saving of our wildlife and wild land, the preservation of our historic landmarks, the cleansing of our air, the restoration of our countryside and the redesigning of our cities and suburbs."

In the original Renaissance an indispensable role was

played by the princes of the Italian city-states whose economic
privileges enabled them to commission the work of the
inspired artists the times produced and who had the taste to
recognize and demand the best. The post-Civil-War period in
the United States saw a vastly enhanced economic power
gathered in the hands of a set of businessmen whose bold
acquisitiveness, techniques of acquisition and addiction to the
material symbols of position gave them something in common
with the Medicis, Sforzas, Estes and Gonzagas. There, perhaps, ended any resemblance between America of the so-
called robber barons and Renaissance Italy. The manners and
tastes of the men who amassed the great fortunes of two or
three generations ago and who showed their quality in the
great summer resorts of Mount Desert, Newport, Saratoga,
Woodstock, Southampton, and Palm Beach are not held in
high esteem today. Yet when we compare their handiwork
with what has followed we may have second thoughts.

East Hampton, which might also be included in the
category of the great resorts though less grand than the others
(while still being grand enough), is the only comparable
settlement I know at all well. And I must say I know no
other in the United States that I find more beautiful. Its great
houses were commissioned by men who thought in terms of
the enduring, who respected what had gone before and meant
to create that which would inspire respect in long years to
come; and whatever their ethics in making money (about
which I am in the dark) they had the instinct of integrity
when it came to employing it. White colonial in style or of
dark, brown-grey weathered shingle siding, of an expansiveness
but little inhibited by cost, the domiciles they ordained
have a mountainous air owing to their bulk and to the
proportion of the whole accounted for by their imposing
roofs. They have the reposeful assurance of lions couchant.
Those along the beach—loaf-shaped mansions—carry out the
lines of the dunes from which they rise as if the two had
been designed together. In the distance, as you look down
the shore into the dusty glow of a sunset, their hazy forms in
the romantic scene remind you of great haystacks.

And, back from the beach, what trees there are everywhere in this place! The trees are above all what make it—
the trees and the rhododendrons two stories tall, the hillocks
of azalea, the walls of privet, wisteria climbing the houses,

ten-foot hedges of lilac, roses and trumpet honeysuckle on the split-rail fences, yews that spread tree-sized fans of foliage by the public library. Most of the elms on Main Sttreet—so celebrated they are mentioned in encyclopedias—went down before the once-in-a-century equinoctial hurricane of 1938, but several remain among the replacements and one, just before the beginning of the shopping district, is the biggest elm I have ever seen; you would think it three elms in one to judge by the bole and the number of subtrunks into which it divides, and gazing up into the prodigal spread of its branches you would imagine yourself looking high and higher into the realm of ethereal events wholly unrelated to mundane affairs on your level. The trees stand throughout in godly occupation, enormous, burr-shaped beeches, green and copper, out of the Forest of Arden; sycamore maples, sugar maples, Norway maples, silver maples (the elms of the maple tribe in their vaselike growth); cylindrical, tassel-foliated Japanese temple cedars *(Cryptomerias);* Atlas cedars with tufted, blue-green needles; lindens (the lime trees of English novels); spruces of the north and pines of the south; and below the spread of the giants, lacy Japanese maples, dogwoods, flowering cherries and flowering crab apples, and rich, lustrous English hollies. You feel you are in a land of master houses and tree-kings only incidentally inhabited by undersized human beings, and sparsely enough by them except on weekends and in the summer.

Estates like East Hampton's are not brought into being and kept up without money. Money was required, too, to build the East Hampton Free Library, in which one could comfortably and happily spend the better part of a lifetime. It was required to erect Guild Hall and its attached hexagonal theater, the site of art exhibits (a show of the first importance could be put on comprising only canvases produced within seven miles of the corner of Main and Dunemere) and of performances in the drama, music and the dance not to be expected away from a major population-center. But money alone can do more harm than good. Dollars aplenty have gone into the new houses along the beaches between Southampton and Westhampton, but confronted by them one feels only glum and disoriented. Their styles are without coherence, without reason, without restraint. The houses of East Hampton were built when there was a powerful indige-

nous tradition in architecture, which was an honest expression
of man's experience on the land, but these are the outgrowth
of nothing in nature or in the human past. They are merely
attestations of what machines make possible: anything that
can be constructed *will* be constructed.

"They give an effect of lack of permanence," said Vera.

They did. One looked like a concertina, another, built of
glass-sided blocks, like a toadstool—truly. Several tall, concrete
structures had roofs of a succession of hemicylinders, as if
lined up for an ice-skater to overleap. A number were of
alternating panels of glass and plastic, or what looked like
plastic. So was an apartment building of four units in a clover
pattern resembling tanks at an oil-refinery. The structures all
looked temporary and expressed the impermanence of values
of the society they sprang from. You felt yourself in the
presence of a culture flying apart in all directions. (Well, we
were not there to look at houses and tried to avoid doing so.
Behind them, between the road and the salt meadows bordering Shinnecock Bay, was a scrub-growth of bayberry, beach-
plum and groundsel-bush still bearing its pallid green
foliage, though it was near the end of November, and there
were patches with a reddish cast where the wild rose stood
with its crop of hips. Several times great blue herons rose
from the marsh before us, lifted into the wind with a few
easy strokes of their great sails. On the beach were sanderlings, the little winter sandpipers of the eastern beaches. They

are nearly white with a dusky upper surface scarcely darker than the sand, but their eyes, bills and legs are black. They pursue the receding waves and retreat from the incoming, scurrying twinkle-footed as if over a hot-plate. They are always in a hurry except when they stop and seem forgetful of what they are doing. They dart forward, then whirl, probing the wet sand with desperate haste.)

Just north of Babylon—and I mean the one on Long Island, of course—the Southern State Parkway passes between lines of full-bodied white pines and Norway spruces. Presumably these once presided over the entranceway to the Belmont estate, which is now one of Long Island's 14 state parks. Not far from it, occupying a bulge in Great South Bay, is another, Heckscher Park. The size of its picnic grounds and of its parking plazas, on which regiments could parade, tells you what the crowds must be that the park draws in summer. On the winter day when I was there, however, the beaches and the waters that washed them were the sole province of a northwest wind—though six miles away, off the corner of shore called Blue Point and famous among gastronomists, ramshackle oyster-dredges were plying, raising the scrapings of the bottom on conveyer belts. The lovely woods covering most of the flat parkland had temporarily reverted to the possession of squirrels, crows and chickadees. The readiness with which one could imagine oneself in a landed gentleman's preserves and the example of the fate of the Belmont property called to mind the obvious truth that it has now been left to the state—which is to say the electorate—to take over the role once performed by a privileged upper class in acquiring tracts of land and managing them to best advantage to lift the tenor of life. The great estates today are people's estates.

The powers exercised by the princes of the Renaissance would be criminal in the view of current political morality. So would those of the haughty noblemen whose cultivated acquisitiveness led to London's present magnificent endowment of parks. Even the society that produced East Hampton has vanished—taking its servants with it. Perhaps the nearest thing to such a town the future is likely to bring is the planned satellite community of which examples are being built today, materialized all at once on vast tracts, complete with commercial and residential areas, lakes and parks, by builders with financing which would have startled even John D. Rockefeller and J. P. Morgan. Even so, East Hampton has a lesson to teach which the nation must learn if it is to be livable in years to come. It is one that does not depend on our being rich, or any richer than the economists allow that we are going to be. If the very trees of East Hampton seem to bespeak wealth— especially the fat-trunked, smooth-skinned beeches with their enormous bursts of a myriad fine branches—these trees in fact cost little when they were planted. You can grow a beech from a seed, for nothing. What counted was having citizens who could see what would come from planting trees and who cared. They loved the village well enough to look three-quarters of a century into its future and plan for it. If the costly mansions contribute incalculably to East Hampton's character, it is also true that there are no more captivating houses in the community than the modest little dwellings on the far side of the pond, bordered by a row of horse chest-nuts, that is your first sight as you come into town. The two oldest houses are here, above the slope of the old graveyard where, in a sarcophagus topped by the recumbent figure of a knight in full armor, lies the first English Long Islander, Lion Gardiner. (Gardiner's Island, which was given to him to for-tify, is still owned by his heirs, to whom one of East Hamp-ton's finest houses also belongs.) The Mulford house (still occupied by Mulfords) and the adjacent house in which John Howard Payne wrote *Home, Sweet Home* while teaching in the academy (now a museum) across the street are simple, shingled structures of the lean-to, or salt-box, style with the small windows of the days before central heating. A fire-in-surance underwriter indifferent to their three-hundred-year-old associations would not assess them at the cost of a three-bedroom rambler. Yet a town of houses their equal would be rich indeed.

What money has done primarily for East Hampton is to give its possessors the incentive and the strength to stand off the elements that have wreaked havoc on almost all other communities in the nation—the dollar-hungry speculators, land-sharpies and construction interests. Money produced a large upper class in East Hampton with beautiful homes to fight for and time to give the fight. Eighty years ago the Ladies Village Improvement Society was formed, and it has proved a force to be reckoned with. The L.V.I.S. said that zoning would be tough, and it has been. It said there would be no billboards, and there are none in the village; moreover, after a grace period granted five years ago, even those in the outer township are scheduled to come down this year— bitterly though real-estate interests are resisting. It decreed that the trees would be protected from those who for one reason or another might find them inconvenient and would be cherished, and they have been. In all this and more the defenders of the town's character have had the backing of a highly literate weekly, the *Star,* which addresses itself with equal tartness to national departures from principle in Southeast Asia and the matter of local trash-disposal. The novelty of East Hampton is that livability rather than marketability has been the criterion. The commercial district is subdued, the municipal parking area out of sight. The past has not been sacrificed. The old homes have been kept intact and so have the old windmills, shingled, saltcellar-shaped structures once crucial to Long Island's economy. Between the village and the beach is a wooded park with a nature trail through it along the waterway leading into Hook Pond. Hook Pond, which was a bay until closed off by the formation of the barrier beach, is itself a wildlife sanctuary. It is home for mallards and mute swans the year around. On migration it is visited by droves of Canada geese, green-winged teals and widgeons— a pretty species with a bottle-green lozenge extending backward from the eye and a crown of vanilla ice cream (in the drake, that is) and the piping voice of a rubber doll with a whistle for a navel. Coots feed like chickens on the fairway of the adjacent Maidstone Country Club, where gulls stand in sober convention. Hunting is, in fact, prohibited throughout the village and its environs, and ring-necked pheasants pick their way about the lawns and roadsides in a semitame state, the cocks magnificently liveried, crimson-faced retainers who gather their dignity about them and lope off when it appears that an intruder means to proceed on his disrespectful course. ("Why do they appear to be lacking arms?" I remark to Vera. "Because," she says, "they have white collars, like clerics.")

Yet I do not believe that wealth has been the indispensable ingredient. In other towns the battle has gone to the moneygrubbers by default. It has been the lack not of wealth but of purpose and persistence on the part of those who

stand to lose by the prostitution of the community. They do
not care, or care enough. In the suburbs, which increasingly
are Residential America, they are apt to be transients in any
case. The profit-grabbers, spurred by one of the strongest of
all human motives, give full thought to their designs. Fighting
them is not an idle-hour, off-and-on-again operation, and the
issue almost always depends on their defeat.

One tells oneself that there is hope. Our economic productivity, which is in large measure the source of our trouble,
could provide the means of a partial remedy anyway. When
we can clearly afford to do so, it should be possible to preserve far more of our land, adding it to the public domain,
and of the monuments of our past association with it. Leisure
and economic security have in the past led to improved tastes
and the cultivation of the arts on the part of the successful
few and their heirs, and maybe they will do so in the case
of the successful many tomorrow. It could even be that with
incomes growing ever higher (if they keep on doing so)
profit-making will cease to be esteemed by us as man's primary purpose on earth and we shall prove less willing to
sacrifice all else in its favor. The achievement by urban voters
of the representation they are entitled to could also make a
difference, for it is in the cities that the need for conservation
is best appreciated.

Some grounds for encouragement may be found in the advances the cause of conservation has made on most fronts in
the past few years. Steps have been taken to safeguard remaining areas of wilderness—a legislative near-miracle. New
National Seashore Recreation Areas have been authorized.
Congress has put the Federal Government squarely into the
battle against pollution of the atmosphere and the rivers,
which hitherto has been less a battle than a rout of the public
interest. An American President has recognized that "the
explosion of the world's population" is of concern to our
Government and has undertaken to "seek new ways to use our
knowledge" to deal with it. The Senate has taken under consideration measures to "coordinate birth-control information
and make it available upon request in the United States and
overseas." Actions have been taken by most states to carry
out such measures within their own jurisdictions. An American
President has declared that "association with beauty can enlarge man's imagination and revive his spirit" and made the

crucial decision that "the beauty of our land is a natural resource" and that "to rebuild and reclaim the beauty we inherited" must be a national aim.

Of our National Seashores, all but Cape Hatteras have been established since 1961. Fire Island, which acquired this status in August 1964, was the fifth. Thirty-two miles long, it makes up the center section, and more than one-third, of Long Island's south shore. The wonder is that by the time salvation came there was anything left to save, for Fire Island's western end lies only fifty miles from the center of New York City and sixteen million persons live within a hundred miles of its fine beaches. What preserved it was its relative inaccessibility. There were, and are, no roads on it. Until April 1964 its only connection with the mainland was a bridge at its outer end, and this led only to the parking lots and bathhouse of a county park. In that month, however, a causeway and bridge were opened to Fire Island State Park, which occupies the western five miles of the island. The decision to construct the western link (a much longer and more expensive one) was ominous. The immediate purpose was to prepare the 1,000-acre Fire Island State Park to take the human overflow from Jones Beach, where even the mammoth facilities which had once made it a model of its kind were being swamped. Parking spaces for twelve thousand cars were laid out to handle the traffic the bridge could be counted upon to bring. (Bathhouses with 850 lockers, picnic grounds and a snack bar and souvenir shop were already in existence, serving ferry-borne crowds.) But the bridge was to be only a beginning. A proposal had already been launched to build an "ocean boulevard" the entire length of the island. This high-speed thoroughfare was to have four lanes and a right-of-way of three hundred yards, and for long stretches this would have taken up half the width of the island, which has the proportions of a strand of spaghetti. *Life*'s comment was that "It is all too easy to equate the public interest with that version of the 'mass interest' which turns out to mean more automobiles and hot dog stands." The chief proponent of the highway plan was, of all things, the Temporary State Commission on Protection and Preservation of the Atlantic Shore-front. The Secretary of this body was New York's well-publicized Parks Commissioner. An urge to bequeath imposing monuments to posterity seems to seize upon those who have been long in office—and the Commissioner's modesty had already been so far overcome that Fire Island State Park had been renamed for him and the new causeway to the island named for him too.

Fortunately, local opinion was strongly in favor of saving Fire Island from the proffered Protection and Preservation. Conservationists all over the country, moreover, rose to its defense. The highwaymen were put down. Under the bill passed by Congress, Fire Island National Seashore will remain free of roads and motorcars. It will include twenty-six miles of ocean beach, extending from Fire Island State Park (as I shall continue to call it) to the eastern tip of the island, together with 18,700 acres, of which 4,500 are land. Most of the western half of the island, other than the beach, will remain outside the reservation; except for the state park, this half is largely taken up by fourteen villages.

While everyone who lives on Fire Island is dependent upon private boat or public ferry in getting to and from his abode and always has been (and now, we may trust, always will be), the island has been a resort at least since 1855, when a big summer hotel was built at its western tip—or what was then the western tip, four miles short of where it is today. The Surf was a long, three-story structure with covered boardwalks connecting it with auxiliary quarters and with both waterfronts, also with a pier to which a side-wheel steamer brought guests from across the bay, among them, one reads, Jay Gould and Lillian Russell, *à deux*. Since the Surf burned down just before World War I, nothing anywhere near so grand has been seen on the island. Just about everything else in the way of human *divertissement* has been, however.

It was the dead of winter when I first saw it—and what I saw were only the parts around the two bridges to which I could walk. From the causeway, the ice on Great South Bay extended as far as one could see, though there were black ducks and scaups as thick as flies where there was an open lead. Against a sky hung with clouds in heavy folds, between which a peach-colored, early-morning sunlight filtered, the gulls were ghost-white. Few scenes are more desolate than vast, bare accommodations for an absent public, and that was how the state park was with its asphalt plains and sprawling bathhouses. At Captree State Park work was already under way on some of the charter-boats and excursion-boats

which by mid-March would be taking fishermen out for
flounder, twenty to fifty or more in a load. (Captree occupies
the outer end of Jones Beach Island, with which the inner
end of Fire Island overlaps; you cross the one in going to
the other.) On Fire Island, even the Coast Guard station
seemed unoccupied. However, three swarthy youngsters were
batting a baseball to one another on the beach with the
exaggerated mobility of youth possessing energy to spare.
Truants from school, they must have been, and truants un-
abashed by their truancy—maybe even dropouts from high
school who would pay for it in later life. But it did one good
to see the human spirit rebellious of confinement—suffi-
ciently so to be attracted to this winter-bound and deserted
spot—and so bouncy. They scooped the rolling ball from the
sand and flung it with loose-limbed fluidity of movement.
Probably they would heave beer cans into the scenery with
equal nonchalance, I had to remind myself.

On the bay near the shore, where buffleheads were diving
at the edge of the ice, were a dozen red-breasted mergansers.
These are to other ducks as those prodigiously spare race
horses of early-nineteenth-century prints are to workaday
horses. The drake, dressy in white collar, carries his dark-
green head as proudly as a prancer on a checkrein, the plumes
of his war bonnet stirring in the breeze. There were also the
three birds that most temper the severity of the winter beach
with their cozy air—sanderlings, to begin with, which, with
their short necks and long, shorebird's legs, have the immature look of colts. In flight they are long-billed bullets
flashing by on scimitar wings which show a white median
stripe. The speed and dash of shorebirds in the air does not
seem to go with their soft, tremulous personalities and
plaintive notes, but frequenting a terrain without cover as
they do, a favorite hunting-ground of falcons, they have no
choice but to be fast and tricky.

The horned larks, with their incongruous, rather Tartarlike
black-mustachioed, black-browed and -horned little faces, feed
back among the grasses. Their motions are sudden, unsure
and jerky, like those of a wound-up toy, but they pirouette
almost as smartly as the sanderlings on their short legs. When
disturbed they take off as if suddenly aware that what they
are seeking is somewhere else altogether, sending back a
chorus of timid cheeps and chipperings. Snow buntings,

possibly because they look as fat as little seals, appear to
have come straight down from the Arctic, as they have. A
flock had swirled up from the hillside when I turned into
Acadia National Park and another had swung erratically by
over the dunes at Ipswich, their plumage a fair approxima-
tion of the white of the sand, the tawny of the beachgrass and
the black of the beach-plum. Upon alighting, snow buntings
stand stock-still in case a predator had spotted them on the
wing. They will take a little run, stop and look up at the sky.
And they are continually looking up as they walk about. Yet
they twitter away musically as if they were in on some redeeming
secret about the cosmos.

Remaining alive is clearly a full-time occupation for most
creatures. Among the exceptions are the gulls. One of the
consistent impressions you bring back from the shore is of
the ennui of the gulls. At least it looks like ennui. All up and
down the coast, on favored spots on the beach, more commonly on grassy expanses back from it, on school playgrounds,
in city dumps, even on the flat roofs of depots in Jamaica
(Long Island, again), masses of gulls stand stolidly, some
asleep, like elderly club-members for whom life has lost its
challenge. They stand in similar guise, individually, on seaside
telephone poles and even on the cables slung between them:
just stand and stare, whether with anything on their minds it
is impossible to say. Gulls, in current parlance, have it made.
"Getting along in the biosphere," Marston Bates observes,
"has come to mean getting along with man." After having
been harried ruthlessly by eggers, plume-hunters and target-
practicers, gulls since the turn of the century have been on
the right side of civilized man, protected for their value as
scavengers of organic refuse and because civilized man's heart
has been softened toward objects of natural beauty. Herring
gulls especially, which breed around the whole Northern
Hemisphere, have greatly prospered and have extended their
range southward (or reoccupied parts from which they had
been driven) both in the United States and in Europe. They
have, indeed, so multiplied as to cause serious trouble for
the terns, whose habitat they share and whose eggs and young
they feed upon. Worried wildlife-management specialists have
even resorted to poisoning to reduce the numbers of herring
gulls. As almost always happens when an animal species
threatens to burst its bounds, a natural check has appeared,

and one which may help restore the balance, though it has not yet done so. Behind the herring gull in its surge of numbers has come the larger and more authoritative black-backed gull, also with a taste for eggs and young birds, among them those of the herring gull. From having when I first knew it, in my boyhood, been a bird worth reporting to ornithological headquarters when winter brought it south to the vicinity of New York, it now ranges down the coast through half the year as far as North Carolina and even breeds on Long Island.

In late January, Fire Island was as desolate around the outer bridge as around the inner but—once you got away from the installations of Smith Point Park—with a wild and barbaric air, challenging you to face it out. The sky was filled as if with smoke by the unwearying easterly. The few gulls took off from the beach far ahead, unsure of man in this lonely spot. With the dunes having the form of gale-tossed waves, the very shore appeared to be storm-born and tumultuous. One felt one had intruded between two arch-beings rapt in a blindly watchful, age-old confrontation, the frowning land boldly matching its static solidity against the perpetually assailing, fluid sea. The eerie feeling engendered by the contest between two such powerful yet lifeless personalities was intensified by signs of man's abandonment of the scene. Rising a foot or two from the sand of the beach were two rows of pilings—pine trunks rotted away but for their cores. These and some twisted, rusted link-fencing were all that remained of a pre-hurricane Coast Guard station. As well as commemorating a day when man had a more intimate and precarious involvement with the sea and beach-patrols were regularly maintained, they gave evidence of the recession of the shore, of which I had read. Fire Island, as is said to be the case with some other barrier beaches, may be moving back toward the mainland. Long-time residents say the beach is much narrower than it used to be. The wreck of the steamer *Franklin,* which was driven ashore a little farther up the island from where I was walking, is still to be seen at low tide, I had read, but half a mile off shore, the beach having presumably retreated as much as that since the old side-wheeler went aground in 1854.

Joseph Conrad tells in *A Personal Record* of the ordeals of his successive examinations on the way to a master's certificate, the examiner in one placing him in an "imaginary ship [that] seemed to labor under a most comprehensive curse. . . . Finally he shoved me into the North Sea (I suppose) and provided me with a leeshore with outlying sandbanks—the Dutch coast presumably. Distance, eight miles. The evidence of such implacable animosity deprived me of speech for quite half a minute." At the site of the old Coast Guard station I recalled that passage, as I had many times on the beach. When you are by yourself at the shore on winter days of a stiff wind from off the sea, such as this one was, the ghosts of ships in their mortal hour are present and the all but audible cries of the despairing seamen carry to one.

The south shore of Long Island is not quite such a charnel house of ships as the shoals below Cape Cod and those off the Outer Banks, but with its outlying bar it would be found gruesome enough by eyes which could penetrate the waters and the sands. That is clear from the account written by Jeannette Rattray of East Hampton. It was the frequency of wrecks along these strands that caused the first Fire Island lighthouse to be erected in 1825. Four years earlier the first steamship to cross the ocean had gone aground and been broken up on a November day somewhere along the stretch of coast before me. (The single-cylinder engine turning her collapsible paddle-wheels developed only 90 horsepower, but it drove her for the first four days of her maiden twenty-nine-day crossing, at six knots.) I peered at the running waves of the grey sea as if by an act of will I might divine *Savannah*'s place of burial. She had been known to me from childhood; my father and mother were acquainted with some of the heirs of her first owners, in the city she was named for. . . . It is strange with what emotion one thinks of finding and resurrecting the remains of such a vessel, as if in raising them in triumph—behold!—one would snatch a victory from the consuming medium!

Probably the most famous victim of shipwreck on Fire Island was Margaret Fuller, early champion of women's rights and erstwhile literary editor of the New York *Tribune.* When the vessel in which she was sailing, *Elizabeth,* was driven onto the bar in 1850, she saw her little son drowned with a sailor who was trying to swim ashore with him, then was drowned herself, lashed to a spar, as was her husband. "I accept the universe!" she had once declared, hardly foreseeing, one may be sure, how that odd, presumptuous faith would someday be tested.

It was to the west, near the inner end of the island, that *Elizabeth* was lost. In the other direction was the site of a shipwreck that, of all on this stretch of coast, was one of the most tragic in the needless loss of life it entailed and in the conclusion it wrote to the sad history of those to whom the coast had formerly belonged. The vessel was the iron sailing ship *Circassian,* which had been a blockade-runner during the Civil War before being captured by the Union. When she went aground on the bar in December 1876, there had been no difficulty in getting her company ashore. The trouble came later, during the attempted salvage. A storm struck. The salvage master, confident that it would float the prize off the bar, held his crew aboard—until too late. Of the thirty-two men, twenty-six were drowned, including ten of the last full-blooded Shinnecock Indians.

To see very much of Fire Island, I had to wait until I could ride down it with a Park Ranger. None had yet been assigned to the projected National Seashore, and I did not have my tour until I had long been back from pursuing winter down the coast to its southernmost holdings and winter itself had withdrawn to its Arctic fastnesses.

It takes the ocean off the northeastern states a long time to warm up after it has cooled off. While it is doing so, those who choose to dwell upon the shore are like investors who surrender immediate gratifications for the sake of future returns. Sunlight is poured into the bank of the sea at the cost of a late spring and its warmth withdrawn later for the advantage of a protracted autumn. It must be remembered, however, that the ocean does more than delay the advent of the warm and cold seasons. By acting as a break upon them it moderates both. Montauk is not only relatively cool in summer (as one might expect); its frost-free season is reported to be three weeks longer than that of Roslyn, at the other end of the island, on the Sound. Of course, temperature is not everything. Once at Montauk the lighthouse-keeper's wife, upon whom had temporarily devolved the duties of the post, had to creep up the hill to the beacon on her hands and knees to keep from being blown off it, while chimneys and roofs have repeatedly been swept from it and one wind carried an entire barn to sea.

On outer Long Island, the only truly warm spring days are the still ones. Winds from the northern quarter bring down the cool air of Canada while those from the southern come chilled by the sea; they feel like the flow from a refrigerator. In early June the ocean at East Hampton, I found, was still so cold it gave you an electric shock when you lunged into it—while a breaker perfectly innocuous-looking to an eye attuned to winter's plungers knocked you head over heels. In April and May, temperatures registered by our thermometer were regularly 5 to 10 degrees below those broadcast by the radio station at Hartford, Connecticut. The spring blooming season is thus delayed. Measured by the dogwood, outer Long Island in early May is about ten days behind that part of Westchester County which is of the same latitude. Inasmuch as the difference is greatest early in the season and lessens week by week, spring is telescoped; forsythia and tulips will still be blooming when rhododendron comes in.

On Fire Island the compressed flowering season must be at its peak in the second week of June, or so I decided when I saw it then. (I am now going on ahead of my narrative.) The beach-goldenrod, which perhaps showers the sands with more radiance than any other plant, would not be in bloom until much later, and the flowers of the beach-plum, which encase the scrawny black limbs in glowing, snowy sleeves, were all gone. But on the outer ramparts of dunes, the trailing, rubbery-leaved beach-pea had erected its standards, pink fading to bluish, and the cushions of wormwood *(Artemisia)*, with its indescribably lovely pale, soft, blue-green foliage, were small forests of stalks hung with petalless yellow flowers. On some dunes the salt-spray rose marched down the inner slope bearing its white or magenta saucer-flowers. Behind the outer dunes, the pads of beach heather were brilliant butter-yellow with little five-petaled flowers, and yellow were the flowers of the four-foot-tall thistles. Among the compactly vegetated dunes of the second rank, more salt-spray rose in bloom, with it that other Asian immigrant, multiflora rose, with its clusters of flowers like yellow-stitched white buttons, and the pink-flowering native rose, and so too were most of the woody plants—wild cherry, poison ivy, Virginia creeper, blueberry, sassafras and, where it grew in protected places, holly.

Holly is the tree that comes to mind when Fire Island is mentioned—not because it is typical but because, incongruous

as it is, it is represented in one particular place there by
patriarchs of its kind. It may seem curious that Fire Island
should be celebrated and especially cherished for a feature
out of character on a barrier beach and commonplace over
most of the rest of the East—a woods. It does not seem so
when you have seen it, however. The famous sunken forest,
a fifth of a square mile in extent, is located in a section of
the island of no more than average width but it is protected
by dunes among the island's largest, up to thirty feet in
height: camels' humps, they reminded me of. To reach it,
you climb the inner range, up a sandy slope sheeted with
bearberry. The top of the forest stretches away on a level with
the top of the ridge; you might think you were looking across
a brush-grown plateau. The first invader must have been
astonished to find himself descending into a darkly wooded
glen. Entering it, you feel you have chanced upon the secret
hoard of that pitilessly exposed, outlying isle seared by sun,
wind and salt-spray, as if you had come upon an eagle's nest
and had your eyes opened to its fierce guardian's capacity
for protectiveness. As man's essential humanity may come
out most affectingly in conditions least propitious to it, as at
times of natural disaster, so may the ·essential quality of a
woods in the unlikely setting of sand dunes. After the glare
of the beach and the shimmering sea I thought as we de-

scended the path into the sunken forest that never had a
sylvan stillness been so trenchant or been parted so sug-
gestively by a rustle in the undergrowth or the flutter of a
bird's wings, never sun-spangled shadows more beckoningly
receding, never mute tree trunks more inviting of touch,
never more silencing a softness of leaf mold underfoot,
never more rich a bogginess as in the small depression at
the bottom of the path. Red maples, pitch pines, black tupelos
and sassafras trees almost as big as any I had seen (granted
that they are small trees at best) made up the forest—with
the hollies, some of which were a foot through at the base
of the trunk. "Dr. Murphy says this one may be 150 years
old and is probably the oldest of all," said our guide. William
R. Oakley, " 'Sunken Forest' Guard," as he was identified on
the card he gave me at parting, looked as if he might have
stepped out of the clipper ship depicted on the card. He
lived by himself at the edge of the forest amid gleanings of
the beach that must have taken years to accumulate; the
place resembled on old farmyard on the eve of an auction.
A guard was needed. Even with one, as he pointed out, young
hollies had been slashed into and other small trees felled for
firewood. That the sunken forest has been preserved is owing
to the public spirit of a group of private citizens mostly of
the adjacent village of Point O'Woods, the oldest and most
high-toned on the island, who, to prevent its being sliced
up into lots by developers, purchased seventy-five acres of it
at a cost of $150,000. This and the other fifty acres of the
forest will be part of the National Seashore.

That day, as I so often am, I was pierced through by
admiration—the expression is really not too strong—of those
who in defense of the patrimony of the nation set their sights
on finite, concrete objectives and then go after them with
whatever it takes to achieve them. They are not, like me,
demoralized and defeated at the start by the magnitude of
the problem. Simply because they cannot save all or even
much of the remaining climax woodland in our country or
of the remaining un-built-over beach they are not discouraged
from setting about to save what they can, even if it amounts
to only a few score acres or a few miles. They organize, they
campaign. They give time and money they could spend far
more pleasantly in other ways. While I am in retreat before
our all-consuming commercial civilization, seeking out places

where I can forget it, they are doing battle with it, attending zoning meetings and legislative hearings armed with facts and taking the issues to the courts. They work in and with conservation organizations, and when an island is threatened by an ocean boulevard, a redwood forest by a state highway, a canyon or river valley by a dam, a National Park by over-development or defection of its water supply, a national monument by real-estate promoters, a scenic vista at the heart of the nation by ten-story apartments or a sewage-disposal plant, or disappearing birds or mammals by shoot-ing, pesticides, poisoning or invasion of their breeding grounds, they raise the alarm and mount the counterattack, and they never give up—while I, like the enraged King John at Runnymede, gnaw at sticks and hurl imprecations in the general direction of the human race. They are the officials of executive agencies who year after year patiently and exhaustively present before Congressional subcommittees headed by martinets the case for measures to conserve beaches, dunelands, forests, prairies, waterways and the land-marks of the past; or conversely, they are Congressmen whom such measures may not help at all in the ordeal of elections and who yet take precious time to battle for them, session after session if need be. I fulminate against parents who, in a world already feeling the pinch of numbers, heedlessly or complacently go on multiplying themselves, like occupants of a lifeboat insistent upon obtaining more than their share of limited provisions; but *they* are out forcing upon the notice of the public the disasters a swarming population has in store for the nation and the world, establishing birth-control clinics, giving tangible help to foreign countries condemned to poverty by the ungoverned reproduction of their inhabitants. God be praised that there are such persons.

It was only in the nick of time that they won the day for Fire Island. Not only was the Park Commissioner's blunder-buss sighted down it, but the builders were hard at work. The villages were spawning more houses, "boatels" were ap-pearing and more squatters' huts were cropping up deep in the still-virgin duneland, often constructed at little cost of materials, mostly picked up on the beach. (I have never seen such a shore for attracting drift lumber as Fire Island—not only the great creosoted timbers at the inner end but every-where a profusion of planks and a bewildering number of

cargo platforms, used with fork-lifts.) The prospect that Fire
Island would be made a National Seashore only stimulated
the rash of building. Choice lots, which would be surrounded
by parkland, were snapped up by those whose only concern
was to snatch what they could for themselves and to hell with
the public interest. Applications for building-permits poured
in. Brookhaven township, which includes most of the settled
part of the island, denied them but the denial was upset in
the courts. It was a memorable pageant of self-seeking. The
act calling for the creation of the National Seashore set July
1, 1963, as the cutoff date for new construction in the undeveloped parts. Any house begun in such parts after that
date was to be subject to condemnation—but at full cost to
the taxpayers, of course. (There is no restriction on building
in the areas excluded from the Seashore provided zoning
criteria set up by the Secretary of the Interior are complied
with.) The inspection trip on which I was accompanying the
Park Ranger took us into a number of houses marked for
condemnation near Cherry Grove. Elevated on scaffolding,
they were very contemporary in their cubical forms, glass
walls and modern equipment and were connected with one
another by high boardwalks. But most of them had been
broken into, fixtures made off with, toilets clogged, floors
littered with literally hundreds of cigarette butts; evidently
they were used as places of assignation.

Cherry Grove, the "Official Guide to Fire Island," published
by *The Fire Island News,* explains with startling candor,
"is the only Island community—and one of the few in the
world—in which homosexuals constitute a substantial proportion of the inhabitants." That the fact of there being only
one such community on the island should be considered
noteworthy tells a good deal about this peculiar locale. Unquestionably the young men strolling on the beach or the
boardwalks comprised most of the visible population. They
were personable on the whole and above average in physique,
and if there seemed a quality about them of being a little
blurred or wraithlike, that could have been my imagination.
The Ranger told me that there was a masquerade party at the
end of the season at which it was said to be impossible in
some cases to tell which of the women were *bona fide* and
which were men, and those which were women were quite
likely to be variants themselves. A clean-cut, outdoors young

man only two years out of Montana State University, he must have been goggle-eyed at what fate had dropped him into the midst of—and not in Cherry Grove alone—when he was delivered to his post two months earlier. However, he took it in stride now, though his regard of the bikini-clad young women farther along at Ocean Beach may have been, as mine also may have been, a little more sidelong than that we bestowed upon, say, the small flocks of great black-backed gulls entering their second year which to my surprise outnumbered the herrings we saw.

Male and female homosexuality and transvestism were only some of the directions sex took on the island. There was also exhibitionism, again both male and female. If I understood correctly, the next issue of *The Fire Island News* was to have a story on a girl who made a practice of flying a kite from the dunes in the nude. Most of all, of course, there was straight sex. "Open covenants openly arrived at" would apparently describe much of it. "Groupings," as the term was for the foursomes and sixsomes who banded together to take a house for the season in order to circumvent the exorbitant rentals, were often enough of mixed sexes with the participants brought together simply through the want-ads. Love-making in virtually all stages, if indeed not quite all, was an ordinary sight along the beach; there was no time, and for many no place, for decorum. Harried New Yorkers had to take their frolics, like their cocktails, at a gulp.

Ocean Beach, the most populous and boisterous of Fire Island's towns, is also the most notorious for the quick pick-up and the compact orgy for weekenders. As well as the revelry of Manhattan and of a South Sea isle could be combined in half a square mile of cottage-dwelling beach community with seven bars in a small commercial quadrangle, Ocean Beach combines them—with the understanding that Fire Island is not for everybody; money is required to reach it and put up on it. According to the proprietor of one of the bars, at which we had a sandwich lunch, the town's permanent population of 150 is increased a hundredfold on big weekends in the summer. (For the island as a whole, the figure probably reaches 40,000.) Most of the holidaymakers come from New York offices, business and professional; some are from the colleges, some from the varied fields of the arts. Luminaries from the theatrical and entertainment worlds

burst in around the witching hour on Saturday, having crossed
the bay by speedboat, and head for the raucous, all-night
parties just then hitting their stride.

"I'll be interested to see what exposition of the human
community the National Park Service offers in its visitor-
orientation center," I remarked to my escort. But he was not
to be baited.

It is too bad that the subject will doubtless have to be
eschewed, for the human side of Fire Island is not lacking
in instructiveness. Like the metropolis of which it is an off-
shoot, Ocean Beach stands as a high-water-mark of man's
progress in the subordination of nature. This is a way of life
of man's ordering. The restraints imposed by the natural
order and the restraints imposed by tradition—the modes and
mores established during a period of equilibrium between
man and nature—have been left behind. But life without
restraints is life without form, and life without form leads,
pretty surely, to demoralization. Whatever else may be said
about the pursuit of happiness by the sybarites of Fire Island,
it seems safe to suppose that it is not brilliantly successful.
One is sometimes tempted to believe that human beings can
endure anything but that which they most persistently seek
—freedom. The value of freedom is not to be doubted, but in
the end its value, one might venture to guess, lies in the
opportunity it gives us to choose which discipline we shall
yield it to. Perhaps after all my difference with the nuns of
Salveregina College is only that I should make a different
choice from theirs.

Point O'Woods, a settled, self-respecting colony of traditional, two-story frame houses of brown-shingle siding which
was established in 1890 as the Long Island Chautauqua Association with all the land and utilities jointly owned (as they
still are), has separated itself from Ocean Beach and its
satellite communities by a high link-fence topped by several
strands of barbed wire, and one can understand why. Yet I
must not do Ocean Beach injustice. There is about it a most
potent charm. However it may be when the diversion-hungry
crowds pour in on Saturday, on a weekday it seems a quiet
enough resort of ordinary people who with industry sparked
by desperation have contrived a small retreat from New
York's heat-oppressed, fumes-asphyxiated, savagely noisy
summer. The one-story cottages are closely planted with

shrubs, the horizon is low and wide and the reduced scale on which the village is built is beguiling. But it is less in what Ocean Beach possesses that its charm lies than in what it is without. It is without motorcars. There are no motorcars and there is no provision for any. Well, there *are* utility vehicles, a police car or two, and a fleet of ten beach-going taxicabs, which the island would be better off without, and these can navigate the sandy, rutted passageways between the rows of houses, half on the concrete walkways, where such as these exist. But private cars are missing. And to come to a village where this condition prevails, where the incubus of the automobile has been lifted from mankind, is like waking from a bad dream. It needed only an introduction to that snug, humanly-proportioned little town, in which people are visibly what counts, and a glimpse of the row of little carts, kept chained at the landing, in which the inhabitants haul their baggage and groceries, to convince me doubly of what I was already sure enough: that I should willingly forgo the chance ever to ride in an automobile again if everyone else would do so too. If such a revolution could ever take place it would be like the liberation of a land from a foreign army of occupation. We should rub our eyes and rediscover our fellow men.

"How are you going to keep Fire Island from becoming another Jones Beach?" I asked the Ranger.

"You know," he said, "everyone asks that question in those very same words." He reminded me that there would be no roads giving access to the beaches away from the bridges. There would be trails leading off from the parking areas and a bicycle path running the length of the island (a wonderful idea, in my view, which would bring me back to Fire Island without fail unless an act of God prevented) but no masses of people were going to go very far by those means. The capacity of the ferries that would take visitors down the island to landings along the bay shore would be restricted. That would insure that the island would not be overrun. His main concern seemed to be with the damage that even a small amount of foot-traffic could do the dunes.

"You see there the paths that have been worn across them? That's all it takes to start a blowout, and before you know it the dune's finished. The people who live here understand that and do their best to protect the dunes, but we're going to have a job getting the point across to tourists."

The Secretary of the Interior foresees for Fire Island National Seashore an annual incursion of six million visitors. One can only hope the Ranger is right and that the pressures sure to be generated for ready access to all parts of the reservation can be withstood.

Down the Coast
to Assateague

IT WAS the first day of February, four months before I had
my tour of Fire Island, and I was driving through New York
on my way south. My resolution to look hopefully and con-
structively toward the future was as usual proving unequal
to the experience of traversing the metropolis. The two-hour
wide traffic congestion was too much for it. So was all the
construction that was going on, which, recognizably only a
frantic response to mounting needs that would overwhelm in
due course whatever was built to contain them, was as temporary as the buildings of the World's Fair beside the Long
Island Expressway. So was the thought of the relentless
demands New York made upon one's success-achieving potential. In the world man left when he moved to the city,
what counted was to be alive, holding your own against the
elements. You felt it on the beach, and as if it woke a power
in you. But in the metropolis, where your contest was not
with nature but with the human crowd, it was by no means
enough to be alive. You had to be on top of the heap or the
heap would be on top of you.

"We know," says Constantinos A. Doxiadis, internationally-
noted city-planner, "that a century from now the average
city will have 20 times more people, 100 times more income
and 200 to 300 times more cars and machines." That was
surely what lay ahead. But whether we should get there was
another matter. It was in my mind that metropolitan civilization might be likened to a balloon which we are constantly
blowing bigger, increasing the tension and the pressure within,
and that if so a limit must sooner or later be reached. The
balloon would start to blow back in our faces and would
collapse, or it would explode. And the sooner the catastrophe

came the better, I thought—the more plants and animals there would be surviving to restore the earth's rich life and the better prospect there would be that a portion of the human race would remain unspoiled to carry on.

However, driving up the shore of the harbor, I almost repented of the sentence I had passed upon the city. The Verrazano-Narrows Bridge is alone nearly enough to justify New York's sins against nature. The twin pylons carrying the 6,690-foot-long suspended roadway caused me to gape, awed and marveling and troubled of heart as by an intimation of the supernatural, as an untraveled *fellah* of ancient Egypt must have gaped when first he stood before Cheops. You can hardly think of it as the artifact of ordinary men, your fellow pygmies whose essential objectives in life are tenderloin steak with French fries and a fair partner in a soft bed. It seems rather the creation of impersonal, earth-shaping forces such as those which produced the moraine, the ends of which, here where it was sundered by the Hudson River, the bridge connects—and not unworthily. Then, across the Narrows above the bridge, at the Staten Island piers, are the big tankers from Maracaibo and Bahrein. On your own side of the harbor, where the Belt Parkway cuts behind the Brooklyn docks, are the derricks and funnels of the workaday freighters and, when you have passed through the tunnel to Manhattan's Battery and the West Side Drive, the piers at which the world's great passenger liners are berthed, white palaces on hulls black or grey. It comes to you, as with the smell of brine, hemp and spices wafted from the docks, that New York is not entirely the inward-turning, self-absorbed financial and cultural capital you picture but a trader gazing seaward along the shipping lanes to Southampton, Cherbourg, Naples, Piraeus, Valparaíso, Capetown, Bombay, Singapore and Yokohama—a great and romantic port.

But no, it does not help. The Verrazano-Narrows Bridge is dedicated to Baal: only motor vehicles may cross it; it is barred to the walker. A curse on it! And what does it mean today to be a port? Ships have lost place to airplanes, which every year fly bigger crowds to less differentiated parts of a more shrunken globe. A generation is foreseeable which will have traveled everywhere and have never known what travel is, never known the sense of vast distance traversed, the deliciously prolonged suspense of a protracted voyage at sea

while you are held, as it were, in lightheaded abeyance, or
the chance to be a different person that a strange and unpredictable land far removed from your familiars affords. . . .
Still, all is not lost! Even if the worse comes to the
worst, there will be times of day and seasons of the year that
are uncongenial to the multitudes. Like an animal forced to
the edge of its environment by a more powerful invader, you
can be abroad at dawn and afield in winter. And, assisted by
evidences of the time-span of geological change, you can take
a long view and consider that over-dominance of the environment, such as our civilization has achieved, seems inevitably
to set countervailing forces in motion which in the end restore a balance—even if civilization is not like a balloon.

Across the Hudson there are the Palisades. For twenty
miles these spectacular cliffs, between three hundred and five
hundred feet in height, form the western bank of the river,
which for this distance is not truly a river but a cleft in the
continent into which the sea has flowed. They owe their
origin to the instability of the crustal rocks following the
uplifting of the Appalachian mountains some two hundred
million years ago. While sediments from the new range were
being deposited off shore and recompacted into rock, a fissure
was opened in the earth's crust and basaltic magma from
the depths forced its way between the bedding-planes of the
newly-formed red sandstones and shales and solidified. An
immense basaltic sill was formed, like a tabletop sloping
down to the west. The Palisades are its cutaway eastern edge.
They derive their name from the prismatic form taken by the
congealing magma. "Trap" is a term commonly given to
rocks of this structure, from the Swedish word for steps.

From the New Jersey end of the Lincoln Tunnel the highway cuts through the black rock of the Palisades and about
five miles farther on through the equally black rock of Laurel
or Snake Hill, a remarkable outcropping, steep and abrupt,
above the Hackensack marshes, the feeder-pipe of an ancient
volcano. Disfigured by the symbols of Greek-letter fraternities
painted on it, encumbered by the ruined brick buildings of
the former County Work House and Poor Farm, it is also,
alas, being quarried away. I have a block of the basalt of which
it is formed and am given pause by its presence in the room
with me after the events it has come through, which have
seen the face of the earth transfigured, since its birth in a

cataclysm of eons past. (I picked it up on my return trip at some risk of being piled into from the rear by a truck as I whisked the bus off onto a suddenly-appearing shoulder in the cut the New Jersey Turnpike makes in the side of the outcropping.)

The thousands of acres of tasseled reeds *(Phragmites)* in the alluvial plain of the Hackensack River through which the Turnpike passes have been greatly reduced by fill for railroad yards, junkyards of cars, trucks and buses, chemical works and other plants and are being further steadily encroached upon by plateaus of refuse. You still, however, have reed-fields beside you as you drive on past the Newark port and airport and beyond, in the region of the oil refineries around Elizabeth. There, where the storage tanks are scattered over the denuded landscape like checkers-men, the steel entrails of the machine age are laid bare in miles of pipes, and a sweetish reek hangs over all. Towers of steel scaffolding carry power-lines across the plain. I drove past tall chimneys from which smoke funneled up, some black, some white, to merge into the tarnished silver overcast. Fire was bellying out of some, billowing and trailing off into the sooty vapor. A black river flowed between banks equally black, passed over by all but a few gulls which stood, somehow unsoiled, in the poisonous mud. Over a sere, thankless-looking field a rough-legged hawk was hunting. It displayed the white rump of its kind and was hovering on bent wings as a roughleg does— a feat of aeronautics, one would think, for a bird with great pinions meant for soaring. (Its legs are rough only in being feathered.) An attractive aspect of birds—and one that makes Jamaica Bay for all its degradation a place of escape from the city—is that they are uncompromised by their surroundings. A roughleg against this pestilential background is no different from what it would be above the moorland of Cape Cod, with which, as with all its primitive homeland, it serves as a link. As for me, I felt sure as I drove on to Sandy Hook that I should be anything but uncompromised if I were required to inhabit the squalid outskirts of the New Jersey industrial region. . . . I saw myself occupying a hollow-eyed house of fake-brick asphalt siding, an old car on blocks in the bare yard with motor removed, and down the way a false-front, cinder-block roadhouse with advertisements for beer in neon script in the dusty windows. The long view of

geological time would not save me. An alcoholic, a devotee
of sex or violence, a political extremist, a religious fanatic,
a television-addict: I doubted that I should escape being one
or another.

The beach at Sandy Hook turned out to be rather forbidding, all things considered—one of them being that a thin,
driving snow was in the air. A low, narrow, shrimp-shaped
peninsula jutting up into Lower New York Bay, Sandy Hook
extends to within five miles of Rockaway Point on the other
side of the bay. It, the hook of Cape Cod and the upper
prong of Nantucket are the only considerable spits on our
Atlantic coast formed by northward-flowing currents. Apparently the central New Jersey coast, like the Upper Cape and
Nantucket, breasts the seas and parts them, causing currents
to go off in both directions. The fact that the northern New
Jersey coast is in the lee of Long Island, as far as the prevailing down-coast current goes, doubtless accounts for a great
deal. Because Sandy Hook is the site of a military post—
Fort Hancock—the public is admitted only as far as the state
park at its base, and the gatekeeper could not understand why
I was willing to pay fifty cents to visit this at such a time.

From the beach, strewn with the white shells of surf clams and quahogs and bruise-colored shells of moon-snails, a towboat could be seen on the horizon of the leaden sea pulling three widely-spaced barges, but these seemed as static as so many Fort Sumters. Behind the beach, snow-fencing and an abatis of discarded Christmas trees had been erected to hold the sand, which evidently was drifting inland. Dead and dying trees rose from the dunes, including hollies holding grimly and gamely on to life though bare at the top. Yet cheerless as was the prospect, the sight of the sea brought a kind of redemption from what had gone before, an intimation of momentousness and grandeur in what passes on this earth.

Low hills come down to the shore at the foot of Sandy Hook—the Navesink Highlands—and these are the last that do so from here on. At this point the coastal plain begins to emerge from the sea and fan out southward, the Piedmont retreating as it does so. Originally, the coastal plain was a ledge of sedimentary rock formed under the sea out of the silt and sand washed down from the eroding Appalachians at a time when the ocean lapped at the edge of what is now the Piedmont. (The Appalachians themselves are composed chiefly of rock which was formed in the same way, as an ocean bed, out of eroded material carried down from an ancient and evidently mighty range of mountains and subsequently upreared and buckled. In their case, however, the silt and sand that formed the sedimentary rock was brought down by westward-flowing rivers, from mountains to the east, of which the present Piedmont marks what was their western edge. If, as there is reason to believe, the continents were once joined together and have since drifted apart—islands of granite on a sea of basalt—opening up the Atlantic Ocean as a great fissure between the Americas on one side and Europe and Africa on the other, then the roots of the primeval range are perhaps to be found not under our Atlantic seaboard and the waters off our coast but in Europe.) The broad ledge of new rock extending out from the foot of the Piedmont emerged as the coastal plain, reaching from Georgia to beyond Nova Scotia, with a retreat in the ocean. Then, when the ice sheet had first depressed the land and subsequently, as it melted, released the stupendous quantities of water it had contained, a partial reversal took place. The coastal plain was submerged again north of the bay of New

York, decreasingly so to the south, where, however, the ocean covered the outer margins of the plain and advanced up the valleys that had been etched out by rivers. The lower courses of the rivers were thus converted into estuaries, or arms of the sea. The Susquehanna, Patapsco, Patuxent, Severn and Potomac of western Maryland and their matching streams in eastern Maryland, together with the Rappahannock, York and James of Virginia, were once branches of a single fresh-water river; now they flow into separate tidal estuaries up to fifty miles long which are all branches of one much larger tidal estuary, Chesapeake Bay.

As the coastal plain widens southward, the fall-line stands farther inland. This is the line on which, from New Jersey southward, the rivers tumble from the hard granitic rock of the Piedmont to the beds they have cut in the softer sedimentary rock of the coastal plain. Below the fall-line, rivers are tidal and navigable. Because transshipment of cargoes must take place at the fall-line, it is natural for towns to grow up there. Trenton, Philadelphia, Baltimore, Georgetown (now part of Washington), Richmond, Raleigh, Columbia, Augusta, Macon and Montgomery are among those that did so. From New York northward, where the land was sunk right down to the sharply rising terrain of the Piedmont, the sea made much less additional progress up the rivers. With one exception, the fall-line in the northeastern states lies much nearer the coast, the two being scarcely distinguishable north of Massachusetts. The exception is the valley of the Hudson, which was relatively level for a long way inland so that the ocean advanced far up it; the tides today are felt all the way to Troy, 150 miles from the river's mouth. (This, of course, greatly influenced history. Of the initial Dutch settlements of 1623, the most populous was at Albany, I learned to my surprise. The Hudson subsequently became a great avenue of commerce through which was funneled the trade of the northern Midwest and the Great Lakes.) The bed of the Hudson in cross section has a broad upper portion and a keel-like lower, which was the gorge through which the river flowed before the sea's invasion. This gorge runs to the edge of the continental shelf and down its front for a distance of four hundred miles from the shore and would be one of the most spectacular features of the country if the ocean returned to its proper bed below the shelf.

When you follow a terrain feature like the coast rather than a main highway you come upon much that is unexpected. Long Branch was one of the surprises I had. It was a resort which once, at least, opulence had made its own. Ocean Drive, which passed through a succession of beachside resorts, was here paved in buff-colored brick. The mansions fronting it, mostly white and many in a Spanish style with red, barrel-tiled roofs, were spread out expansively, displaying the architectural extravagances of deep porches, multiple dormers, bay windows and conical turrets that few persons since our grandfathers' day have had the ingenuous self-assurance, even if they have had the means, to indulge in. Presidents Grant, Hayes, Harrison and Wilson all came to Long Branch, and so, over half a mile of railroad track laid in the course of a single night from the station to his cottage, did the wounded Garfield, to die lingeringly. This I learned from the W.P.A. Guide, as I did also that Colonel Jim Fisk, who with Lily Langtry, Diamond Jim Brady, Lillian Russell, Josie Mansfield and Ed Stokes had added glitter to Long Branch, had drilled a private regiment in gold braid on the Bluff Parade Ground. And I had barely heard of Long Branch. The Parade Ground has gone now and so have the bluffs and two earlier Ocean Drives, so seriously has the sea been wearing away this section of the coast.

As on Long Island, the sea with its spoil of sand has formed barrier beaches across the bays on the New Jersey coast, sealing off many and converting them to fresh-water lakes. And these, like their counterparts around East Hampton, now afforded one of the pleasantest sights imaginable. On the ice that covered them, children on skates, all in bright colors, swarmed as densely and as intricately interweaving as a host of gnats. The scenes had a wonderfully old-fashioned air. I could not remember when I had last seen children in such numbers enjoying themselves spontaneously and on their own. It was as if station-wagons, television and the billion-dollar toy-industry had never been invented. The skaters screamed, skidded and swung on one another, and the misting-over of the vista by the fine, falling snow made it seem even more a picture found in an attic come to life. One of the lakes—Shark River, at Belmar—was shared between some hundreds of children and as many mallards in an opening by the outlet, while beside the bus as I brewed a cup of

tea a close band of rotund little coots was snatching a meal
from a lawn. Someday, perhaps, shame at the way we have
treated our country's wildlife and a realization that such of
it as survives does so only through our active fostering may
bring about a truce between us and the remainder. Should it
do so, we could expect that the waterfowl, game-birds, hawks
and others that now generally flee for their lives at our approach would become as little fearful of us as many already
are where they are protected—like the coots beside the bus.
Here and there, at any rate, the depleted, crowded planet
would have an aspect of Eden.

The coast of New Jersey is like that of Long Island not
only in that the beaches start out at the upper end at the foot
of hills and as an integral part of the land and then go on to
enclose lakes that once were bays; they also, still farther
down, stand off from the land as barrier islands fringing bays
and marshes. And this, with the marshes cut by tidal rivers,
is more or less the character of the coast from New Jersey
southward. From here on, the limitations—and attractions—
of a flat, sandy coast being what they are, the only towns on
the ocean are resorts like Long Branch or playground cities
like Asbury Park, just beyond it, a place of hotels, dineries
and amusement parks and especially of Convention Hall.
(This big bandbox built out over the ocean gave me a feeling
as of my heart skipping a beat when I passed it. However, it
was not a heartbeat that was missing but some twenty years.
During World War II I had studied in an Army communica-
tions school in Convention Hall—looking out of a window to
the beach, literally within a stone's throw, on which the burning *Morro Castle* had gone aground in 1934 after 122 of her
passengers had died.)

Another consequence of the character of the coast from
here on is that it has made possible the Intracoastal Waterway, a water route inside the shore which, making use of
bays, salt rivers, artificially deepened channels and a few
considerable canals, will take boats of up to seven-foot draft
to Florida and along the Gulf Coast all the way to the
southern tip of Texas. The entrance to the Waterway from
the ocean is at Manasquan Inlet, twenty miles below Sandy
Hook. (There is also a northern leg from New York up the
Sound and through the Cape Cod Canal to Boston. The total
length of the Waterway is thirty-one hundred miles.) I rather

expected a special portal at Manasquan, like the Gateway to the West at St. Louis, and while none was to be seen, there was, immediately to the north at Sea Girt, a much more remarkable attraction. In a park just back from the beach was a forest of full-grown hollies, the only one I had ever seen, and all along the street there were hollies as shade trees in front yards.

That night I thought how much I could wish for everyone the chance to get away as I had and take potluck on the road. Having cleaned up after dinner—which is to say stuffed a can and a paper plate in the trash bag and washed a saucepan, a cup and a spoon—I was stretched out in near-perfect repose. It was snowing furiously, a copious, seemingly inexhaustible snow rushing past the windows blindingly, but since the wind seemed to be from the southwest I had hopes of its letting up. If it did not, morning would find us in snow over our hub-caps, I knew not where. Technically I did know where—on the parking grounds of a lifeless, black swimming pavilion in Island State Park on one of the long, narrow barrier islands framing Barnegat Bay, New Jersey's equivalent of the Outer Banks—but it was to me only a place on a map. Being disengaged and footloose of course has its risks. It can quickly lead to demoralization. Anyone intending to go vagabonding by himself in an off-season should probably have a concrete objective. He could be collecting minerals or completing a monograph on eighteenth-century farm buildings. Given such a purpose—and learning about the beach in winter seemed to serve—the constant uncertainty of what you are going to come upon, the freedom from commitment to an itinerary, even the question of how and where you are going to spend the night, give the passing moments a vivid freshness. The mistake we are apt to labor hardest at making is foreclosing possibilities, without which life is not life.

The snow stopped during the night but it left an accumulation sufficient to transform into an etching the landscape of beachgrass, bayberry and flattened holly and juniper. The low-pressure area could actually be seen in retreat in the east, the sky in that quarter and the sea beneath it being positively brown. I walked for an hour on the beach, exhilarated by the virgin morning and thinking, as I so often had occasion to, what a privilege it was to have the vast arena of sea and

sand all to oneself with only such company as one would
willingly share it with—in this case gulls, sanderlings and
long-tailed ducks. The last were speeding southward in flocks
of fifty and more. Never prepared for the dash and limber-
ness with which the longtails fly, and with my binocular
steamed over with the cold, I first mistook them for some
large, pied shorebird.

Barnegat Bay was ice the color of dishwater from shore to
shore. Frozen too were the salt-grass and cord-grass marshes
of the 26-square-mile Brigantine Wildlife Refuge, just north
of Atlantic City. Brigantine is known especially for the brants
that congregate there in winter. This small goose is a distinct
personage in the bird world. It nests as far north as there is
land, on Ellesmere Island and the northern coasts of Greenland, spending the winter on the Atlantic coast from New
Jersey to North Carolina. It is uniquely a salt-water goose,
and if it repairs to dry land to nest, the young make for the
sea as soon as they are hatched. In the 1930's, the survival
of the species was problematical. At that time the eelgrass,
which made underwater meadows of the shallower bottoms
of bays from Newfoundland to North Carolina and on which
the brant chiefly subsisted in winter, was very nearly wiped
out by a blight. In vastly reduced numbers the brant managed by switching to a diet of sea-lettuce to tide itself over
until the eelgrass blight had run its course. With the recovery
of its staple, it has made a full comeback. It remains, however, an illustration of the dangers of specialization—fortunately not so somber a one as the Everglade kite of Florida
which has been practically exterminated as drainage canals
have destroyed the habitat of *Ampullaria,* the large fresh-
water snails on which it depends entirely for food. But of
course the story of evolution is the story of the Everglade
kite endlessly repeated. If we pare nature down to its essen-
tials, what we end up with, I sometimes think, is irony, or, if
we prefer, an inescapable and implacable balance by which
ultimately everything comes out even. The competitive conditions of existence press all living things in the direction of
specialization, for in specialization is efficiency; the Everglade
kite's long-tipped hooked beak is wonderfully adept at ex-
tracting *Ampullaria* from its shell. Yet the more highly specialized the form, the more vulnerable it is to a change in its
environment. From the pteranodons of twenty-foot wing-

spread to the flightless giant moa, the history of life is a history of the sloughing-off of the specialists, though this is probably much more true of the land than of the sea, where the environment is more stable. Every creature that has been cock of the walk in the past has been humbled—and always, I should imagine, by less specialized competitors. The greater the success, it sometimes seems, the surer the downfall. Man has thrived in part because he is a generalist, inherently unspecialized and adaptable. He is an animal with forelimbs which never evolved into flippers, claws, hoofs or wings; these would have committed the species to a single narrow mode of existence. Instead, he developed versatile hands and to command them, in place of an inflexible set of instincts, an improvising brain. Thus he has become able to complement himself at will with oars, knives, domesticated horses and finally airplanes as well as other adjuncts which could be set aside when they had served their purpose. Yet there is a catch. There always is. The history of human life too is one of successes which have failed—of vanished societies. Mankind has avoided specialization as a species while gaining its advantages through civilizations based upon the specialization of the individuals composing them. The more highly evolved a civilization, the better able it is to command its environment but the more susceptible to disruption it grows as the conditions of existence it affords its citizens, and on which they depend, become ever more refined and complicated. When a man can support himself only by making shoes, or a certain component of shoes, or by the keeping of accounts, and depends upon food, water and fuel brought from a hundred or more miles away, and society is chiefly composed of such men, then it had better be sure that nothing can arise to upset its precarious, if productive, internal economy. The development of civilization would seem to be a kind of race. Can society's increasing effectiveness keep ahead of its increasing vulnerability? For every civilization the race has finally been lost—up to our own. Western civilization has gone much farther than any other—in effectiveness and, one must suppose, in vulnerability.

But back to the brant, which in its extremity squeaked by on the bare minimum of resilience and now is safe: as many as 170,000 have been recorded at one time in the Brigantine Wildlife Refuge. None was to be seen when I was there,

however; the marshes were a snowbound Arctic tundra. A
rent in the ice of an impoundment in the distance was crowded
with ducks, though. I had scarcely noticed this as I drove
along the dike when most of them suddenly took to the air
and came speeding overhead—a sheet of black ducks. The
trouble was evident. An Olympian bald eagle, white of head
and tail, was winging in. Then followed a performance the
like of which I had never before seen. The eagle repeatedly
dropped upon a duck, the duck each time diving at the last
instant, the eagle rising eight or ten feet with much flapping
and trying again. (The blacks had obviously cleared out
because they are non-divers.) It ended with the eagle standing on the ice, whether having caught its prey I could not
make out. But I doubted that it had. It was ill-equipped to
overcome such a quarry and I thought the hunting must have
been poor to account for its putting so much energy into the
attempt.

I caught up with the brants on the outskirts of Atlantic
City. There were hundreds, perhaps several thousand, only
a little off the highway on Absecon Bay, and they were as
dainty little geese as they are reputed to be. Short-necked,
buoyant and active, they looked like mallards seen as through
a glass darkly, but a glass permitting their pale underparts to
show up in bright contrast with the charcoal of their heads,
necks and breasts. The flocks, blooming with cottony patches
as their members tipped to feed from the bottom, exposing
the snowy feathering beneath their tails, kept up a subdued
honking, sounding like a chorus of swamp tree-frogs in a bog
in March.

Atlantic City is a natural site for a resort, winter as well
as summer. The beach here, as it does nowhere else between
Long Island and Cape May, faces more south than east and
thus is somewhat protected from winds and currents from
the north. In addition—which seems not to be generally
realized—Atlantic City lies as far south as the upper corner
of Virginia. However, after traversing the city's outskirts and
walking on the grey beach of adjacent Brigantine, where
hordes of gulls stood sated from the unaccountable quantities
of surf clams washed up on shore, I decided to forgo the
rest. I thought I had become inured to our national capacity
for commercialism, but the approach to Atlantic City taught
me I had not. The last mile of U. S. 30 is a hallway between

uninterrupted ranks of billboards touting the resort's tourist-hungry procuria. I suppose the exhibit is not much more debasing than that put on by other American communities but it seems so because Atlantic City's only excuse for being is to be attractive and because it has so much to work with, including a scenic prospect of wide salt marshes and tidal inlets that the highway leading to it *could* afford. After all, even acknowledged prostitutes should be expected to have sense enough to affect some concealment of their purpose and to make the most of their charms.

The next morning I knew before I was half awake that it was cold. At five-thirty I leaned out of my sleeping-bag and, feeling myself instantly in an icy embrace, lighted the alcohol heater. Ten minutes later I made myself climb out. It was then 15 degrees inside the bus and 8 degrees outside. By the time I had water boiling for eggs and coffee, the various burners had raised the inside temperature to 40 degrees. That was comfortable enough for one who, after a reasonably warm night, had the benefit of morning vitality. However, the jars of coffee, sugar and marmalade, the electric razor and everything else in the bus were still at about the temperature they had dropped to overnight. Holding them turned the hands stiff with cold. But that was a small matter with the new day at hand. There were woods all around me, I found (I had arrived after dark), and they were as beautiful as winter woods always are on a sunny morning, especially with fresh snow on the ground. I was on one of the forested hillsides rising from a small lake that make up Parvin State Park, near Vineland. It seemed hardly credible that a society guilty of the profanations of Atlantic City, forty miles to the east, could so esteem a lovely spot like this as to take it under its jealous care. But so it was, and one was not only grateful for it but grateful for the chance to be grateful and grateful also that New Jersey kept its state parks open in winter and allowed one to camp in them for a mere fifty-cent fee. *Ave Nova Caesarea!*

The cold was such that a layer of frost had formed on the inside of the windows from the condensation of moisture and the windshield filmed over as fast as I could scrape it clear until the car heater had warmed up. But what can be better than a day at the nadir of winter when you spend it driving south, deeper with every mile into the province of

the sun and into country progressively less cramped as it
grows bigger and the towns farther apart? The question answers itself.

If you are following the changing vegetation and making
that your criterion, you will find that the South begins at
Delaware Bay. (Another geographical fact little realized is
that Delaware is almost entirely south of the Mason-Dixon
Line.) There the pitch pine finally gives up the coast, having
descended it from Maine and on its way dominated Cape
Cod and much of Long Island before coming even more
fully into its own in New Jersey: the famous Pine Barrens,
whence the American armies of the Revolution and the War
of 1812 were supplied with weapons forged of local bog-iron
smelted over fires of pitch pine and which, after the exhaustion of the virgin timber a century ago, were for years a
virtual lost world, occupy more than two thousand square
miles behind the coastal marshes in the southern part of the
state.

The loblolly, which replaces the pitch pine on the coast of
Delaware, is a much taller tree with longer needles and cones
and in maturity with a massive head of foliage borne on a
bole that may rise straight and branchless for from thirty to
fifty feet; where the pitch pine is picturesque and meager,
the loblolly is statuesque and lordly. With the loblolly comes
the wax myrtle, a more-delicate-leaved, smaller-berried, evergreen sister of the bayberry. On the beach, behind the dunes,
where the loblolly is as stunted and depressed as the pitch pine
farther north, the wax myrtle grows in the same low, dense
clumps as the bayberry, which it wholly replaces below North
Carolina, but in the woods it forms open shrubs ten feet tall
and farther south becomes a small tree. Also on the coast of
Delaware you begin to come up with birds that in the north
are considered harbingers of spring. In a field near a com-
memorative stone marking the site of a Dutch settlement of
1631 on an inlet below Cape Henlopen, I saw grackles feeding in the stubble, and a little farther on, red-winged blackbirds. (The Dutch settlement, which was wiped out by
Indians the next year and re-established the year after that,
was something else I had never heard of.)

On the beach at Cape Henlopen itself came Bonaparte's
gulls. In the graduated series of the family *Stercorariidae,*
running from the swallowlike least tern to the great black-

backed gull, which puts one in mind of an albatross, the Bonaparte's gull stands less than a quarter of the way along, a most engaging little gull, white on the leading edge of its pearly wings, almost as light and lively in the air as a tern and with a habit of flying with its small, black beak pointed down, tern-fashion. I had seen a few on Shinnecock Bay, but here there were six or seven hundred. They were stretched out on the water just behind the surf for a quarter of a mile along the outer, leeward side of the point. When the waves carried those in front into the breakers they would rise like a flock of white pigeons in a city square and settle elsewhere. Many were looking down and dabbling in the water. Evidently a churning-up of sea-lettuce from the bottom explained the congregation. The lovely creatures in their numbers and behavior seemed tinged with mystery, however, as if this were a visitation from another world, purer and gentler.

The pretty sight was one I felt I had earned, for the incessant and nerve-racking northwester in which I had been walking scorched the face; the temperature did not rise above 25 degrees all that day. The wind was driving straight down the bay, herding the crowded, frothing waves toward the sea, with the result that those along the southern shore broke directly upon the beach on the inner side of the Cape, which juts up into Delaware Bay like a lower incisor tooth in an open mouth. The result was also to illustrate a principle of wave action I had heretofore only read of. Where one might have expected that on the other, leeward side of the Cape the waves would be rushing away from the shore, still obedient to the wind that created them, the peninsula so bent them that all around it they were coming in directly upon the beach, those on the far side squarely into the wind, having been turned completely around. . . . Two calico-patterned shore birds called turnstones, plump, pink-legged and dove-like, took off in the guise of flying chocolate sundaes, emitting katydid cries.

Did it matter that this was rather far north for the turnstone in winter, or what the behavior of Bonaparte's gulls may be, or how the pitch, loblolly and longleaf pines divide up the coast, or that the sand on the beach at Brigantine is dark grey and fine? I thought a bit about the question as I drove along.

The shore in winter is rather spare, to say the least. It is nature with few concessions to the human need for comfort. Its emptiness, where the beach is devoid of any marks of human habitation, will take you back to a past before man appeared on earth and perhaps give you an inkling of what it would be like to find yourself returned to that past beside an ocean that had never known a keel, the only one of your kind in existence. On the other hand, the tokens elsewhere at the shore of man's visitation do not much temper the sense of your isolation. The snow-fencing erected to hold the sands (of which there must be a thousand miles along the Atlantic coast), the interminable lines of telephone poles with the wires sagging between them, the uninhabited and dissipated-looking cottage warrens created a more sordid desolation. The seasonal ebb of the human sea from the shore leaves hundreds of miles of resorts nine-tenths deserted.

Cape Henlopen presented a special case of dereliction. There was a sentry-box and then one barracks after another and street after street of other barracks and smaller houses— officers' quarters—all deserted and silent. This was Fort Miles, now decommissioned and acquired by the State of Delaware. It was, I am glad to say, to be converted into a park which would include the whole cape and the coast for two and a half miles south of it, but the conversion had not yet started. The street signs, beginning to rust, still stood at the intersections. Of a few buildings, only charred ruins remained. Evidently vandals had got to them. One authorized demolition crew was at work. Of other sign of life there was none except for a man climbing a concrete tower overlooking the point. This stark, cylindrical structure, cut with a slot or two like those in a knight's visor, was incongruously capped with an endearing little clapboard cottage which, to judge by the wind vane and anemometer atop it, was a weather station.

Similar towers, resembling concrete silos, stood at intervals down the coast, relics of the war like helmeted giants still gazing out through those narrowed apertures across the sea, too mindless to grasp that the danger had passed. On the coast of Maryland the summer cottages, many in pastel shades, overshadowed by big apartment motels, occupied the shore five ranks deep, mile upon mile, back from an ocean and beneath a sky that alike were hard, bright and cold as the bitter wind that still was blowing. I have never beheld a scene of human abandonment on such a scale as that from Bethany Beach to Ocean City—not that it was not greatly to be preferred to the same scene in summer when, I understand, proclamation-bearing aircraft and boats blaring through loud-speakers patrol off shore advertising local night spots. Locked-up churches and empty gas stations witnessed the completeness of the evacuation.

So it is that traveling along the shore in winter by yourself you are apt to discover your capacity for loneliness. If at the same time you discover that your interest in the nature of the outer world is undiminished you can account yourself fortunate. That was the answer that came to me to the question of whether the succession of plants and birds, the physics of wave-motion and the varying structure of beaches were important; if you thought they were, you had much to be grateful for—and whether you did was likely to depend (to be realistic about this) upon whether you had associates who thought they were and would willingly listen to what you had to report about them. In that, I knew myself to be especially well off.

But of course the question could be pressed further. Suppose the circumstances of the wintry shore were carried to their logical extreme and one found oneself at sea in a sinking ship beyond hope of rescue. Would one then have an eye for the processes of the universe? I should have liked to

think that, failing an ability to execute in the time remaining
a stanza of verse that would epitomize man's experience on
earth, I had it in me to absorb myself during that final
ordeal in taking notes on the performance of such birds as
might be present (shearwaters would be a possibility even
in mid-Atlantic) with a view to plugging them in a bottle
addressed to the Secretary of the Smithsonian Institution
before the waters closed over me. My recognition that I
should be as little up to the one as capable of the other did
not perturb me as it should have done for the simple reason
that I had grounds for more immediate concern. I fell far
short at the best of times of such reasonable standards as
those set by Sir Thomas Browne. My observation of nature
was desultory in the extreme. I had engaged in precious little
"judicious enquiry" into God's acts or "deliberate research
into his creatures." I had not been one of those—much as I
applauded them—who in doing so "highly magnifie him."
We are not all equal to exacting disciplines. I was one of
"those vulgar heads that rudely stare about, and with a gross
rusticity admire his workes." Still, it could be argued that
admiring his works with a gross rusticity is preferable to not
admiring them at all. And I could testify that finding them
admirable makes a difference in the state of mind of a
traveler in the realm of the winter sea, even if it might not
alone sustain him in the final pass—since, as Sir Thomas
points out, "the long habit of living indisposeth us for dying."

On Assateague Island, I found, admiration came easily
from the moment of my arrival. When I had marched through
the dunes to the beach the ocean lay before me like a deep-
blue plain, quieted beneath the stroke of the daylong, offshore
wind, its surface disturbed only by the low swells from the
far distance that appeared as darker lines upon it and spent
themselves on the beach with a small, last-minute crack or a
mere tired collapse. It was quiet enough for a flock of gulls
to be settling upon the water, apparently for the night. Across
the whole expanse of the ocean the front of each wavelet
reflected evanescently the indescribable soft orange that
glowed above the horizon before fading into the azure. It
was a sea of molten gems which fluidly expanded and con-
tracted in the agitation of its surface, a sea of fable beside
which one might have expected a mounted knight to appear
to contemplate it, casque in arm. Behind, the thinnest paring

of a moon hung over the darkening woods. These were part of the great loblolly and dense deciduous forests rich in hollies up to thirty feet tall of the mainland coast of Maryland. In passing through them on the road from Berlin there had been a feeling of remoteness—the first I had had since leaving Maine—by which I had known that I was truly in the South.

Assateague is a southern Fire Island. The similarities are remarkable. Both are thirty-three miles long, though the former, being wider, contains 18,000 acres (almost thirty square miles) to the latter's 5,700. Both are edged on the outer side by an excellent beach (Assateague's magnificent in its breadth) and on the inner, along the bays they enclose, by salt marshes, ragged in shoreline. Both islands had been separated from the barrier beaches above them, of which they had previously formed a part, by a storm, and the storms that cut the new inlets occurred within two years of each other, in 1931 and 1933. Both have since then been accessible until recently only by ferry, which impeded their settlement. The lower tip of each, for four miles, is a state-operated public recreational area, a state park in the case of one and, in the case of the other, Federal land leased to an agency of the state—the Chincoteague-Assateague Bridge and Beach Authority. But here is a difference: the lower nine miles of Assateague, comprising all the portion in Virginia and half the acreage of the whole, has been in Federal ownership for some years—since 1943, to be exact—having been purchased with the proceeds of duck-stamps and designated (by a misnomer) the Chincoteague National Wildlife Refuge. In the past several years, both islands have been connected with the mainland by two bridges each, and in each case one bridge is a few miles from the lower tip and the other about a fifth of the way down from the upper bridge—a small county park in one, a two-mile-long Maryland state park in the other. In both cases the major bridge was opened in 1964. In both the plans for the bridge precipitated the question of the island's future and joined conservationists and exploiters in a battle that resounded across the country. The objective of the former in both cases was the designation of the island as a National Seashore. In both, private interests pressed for building permits till the eleventh hour and by recourse to the courts defeated the efforts of the state executive to deny them.

Fewer permits were issued for Assateague, but they included permits for a motel and a $100,000 tavern.

But there have been significant dissimilarities. The occupation of Fire Island was started several generations ago but remained confined mostly to the lower half of the island. Only in the 1950's did real-estate promotion begin on Assateague—but it got under way then with a vengeance. Buying up the land at a reputed fifteen to thirty dollars an acre, a developer laid out a fifteen-mile-long subdivision consisting of 6,000 half-acre lots (1,268 zoned commercial) and occupying the middle half of the island. Calling the development Ocean Beach, he constructed a sand-asphalt road through it with a spur to a ferry-landing. Prospects, a bitter witness recalled to a Congressional subcommittee, "were swayed by high-pressure advertising, whole-page advertising, Mister, 'God is love; love thy neighbor as thyself,' at a cost of $2,000 to $5,000 per page." The developer, he recalled, "used to have a prayer meeting every time he held a sales meeting." Whether by these or other methods, lots were disposed of to 3,200 buyers and summer cottages began to be built. The hope of bringing the island into the National Park system, which went back thirty years, would surely have been doomed but for the intervention of Providence. In March 1962 a violent storm struck the coast, inundating much of Assateague, destroying thirty-two of the houses so far constructed and damaging seven of the remaining eighteen. The doubtful feasibility of the kind of settlement of the island called for by the planners of Ocean Beach seemed to be demonstrated; said a survey prepared by the Bureau of Outdoor Recreation, "A large part of the central section of the island is 1.5 feet above mean sea level (only a few inches above mean high tide) which would seem to indicate that in times of rough weather a substantial portion of the island is awash." Circumstances which led to the suicide of Ocean Beach's developer gave the conservationists a second chance.

The battle was to run for three and a half years. Whereas Fire Island's inhabitants stood to gain by the creation of a National Seashore which would be confined to the largely unsettled portion of the island and supported it, the lot-owners of Assateague would be prevented from becoming inhabitants by a National Seashore which would necessarily require their holdings, and they fought it. In the metropolitan area of New York, where open space is a rarity, a sophisticated and informed public could appreciate the value of a seashore park. In rural Worcester County, in which the Maryland portion of Assateague is situated, opinion was formed by small businessmen and property-owners concerned for the tax-base.

The verdict of the storm was by no means accepted by the local interests. They contended that the seaside resorts to the north had been hard hit by the storm but had weathered the damage. They were unmoved by the rejoinder of the publisher of *The Worcester Democrat,* who pointed out that in Ocean City, which had had the benefit of over seventy-five years of private development, the damage had been repaired only at a cost of a million dollars in state funds and of hundreds of thousands in the work done by the Corps of Engineers in the restoration of the dune line. They were not interested in the opinion of the Maryland Board of Public Works that to render Assateague suitable for a development like Ocean Beach, between seventeen and nineteen million dollars would have to be spent in installing utilities, raising elevations and erecting dunes—for which six hundred waterfront lots would have to be sacrificed—and that this figure would not include the 50 per cent of the cost of erecting the dunes that the Federal Government would be asked to pay.

At bottom, the issue was what it always is when conservationists and local investors clash: what kind of country are we going to have? The Worcester County Commissioners made no bones about their preference. They asserted that "the overwhelming part of the public which desires ocean front entertainment is invariably drawn to large population centers where comfortable hotel and motel accommodations are available, as well as shopping facilities and evening entertainment activities such as nightclubs, shopping areas, and amusement areas. . . . Worcester County believes that Assateague Island should be privately developed with private capital, initiative and energy in the American way, and not by socialistic bureaucrats desiring public ownership for the satisfaction of those few who do not have the industry and energy to provide for themselves." The Commissioners did not believe that the National Seashore "would become anything but a barren wilderness useful only to bird watchers." Even appeals to their enlightened material self-interest were

futile. Congressman Roy A. Taylor of North Carolina spoke
fruitlessly of the economic benefits that Cape Hatteras National Seashore had brought to adjacent communities. Senator
Daniel B. Brewster of Maryland reminded them in vain that
"estimates by competent independent economic consultants
show that if the National Seashore is established, there would
be an increase in the assessed valuation of the surrounding
country that would add $20 to $25 million to the tax base of
Worcester County. Even the most optimistic estimates of
private developers pressuppose an increase of only $18 mil-
lion."

With the lot-owners themselves it was impossible not to
sympathize, up to a point. "These people feel they're being
cheated," a local businessman declared. "They're being
cheated just after their bridge has been completed which,
incidentally, they worked long and hard to get, and finally,
when they thought that they'd at last be able to build on land
they purchased some fifteen years ago, they are stopped."
He added that he did not think they would be cheated
monetarily by the Government, but, as one of the lot-owners
exclaimed, "There's no price tag that you can hang on my
dream." It was the American dream, certainly: a place of
one's own away from it all. But we cannot eat our cake and
have it too. If the lot-owners correctly identified the cake-
eaters—those responsible for the increase of our population
by three million a year and for the annual racking-up of 10,000
or 20,000 miles on ever more millions of motorcars, among
whom are doubtless included many of the lot-owners themselves—they did not indicate it. Yet just as the interests of
those who "might otherwise have had an opportunity to see
a small portion of the land as the forces of nature originally
shaped it"—as Robert L. Dwight of the Citizens Committee
for the Preservation of Assateague Island put it—would have
been sacrificed had the lot-owners been able to realize their
piece of the American dream, so their piece of the dream
must also have been sacrificed in time to the spreading human
swarm. Indeed, at a public hearing in Baltimore, as Mr.
Dwight recalled, "the spokesmen for the property-owners,
themselves, pictured the ultimate creation of another Ocean
City or perhaps even a Miami. They said it would just take
a little time. The 3,000 houses would then get torn down to
make way for this."

Had the prospects for the Assateague National Seashore been poor in February 1965 I could not have brought myself to visit the island. As it was, half-a-dozen bills authorizing the Seashore had been introduced in Congress and their objective had the active support of sportsmen's organizations, garden clubs, civic associations, labor unions, every conservation body in the country, local opinion in Chincoteague, both Maryland Senators and the Maryland and Virginia Congressmen concerned. The expectation that Assateague would be preserved gave one license to enjoy it.

I parked the bus overnight at the edge of the parking plaza in which the highway ended immediately after crossing the new 1.5-million-dollar bridge at the Maryland end. After breakfast by lamplight I was off before the sun had cleared the horizon, encouraged to see it rise large and orange above an ocean dappled with the peach color of the eastern sky. The inevitable telephone poles led off in both directions and the sandy lane beneath them was rutted with car tracks— to be expected even on a barrier island where footprints are few. In the distance in either direction one or two houses were in view. But on the whole the island seemed wild and unaltered; and with no other human figure to be seen on that broad, flat strand I felt like a castaway. The thermometer stood at 12 degrees and my hands and feet were like stones. Even if my binocular had not been as stiff as a single casting I could not have manipulated it for a better look at the horned grebes off shore, forty-five in one flock, more than I had ever seen before in one place. (An habitué of the coastal waters in the cold half of the year, the horned grebe in its drab winter garb might be likened to a delicate, diminutive Canada goose with its markings faded out and the suggestion of a beret on its head.) Everything was frozen: the silvery beach where the retreating waves had left it wet and the salt marshes on the other side. A few song sparrows keeping company with a band of myrtle warblers were puffed up against the cold. But the whole universe seemed united, as under the baton of a supreme conductor, in that dayburst, and the icy air, making one more appreciatively conscious of the warmth harbored within one's overcoat, made one also more aware—as the severity of the winter beach generally did —of how little to be taken for granted is the gift of life and how greatly therefore it is to be esteemed, not for what rare and exotic confections it may bring but as a moment-to-moment boon in itself. If the shore at its bleakest tested one's spirits it also invigorated what it tested. Perhaps Sir Thomas Browne would have been less prone to count the world, as he said he did, "not an Inne, but an Hospitall, and a place, not to live, but to die in," if research into God's creatures had required of him more physical exertion in an intractable out-of-doors.

The sun must soon have made a difference in the temperature. At least I cannot remember thinking about the cold very long after the start of the three-hour walk I took down the island. I might not have gone so far but for the unexpected sight at a distance, by some loblolly woods, of a large, conventional, two-story house with gable roof and attic, paintless and, as my glasses showed after another ten or fifteen minutes, its windowpanes gone and its roof partly fallen in. I was told by two other visitors to the island whom I encountered that it was a former hotel, from half a century back, which had failed and been abandoned. These two, men in their sixties, were driving a fifteen-year-old, soft-tired sedan and had been stopping every quarter of a mile or so to get out and walk off into the brush, hallooing in a puzzling fashion; we had alternately been overtaking each other. They explained that they were looking for an eight-month-old, black-and-tan foxhound which had strayed from a pack they had been out with the evening before and asked if I had come upon him. But all I had seen were some of the famous Assateague ponies, eight of them, including a white and several piebalds, small, short-necked and with forelocks hanging down their foreheads; rather listless, they seemed.

I found the old hotel gutted and the interior strewn with lath and plaster. In the surrounding scrub growth were a rusting bedstead or two and similar hardware. Sitting on a fallen beam in the warming sun with a cup of coffee from a vacuum bottle and a package of graham crackers, I felt on extraordinarily good terms with the world, lighthearted and carefree, as I had on the road to Sankaty Head. One more degree of liberation and I should have dissolved in the limpid ether.

One might have hesitated to take it on oneself to decree the bankruptcy of the hotel and the destruction of the cottages hit by the storm of 1962, but that did not mean one had

to repine over the wreckage, and I spared myself the distress
of doing so. I am afraid I beheld even with composure the
remains of the asphalt road that made Ocean Beach possible;
they resembled strips of tread from a gigantic, blown-out
tire. One cottage in this section, built on stilts just back from
the beach, had survived intact to do disproportionate damage
to the landscape, but the others were in ruins in various
degrees. The best-preserved of these was a kind of town hall
by the pinewoods which had been only displaced and left at
an angle. The pines themselves, though twenty to thirty feet
tall and a third of a mile from the sea, were browned from
salt burn or dead at the top. Of some of the cottages, only
pipes and other metal parts remained, maybe a hot-water-
heater or the electrical connections. A ruptured wooden-stave
water tank on low pilings with the rusting corpse of a Jeep
pickup truck at its feet, evidently caught there by the storm,
recalled photographs of the dust bowl of thirty years back.

Despite the cold, this was clearly a southern beach, and
there was a jungly feeling about the dense hummocks of wax
myrtle and stunted pines with a few bear oaks among them
that rose behind fields of pale, silky, knee-high grasses.

After I had returned to the mainland to drive to the lower
end of the island, signs of the South multiplied. I had hardly
crossed the bridge before I ran into a flock of tens of thousands of grackles pouring through the woods and alighting

on the grassy shoulders of the highway. (It was probably as many birds as I had ever seen at one time, and in the rustling of the myriad sable wings I must say there was something a little disturbing.) Even while the frosty air nipped your face and the glazed snow glistened in the furrows of the plowed fields you knew that this was a hot country in summer. It may have been the turkey vultures balancing on the air currents like tightrope artists with arms outstretched as they coasted over the treetops, or the sheen or pallor of the blue winter sky or the strength of the sun even on a freezing day. . . . On the other side of the Virginia line the woods were green with holly, wax myrtle and red bay—a skimpy little tree with leaves like the mountain laurel's. The curious farmhouses of eastern Virginia, only one room deep but two broad and two stories high, put in an appearance, and with them occasional plain white, lonely churches. The town of Chincoteague itself greeted one with a shabbiness that economic adversity in many forms has made also characteristic of much of the South. This was made more evident by contrast with the depersonalized, affluent neatness of the distant barracks, office buildings and huge saucer antenna of the Wallops Island missile launching site which you see before the highway takes off across the marshes for Chincoteague Island. (The succession of islands below Chincoteague is Wallops, Assawoman.)

Lined up along the bay and the channel separating it from the marshy island over which one crosses from the mainland, Chincoteague is a well-sited town. Had it, like so many fishing ports, had the benefit for the past two or three generations of a well-to-do population of devoted summer-home-owners, it might today remind one of, say, Wellfleet or even of a minor Provincetown. As it is, it has had to depend on the harvest of oysters and clams, from which the returns are not great or easily come by. (Oysters are grown mostly on private beds planted with seed oysters dredged from public rocks by commercial fishermen. Clam beds are also seeded, the adults being garnered by dredging in winter and in summer by waders who locate them by signs in the mud or by feeling them underfoot.) In urging his constituency's need of the Assateague National Seashore, Congressman Thomas N. Downing stated that "when Chincoteague Naval Air Station moved out in 1959, this just put a blight, an economic blight, on the entire countryside." He went on to say that 55 per cent of the families in the area have an income of under $3,000 a year, that farms in the area were reduced by 25 per cent from 1950 to 1960 and the population by 13 per cent. What the National Seashore could mean, Chincoteague has in recent years had a chance to discover in the annual windfall of tourist dollars the July roundup of ponies brings. This nationally-reported event, managed by the Chincoteague Volunteer Fire Company, attracts more thousands every year to see the several hundred surplus animals herded, swimming, across the channel from Assateague to Chincoteague, where they are put up for auction.

On the waterfront at Chincoteague were piles of oyster shells like centuries-old middens, one the size of a two-story house. (Actually the shells are redistributed on the beds every season to give the young something to attach themselves to.) But the yards of the dealers, which dominate the main street, were trashy with bottles and papers, and the wharves and fishing boats, while they could be respected as genuine—they were not the toys of the idle rich—seemed run down and ill kept.

Chincoteague being famous for its oysters, particularly those of Tom's Cove (now part of the Refuge), I decided to suspend my rule of eating in the bus and have half a dozen of the delicacies. But the plump waitress behind the counter in a restaurant advertising sea-food specialities seemed bewildered by an order for raw oysters. "Oysters on the half-shell?" she asked. "That or any other way they come uncooked," I said. She went and consulted with the owner, who pulled down the corners of his mouth and shook his head. In a booth two teen-agers sat with mouths agape listening addle-brained to a jukebox that thundered like the organ of a movie cathedral; one would have thought the instrument an artificial heart on which they depended for their lifeblood. . . . Another restaurant boasting that it served "all kinds of sea-food" was closed for the winter. I gave up.

But I should not construe too much from this experience. Thanks to the efforts of fifteen women of the town, an oyster museum will tell the full story of the oyster biologically, historically and commercially, with living exhibits, and the embassies of other oyster-producing countries have promised cooperation. Chincoteague, it would seem, is getting the idea. It could well be transformed by the National Seashore.

Meanwhile, if the town has the shortcomings of a community in the South bypassed by prosperity, one must acknowledge that it has also the virtues of a Southern community. The girls on the street were trimmer and prettier than those I had seen in comparable towns in the north, including Mount Desert and Cape Cod. And while the municipal dock was earth-filled and crude (I had developed a pretty taste in municipal docks) the policeman who directed me to it took me fatherly-fashion by the arm and made me welcome to spend the night there most cordially. More surprisingly, there was a clean, heated public toilet; the public toilet in the park at Bar Harbor was disdainfully closed for the season and I had seen none other anywhere.

In the South you are generally nearer the traditional or the primitive than you are in any other part of the country I know. This can be for the better and it can be for the worse. It is for the worse in my view, since I do not care to live in the atmosphere of a battlefield, in the persistence of the widespread Southern addiction to hunting, in which many rural Southerners are little disposed to suffer the interference of the law. The Ranger who drove me around the Chincoteague Wildlife Refuge—a tall young man with a narrow build and a narrow face, from Memphis, Tennessee, a graduate of the University of Mississippi—did not like to dwell upon the trouble caused by poachers; it was the business of the Refuge to get along with the public and win its good will. He could not, however, conceal his regret for his days in the Northwest where, as he said, the level of education was high and public support for game regulations strong. And from an acquaintance of mine who was informed about the local situation I had heard something of the lawlessness of the gunners in the area. Shooting over baited fields was habitual —even state legislators in Maryland, as I knew, being repeatedly caught in this practice. Shooting out of season and shooting in the Refuge were also common, and the Refuge wardens were in real danger. One had been shot a few years before and would have been killed by his assailant had not the latter's gun misfired when he came up to deliver the *coup de grâce* by discharging it into his victim's head. For his offense he had been sentenced by the local court to a year in jail and was now to be seen in the streets of Chincoteague, an accepted citizen of the community. It was my friend's opinion that anyone who killed a warden in this part of the state would have popular opinion on his side. I asked if the hunters could not see that it was to their advantage for wildfowl to have sufficient protection to provide hunting in the future. He scoffed. "If the world's last female duck were in range of one of these pot-gunners he'd shoot it without a moment's hesitation."

The Ranger escorting me admitted that the use of fixed traps in the Refuge for catching ducks for banding had had to be abandoned owing to the frequency with which the captives would be lifted by some of the local inhabitants who also—illegally—set traps of their own. There was a lively black market for game and a delicacy like a black duck would bring four dollars, which was well worth stealing for, or otherwise breaking the law to get. Perhaps in this too the opportunities the National Seashore will bring will make a difference. At least I can imagine that law-enforcement may be more difficult when a quarter of the labor force is unemployed, as Congressman Downing says it has been at times in the Chincoteague area. Anyway, the Refuge now relied upon cannon-traps in snaring waterfowl for banding. These, by means of a bank of mortars, fired a net over a baited area. A few days before, 446 birds had been captured at one time with this device. The Canada geese had to be handled with care. The trick was to grasp their wings together at the base and hold them away from you. Their bite was not so bad but a blow from one of their wings could hurt. The herring gulls, on the other hand, had a bite that drew blood. Like other wildfowl men, the Ranger had little liking for the gulls.

At its lower extremity, Assateague ends in a hook much like the one in which Cape Cod ends at its upper. Just before the start of the hook it achieves its greatest width, one of over two miles; the end of the island rather resembles an open harness-clasp. Debouching from the bridge onto this part you come to a pine forest which in beauty is second to none I have ever seen, though admittedly I saw it at probably its uncommon best, with a low sun flooding it from the side with a ripe, rich light and glistening on the ice-encrusted snow, turning it to citron. A circular trail has been laid out

through it. The terrain is steeply hilly, being formed of old
dunes which rise to a maximum height of forty-seven feet,
and some of the loblollies that largely make up the forest
have a forty- or fifty-foot spread of massive limbs and trunks
too big to encircle with your arms; for trees on a barrier
beach these are giants. Among the hollies, myrtles and bays
of the understory are bear oaks, some of which have trunks
you can barely encompass with your two hands, which makes
them giants too, of their kind. The forest might be the grounds
of a Buddhist temple.

The pines extend northward along the inner side of the
island but in diminished size, and the ones I saw where the
land was narrower were browned like those at the Maryland
end. The storm of 1962 had been the most damaging in thirty
years. The former Coast Guard station up near the Maryland
line, which had been in use by the Refuge, was wrecked.
Where the seas had poured in on the southern portion, the
island was bare and gaunt, a place of desolation. A line of
dunes had now been constructed behind the enormous beach
to stand off future storms—though of course no such defense-
works could be wholly proof against the assaults of the sea.

In addition to the dunes, miles of dikes had been erected to
create impoundments of fresh water and were being extended.
It cannot have been much fun working on the dragline—a
cranelike machine with a free-swinging bucket at the end of
a boom which I saw parked by a ditch and which made me
think of the picked-over carcass of a brontosaurus. "The sand
gets in your hair, your clothes, your teeth, everywhere here,"
said the Ranger. His heart was unmistakably in the Northwest, even more in Alaska, to which his passion for wildfowl
had led him to work his way before he had enlisted in the
Fish and Wildlife Service and to which he was pining to
return. "You ought to see the Mississippi Flyway," he said.
"You can see a hundred thousand ducks at a time there. Lakes
the size of these are covered solid." I had exclaimed over a
dense line of black ducks on an unfrozen part of the impoundment. To me at least their thousands were impressive, as
were the twenty snow geese and ten whistling swans that were
with them. The male swans, their mating instincts already
awakening, were sparring with each other. Two would stand
erect in the water, face to face, enormous wings flailing the
air, magnificent as embattled stallions. They recalled, too,

figures in a coat of arms; one saw them supporting a shield between them. Even the Ranger was moved by the sight we had from the tip of the hook, wondering for a moment if we were really seeing what we thought we were—a low-lying cloud of birds a mile away across the bay. It was indeed a flock of birds, immense as their numbers had to be to account for the mass. They were brants. When they put down on the opposite shore, the Ranger, after counting a minute fraction of the flock through his binocular and multiplying it by the denominator, came up with an estimate of fifteen thousand birds.

The nearly five-mile-long hook was the most monstrous unrelieved sand-waste I had yet met with. There was virtually nothing on it but whelks, but it was whelks from end to end, such a littering of whelk shells as one was stumped to find an explanation for—whelk shells the color of peach ice cream deepening to orange-pink on the inside of the coil and others dark grey with peach showing through. And they were all of full size, eight inches long and five wide at the maximum extent of the spiral.

In summer, according to my guide, the sand of the hook was so rutted with the tracks of beach-buggies it was hard to walk over. One can imagine the damage that must have been done to Assateague if the Refuge had not been in existence to seal the island off when the bridge from Chincoteague was built in 1962. As it is, just above the complex at the base of the hook, where the road from the bridge ends—restaurant, bathhouses and souvenir shop, all under the Bridge and Beach Authority—a fence across the beach keeps the buggies out of the Refuge proper, admission to which requires a permit. Robert Murphy, the writer, told me that when he had been there in August he had found it like Times Square on New Year's Eve.

We drove back to this spot at a good clip, it having been noticed that the needle of the pickup truck's gas gauge stood at "E." We made it as far as, but no farther than, the deep sand of the ramp over the dunes leading to the paved road before the engine commenced to falter. The Ranger turned it off at once, observing that if you ran a car to the last drop of fuel you could wear the battery out getting it started again after you had replenished the supply. Snapping on the radio transmitter in the dashboard, which gave out with a raucous blast, he reported our situation to headquarters. Replied a waggish voice from the receiver, "By the restaurant, eh? Ummm. I can't seem to find a map that would show where the restaurant is. Why don't you just walk back?" Nevertheless, a truck with a can of gas soon arrived.

Do not feed the ponies, said a sign beside the road. Why not? I asked. "For one thing, the ponies bite," the Ranger said. "For another, feeding them from cars would cause them to congregate on the road. They have pretty thin pickings and don't need much temptation. You notice how their ribs show." They were, to be sure, a somewhat lackluster lot. Here and there were some of them standing about, seemingly always well apart from one another and apathetic. They did not much suggest the thundering herd, wild with the love of freedom that one has been led to picture. But the actuality is not what counts. Thanks partly to a rather loosely imagined novel about the ponies by a writer of popular juveniles and the motion picture that followed it, they are championed by children all over the country, and consequently by adults as well. Though they compete with the native wildlife for forage, eking out a living on marsh grasses, the Refuge is stuck with them. The bill to make a National Seashore of Assateague introduced in the new Congress by Thomas N. Downing, about which I heard on the radio at Chincoteague, expressly stipulated for the preservation of the ponies. And there can be no doubt, as the past chairman of the Chincoteague Fire

Company's Pony Committee testified, that "the tourists who come to the Chincoteague area to see these pony herds contribute greatly to the economy of this depressed area." In 1965, no less than fifty thousand were reported to have come to see the roundup and sale. One wonders how many, by contrast, came to see what is native to the country: the waterfowl from millions of square miles of the northern half of the continent hard-pressed for the food and shelter offered by the Refuge, which is strategically located at the neck of the funnel of the great Atlantic corridor; the shorebirds for which Assateague is a concentration point on their astonishing hemisphere-to-hemisphere migrations, on which many fly fifteen thousand miles a year. Before Cape Hatteras National Seashore was created there were also wild ponies on Ocracoke Island, their origin explained by similar romantic stories (their ancestors were put ashore by Sir Walter Raleigh, or by pirates, or had swum ashore from a wrecked Spanish or Portuguese galleon), but there the Government got to the animals before fame did and rounded them up to keep them from destroying the grasses then being planted to stabilize the dunes; their descendants may be seen in a corral maintained by the Boy Scouts, for whom they make possible the novelty of a mounted troop.

I found myself much more drawn to another hoofed animal introduced to Assateague which, though less celebrated than the horses, seems to thrive better on what the island has to offer. At least the sika deer give that impression and seem to fit more naturally into the habitat, which is doubtless why I feel differently about them. If you keep your eyes open in the woods or along the edge of the woods you are more than likely to see a family-sized group of them. They are the size of the native white-tailed deer and have the whitetail's habit of standing stock-still and staring at you, inoffensively. But the sika is a quite different beast, of the genus *Cervus,* to which the American elk also belongs. Its face is shorter than the whitetail's, its eyes wide apart like a cow's, and it has a deep body and a dense furry coat with white spots down the spine and a white patch around the tail. The Ranger observed that as a result of the Imperial Japanese partiality toward sikas as gifts, the species is now found around the world. Partly because they are very thrifty feeders—as I could believe, seeing one browsing on wax myrtle—they quickly build up much larger and denser populations than the native deer, he said. Even heavy hunting may not keep their numbers down, for which reason their importation into Maryland is forbidden. Because the Chincoteague Wildlife Refuge was becoming overcrowded with sikas, an open season had been declared the preceding fall and 246 bucks, does and fawns been killed by local gunners. The Ranger approved of the hunt, being in favor of all "compatible" uses of refuges which would demonstrate their value to local sportsmen and win public support. (The Chincoteague Refuge is ordinarily completely closed to hunting because of its narrowness.) Given the inadmissibility of reintroducing wolves or even cougars—the preferable means of dealing with the overabundance of deer anywhere, in my view—I did not know what solution I should have proposed. But I was glad not to have been on hand to hear the cannonading and to see the faces of those who thought the sport enjoyable.

Speaking of the bill to create the Assateague National Seashore, Senator Brewster said on July 23, 1965: "If Congress fails now to complete action on this measure, there is little likelihood that private development can be longer forestalled. The American people will have lost the largest remaining undeveloped seashore between Cape Cod and Cape Hatteras and one of the very few remaining such areas in this country."

In September an Assateague National Seashore was authorized—but at a heavy price. In addition to the southernmost four miles of the island, which will remain leased to the Bridge and Beach Authority, and the two miles at the upper bridge, which will remain a Maryland state park—both these areas to be developed for "intensive use"—another six hundred acres below the state park will be leased out for commercial development, *and* the construction of a highway running the length of the island between the bridges is mandatory. Congressman Rogers C. B. Morton of Maryland stood on his "insistence" that the road be built. Such a road, said Congressman Downing, "would mean that those fifty million Americans we have been talking about [to whom Assateague would be accessible] could travel by automobile and really enjoy the island."

The Outer Banks

WHAT Mount Desert Island is to the rocky shores of the Northeast, the Outer Banks are to the barrier beaches of the coastal plain—the ultimate expression. A string of sand-reefs 180 miles long (more than 210 if you include the projection extending west from Cape Lookout, at the southern extremity of the chain), the Banks bulge out into the ocean to a maximum distance of over 25 miles from the mainland and enclose a shallow, brackish, almost-tideless sea which is much larger than Long Island Sound and comparable in size with Chesapeake Bay. This sea is made up of Pamlico Sound and its branches, chief of which are Currituck. Albemarle and Core Sounds.

The farthest-protruding sector of the Banks consists of Hatteras and Ocracoke Islands. The former, 50 miles in length, forms the notorious cape where it bends sharply from the south to the southwest. The latter, which once was a continuation of it, is 18 miles in length. The two islands, to which alone the name *Outer* Banks should perhaps properly be applied, together with the lower nine miles of Currituck Banks, north of Hatteras, make up the Cape Hatteras National Seashore Recreation Area, which was authorized in 1937 and established in 1953. Since my visit, I am glad to say the islands to the south—Portsmouth Island and Core and Shackleford Banks—which make up the remainder of the chain and total 58 miles in length, have been incorporated in a Cape Lookout National Seashore, bringing the length of shore under Federal protection to 125 miles.

You are only a little more than fifteen miles from the start of the Banks when you cross the mouth of Chesapeake Bay going south. (And an extraordinary crossing it is, via the new

eighteen-mile-long bridge-tunnel combination, giving you the initial feeling of putting out to sea by motorcar; you could as well imagine yourself bound for Europe as for Norfolk.) At Cape Henry, on the southern side, you are also, from the point of view of vegetation, having a first foretaste of the Deep South, for this is where the evergreen live oaks begin. There are groves of them along the shore, small trees here with crooked trunks branching from the ground and the foliage leaning back from the sea like wind-swept flame. On the dunes, holding down the sand, are the first sea-oats, too. They are taller than the beachgrass, which they progressively replace to the south, and highly decorative when they are bearing their tall, nodding, plumelike panicles of flattened grains—too decorative for their own good and for that of the dunes, from which they are too often yanked to gather dust in vases.

Captain John Smith put ashore at Cape Henry on his way to the founding of Jamestown in 1607. Had Chesapeake Bay been known to the English twenty-three years earlier, when Amadas and Barlowe explored the North Carolina coast for Sir Walter Raleigh and glowingly reported the Banks to be "most beautifull, and pleasant to behold, replenished with Deere, Conies, Hares and diuers beastes, and about them the goodliest and beste fishe in the world, and in greatest abundance," the permanent English settlement of the New World would probably have had an earlier beginning. (In at least one of their claims for the islands the explorers were not exaggerating; a greater variety of fishes is said to be found in Dare County—which takes in the outermost half of the Banks and the adjacent bulge of the mainland—than in any other county in the United States.) Roanoke Island could only have been picked as the site for the first colony by men who knew no better, for it lies just inside the string of barrier reefs that presented the most exposed and dangerous stretch of coast the newcomers could well have found.

I could have wished Smith's three vessels such a morning at Cape Henry as I had, with gulls and boats white as china against the blue of sea and sky and with cardinals and red-winged blackbirds singing in the green woodland of Seashore State Park undeterred by the snow on the ground and the sub-freezing temperature. Had Smith been vouchsafed a pre-vision of Virginia Beach, where I had spent the night, he

would without question have thought himself in fabled
Cathay, to which the early navigators were prone to believe
every seeming gap in the east coast of the Americas led.
(Verrazano, discoverer of the Outer Banks, had no doubt that
the body of water he beheld on the other side—Pamlico
Sound—was "the oriental sea" and sought in vain a strait
through the "isthmus" which his vessel would "be able to
penetrate to those blessed shores of Cathay.")

Virginia Beach, which lies just south of Cape Henry, may
well be, as it asserts it is, the largest oceanside resort in the
world. Magnificent motels in the form of jewelry boxes line
the shore, affording such a picture as a deprived child might
imagine would meet the eye on the other side of the Pearly
Gates; you mentally supply *In a Persian Garden* for background music. It having been my fifth day out and high time
for a bath, I drove up and down the avenue behind the
ocean looking for a motel that served the simple purpose for
which motels were originally designed and looking in vain.
Reduced to inquiring finally of one of the shrines of luxury,
I found that, the month being February, its scale of values
and mine were not unbridgeable after all; I was given for $5
a huge double room and bath that brought $17.50 in season.
When I had settled in and had dinner I took a turn on the
deserted concrete walk elevated above the beach. There was
little separation between the ornate if at present largely
lightless pleasure domes on one side and the sea on the other,
where in the darkness the lights of ships bound to or from the
far reaches of the Atlantic showed faintly in the distance.
The longer I walked the more uncanny seemed to me the
juxtaposition of the two spheres of human existence, as if it
were not to be expected that they could be accommodated
one to the other and there must be a kind of coming-apart at
the seams somewhere. Perhaps I should not have felt this,
or felt it so strongly, had it not been that the last time I
had been here I was in uniform, stationed a few miles away
at Camp Pendleton, and the beach below me on which the
black waves were piling in to give up their ghosts in pale
breakers was rimmed deep with oil from the bunkers of
torpedoed vessels.

For years a highway down the shore from Virginia Beach
has been talked of, but so far there is none. To reach the
Outer Banks from the north by the most direct route you

drive south some sixty-five miles from Norfolk to a trestle across the mouth of Currituck Sound. Another highway crosses to the Banks twenty-five miles farther on, bridging the juncture of Albemarle and Pamlico Sounds, in which Roanoke Island lies. This route, swinging deeper inland, is more circuitous. However, it affords not only a chance to see the foundations of Fort Raleigh (a National Historic Site), constructed by the colony of 1585-6, but also a view, albeit one limited in depth, of the vast swamp forest making up much of extreme eastern North Carolina, of which the Dismal Swamp, lying half in Virginia, is a northern extension. In fact, it traverses three counties that, occupying the northern half of the great broad peninsula between Albemarle and Pamlico Sounds, are predominantly swamp and contain only three or four paved roads each. From sea-level, the land through here rises only one foot per mile. For long stretches the highway is built up on fill and bordered by a canal which is the incidental result of excavating the earth needed for it. Such canals are a feature of this part of the world and are useful to fishermen, who sometimes have small boats on them. At the Alligator River, one of the broad estuaries with which that country is parted, I picked up one young fisherman who was signaling for a ride. A boy of perhaps fourteen wearing rough, country clothes and rubber boots turned down under the knees, he spoke with an accent that made him almost as difficult for me to understand as the woman to whom I had given a ride in Maine. Fair-haired and with an animal-like simplicity—he talked as if his kind of life must be as familiar to me as to him, as if there could be no other—he might have been a boy with the baggage train of Harold the Saxon at Hastings; I am sure he would have been more at home in Harold's army than in cities less than a hundred miles away. His world seemed to consist mostly of fishing and hunting. He explained that he seldom had a chance to bring down anything big because he had only a single-shot .22 though it was one which, he asserted, shot very true. Squirrels and "sage chickens"—whatever they can have been—were his usual game, he said. Calling my attention to a sign pointing up a side road—one of the rare ones—to "Buffalo City," he told me that there were only a couple of houses left there, all the rest having fallen in; at least that was how I interpreted his meaning. And Buffalo City was one of the only four communities shown on my road-map in the entire three-hundred-square-mile extent of the mainland portion of Dare County.

I was sorry to lose my passenger after only a few miles. I should have liked to learn more about him, if I could have, for he belonged to a generation that, barring a drastic setback to our civilization, will probably be the last in the nation to exhibit any significant regional differences. All of us deplore the trend to national (and international) uniformity and all of us support one or another set of agencies, liberal or conservative, that make it irresistible. So more and more, in a country where the towns and villages would differ as widely as those of Scandinavia and Arabia if differences in physical geography were matched by those in human geography, we find everywhere pretty much the same houses, the same gas stations, the same products advertised, the same trucks delivering the same soft drinks, the same hardware stores, magazine stands and motion-picture houses with the same bills on the same main streets and the same kinds of clothes on the same-looking people. And even though we know we should have expected nothing else we feel let down when we travel, and cheated.

While inevitably the inhabitants of the Banks will increasingly be subject to the same influences that shape the rest of us, they start out from a base that is distinct enough. There is nothing in the United States quite like the remote, meager and frequently storm-swept rope of islands on which for generations the Bankers managed to support themselves by fishing, stock-raising, a bit of farming, pilotage and beachcombing for wreckage with the help, beginning in the post-Civil-War decades, of Federal payrolls, which their manning of lighthouses and lifesaving and weather stations brought. If a world apart, the Banks can hardly, however, be said ever to have been isolated since they were settled in the latter half of the seventeenth century. Long even before then, indeed, they were the scene of much activity. Between 1584 and 1591 they were visited by seven expeditions under captains as eminent as Sir Richard Grenville and Sir Francis Drake— whose fleet numbered no less than twenty-three vessels—in connection with Sir Walter Raleigh's effort to establish a permanent English base on the coast of "Virginia." In the full flowering of the age of sail no inconsiderable part of the world's argosies passed within sight of their shores, of which few in the world were so menacing to them. Even by 1790 so many ships were being driven upon the sands of the Banks that "Vendue Masters" were appointed to take custody for the owners of the salvageable property—in the performance of which duty they were more often than not frustrated by the forehandedness of the Bankers.

For two centuries, until the 1890's, when the Albemarle and Chesapeake Canal opened an interior water route between the Chesapeake Bay and North Carolina's eastern towns, most of the state's sea-borne commerce passed through the inlets of the Banks, and the little communities of Portsmouth, Ocracoke and Hatteras were in turn its chief ports of entry. Unwelcome attentions came to the Banks too. In the second and fourth decades of the eighteenth century pirates descended on them, native in the first period, Spanish in the second. The British in the Revolution raided and revisited them repeatedly in a vain effort to keep the inlets blockaded. The Union forces in the Civil War had better success. The Confederate forts on the Outer Banks fell early in the struggle, and through Hatteras Inlet in January 1862 passed one of the great armadas of the time, a fleet of eighty Union vessels moving against eastern North Carolina—but not without paying toll: a storm delayed the passage for two weeks, destroyed a number of the ships, dispersed others and nearly put an end to the expedition.

The impression the Banks make upon you, growing from the time of your arrival as your acquaintance with the attenuated isles is extended mile by mile, is one of enormous vacancy. The feeling that gains upon you is one you may have had in minute measure before in coming to a house from which everything is removed. Here the evacuation has been by nothing so picayune as human occupants and their appurtenances but by the world to which human beings are attuned. The Banks could well be—and for that matter may literally be—the long, thin rear guard of a continent left to face the sea in the sea's own alien realm by the continent's retreat over the horizon behind them. The state of mind they induce, at least in the newcomer, is partly queasy, partly awe-struck and partly fatalistic. So it must always be before the naked sweep of agencies that take little account of man, but here the land itself has a quality of the hypothetical, doubtless owing to its seemingly unnatural configuration and to the improbability, as one conceives it, of its being here at all.

If, coming onto the Banks from across Currituck Sound, you delay proceeding southward to the National Seashore and turn left onto a secondary road, you will come within three miles to the end of the asphalt, to the hamlet of Duck and—much more quickly than if you had taken the conventional turn to the right on the main highway—to the Banks as their natives have generally known them. The location of Duck itself speaks of the chronic problem of life on islands so exposed to the sea. Its score of fishermen's worn little houses are strung out, obviously for the shelter they find there, where the road winds through an unusual formation of quite considerable forested dunes. The woods are heavy on the slopes but not tall and some of the squat live oaks that stand out in it, with butts two feet in diameter, must have been there when the first white settlers came. On several of the dunes, however, the sand has broken loose, doubtless because the natural cover had been disrupted, and is spilling down the sides; you wonder if it can be held or the dunes will roll on through the community.

Beyond Duck the land flattens out and narrows. The low dunes beside the sandy road and their copious vegetative cover are safeguarded from any human intrusion by the presence among them of unexploded shells, of which signs warn; this is a naval aircraft firing range. Humped thickets of wax myrtle and live oak and smaller ones of bayberry recapitulate the form of the dunes and are tangled with evergreen bullbrier smilax of pear-shaped leaves and pretty little spherical clusters of blueberrylike fruit. Currituck Sound is on the left, dazed with space, a domain of boundless water and brown salt marshes, flat, dense and even-textured as sheets of gingerbread. On the right the beach is out of sight behind a high sand-dike.

I climbed the dike where there was a ramp and thought I had never seen the ocean so enormous. It seemed the more so, no doubt, for its quiet. And quiet lay upon the Sound too, which was still enough to permit a solitary fisherman to be standing up in his rowboat. To have such profound quiet over so vast a scene was queer, and I had that sensation the Banks evoke, as of something momentous in nature having been arrested or removed. Farther on the silence yielded to a faint chorus as of tiny trumpets. I came up with a line of whistling swans strung out on the water. There were eighty-two of the monumental birds, more than the total of those I had ever seen up to then. The punishment visited by man upon the wildlife of the east has been so harsh that anyone accustomed to the consequences could only be amazed that creatures so splendid and conspicuous could coexist with man in any degree. At closer hand their intermittent vociferations sounded like yelpings of a small-dog kind.

While there was still ice on the Sound along the shore, little snow remained. The temperature rose to a blessed 50 degrees. A catbird and a towhee called, two of the numerous myrtle warblers dashed out onto the road after insects, and during lunch, unbelievably, it grew so warm in the sun-heated bus that I had to open a window.

In the other direction, south from the bridge over Currituck Sound through Kitty Hawk and Nag's Head to the bridge from Roanoke Island, where the National Seashore begins, you pass through twenty-five miles of conventional seashore development, of beach cottages, inns and motels, shops and gas stations. However, at Kitty Hawk (called Chickahauk on the early maps) the Banks expand to triple their prevailing width of less than a mile and there, as at the Cape, where they are equally wide, there are fresh-water ponds and forests on the inner side in which you would suppose yourself on the mainland. South of Kitty Hawk, back from the ocean, are the famous great dunes, the largest coastal dunes in eastern North America. The height of the tallest, Engagement Hill, is given as 138 feet, but their heights, like their locations, may vary as the wind works over them. The huge sand-mounds seem almost unreal, as if they could hardly have risen by natural processes from that generally low-lying barrier reef. Among them are the Kill Devil Hills (their names apparently combining the early settlers' terms for a body of water and for a ridge) where, as Ogden Nash put it, two Wrights made a wrong. The hill associated with their three years of experimentation and their achievement of the first successful flight of a powered aircraft in December 1903 was stabilized under a cover of sod in

1932 (though not before it had moved several hundred feet since the time of the Wrights) and crowned with a granite pylon. The monument is about as suggestive of winged flight as a giant gravestone would be, and that is what it resembles—perhaps not inappropriately in view of the millions of people whose deaths were foreordained on that spot. However, if the airplane had not been launched on its career from the Banks (to which the Wrights were drawn because the winds there were advantageous for gliders) it would speedily have been launched on it elsewhere. And if the Banks were the scene of another ill portent for humanity written in the skies thirty years later, when bombers of the Air Service under Brigadier General Billy Mitchell proved the efficacy of aerial assault promptly after taking off from the flats below the Cape by sinking two retired battleships lying by Diamond Shoals, still it must be said that if surface vessels were vulnerable to bombing, it was better to know it.

Though for the first four miles you continue to have beachside resort off on your left, there is an immediate change when you cross the boundary of the National Seashore, a wholly different atmosphere. It is like passing from Broadway into a church or museum. The mantle of protection thrown over the natural scene is almost palpable. The very shoulders of State Highway 12 are different—grassy and without litter. You are on the Sound side of the Banks, where the marshes are. These marshes are characteristically of cordgrass on the outer portions and, on the inner, where the flooding is less deep, of black rush, which has dark-green, wirelike leaves three feet long tapering to a sharp point. In winter there are likely to be snow geese soon after you enter the reservation. *Chen hyperborea*, the Goose from Beyond the North Wind, is stocky, the adult spectacularly white (even if often stained on the face as by rust) with black outer flight-quills and bright-pink legs and bill, the latter with dark patches on the side which give it, incongruously, an expression as of baring its fangs. A score of them were so close to the road when I drove in that cars were stopping for a look at them and to take photographs, as they do in other National Parks when there are deer or a bear beside the road. It was another case of the quick response of wild animals to protection, even when the protection is only temporary. Shooting was permitted in the season in some parts of the

National Seashore, I was told by a man who had driven up with his wife and turned out to be a National Park Ranger Naturalist dressed in mufti, it being Saturday. He admitted he could not get used to the blazing-away of guns on lands under the Park Service. "There seem to be far more people interested in watching birds than in killing them," he observed, "but somehow the ones who want to kill them are the ones with the most voice." From the marshes came a constant gabble. There were hundreds of snow geese out there. They seemed to be as loquacious as the Canada geese and had the same scandalized intonation but their voices sounded a little thinner.

Nine miles after entering the park you come to the end of what is still called Bodie Island, although the inlet separating it from Currituck Banks on the north closed over many years ago. The bridge over Oregon Inlet was opened in the same critical twelvemonth that saw Fire and Assateague Islands' isolation ended by similar modern spans. It is named after a Congressman from Washington, North Carolina, demonstrating again that the tastelessness of our age, which permits living politicians to have their names attached to monuments built with taxpayers' money, gives added impetus to the construction of costly public works. It is a beautiful bridge, two and a half miles long, curving gracefully in the horizontal as well as the vertical plane. But arriving at Hatteras Island today is no longer the experience it was when you disembarked at the end of a half-hour crossing on the open deck of an iron ferry, swinging wide around the shoals, while the gulls, beating lustily over the stern, took bread almost from the hands of the children.

Still, there is hope that the bridge will not prove an unqualified success even by prevailing standards. South of Oregon Inlet, off to the right near the Sound, is a mysterious-looking section of wooden trestle. Once it bridged New Inlet. But New Inlet, after an off-and-on existence of two centuries, closed over more or less decisively in 1944, leaving the trestle bridging a mere bay. It is normal on the Banks for inlets to open and after a longer or shorter period to close again. As David Stick, their historian, observes, there is hardly a section of the Banks that has not, at one time or another, been cut through by an inlet; there is always a mass of water seeking an outlet from the Sounds, into which the United States

Geological Survey estimates that fifteen billion gallons are emptied by their tributary rivers every day. (In the long-ago, charts did not keep up with the changes and since—as Stick also points out—a newly-sanded-over inlet had much the same appearance from a rough sea as a still-open one, it is feared that more than one master seeking the protection of the Sound in a gale ran his ship squarely upon the beach.) In addition, because the southerly drift current along the coast despoils the upper ends of barrier beaches of sand and deposits it at the lower ends unless prevented by extraneous interventions, the inlets tend to move down the Banks. Since its appearance during the fearsome hurricane of 1846, Oregon Inlet—named after the first vessel that felt her way through it—has in fact moved a mile to the south. Whatever its intent with respect to future migration may be, there is evidence that it is even now shoaling up—with the piers of the new bridge being the cause of it! That the bridge may eventually cross land standing high and dry above the sea, a four-million-dollar monument to the vanity of man, and of publicity-mindedness, is probably too much to look for. But at least one may hope that the engineering task of keeping Oregon Inlet as it is and where it is will be such as to discourage the bridging of other inlets to the south, for which we need not be surprised to learn there is already agitation.

For miles after you descend to Hatteras Island you have on your right a dun-colored savannaland on which there are clumps of yaupon, groundsel-bush and dusty-olive wax myrtle dense as upended brushes. In the grass, like antelopes on the plains of Africa, Canada and snow geese are grazing. This is Pea Island Wildlife Refuge, which is 12 miles long. As you drive on, gulls rise before you from the scallops they have dropped on the asphalt; those the gulls have finished with are sometimes being picked over by boat-tailed grackles, so large in northern eyes, so odd in the light-brown hues of the smaller females. Waddling meadowlarks feed on the shoulders of the road. On one drive I took through here I followed a short-eared owl as it coursed along the dunes, altogether as mothlike as owls are habitually said to be in its soft flight— a flutter of irregular, deep wingbeats—the sudden turns it made, in its rounded head and body forming an integral, bullet-shaped whole. Too intent upon the hunt to notice me, it crossed the road ahead and continued hurrying on over the beachgrass of the lower dunes. When suddenly it banked and plummeted, disappearing, I put on the brakes, jumped out and got to the top of the ridge in time to see it rise on its brown-barred wings and make off carrying a large rodent with a white belly. Putting down again a hundred feet away, its back toward me, it fixed me over its shoulder with the unaltering and unalterable owl stare, its dilated yellow eyes with round black pupils rather close-set in a human face. There was a hint of magic in the proceedings, a suggestion of Merlin's presence.

By the hour (assuming that you stop from time to time) the ribbon isle leads on, threadbare, wind-pinched and oppressed in the inhuman immensity of water and sky but dogged, sullenly persistent too. Between you and the ocean are the dunes, hirsute with silk-hairy beachgrass and the more abundant, darker sea-oats, which grow in woolly clumps; those in which the seedstalks are not yet wholly bare resemble archery targets crowded with arrows. On your other side there are sand flats usually grown up in grasses, especially salt-meadow cordgrass, a tall thing of a few pencil-line-thin blades and an equally fine stalk from which the seedheads jut off like raised arms of a thicker line.

Where the island widens, hills and ridges of vegetation are formed by live oaks. The oaks are likely to be particularly prominent where the towns are, or vice versa. The towns occupy privately-owned strips, five in number, confined mostly to the Sound side of the Outer Banks, the National Seashore skirting them on the ocean side. Strangers may wonder why most of the towns have names that sound so unindigenous and that grate so on one's sensibilities. The answer is that they were all renamed by the United States Post Office Department beginning in the 1870's as post offices were established in them. Reading from north to south, Chicamacomico became Rodanthe and its southern outgrowth Waves, Clarks became Salvo, Kinnakeet became Avon, The Cape became Buxton, and Trent became Frisco. North of the National Seashore, Nag's Head (how inelegant!) was briefly changed to Griffin, Whale's Head became Corolla, and Wash Woods became Deals. Frisco and Salvo! One can only hope for a rebellion and the reinstatement of the original names. The towns surely deserve it. Their charm, it is true, is not overpowering. A number of the older houses look as if more had been taken out of them than put in for a long time and the new ones are of an ordinary suburb style or stylelessness. Scrapped cars or a house-trailer—probably of all the products of American industry the one most determinedly repellent in design—are apt to be in view. On the highway along which stretch The Cape and Trent (or Buxton and Frisco as we are enjoined to call them) one could be in almost any less-well-favored section of the southern coastal plain. Yet the two-story, quite plain, traditional Banks houses which have been kept up have a genuine appeal, at least for one who finds the generality of one-story dwellings spreading like a rash over our country a dreary bore, for some reason. Unmistakably, they have always had to count costs, but, their plantings gathered like skirts around them, they face life in the realm of the overvast, wind-swept skies with composure and self-respect.

The live oaks are the royalty of the plant kingdom on the Banks. They are regal in proportions and in bearing, and their wood is the hardest and heaviest of that of all the oaks and outstanding in the finish it takes, which made it prized by shipbuilders for both timbers and interior paneling. Live oaks are resistant to salt-spray presumably because their small oval or elliptical leaves, pale on their undersides, their edges usually rolled, are hard-surfaced, so much so as to feel crisp and lifeless. But here even those farthest removed from the ocean are dwarfed, most of them resembling giant *bonsai*. They have a habit, of which for some reason one never hears, of sending up shoots from their lateral roots and in more forward locations form thickets of thin-stemmed growth that would never be recognized for what they are by those whose idea of the species was formed in coastal Georgia or Florida or along the Gulf; there live oaks have trunks up to seven feet in diameter and such a spread of limbs that from the center of a divided highway they will shade six lanes. In the coastal thickets their habit of growth and even the character of their leaves are akin to those of wax myrtle and of yaupon.

Live oak, wax myrtle and yaupon are the plants that produce one of the phenomena for which the Banks are known. Back from the beach and on the forward slopes and summits of the dunes on the inner parts of the islands, in locations but little protected from the sea winds, in which few other

woody plants could survive at all, these three take dense,
flattened forms, sheered by the blown salt-spray—specifically,
their exposed twig-ends killed by the accumulation of chlo-
rine ions in their tissue. On the windward side, the effect is
of hedge-clipping with the surface of the depressed plant
sloping down toward the sea as each bare twig-end gives
some shelter to the foliage in its lee; the plants crouch
beneath shields woven of their own growth.

Yaupon, or Sea Island holly, the third of the triumvirate of
woody plants without which the Outer Banks would not be
what they are, grows as wax myrtle does, as an open little
tree in the woods and in dense clumps out under the scourge
of the elements, but of the two the yaupon is the tougher; it
advances to the lee of the seaside dunes, forming humps so
solid they can almost be sat upon. With its richly green,
elliptical, slightly scalloped little leaves and with its nearly
white, green-grey branches and tight clusters of small, translucent, almost luminous scarlet berries encasing the twigs of
the female all winter long, it is, in my view, of all our native
shrubs the most admirable. Its leaves contain caffeine, in
about the same proportion as those of its close relative,
yerba maté, the proportion in some specimens equaling that
of tea leaves. The "black drink" of the coastal Indians, called

by them *cassena* or *cassine,* was made by steeping yaupon
leaves, the brewers first "having dried, or rather parched, the
leaves in a porridge-pot over a slow fire," as Mark Catesby
wrote in 1754. Of their "beloved liquor," Catesby went on,
they made "a strong decoction . . . which they drink in large
quantities, as well for their health as with great gust and
pleasure, without any sugar or other mixture; yet they drink
and disgorge it with ease, repeating it very often, and swal-
lowing many quarts." How *Ilex vomitoria* got its scientific
name is evident. *Cassena* as an emetic was held to cleanse
the system. Imbibed for its own sake, it "strengthens and
nourishes the body," Jacques Le Moyne wrote two centuries
before Catesby. Both men described ritual ceremonies in
which the drink figured. Indians came to the coast from
hundreds of miles inland to partake of it. The white settlers,
preparing the leaves as the Indians had, found it palatable and
refreshing. Yaupon gave the Bankers a drink that fortified
them against the pentrating damp winds of winter that assail
their islands and a money-crop for export through the early
decades of the past century. Recovering its popularity during
the Civil War as a substitute for tea and coffee, it helped see
the South through the ordeal of those times. All honor to
Sea Island holly!

Miles before you reach the Cape, the shaft of its famous
beacon comes into view. It stands over two hundred feet high,
the tallest lighthouse on the continent, and is spirally banded
in black and white—because, it is said, of an administrative
error. According to this interpretation, the instructions as-
signing a diamond pattern to Cape Lookout lighthouse were
meant for Hatteras lighthouse to accord with the name given
the shoals over which its beam sweeps in warning, which for
so long have made this corner of the coast known as the
graveyard of the Atlantic.

The United States Coast and Geographic Survey chart
shows a depth of only three feet at mean low tide more than
five miles off shore south of the Cape and of only 13.5 feet
ten miles to the southeast; the 60-foot line swings out as much
as twenty miles off shore, to the east. There are actually
three sets of shoals separated by deeper stretches known of
old to the Banks pilots, and originally only the middle one
was called—by virtue of its shape—by the name now applied
to them all: Diamond Shoals. Navigation in their area,

warns the chart, "is extremely hazardous to all types of craft."
Efforts to place and maintain buoys on the shoals began
long ago, as early as 1822, but they repeatedly failed. Attempts to erect a lighthouse on them in 1891 and 1904 also
failed. A lightship stationed off the shoals in 1827 was driven
ashore by a hurricane three years later. A second one in the
late 1890's met the same fate in two years. Since then, however, a vessel has been maintained there with few interrup-
tions, one of these having been in 1918 when a German
submarine, after warning the lightship without effect to cease
telegraphing word of its presence to other ships, sank it.
Because of the shipping that skirts Cape Hatteras—on an
average day, twenty vessels are said to pass within view of
the lightship—the neighborhood was a favorite with U-boats
in the first years of World War II. A hundred vessels were
sunk in the Battle of Torpedo Junction—and the last victim
had not yet been claimed even when I came to the Cape,
twenty years after the armistice. Five months after my visit
the trawler *Snoopy* out of New Bedford, dragging for scallops off the Banks at twenty fathoms, brought up a great ugly
metal tube in her chain net. "The whole boat was shaking
and quivering from the weight of it," a survivor reported. "I
asked the skipper what was happening and he said, 'We've
got a torpedo.' " They tried to shake it loose below the water
and could not. When they brought it up again, it exploded.
The trawler was blown to splinters and eight of the crew of
twelve were killed.

Of the seven hundred ships of over fifty tons' displacement that the historian at the National Seashore estimates
have gone down off the Banks, probably about half were
accounted for on or around Diamond Shoals. Of them all,
perhaps the most talked of is *Carroll A. Deering*. In the
National Park's excellent little Museum of the Sea at the
Cape there is displayed a photograph of the hulking five-
master taken in the shipbuilding yards at Bath, Maine, just
before she went down the ways. Two years later she was
found aground on Diamond Shoals, her sails set, the men's
food in the galley, the crew vanished and never heard of
again—another *Mary Celeste*. The most famous of the ships
lost here was doubtless *U.S.S. Monitor*, which went down in
a gale off the Cape in December 1862 while under tow. The
towing vessel, the side-wheeler *Rhode Island*, picked up most

of the crew. Of the sixteen lost, the bodies of five were
washed up on shore and were buried by Union soldiers re-
portedly at the foot of a juniper and their common grave
covered with rocks evidently from the foundations of the
first lighthouse, built in 1797. There is just such a pile of
rocks by the rotted stump of a cedar on a likely ridge a mile
west of the lighthouse. The site is on a slope now included
in a special tract of woods and fresh-water swamp inhabited
by cottonmouths through which the Buxton Woods Nature
Trail passes—one of the delights of the Cape; with American
holly, laurel oak, swamp bay and loblolly pine added to the
live oak and the arboreal forms of yaupon and myrtle, the
trees festooned in bullbrier and laurel smilax, and saw palmetto bursting from the ground, the dell when you come to it
in February from the beach and the dunes seems as green
and luxuriant as the heart of a Caribbean isle. The cairn
under which *Monitor*'s five seamen may lie is adjacent to the
trail.

Arriving at the point of the Cape is like reaching the summit of the highest mountain in a great range or a monument
of history around which the tides of human affairs have
poured, the Parthenon, say, or the Tower of London—an
enormous experience if you come at a time of year or day
when you are alone with it. *Here it is,* you say to yourself,
your mind swamped with the actuality of where you are. You
can walk out to the very tip, where the beach slopes beneath
the waves. And there is the veritable point of land that has
been all-important to so many mortals, the name of which
has been on so many lips.

The sun was setting behind low clouds when I drove up to
Cape Hatteras and the light atop the great sentinel was
already on and shimmering like a jewel on its cyclical appearances. When I disembarked at the campgrounds, a mile
and a half southwest of it, the sky was a glowing, metallic
blue behind snowy, coagulating clouds. In the west, a mellow,
yellow effulgence was like the memory of a vanished golden
age on earth, while nearly overhead was the new moon,
which had been the merest sliver at Assateague. Against this
background, as I set out on foot for the point, flocks of snow
geese began to come by, the first ones out at sea. They had
evidently not been long on the wing, for they were still getting
organized, and before their flocks took form there was much

crowding at the front and trailing in the rear, as there is apt
to be among human troops on the march. Their clangor was
like that of the Canada geese, if perhaps with less conviction
and boldness. But to make up for that there was the drama
of their appearance, their pristine white set off by the black
wingtips against the fathomless blue sky and one's knowledge
of their origin near the Pole. The last of the five or six flocks
was the largest and passed directly overhead, making my
scalp crawl. The host came on nearly abreast, a phantom
army sweeping forward, like a charge of winged cavalry in
full battle-cry, the sound of their pinion-strokes the muted,
muffled thunder of spectral hoofs. One bird, much darker
than the rest though white-headed, was unmistakably that
sought-after rarity in the East, a blue goose down from an
Arctic breeding range so remote and so confined that it was
not discovered until 1929.

Walking on with the beam of the lighthouse on my left
flashing by every fifteen seconds, I passed the bodies of two
gulls, a red-breasted loon and a porpoise. The narrowing
beach was littered with treetrunks, boards and ships' timbers,
most of the last perhaps from an ancient victim of the shoals
of which only the prow remained visible and in one piece.
It rose from the sand barely recognizable for what it was.
As in the hulls of the other wrecked wooden ships one came
upon, the oaken ribs were a foot square in cross section and
laid side by side. You could believe the figures of 1770 cited
by Robert Cushman Murphy in explaining the early defor-
estation of Long Island which show that a seventy-four-gun
frigate required the lumber of twenty-two hundred trees,
estimated to be the normal cover of forty acres of first
growth.

I have seen waters that are frightening or appalling but
until I had stood looking seaward from the point of Hatteras
I had never seen any that were eerie. On either side of the
shoals the ocean was placid. To their west, in the bight
formed by the point, a school of porpoises was advancing
calmly, their backs showing like the rims of slowly turning
mill wheels as they arched above the water. The serene scene
included also two skimmers that went by with their loping,
tireless-seeming flight—dark-backed terns that would be
beautiful were they not bill-heavy, like pelicans. But off the
point an entirely different order prevailed. The sea there was

roiled and tormented. Low breakers were suddenly thrown up and as suddenly flattened in the troughs of others or flung headlong into breakers tumbling in from the other direction. As far as the eye could reach the ocean was a riot of leaping waves and frothing whitecaps—and with no agency detectable in the windless calm to account for it. One hears much of the collision of the coastal current and the Gulf Stream at Cape Hatteras, but the latter passes twenty miles off shore, and even if the two drove directly upon each other their combined rates of flow would fail by far to produce such a turmoil of waters. So the authorities of the Park Service point out. It is their view that the explanation lies in the effect of the shoals upon the waves; as I had seen at Cape Henlopen, waves coming in from the distance are bent 180 degrees by the shallow bottom—turned completely around—only instead of breaking on both shores of an intervening promontory, they here, where the promontory is under water, pile into each other. I can think of no other explanation. Yet to witness the phenomenon where there are scarce any stirrings of air and no incoming waves of apparently sufficient size to account for it is uncanny. One could have thought that a huge school of giant fish was thrashing about just below the surface.

And beneath those tortured seas lay the ocean's bottom and its gruesome treasury. It is bad enough to visualize the black remains of vessels lying in filtered light under six or eight fathoms of water, but staring out from the point it was somehow worse to think of all those with their pathetic souvenirs of hopeful human life that were irretrievably entombed deep beneath the crushing weight of the inexhaustible sand of the shoals, into which ships sink without a trace. If such things as ghosts existed, I told myself, I should not sleep that night. Probably I should not anyway, I reflected, in the deserted campgrounds thinking the thoughts that that fell shore gives rise to.

But ghosts, if there be such, seem seldom to trouble the living, and the living, for their part, seldom lie wakeful over the fate of the unknown dead. Only the sprinkles of rain accompanying a wind that had risen in the east disturbed my sleep, and the next morning, elated at being able in the mild air off the Gulf Stream to doff my wrist- and ankle-length thermal underwear, I had a chance to see what a fair breeze

could kick up on Diamond Shoals. It took the seas a little
while to build up. The ocean, on which a pallid sun gleamed
fitfully as it faded in and out through the rift of cloud, was
green marble but, whipped by the wind, it soon began to
work up a surf and to turn milky. Within two hours,
champing breakers were thundering in upon the beach on one
another's traces and the frothing sea was brilliant-hazy to the
horizon with the peculiar bloom a southeaster imparts to it.

This was the heavy onshore wind that sailing vessels had
cause to dread. It was easy, in the teeth of it, to call up a
picture of a storm-wracked schooner rearing stiffly above the
churning sea in brute agony, helpless to beat her way against
the gale driving her in upon the shoals. At the point was a
spectacle I had never thought to behold: that of the sea in
pitched battle against itself. Wave systems were coming in
from both northeast and southwest to smash full force into
each other, and from the impact sheets and geysers of foaming waters erupted. The shoals acted as a fire under a caldron,
and the chaotic pitching of seas extended to the limit of
vision. It was like a leaderless and hysterical rebellion of
the waters. Frantic, demonic, rushing waves sought to claw
one another down. They were colliding and breaking pell-
mell directly before me in torrents of flying spray, sending the
water racing up the beach boiling with foam and sending me
fleeing.

I spent a long time watching it and, hardly able to stay
away when I had left, was back again in the last hour of
daylight, though I felt contrite at putting to flight once more
the flock of gulls that hung out around the standing water by
the wreck. The waves were still surging in though with
diminished turbulence; the wind had fallen and with the tide
out the water was less deep over the shoal. But a pelting
rain kept me from seeing well, hiding even the lighthouse
until the beam suddenly came on, high up in the grey ob-
scurity, effectuating God's *Fiat Lux*. It pattered loud on my
raincoat and was funneled onto my trouser-legs, in accordance with the purpose for which raincoats are evidently
designed.

Hatteras light reaches twenty miles to sea, and so do
the impulses from the Loran station, which are transmitted
from the thinnest possible tower of red steel scaffolding
standing at some distance from the lighthouse and standing

higher. (Efficiency, not grandeur, is the watchword of our times.) And Loran operates as well by day as by night and in the thickest weather. It is not alone because of the replacement of sails by steam that Hatteras's menace to shipping has been so greatly reduced, as the officer in charge of the Coast Guard Station pointed out to me. It is also because of Loran. In the past, ships dependent upon a magnetic compass during overcast weather when the sextant was useless —and such weather could last for ten days at Hatteras— were in great danger of going off course when passing through the shipping lane, which was sixteen miles off the Cape, for a magnetic compass was fallible. Upon my asking why, then, ships had not given the shoals an absolutely safe berth, say by a margin of fifty miles, he replied that ships carried as little fuel as they could do with, since fuel took up space otherwise available for cargo, also that time was money to the owners. (He did not mention it, but I dare say that ships southward-bound past the Cape have always kept close in to avoid having to buck the Gulf Stream's four-knot current.)

The officer went on to explain that the Coast Guard's burdens have also been eased by the helicopter and, especially on the Banks, by hard-surfaced roads along the coast; the two innovations together enable a station to cover much more ground, and the number of stations between Ocracoke and the Virginia line administered by Cape Hatteras has been reduced from twenty-three to nine. The tasks of those remaining are chiefly taking care of fishing and pleasure craft. Most seagoing boats today are equipped with radio and can get word of storms in time to run in before them, but it is still necessary occasionally to go out in a blow on a rescue mission. He had confidence in the ability of the Outer Banks patrol boat—a ninety-five-footer stationed at Ocracoke—to meet any weather it might run into. The problem was in getting out to face it, for the inlets are in effect much shallower when seas are running high; for example, a mean depth of eleven feet does not help much when waves are so high the troughs are only five feet from the bottom.

But if electronics have enormously lessened the dangers to which ships were exposed when they had to run blind, it would appear that the sea is far from tamed. Of the world's approximately 24,000 merchant ships of five hundred or more tons, according to a report of the Liverpool Underwriters

Association, 148 were lost in 1963 and 117 in 1964, while
those disabled by collisions, damage from weather, stranding,
"contact damage," damage to machinery, fires and explosions
amounted to more than a third of the remainder; the per-
centage, moreover, has been creeping up year by year. The
United States Coast Guard reports that in 1964 it saved
almost three thousand lives and rescued ships worth, with
their cargoes, more than two billion dollars.

If the Outer Banks today see far fewer ships fall prey to
the sea's hunger than in the past, they seem themselves in
recent years to have suffered more from it. Despite the dune-
dike built and maintained along the inner edge of the beach
by dredging, bulldozing, snow-fencing and planting, the Outer
Banks are losing two feet a year to the sea, on the average,
and probably more—in places much more—according to the
authorities at the National Seashore. The shore may have as
much as two hundred feet sliced off it in a single storm, while
in a sector near the village of Hatteras it has been cut back
eighteen hundred feet since 1937. The rate of erosion is such
as to raise the question of how there can be any Banks still
in existence—which in turn raises the question of how there
happened to be any Banks in existence in the first place.

The favored explanation, as it would seem to be, is twofold.
First, it is represented that the barrier beaches standing off
the coastal plain today, including the Banks, were the coastal
dunes of the Ice Age, when the ocean was shrunken and the
shore lay far to the east of its present location. This theory
holds that as the ocean rose with the melting of the ice-sheet
the dunes were progressively built up by the waves, which
piled sand on the beach below them, and by the wind, which
carried the sand up their slopes, in the conventional dune-
building process; at the same time the sea flooded the margins
of the coastal plain behind the dunes.

The other element believed to enter into the constitution
of the Banks (as of other barrier beaches) is the drift current that deposits sand as it moves along the coast, picks it
up again and carries it on, usually replacing what it removes
with more sand from some continuing source of supply. The
source of supply for the Banks would be, I should judge, the
sediment carried by the rivers that empty into Chesapeake
Bay after draining five hundred miles of the Appalachian
Mountains. On the map, indeed, the Banks suggest a thin

stream poured out of the bottle of the Bay. An odd feature of the stream, however, is that at Cape Hatteras it angles sharply to the west just as if—to stay with the analogy—it were glancing off an obstruction. And something of the sort may be the case, with the obstruction consisting of offshoots of the Gulf Stream.

This river of the ocean, forty miles wide and two thousand feet deep, moving with the volume of a thousand Mississippis, follows a course conforming roughly with the edge of the continental shelf—which was the great granite island's original shore. Skirting the southeastern coast of Florida in the area of Miami, it parallels the coastline, its inner edge thirty or forty miles off shore, until it passes Cape Hatteras at a distance of only twenty-five miles, after which its separation from the coast progressively widens. Off the Cape, possibly because it here encounters the southward-moving littoral current, streams peel off its inner edge to curl around like shavings. These, it is possible, crowd the littoral current, deflecting it sharply westward so that, below Cape Hatteras, it causes the shore to arc inland. At the same time, its encounter with the tendrils of the Gulf Stream may account for the deposit of sand forming Diamond Shoals.

A possible objection to this explanation of the bend in the Banks at Hatteras is the fact that they bend even more sharply farther south, where Core Banks and Shackleford Banks form an approximate right angle (even an acute angle) with Cape Lookout pendant from the place of juncture like the head of a harpoon. Is this deflection of the stream of sand also caused by offshoots of the Gulf Stream—earlier ones? Does it reflect the original configuration of the coastal plain, and is that also the explanation of the bend at Hatteras? Is the shape of the Banks to be accounted for primarily by the fact that the estuaries opening into Pamlico Sound (which is framed by Banks running predominantly north and south) empty toward the east, whereas those opening into the sounds behind the Banks at the lower end of the chain (which run east and west) empty toward the south?

All I feel fairly sure of in respect of the origin of the Banks is that if their existence were unknown, no one would expect them to be there. And if it were hypothesized that there was such an extraordinary string of sand reefs, I for one would certainly argue that either they would have been expanded by the forces that brought them into existence or, contrariwise, eliminated by the forces that prevented their expansion. As it is, one is left to wonder how so precarious and delicate an equilibrium has been maintained between influences of such dimensions and such might.

A knowledge of what lies beneath the Banks does not conduce to any stronger impression of their security. The bedrock of the continent—the "basement," as the geologists call it—which is near the surface at fall line, slopes down at an accelerating rate toward the coast. By the time it has declined to twenty-five hundred feet below sea-level, it is dropping off at better than a hundred feet per mile. At Cape Hatteras, it lies nearly ten thousand feet down. This was discovered when Standard Oil of New Jersey drilled a test well at the Cape, commencing at the end of 1945—the deepest ever sunk on the Atlantic coastal plain. For the first fifteen hundred feet the boring encountered only sands, clays and shell-gravels. From that level on there were more sands and clays and also limestones (formed of the shells of marine organisms), then sandstones, shales and more limestones—and more sands. Only when the drill had gone through nearly two miles of these sediments and sedimentary formations did it bite into a really solid foundation—the evidently "highly weathered" granite of the bedrock. Even among the lower deposits there were "massive beds of porous sand," according to a report of the drilling of the well, "North Carolina Esso No. 1." One almost wonders why the Banks, which constitute a kind of barely-elevated rim of a shelf of sand extending out from the coast, do not simply slide off down the edge of the continental shelf, which falls off very abruptly to their east.

The power of the hurricanes' destructiveness makes the survival of the Banks seem more wonderful still. Storm waves crashing in on the abnormal tides destroy dunes and pour across the sand flats beyond them. The winds may reach 125 miles an hour or more. Unless accompanied by rains, as fortunately they usually are, they poison vegetation all across the island with the salt-spray they whip from the breakers and they sandblast the stems and foliage, opening them to invasion by salt, and shred the beachgrass. Of the hurricane of September 1846, it was recorded that the inhabitants "in the morning . . . saw sea and sound connected together, and the live oaks washing up by the roots and tumbling into the ocean." And between the cyclonic storms there are the ordinary gales. The northeaster of March 1962, which wreaked such havoc upon Assateague, cut a broad new inlet just above Hatteras (subsequently filled in by dredges of the Corps of Engineers), washed out and buried parts of the highway, wrecked a fishing center and demolished the Oregon Inlet campground and its site, leaving the beach strewn with chunks of asphalt. I was shown a photograph of a contractor's dragline which it had buried to its boom.

If man has taken second place to the elements as a destroyer, he has added his handiwork to theirs and left the islands more exposed to their onslaughts. As in the case of Outer Cape Cod there has long been disagreement as to how well wooded the Banks originally were. A special study of the question by Clair A. Brown, part of a larger study carried out by Louisiana State University for the Office of Naval Research, concluded that in any event forests covered a much wider area in years past than they do today. For two or three miles along the beach at Wash Woods, near the Virginia line, there are stumps of red juniper, live oak and red mulberry, while near Rodanthe a hurricane of 1955 uncovered similar remains of a forest of southern yellow pine where the beach now is. Shackleford, the most southerly and best protected of the Banks, was certainly once very different. A visitor in 1917 wrote:

> In the memory of living inhabitants, the Bank was well wooded over its entire extent, the strand separating the forest from the ocean being so narrow that it was "possible to sit in a tree and cast a fishing line into the water." Before the Civil War, however, cutting of timber, coupled with forest fires, and the grazing of cattle and sheep, and the inroads of gales, had broken the protecting wall of vegetation and allowed the sand from the beach to blow in on the trees. Slowly at first, and then more and more rapidly, sand was blown in on the vegetation, killing or covering the existing plants.

Today there are ten vacationers' cottages on Shackleford where a century ago there was one of the largest villages on the Banks. Diamond City, named for the pattern of alternating black and white diamonds in which Cape Lookout lighthouse is painted, had five hundred inhabitants who supported themselves chiefly by whaling. When in 1899 a hurricane brought the ocean into the village streets, however, they moved out, taking the remaining houses with them. Nothing is left to show where Diamond City stood but a small graveyard.

Vegetation was similarly destroyed on the Outer Banks. Wherever dry sand was exposed, the winds to the limit of their strength picked it up and moved it forward. The bare dunes rolled with the wind. In some cases they did not finally stop until they had crossed the island and poured into the Sound. Inching forward, sometimes quickening their pace under a howling wind after a dry spell, stabilized for longer or shorter periods, then resuming their march, like zombies, they would bury houses or smother all vegetation in their advance, leaving ruins to be discovered perhaps many years later or forests of skeleton trees. When a storm of March 1846 tore away a range of dunes just below the Virginia line it exposed a grove of dead junipers which, with their "gigantic arms stretched impressively heavenward," were recognized by one of the older inhabitants; in the War of 1812, screened by their foliage, he had conducted beneath them his business of boiling sea water for salt, and now, scratching a little below the surface, he uncovered two of his three-by-six-foot pans just as he had left them thirty-four years earlier when the sand blew in. The stumps of Wash Woods are believed to include those of the same junipers.

By 1936 the erosion of the denuded Banks had reached such a pass that the sea was almost lapping at the foot of the Cape Hatteras lighthouse. Standing more than half a mile from the sea when it was constructed in 1870, it now had to be abandoned. At this point the Federal Government stepped in with countermeasures. A tract of 1,200 acres at the Cape, a gift of J. S. Phipps, had been made into a state park and was to be included in the Cape Hatteras National Seashore, authorized the next year, and it was here that the operation began. Brush fencing set out experimentally was soon found buried to its tops—in sand it had stopped and held. In the next four years, under the supervision of A. Clark Stratton of the National Park Service, men of the Transient Camps—mostly veterans of World War I and the Bonus March—with youths of the Civilian Conservation Corps under Emanuel J. Byrum, erected 557 miles of brush fencing, planted on the resultant dunes enough grass (chiefly American beachgrass, sea-oats and salt-meadow cordgrass) to cover 3,254 acres and set out two and a half million trees and shrubs, mostly live oaks, yaupons and wax myrtles. Meanwhile, the free-ranging cattle and horses (except those of Ocracoke) had been rounded up under a new state law. By 1940 the lighthouse had manifestly been saved, although it was not reoccupied until ten years later. Wind erosion had been arrested and reversed and substantial barriers erected to incursions of the sea. It was a tremendous achievement.

No fortifications of sand can, however, withstand the ocean's mightiest blows or resist its pressure if this is consistently maintained. And the Banks today, while in some sectors accreting, are on the whole markedly receding.

One theory is that as they are worn down on their outer side they are augmented on their inner, in other words that they are slowly migrating inland. It would certainly seem that sand, carried by the wind, moves regularly westward from the beach to the sound, as the rogue dunes do. Yet the map made by John White, who came with the Grenville expedition of 1585, shows the Banks substantially as they are and where they are at present. My guess would be that as sand is blown inland from the beach it is normally replaced by sand deposited by the sea and that if the sounds do not fill up (as Peter Farb in *Face of North America* says the bays behind barrier beaches all must and will) it is because the ocean has here been rising with respect to the land ever since the last Ice Age. That this rise has been taking place no one questions; a foot a century seems to be about the rate. On a branch of Albemarle Sound, peat has been found to go down forty feet, which means that marsh vegetation was once growing as far as that below its present level.

Opinion at the National Seashore headquarters is that the Banks may depend upon a continuing supply of fresh sand to offset losses—which would certainly be the case if they are to any great extent the creatures of the littoral currents —and that the supply may have been failing. This, it is suggested, could be the result of the damming of the rivers that feed the Banks which causes their load of sand to be precipitated in the impoundments before it reaches the sea. The solution proposed by the Corps of Engineers is to dredge sand up from the depths to which the currents carry it and restore it to the shallows for the replenishment of the beach. This device has saved other beaches. It is also possible that the Banks have always been subject to periods of erosion and that these normally alternate with periods of build-up. It occurs to me that the current depletion of the Banks could be the result of the prolonged drought from which the watershed of Chesapeake Bay has been suffering, which has greatly reduced the flow of the rivers emptying into it. If so, the rainy phase of the cycle should see the damage repaired—unless man's interference with the flow of the rivers comes to the point of seriously impeding the delivery of sand.

It was because the State of North Carolina sensibly recognized that only the Federal Government can carry the burden of reconstituting the natural defenses of fifty-eight miles of barrier beach that it offered to donate to the nation most of the land of the Lower Banks, which it had bought up. Public opinion in Carteret County, in which the Lower Banks lie, was in favor of Federal acquisition, in happy contrast to that in Worcester County, Maryland. Actually, the land for the Cape Hatteras National Seashore was also donated. Through the Old Dominion and Avalon Foundations, Paul H. Mellon and his sister Mrs. Mellon Bruce each contributed $409,000 to make the donation possible—most of it in 1954—with North Carolina fulfilling the condition of their grants by putting up an equal amount.

The boom in vacationing has been timely for most shore-based economies, for the technological progress that created the boom by giving us wealth, leisure and motorcars had undermined the coast-dwellers' traditional means of livelihood. Without the mounting flood of vacationers, the Banks might have become depopulated. It has been a long time since wrecks have spread much largesse on their strands. Shipping deserted the Banks ports generations ago; the last commercial freight vessel to pass through Hatteras or Ocracoke Inlets did so in 1895, and Portsmouth has practically ceased to exist. Coast Guard lifeboat stations have been drastically thinned out. The waterfowl that once thronged the Sounds "in numbers exceeding all conception of any person who had not been informed," as an observer wrote a century ago, are part of a vanished America. Hunting as a way of life became a victim of technology with the invention of machine-weapons. When, armed with repeating shotguns and miniature cannon called punt guns, two men could kill 892 ruddy ducks in a single day and a team of four 2,300 in a month—granted that these were record bags even for the North Carolina Sounds—the end of an era was obviously at hand. In 1918 market-gunning became illegal under the Federal Migratory Bird Act. The Bankers still had what had always been their chief source of income, the produce of the sea, or rather of the Sounds, but the facilities their islands could offer fishing fleets could not compete with those available elsewhere. There is today a little shrimping out of Banks ports (Pamlico is the northernmost shrimping ground on our coast) but a good deal of crabbing, but boatmen are turning increasingly to the more profitable business of catering to sports fishermen, hiring out for Sound-fishing and also for trolling for marlin and tuna out in the Gulf Stream. And no doubt raking for clams and tonging for oysters when the wind is raw lose some of their appeal when contrasted with a better-paying and more comfortable berth in a service station or grocery store. The money that vacationers bring not only compensates for the decline of traditional occupations, it hastens it. It is the old story: the national economy, which offers everyone from Seattle to Key West the same rewards—same elaborately equipped motorcars, same electrified kitchens, same spectral entertainment of the television screen—in exchange for the same offices rendered, is seldom resisted.

It is the old story in another aspect as well. An out-of-the-way place is discovered which has the appeal and excitement of the remote and primitive. Visitors begin to come. The influx swells; for the Banks it may be said to have got under way with the bridging of Currituck Sound in 1930. The clamor rises for comforts and conveniences and for ease of access which will as far as possible transform the area into the likeness of every other. And sooner or later the clamorers have their way.

One hears that by no means all the Bankers are on the clamorers' side. This may explain why I could not seem to find a crabber who was going out to tend his traps and would be willing to take me along. Or it may be simply that none was going. The two or three I approached on the quay at Hatteras village, big men in their middle years, could not have been described as communicative. Neither could the proprietor of the packing plant beside the quay, a tall, well-proportioned man, on the dark side in complexion, whose very neat and clean establishment I visited twice to replenish the ice in the bus's refrigerator. Reserved and withdrawn, he spoke and bore himself with marked courtesy, which I took to be the courtesy of a proud man who accords others the respect he takes without thinking to be his own due. He made an impression on me. He might have been the heir of an ancient and noble line whose ancestor, fleeing a conquered homeland, had been shipwrecked on the Banks and elected to remain—a mode of arrival that legend assigns to many founders of Banks families without, it is to be feared, much warrant. His antecedents might have included a scion of the chiefs of the Hatorask Indians. He said the ice would be twenty-five cents.

"I'd have to pay double that for the ice anywhere else," I said, already embarrassed at having interrupted his sweeping out of the plant for so small a purchase.

"Twenty-five cents is all I expect," he repeated with an inclination of the head. "Sir."

I had it from a very different sort of person that local opinion is anything but unanimous in favor of the tourist invasion. This was the driver of a pickup truck, genial and shrewd, with whom I talked on the ferry back across Hatteras Inlet from Ocracoke Island, the employee of a real-estate operator (in Norfolk, I believe he said) whom he described as a millionaire with large interests in Ocracoke. He said he expected the bridge across Hatteras Inlet to come within five years. Upon my expressing regret and asking how on earth the village of Ocracoke could possibly accommodate the traffic a bridge would bring, he remarked with a kind of cynicism that I ought to see it in summer as it was. He said the inhabitants were opposed to the bridge, having no other desire than "to be left alone to fish and fornicate," and the former only enough to permit them to indulge in the latter and take it easy.

The opinion was one he might have hesitated to express in the company of the next person of whom I inquired about the matter, whose hands rested on a desk they could well have splintered—or so their appearance indicated—if he had swatted a fly on it. The Chief Warrant Officer in charge of the Cape Hatteras Coast Guard Station had a broad face with a somewhat flattened nose (and I should not like to have been the other man if he received it in an exchange of blows), greying hair and a square frame. I am diffident about barging in on strangers but he responded to my intrusion with patient politeness and a very acceptable invitation to have coffee with him in the mess-hall, which proved to be immaculate. Having come to ask about the work of his station, I raised the question of local opinion about the proposed bridge only when I learned that he was a native of Ocracoke. In the same conversational undertone which had astonished me at the start by filling the station house with its volume, he said he thought feelings on the island were mixed. I had the impression that he considered it not his business to elucidate the question or mine, necessarily, to have it elucidated. The coincidence of his being stationed so close to his point of origin surprised me much more than it did him for I was only in process of discovering that the Coast Guard is a kind of family enterprise to the Bankers. It was not difficult to see in the man across the table from me the generations of his ancestors whose world was more of water than of land, who ran before the squalls in their shad-boats, sharpies and skiffs and, from the Coast Guard stations they manned, put the heavy lifeboats through the surf of the worst of storms. It is said that, of all the lifeboat crews on the Banks—and at one time there was a station every six miles from Virginia Beach to Cape Lookout—never did one fail to respond to the call of a ship in distress, however towering the seas. On Long Island even today they speak of the Coast Guardsmen from the Banks as being set apart by the tradition they were born to that pitted men barehanded against the surf.

The Cape Hatteras campgrounds are spread out behind the dunes on the Cape's wide, grassy plains. These present a vista of browns as the ridgeland behind them exhibits all the shades of green: the olive drab of wax myrtles; the grey-green of live oaks; the yellow-green of loblollies; the avocado of yaupons; the deep, ceremonial green of junipers; the anemic green of that understudy of myrtle and yaupon, the silverling or groundsel bush, which in the autumn, with its down-covered fruit, looks as if it were mantled with a wet snow. The campgrounds, like the other six of the National Seashore, are bare to a degree that must shock tenters used to the forest parks. Nothing stands above the grass but picnic tables and

trash cans, a boxlike toilet building (closed for the winter)
and a few privies.

While the National Seashore has nearly a million "visita-
tions" a year, I had company only one evening. A pickup
truck with a covered rear was parked a few campsites away
from me with two men in the front seat immobilized by the
rain; it was the evening of the downpour. I thought how
enviable I must appear, able to stand and move about in the
bright and cheerful little bus, a cup of hot chocolate on the
table and a book beside it and my soaked corduroys drying
on a hanger in the heat from the incandescent globe of the
gas lantern below. How delicious these privileges seemed, set
off by the rainy gloom and the proximity of that ominous
shore! I felt sorry not only for my neighbors but for most
of the rest of the world, including three song sparrows which
had been still hard at it foraging for seeds when I had crossed
the dunes on my way back from the point. Before I had set
out, ten of them feeding near the bus had suddenly dashed
for the cover it provided. A female marsh harrier, long of
wing and tail, had appeared, flying close over the ground. She
made a stab at a remaining sparrow but did not persist when
it took evasive action and fled to the bus to join the others.
She knew her limitations and had no time for gestures. Poor
thing. One could feel the urgency of her quest for something
to stay the pangs of hunger before nightfall and, observing
the trembling of her wings and the continual readjustments
required by the gusty breeze, tell that flying is not as effortless
as it usually seems.

After the men in the truck had given up whatever they had
had in mind and driven away, the wind blowing the rain in
from the sea began gently nudging the bus, giving one the
feeling of having palpitations. Later, harder flurries of rain
struck, driven by stronger gusts. They sounded like grapeshot
on the roof and I wondered if I were going to be able to sleep
through them. However, the rain must have slackened off
after I turned in for until I was roused at four o'clock by the
drip from a leak on my sleeping-bag I awoke only once—to
the rumble of thunder. Winter had ended for me as it had
begun at Mount Desert.

The winter beach in any case went no farther than Cape
Hatteras. At nearby Buxton a few oleanders were growing, a
crepe myrtle was heavily draped with Spanish moss and there

was saw palmetto in the woods. This was the frontier of the Deep South. I had no call to go beyond it, but I still could not forgo the chance to visit Ocracoke, the outermost town of our eastern marches.

I did not make it that morning. Hatteras Inlet was fog-bound and I gave up waiting for the ferry to find its way back from the other side. But sitting in the ferry office with half-a-dozen employees of the agency (under the State High-way Commission) I did pick up some scraps of information from the gossip. I learned that it was a matter of amusement to my companions that their colleagues should be hung up on a bar, if that was the cause of the ferry's delay; the metal-lic barks emitted erratically by the radio receiver were enigmatic. I also heard the patriarch of the group, a stocky sixty-year-old on the verge of retirement, speak of the pros-pects of a coastal highway down the entire length of the Banks with a certainty of expectation that made my heart sink. All the remaining houses and privately-owned tracts in Portsmouth, he indicated, had been bought up on speculation in anticipation of the time when the tourist throng would be able to get across Ocracoke Inlet—the only inlet, by the way, which has been open continuously since the arrival of the white man.

Portsmouth's decline had begun over a century ago when Ocracoke Inlet partially silted up and shipping largely aban-doned it in favor of the newly opened inlet to the north, Hatteras Inlet. By the mid 1950's the population had been reduced from over 500 to 17. An official of the Corps of Engineers whom I subsequently met told me of visiting it then and finding the experience one of the queerest of his life. All the remaining inhabitants with one exception were over sixty but they were chipper enough and declared they would live nowhere else. "What do you folks do for church services?" my acquaintance—a Southerner—asked. The eldest citizen and spokesman for the band replied that they had had a preacher but had not liked him and had sent him back to the mainland, since when they had done the preaching them-selves, taking it by turns. The visitor, hearing that the post office was still in business, expressed a desire to buy some stamps, whereupon one of the women detached herself from the group to hurry to the post office, which was located in the general store, to open it up. The stamps were forthcoming, but it turned out that the shelves of the store itself were as bare as the day it was built. Of the thirty-some houses, most were of course unoccupied.

The survivors of those whom the Army Engineer had met must finally have had to be removed to be cared for, for the retiring ferryman reported that the town was now occupied by only a woman and her daughter and a Negro man; another Negro had not long before been found dead in the skiff with which he was accustomed to meet the mail boat.

Later that day the historian of the National Seashore confirmed to me that these three did indeed make up the present population of Portsmouth (and according to the National Park Service the population of Portsmouth makes up the entire permanent population of the Lower Banks apart from the Coast Guard personnel at Cape Lookout). Was there, I asked him, any chance that he or another Park Ranger could be prevailed upon to cross over to the island in the next day or two and take me with him? He replied that the headquarters had no boat available to it, but not before his secretary had announced that if anyone were going she was going too. I had been introduced to her and been made to sit up and take notice by her name—Midgett. Upon my exclaiming over her possession of a name so illustrious in the history of the Banks, she said that she was a Midgett only by marriage. Nineteen Medals of Honor for lifesaving had been won by those who bore the name. Of the six members of the crew of the lifesaving station at Rodanthe who received gold Medals of Honor for the rescue of most of the crew of the burning British tanker *Mirlo* in August 1918, five, including the Keeper of the station, had been Midgetts.

There was no difference in Hatteras Inlet the next morning except that the ferry was in her slip and ready to depart. Looking back on it, I should say that crossing in a vessel that has to grope her way through a chill fog is the right way to approach Ocracoke to appreciate its flavor. Visibility was limited to about two hundred feet. We kept putting up denizens of the spirit world in the form of red-breasted mergansers which sprinted in long strides across the water and got off fast. Twice we plowed into a flock of cormorants and for a time, as if we had invaded a rookery, the limbo was filled with hundreds of the black forms pattering off the water into the breeze. After the last channel marker had faded away astern, a long sandbar parted the mist and water ahead and instantly we were aground. Only the most energetic backwatering got us off. The pilot put the boat around 90 degrees to starboard and we were soon aground again. However, this time we got off without much trouble. Only when the ferry landing materialized dead ahead (for a wonder) did we emerge from the fog. Before us lay a low expanse of sterile salt flats.

You feel for a fact that in Ocracoke you are midway between this world and the next, at least if you arrive in conditions like these. But the barren landscape, at any rate, does not last forever. Before you have gone half the thirteen miles to the town the road begins to curve and recurve gracefully among pleasant, rolling dunes, and there is hummocky country off to the west humped with wind-sculptured thickets and cut by creeks. I felt breathless in a curious way and as if any emotions I might have would lack validity, so far removed was I from the body of humanity. It was only the temporary effect of the strangeness, I am sure, but when I went into a general store in the town I noticed that I approached the shopkeeper with a kind of hesitant deference, such as a soldier of a rear-echelon unit will adopt when addressing a fellow from the front lines.

Ocracoke Island is shaped like a spanner wrench with its handle to the north and a prong extending on from the jaws. The bight formed by the prong and the upper jaw is known as Teach's hole. It was here, supposedly, at dawn on November 22, 1718, that Lieutenant Robert Maynard with two sloops manned by seamen from British warships put an end to the career of Edward Teach, alias Captain Drummond, also known as Blackbeard, who, before deciding to reduce the scale of his operations, had commanded four ships and about four hundred fellow pirates and in two years had captured at least twenty-five vessels and bought the collusion of the Governor of the colony. It was a bloody, if small, engagement ending in hand-to-hand fighting between Maynard and Teach in which the pirate was felled only after he had been hewn almost in pieces. Between the jaws of the spanner, the tips of which very nearly meet, is the remarkable, capacious harbor of Cockle Creek, rechristened (I suppose by real-estate agents) Silver Lake. Alongside its wharves are sturdy-looking fishing-boats, high-bowed and with the rounded sterns of "Core Sounders," some hung with otter trawls, as the shrimp nets are called. The town borders the harbor.

I should like to have seen Ocracoke a generation ago, before the house-trailers, car-bodies and bleak, commonplace post-war houses put in their appearance. But the older houses are still there, mostly very modest and hidden behind man-high yuccas and flourishing oleanders, beneath live oaks and junipers which alike look as if they had grown up and spread out beneath an invisible ceiling about twenty feet high. The old town still gives the feeling that it is pocket-sized and that the human adventure on earth can essentially be held in the cupped hands. If it were in a different part of the country an imposing monument would have been erected at the putative place where in 1585 Captain Sir Ralph Lane's fleet of seven small vessels "after various adventures that caused delay," as Hakluyt recorded, "passed the Cape Feare on June 23rd and days later came to anchor at Wokokon," thus beginning the English settlement of the New World. But little is lost by the absence of a memorial. This is no place for the display of *hubris*. It is more fitting that a working lighthouse—an engagingly fat, sharply tapering, pure-white one rising from little parklike grounds—should be "Wokokon's" outstanding structure. It is equally so that the historic plaque you remember from a visit is the one appearing on the little picket-fenced enclosure in which, beneath white concrete crosses, are the bodies of four seamen of the British Royal Navy found on the beach on May 14, 1942, at the nadir of the war. Considering the number of those drowned in the surf of the Banks—188 just in the wrecks of *U.S.S. Huron* and *S.S. Metropolis* during the winter of 1877-8—it is surprising that the small adjunct to the Ocracoke graveyard should be so touching, but it is.

The last schooner to meet her doom on the Banks was *George A. Kohler*. While taking a parting walk on the beach I came on what remained, south of Salvo. It was not much compared with the tall, well-composed vessel shown intact in a photograph taken just after her stranding in 1933, to be seen in the Museum of the Sea. Yet it was the most extensive piece of wreckage still to be found on the Banks. Not only were the huge timbers and ribs of the bottom of the hull preserved but also some sheathing, all held together by rusted spikes two feet long. It is possible to buy locally a colored postcard of the skeleton with a pretty girl provocatively displayed beside it. To chance upon it by yourself on the deserted beach, devoid of human life for miles in either direction, in the first chill premonition of darkness, conveys a different impression, however; and it was this impression, as much as any, that I took with me when I left the next morning: an impression of nakedness, of a gaunt breastwork of sand, guardian of an empty sound, the wide, cold sky and crashing, tireless sea—witnesses of infinity—and before me the bare, desiccated bones of human endeavor, as remote now from the warmth of human blood and heart as some unidentifiable carcass cast up from the bowels of the ocean.

At the End

SAID Dr. Carl Jung: "I have treated many hundreds of patients. . . . Among [those] in the second half of life—that is to say, over 35—there has not been one whose problem in the last resort was not that of finding a religious outlook on life." It could well be that that is true of all of us who have passed the halfway point.

Psychology has given us a term which may be enlightening: love-hate. The term seems to me to describe the regard in which, whether we acknowledge it or not, we are likely to hold Creation, or the Creator, if we prefer. The conditions of life appall as often as they enchant us. Every year twenty thousand of us in the United States kill ourselves, and doubtless each one stands for a thousand others for whom existence is mostly pain and sorrow. As pitiable as these are those who hunger for life yet are cut down by accident and disease. "As flies to wanton boys are we to the gods; they kill us for their sport." Not for sport, I should guess, but out of heedlessness.

One can hardly contemplate perceptively a tree, a fish, a deer, even a weed without being reminded of the countless millions of its kind which have been sacrificed to bring it to its present poetry of form. Evolution is a process of continuing, ruthless discard of the not-quite-right in favor of an infinitesimally slight gain toward some ultimate goal. For the grace of deer we may thank the savagery of wolves which have pulled down and devoured those which fell short of the species' best, just as for the sagacity and stamina of wolves we may thank the fleetness of deer which has demanded of their hunters the utmost of which they are capable. The conclusion hardly to be escaped it that the Divinity—or Nature, or call it what you will—is interested not in individuals but in ideas or ideals. To achieve a more sharklike shark, a more rabbitlike rabbit, a more maplelike maple, a more tapeworm-like tapeworm no price in individuals spawned and relentlessly culled, the rejects shoveled into oblivion, is too high to pay. The stones of the groins along the beaches of Long Island are regularly encrusted with rock barnacles. But there are no native stones on the beaches west of Montauk. That the imported stones have been colonized can mean only that barnacle larvae, doubtless in unimaginable millions, are habitually swept along the coast to their doom; only accident has saved the lives of the tiniest conceivable fraction of their multitudes. But the cost of colonizing such chance stones as might appear cannot be considered excessive by the Planner. One day in mid-May the swash marks on the beach at East Hampton were formed of the bodies of dark, red-legged insects resembling fireflies with long, narrow heads—*Bibionids,* or March flies, I was told by the American Museum of Natural History, to which I mailed some specimens. For a mile at least (I did not come to the end in either direction) the high-water-mark was traced by a black encrustation of these insects, like a deposit of oil scum, and the surface of the water was dusted with them. How many millions had died—carried on an offshore breeze and drowned—heaven alone knew. And each was a marvel of intricate organization, down to microscopic detail, in com-parison with inorganic matter hardly less wonderful than a human being. But there they were. There had been a minute flaw in their make-up in relationship to the conditions the species had to meet, and this was how it was dealt with. The survivors would be free of the flaw and a more successful *Bibionid* would be the result.

One has the impression of a Creator of unwearying capac-ity for trial and exploration, of infinite resourcefulness and ingenuity and of the capacity for never being finally satisfied. At one time his prime interest seems to be in an armored, semi-flexible scavenger of the ocean floor, and the seas are acrawl with trilobites. At another it is in animals at home in both great media of existence, and there is a far-ranging development of amphibians. What can be done, he seems to ask himself, through the achievement of motion by weaving through water? And the way is prepared for streamlined, lightning-fast fishes. A recurring preoccupation is with flight:

huge flying reptiles scour the skies; later come eight thousand species of birds, preceded by even more of insects, with infinitely marvelous adaptations; then bats, which are not, or not yet, as well designed for the air as birds, and squirrels, lizards and fish which are capable only of gliding. Another possibility presents itself: success in competition for survival through the organization of individuals of types designed for specialized functions—and a variety of insects equipped with instincts of uncanny complexity and precision are embarked on the road to colonial life. When the limitations of cold-blooded life seem to have been reached, the startling innovation of warm blood is essayed—and the reptiles begin to give way to mammals. A periodic curiosity to see what can be achieved through bulk produces dinosaurs and mastodons, giant squids and whales. Finally comes a great and wonderful conception: intellect. Everything for intellect! And, some millions of years later, from lemurlike beginnings, there is modern man, brought to his present state—like every other living thing—by the merciless elimination, generation after generation, of the second best.

Perhaps the Creator, in his awful loneliness, desired a fellow sharer of knowledge, a being capable of at least some gleams of understanding of his processes. In any event, the consequences of human intelligence were to be revolutionary. The possessor of this incomparable gift has been able, through its exercise, to challenge the donor himself, the Creator, and his rule on earth. Man has upset the natural order. He has brought the earth under his dominion as it has never before been brought under the dominion of a single form of life, and every day sees his grip extended and tightened, man's authority supplanting Nature's. And he has ordained that, contrary to Nature's decree, the individual shall count, that the individual, indeed, shall be the ultimate measure of good, his welfare the purpose of it all. It has been a glorious and triumphant rebellion, a drama beneath the skies the like of which has surely never been seen before on earth or, one would guess, on this side of Alpha Centauri, four light-years away, and perhaps never over far vaster distances than that. Prometheus has broken free of his bonds and set up his kingdom on earth. We may legitimately exult in the incomparable achievements of our puny species. Who would exchange them for any other conceivable earthly satisfactions?

Not I. Yet when I look upon Creation, against which we have scored these successes, I must own to a dreadful foreboding. Says F. L. Lucas, one of the wisest of contemporary voices, "Man has today grown ruthless both to Nature and to the past; Nature and the future may prove hereafter as ruthless to him." It seems terribly likely. We are depleting and poisoning our environment and refashioning it in ways that are torturing to the nerves. Our praiseworthy solicitude for individual human welfare—the humanitarianism we feel most commends us to God's mercy—creates conditions in which the least competent of the species are able to survive and multiply; one wonders whether, given the chance, we should not have arrested human development with *Australopithecus.* By modern medicine and surgery we save the lives of those with congenital defects and susceptibilities to disease. Who would have it otherwise? Yet the effect is to breed weakness and vulnerability rather than strength and resistance into the species, to make it increasingly dependent upon artifices which someday may fail it. Nature is unforgiving.

The mind goes back to the instances in history of societies and privileged classes which have had the means and inclination to devote themselves to the pursuit of pleasure—and how often have they not succumbed to other groups of human beings who, because they have had to work to keep body and soul together or because a strong leader has them in hand or because they are gripped by an overmastering idea, have not the habit of self-indulgence and are inured to hardship and struggle, who in other words are closer to man as he is compelled to be in natural conditions? An unprecedented productivity has provided the population of the United States with the means of self-indulgence on a hitherto undreamed-of scale at the very time that our enthronement of the individual has left scant grounds on which anyone can be denied any gratifications he can afford or restraints be imposed by any agency of society.

It sometimes seems to me that we liberate ourselves from the discipline of Nature only to face thankless alternatives. We may elect a state of things in which the predisposition of human beings toward what is alluring but self-destructive is uncontrolled. Or we may elect one in which an authority is instituted to impose control. And is salvation worth purchasing at the cost of submission to such an authority? I can bow before the elements—the rain and the cold—without loss of self-respect where I cannot before a policeman. Every edict I must obey, every form I must fill out, every permission I must seek subtracts from my manhood. I know that the state must exert more control over what its citizens seek to build if the country is not to become unlivable, but when I must obtain the authorization of an officeholder in a county court-house before adding a room to my home I am diminished. I know that our failure to sterilize congenital mental defectives only burdens society with more criminals, more chronically indigent, more morons. I know that the rate at which the human race is multiplying can lead only to utter disaster, inevitably. Yet if governments had the powers of population-control I believe they must have, what might not the end be? Most of us recognize that the income tax is indispensable and requires the Government to demand an accounting of our personal affairs, but few of us can fail to sympathize with the taxpayer who in that part of the form inscribed *Do not write in this space* scrawled "Who in hell says I can't?"

Perhaps the kind of reckoning I think I see ahead may be avoided. It may be that our inventiveness, which has brought us so far, will see us through. A century ago a society as pleasure-bent as ours might well have been overcome by the tougher, better-disciplined Nazi Germans, Imperialist Japanese, Soviet Russians or Communist Chinese. But the technology that has placed so many opportunities for self-indulgence in our way has also given us a matchless industrial plant and put us in the van of weapons-design so that we are able to stand off our challengers. If technology has made us ever more dependent upon an ever more intricately organized and hence more vulnerable civilization and put in a variety of human hands the means of demolishing it, perhaps the very dimensions of the catastrophe that hangs over it will stay the adventurers and ideologues (or arouse others to restrain them) and enforce sanity upon the human race, which for the first time has a civilization in which all peoples have a stake. I may wonder whether human beings can go on psychologically coping with an ever more complicated environment, for complication produces tension, distraction and confusion; like the experience of trying to find our way through a bureaucracy to an official with the power of decision and being shunted about from one pretentious but powerless underling to another, it arouses in us the urge to smash something. But if technology has created an environment in which strains and frustrations multiply, it has also given us the leisure and access to sundry vacationlands in which perhaps we may escape them. Competition within our private-enterprise economy may serve as does competition for survival in nature and keep us from growing soft. Yet the heart of my concern, I am afraid, remains untouched.

If the individual is the be-all and the end-all, if all that we do is to be done with his promotion and deserts in mind, as seems to be prevailingly the view, then I am left with a sense of futility. For government to make the individual and the aggregate of individuals, present and future, its paramount object of concern is altogether as it should be; it is not government's business to instruct us in ultimate purposes. But for the culture (if one may so express it) to look no farther seems to me fatal. If it all stops with the individual, then in effect it all stops with me, or with me in the form of other individuals. And that is not good enough. The fact that there are several billions of me-like individuals makes no difference. You do not increase the strength of a chain by multiplying its links or the significance of the individual by multiplying his numbers. On the contrary. And our civilization, which makes more of the individual and does more for him than any other has, has gone far in diminishing his stature.

Says a sign on a huge apartment complex near the start of the Long Island Expressway: FOR TOTAL LIVING. The phrase has suggestive overtones. Democratic totalitarianism might be as descriptive a term as any for what we seem to be evolving. Such, at least, is the feeling you get from the interminable lines of apartment-house windows, the interminable lines of Levittown roofs, the interminable lines of automobiles and the human mass, in which each integer is interchangeable with countless others. Driving down the Long Island Expressway on a weekend you may see in the space of fifteen miles ten or more funeral corteges, the mourners being sped along behind the hearse, bound for one of the cemeteries so big and so crowded that at first sight you think you are seeing, in the far distance, a whole vast city within a city, with avenues of grey, slablike buildings. The procession moves at fifty miles an hour. Even in the solitude of death the human particle must keep its place in the rushing throng. The feeling grows upon you that the population you are seeing and of which you are a part is a subject population —subject neither to Nature nor to an autocrat, neither to God nor to man, but to a master at once more lavish and more impersonal. What the population is subject to is a system, the inconceivably complicated, diffuse, steadily more comprehensive and far-reaching mechanism that has evolved through the progressive division, subdivision and sub-subdivision of labor, an abstraction that provides ever more copiously for our wants—in fact for total living—so long as we meet its requirements. What it requires of each of us is that we render it an ever more specialized service, that we remain ever alert to keep in the good graces of the particular mentor through which it manifests itself to us—the organization if we are an employee, the market if an employer—and accept a narrowing field of competence and a diminishing self-sufficiency and independence.

(The great houses of East Hampton, like those of Mount Desert and Newport, were built in disregard of the claims of many mortals doubtless no less deserving though much less fortunate than the builders. Anyone, I dare say, possessed of the means and amenable to the architectural traditions of the day could have wrought as well. Still, I could not help taking a special satisfaction in those mansions with their carriage houses themselves of august dimensions because—I realized finally—they seemed not to truckle to the system, they did not line up like docile troops but stood apart in separateness and pride; they showed what man—*a* man—had in him.)

I count for little to the system, or to myself as its subject. At the same time, it counts for little to me. It is a provider of commodities and services without which I am lost, but that is all it is. It does not dignify or enlarge me. Standing beside the sea's edge on the empty beach of the Outer Banks, beside the bleached bones of one of the vessels casually flung upon the shore with a scream of wrenched timbers, I am not sustained by the thought of it. In that scene, which allows little question of my impermanence and dispensability, it seems largely irrelevant. If I am to find a meaning in life, it must be outside the terms of a civilization which tells me that nothing is more important than I am and insures that I shall have it rubbed into me how unimportant that is.

And where else is there to look? Perhaps to the aims of Creation. But is there any point in that when I cannot conceivably decipher its ultimate objectives or even know whether there are any? Some point, possibly. One's observation may justify one in believing that there is in Creation a consistent idealism. Overwhelmingly one finds in Nature beauty— symmetry and harmony of form and color, in limitless variety and patterns of breath-taking verve and finesse, from stellar diatoms to galaxies of numberless suns, from the spiral ribbon of chlorophyl in the transparent tubes of pond scum to the chromatic paeans of the sunsets. If you ask me if I see beauty in the tapeworm or the moray eel I must reply that I do not —but with the proviso that, even with my limited and self-centered vision, I am struck by the beauty, though it be at times a terrible and awful beauty, of the grand design of which they are inseparably a part.

To be aware of the beauty that is spread before us, to treasure and not despoil the beauty that is in our keeping and enhance it as we can, to create beauty out of our own hearts and minds as it is given to us to do so—this seems to me to put us in accord with what we may believe to be the spirit of Creation. By such undertakings we may also render the fittest and most acceptable tribute to the Creator and show our reverence. The need to cherish beauty and bring it into being and the need to revere that which has given beauty to the cosmos are so deep-seated in human nature that I find it possible to imagine that they have a validity of the kind we might wish them to have, from a source outside ourselves.

Ugliness is immorality: so the architect Frank Lloyd Wright postulated. I believe it in my heart to be true. Says Constantinos Doxiadis, "Nature has never suffered from the city of the past. If anything, it became more beautiful. The Acropolis in Athens, for instance, became a much more beautiful rock when man built on and around it. The Italian hill towns have beautified the hills. But the modern city has spoiled nature." The city that is the expression of contemporary civilization has become a monster of ugliness. The promotion of its cancerous growth is in my belief immortal. It is evil, in the sense of sacrilege. Modern man can find work taxing all his talents and resources—and giving him a measure of the fulfillment and immortality he craves—in taming the city and bringing it into harmony with what is in Nature and what is human.

No sensible person would have us preoccupy ourselves exclusively with beauty. A dedication to beauty, like a dedication to a religious absolute or to pure science, must lead to a chilling indifference to individual lives; history is not lacking in illustrations of the principle—of which Creation, in our experience, is the supreme exemplification. But here a balance should be possible. We should be able, like Merlin, to follow the gleam and at the same time be quick in sympathy and help for our fellow mortals, human and animal, who, sorely tried, meet with failure and with grief, as each of us must in the end—victims, all of us (may one say it?), of the Creator's own restless perfectionism. "We acknowledge the hand of God and His wisdom," said Anthony Trollope in accents sounding a little doubtful on the lips of a churchman, "but still we are struck with awe and horror at the misery of many of our brethren." If one could combine idealism and charity in equal measure one would have it perhaps just about right.

No sensible person would, either, have us "return to nature," to be as the American Indian was, much as one may esteem him. If there were no towns, my hand, surely, would be among the first raised in favor of having them. Again I think it is a matter of balance. And the balance would seem now to be tipped very far to the machinery of civilization. The give-and-take relationship between men and their natural setting, by which each is shaped by the other and acquires something of the other's character, is for the West clearly a thing of the past. The equilibrium has been upset. Increasingly man imposes his ways on nature and is less and less affected by nature or—to put it another way—receives less and less from nature.

The alienation of man from his matrix will, I fear, prove to be the alienation of man from life. Nature is pitiless in its exactions but openhanded in its gifts. The elements instill in me something of which the crowded streets only deplete me—vitality, gusto, keenness, a sense of hardihood and of awakened blood, and finally the peace that comes from weariness gained in a trial of strength in the open air. In societies that are still close to the land there seems to be a spontaneity, an ebullience and a capacity for living in the present—the only time in which one can live at all—expressed, among other ways, in impromptu and volatile music and dancing. One wonders whether any array of luxuries and recreational devices can make up for the cheerlessness that seems to be the lot of metropolitan throngs. "Eat with the Rich but go to the play with the Poor, who are capable of Joy." But the Poor, in Logan Pearsall Smith's sense, we shall probably not have always with us. Though we may soon be living regularly to the age of a hundred thanks to transplanted kidneys and mechanical hearts with built-in sources of power, I am not sure how much singing we shall be doing about it.

Perhaps the view of Nature I have hazarded is a comforting self-deception. Maybe Creation is only a brutal accident. The splendor we think we perceive in the mighty works of earth and sky around us, in the trees, the mountains, the clouds, may be only a potentiality in man. Possibly man is all there is after all, encompassed by a soul-curdling, abstract nothingness. It could well be. But, if so—the more glory his! The nobility, the sublimity that man has found in the masterpieces of Creation would then be in himself! If it be so, I shall still hold that mankind's proper background is a natural one. It is an odd thing—and again ironical—that man should be overwhelmed, rendered ignominious, cowed, even, by the scale of his own works when his works are what ours are but that he should never be so by the works of nature. Never is his stature more heroic than when he is pitted against the elements, the brute force of the universe. It is against the background of the imperturbable, forest-girt mountains or the huge and menacing sea—not against one of glass-curtained office buildings or a street of suburban houses with free-form swimming pools—that man should be depicted if we wish to have a portrait that will bring out his grandeur and inspire us with a sense of his significance.

Who can say which version, if either, is right—or even whether in the final analysis there is any difference; for man is himself the product of Creation, and of it, and what is inherent in him must be inherent in it. I am certain only that the truth—if there is a truth in the human sense of the term —is far beyond my grasp, and would be even if it were meticulously explained to me. And I am well content to have it so. In the end, our ignorance is our refuge. We cannot tell! Not long ago I read and copied a passage from a book the name of which I did not record because I knew I should not forget it, as I now have. The passage offered excellent advice, it seems to me, and an irresistible invitation to relieve the mind of an impossible burden: "A bound is set to our knowing, and wisdom is not to search beyond it. Men are only men."

Twenty-five hundred years ago Nature spoke in an inscription on an Egyptian temple to Neith, a sky-goddess:

> *I am all that is and that was and that shall be,*
> *and no mortal hath lifted my veil.*

One afternoon at East Hampton early in January I thought the veil was perhaps lifted a slit, or was about to be.

The ocean had brought me up short at first sight, it was so still, so bright. I had never seen it so like a lake. Only when they were almost on the shore did the low, weary swells cave in, falling inertly, and each one seemed likely to prove the last. There was the gurgle of the dying breaker, the indrawn breath of the receding wash, and no other sound. A flock of gulls at rest far off toward the horizon stood out conspicuously, so quiet was the water. Filaments of soft, grey-white clouds were gathered in a hazy quarter of the south. On one side the sea was a pale, peacock blue, like metal, reflecting the sky above it from which it was parted by an odd, smoky curtain, like a belt, setting off the ocean's knife-edged rim. For the rest, it was a mirror of the ceiling of white cloud over most of the sky, through which the sun shone as if in a dream. Over all there was an end-of-the-world air, as if a conclusion had been reached and motion gone out of the universe. Plunged into profound but enigmatic meditation, I stood and waited. It was like a pause before a consummation. But nothing happened . . . until my eye was caught by a large bird coming in at an angle to the shore, just clearing the water. It flew unlike any bird I knew. As it drew nearer I saw that it was a Canada goose, but one driving on with abnormally hard beats of its wings. Then the reason became clear. Half the flight pinions on its right side had been shot away. On it came, head high, as it struggled to maintain its clearance of the water. Then as it neared the shore—the shore that always meant danger—it fought harder to rise. You could feel the force that went into those down-sweeping wings to better its maimed and awkward flight, the power of will; there is no self-pity in Nature. And on it came —and higher. It passed well above the beach and in a moment, dropping lower, had crossed the dunes—all that lay between it and the sanctuary of Hook Pond. . . . The stillness and quiet of the far-reaching scene were more suggestive, more eloquent than ever. But all I could be sure of was my own emotion.

Index

Acadia National Park, 19, 35, 42, 44, 57-58; *see also* Mount Desert Island

Accabonac Harbor, Long Island, 145, 152

Albemarle Sound, 265, 269, 270, 293

algae, 27-28, 32, 51, 127, 146, 162-63; *see also Chondrus, Codium,* diatoms, dulse, *Laminarias,* wrack

Amagansett, Long Island, 178, 192

Ammophila breviligulata, see beachgrass

Amory, Cleveland, 19

amphipods, 32

Ampullaria, 240

Andropogon, see broom sedge

Appalachian Mountains, 8, 13, 232, 235

drainage from, 288

arbutus, trailing, 91

Argall, Samuel, 38

Artemisia, see wormwood, beach

Asbury Park, N. J., 238

Assateague Island, Md.-Va., 248-64

Assateague Island National Seashore, 250-53, 256-57, 261-63, 264

Atlantic City, N. J., 240, 242-43

character of sand from, 168

Banks, the North Carolina, 4, 65, 265-67, 271-303, 312

character of sand from, 168

factors influencing the physical character of, 289-94

geological origin of, 288-89

historical background of, 271-72

Bar Harbor, Mount Desert Island, 18-19, 21, 38, 258

barnacles, rock, 31, 32, 306

Barnegat Bay, N. J., 240

barrier islands, *see* islands, barrier

basalt, 43, 58, 232, 235

sand from, 168

Bascom, Willard, 57, 187

Bates, Marston, 28, 216

Bath, Maine, 11, 282

bay:

red, 256, 260

swamp, 283

Bay, Frenchman, 39, 44

bayberry, 64, 69, 73, 123, 177, 197, 208, 239, 244, 273

beachgrass, 63-64, 69, 72, 73, 90, 103, 123, 126, 178, 239, 267, 278

planting of on Outer Banks, 292

bearberry:

alpine, 50

evergreen, 91, 178, 221

beech, 42, 207, 210

Beston, Henry, 93

318

Bibionid flies, 306

"Blackbeard," 301

Block Island, 80, 152, 173

boatshells, 145

Boreal forest, *see* Canadian Zone

Boston, Mass., 79-80

brants, 240-42, 261

"Breakers, The," 137, 138

Brewster, Senator Daniel B., 252, 264

Brigantine Beach, *see* Atlantic City

Brigantine National Wildlife Refuge, 240-41

broom sedge, 123, 125, 197

Browne, Sir Thomas, 49-50, 248, 254

Bruce, Mrs. Mellon, 294

Bubbles, The, Mount Desert Island, 35, 43

buffleheads, 25, 197, 215

buntings, snow, 215-16

Byron, George Gordon, Lord: *Childe Harold's Pilgrimage,* 17-18

Buxton, Hatteras Island, 278-79, 298

Buxton Woods Nature Trail, 283

Buzzards Bay, 87, 128

Cabot, John, 11, 104

Canadian Zone, 8, 22

Cape Ann, 72-73, 74-75

Cape Cod, 80-112, 128-30, 133
    geological origins of, 77-80, 86-89, 128, 175, 234
    life-expectancy of, 181

Cape Cod Canal, 111-12

Cape Cod National Seashore, 86, 88, 89, 92, 95, 101, 102; *see also* Cape Cod

Cape Hatteras, 102, 133, 274, 281-88, 289, 292-93, 297

Cape Hatteras National Seashore, 251-52, 265, 274, 275-76, 292, 297-98; *see* *also* Cape Hatteras; Currituck Banks; Hatteras Island; Ocracoke Island

Cape Henlopen, Del., 244-47

Cape Henry, Va., 267

Cape Horn, U. S. Coast Guard Cutter, 109-11

Cape Lookout, the North Carolina Banks, 281, 289

Cape Lookout National Seashore, 265, 294; *see also* Portsmouth Island; Core Banks; Shackleford Banks

Caroll A. Deering, wreck of, 282

Carson, Rachel, 162

cedar:
    red, *see* juniper
    white, Atlantic, 91-92
    white, northern, 42-43, 91, 126

Champlain, Samuel de, 42, 51, 104

Chesapeake Bay, 236, 265-67, 271, 288, 294

Cherry Grove, Fire Island, 224-25

Chincoteague, Va., 253, 256-59

Chincoteague National Wildlife Refuge, 249, 258-64

Chondrus, 28, 32, 63

Christianity, 47-48, 158-61

cinquefoil, wine-leaved or three-toothed, 51

Circassian, wreck of, 219

clams and clamming, 70, 146, 170, 177, 203, 235, 295

coastal plain, 14, 77, 175, 235-36

Coast Guard, U. S., 109-12, 217, 287-88, 294, 296-97, 300

Codium, 146-47, 170

Coffin, Robert P. Tristram, 61

Cole, Thomas, 18, 19

coltsfoot, 177

Coney Island, N. Y., 182, 191, 195

Connecticut, 7, 141

Conrad, Joseph, 149, 217-18
coots, 211, 238
copepods, 162
cordgrass, 275, 278
  planting of on Outer Banks, 292-93
Core Banks and Sound, 265, 289
Corea, Maine, 60
cormorants, 139, 300
Corridor (of bird migration), Atlantic, 69, 263
Corson, Bob, 38-42
crabs:
  blue, 146
  horseshoe, 148
  northern, or Jonah, 39, 170
cranberry, 73, 85
  mountain, 50
Crane's Beach, see Ipswich, Mass.
creeper, Virginia, 177, 179, 220
crossbill, red, 22
crowberry:
  black, 50
  broom, 91
Currituck Banks and Sound, 265, 269, 272-76, 295

deer:
  sika, 263-64
  white-tailed, 37, 42, 71, 263
  hunting of, 115-16, 123-24, 125, 264
Dennis, Cape Cod, 82-83
Diamond City, the North Carolina Banks, 292
Diamond Shoals, Cape Hatteras, 281-86, 289
diatoms, 162, 163
Distichlis spicata, see grass, salt-meadow
dolphins, 162, 283, 284
Dorr, George Buckham, 19
Downing, Congressman Thomas N., 256-57, 264
Doxiadis, Constantinos A., 229, 313

Drake, Sir Francis, 271
drumlins, 79
Duck, Currituck Banks, 272-73
ducks:
  baldpate, see widgeon, American black, 68, 197, 214, 242, 259
  long-tailed, 117, 240
  mallard, 211, 237
  scaup, lesser, 197, 214
dulse, 28
dunes, sand:
  formation and behavior of, 63-64, 73-74, 101-02, 185-86, 288-89, 292
  stabilizing of on Outer Banks, 292-93
dunlin, 37

eagle, bald, 242
East Hampton, Long Island, 4-5, 148-49, 178, 182, 184, 191, 193, 199, 206-07, 209-11, 237, 311, 316
  climate of, 219-20
eel, moray, 162, 164, 312
eelgrass, 147, 240
eiders, common, 20, 44-45, 94, 117
Eliot, Charles, 20
Elizabeth Islands, 87, 128
Elizabeth, wreck of, 218-19

fall-line, the, 236
Fernald Point, Mount Desert Island, 38
fir, balsam, 8, 9, 23, 44, 65, 92
Fire Island, 149, 173, 213-28, 249-50
Fire Island National Seashore, 213-14, 219, 223-24, 225, 228; see also Fire Island
Fisher's Island, 80
fishing, decline of American, 75-76
Flyway, Atlantic, see Corridor, Atlantic

Forbush, Edward Howe, 71
Fort Raleigh, Roanoke Island, 269
Fuller, Margaret, 218

gannets, 45, 94
Gardiner's Bay and Gardiner's Island, New York, 145, 175, 179, 210
geese:
  blue, 194, 284
  Canada, 23-24, 67, 211, 259, 277, 316-17
  snow, 197, 260-61, 275-76, 277, 283-84
George A. Kohler, wreck of, 302
George's Bank, 15, 111, 131
glaciers, see Ice Age
Gloucester, Mass., 66, 75-76, 124
goldenrod, beach, 69, 139, 178, 220
Gorham Mountain, Mount Desert Island, 51
grackles:
  boat-tailed, 277
  common, 244, 255-56
granite, 43, 58, 75, 128, 141-42, 168, 174, 235, 290
grass:
  high-tide, 67
  salt-meadow, 67
  switch, 67
Great Beach, Cape Cod, 90, 98-99, 104, 180, 181
Great Eastern Rock, 181
Great South Bay, Long Island, 182, 209, 214
grebe, horned, 253
Green (Cadillac) Mountain, Mount Desert Island, 18, 42-44
Green Mountains, 13
Greenport, Long Island, 192
Grenville, Sir Richard, 271, 293
Griscom, Ludlow, 71
groundsel-bush, 208, 277, 297

Gulf Stream, 4, 38, 285, 287, 289, 295
gulls:
  Bonaparte's, 244-45
  great black-backed, 108-09, 217, 244-45
  herring, 25, 39-40, 109, 145, 147, 151-52, 155, 216-17, 248, 259, 277
  Iceland, 115
  Kumlein's, 45

Hatteras Island, the North Carolina Banks, 265, 277-87, 289, 291, 292-93, 297-98, 302-03
Hatteras village, 271, 295
hawk:
  marsh, see harrier, marsh
  rough-legged, 71, 233
  sharp-shinned, 162, 164
  sparrow, see kestrel
harrier, marsh, 72, 298
heather, beach, 70, 73, 178
Heckscher, August, 199, 200, 205
Heckscher State Park, Long Island, 209
hemlock, 10, 42, 65
highways, Interstate, 9-10
Hither Hills State Park, Long Island, 178
holly:
  American, 222, 235, 239, 249, 256, 260, 283
  inkberry, 91
  Sea Island, see yaupon
  winterberry, 71
Hudson, Henry, 104, 192
Hudson River, 38, 195, 231, 232, 236
Hudsonia, see heather, beach
hurricanes, 55, 125, 143, 184, 186, 207, 290-91

Ice Age, 14-16, 59, 77-80, 174-75, 235, 288, 293
Intracoastal Waterway, 238-39
Ipswich, Mass., 72-73, 168, 216

Island State Park, N. J., 239
islands, barrier, 65, 182, 195, 238, 293; see also Assateague Island; Fire Island; Banks, the North Carolina

Jamaica Bay, Long Island, 182, 197-98, 233
jingle-shells, 143-45
Jones Beach, Long Island, 213, 215, 227
Jordan Pond, Mount Desert Island, 35, 43
Jung, Carl, 304
junipers, 70, 127, 239, 291, 292, 297, 301
    mat, 50

Katahdin, Mount, Maine, 13
kelp, 27-28; see also Laminarias
Kennebunk and Kennebunkport, Maine, 61, 63
kestrel, 42, 72
kettleholes, 79, 86, 87, 176
killdeer, 137
Kill Devil Hills, the North Carolina Banks, 274
kinglet, golden-crowned, 22
kite, Everglade, 240
Kitty Hawk, the North Carolina Banks, 274-75
krill, 163

Laminarias, 27, 63, 147, 170
Lane, Captain Sir Ralph, 302
larks, horned, 215
laurel, sheep, 50, 91
Lawrence, D. H.: Sea and Sardinia, 198
lichen, 30, 100
    moustache, 91
    old-man's-beard (Usnea), 91
    thorn, 51, 91, 100
Little Moose Island, 50, 57
lobsters and lobster-trapping, 39-40, 146, 170
Long Branch, N. J., 237, 238
Long Island, N. Y., 65, 80, 143-49, 177-82, 184, 192-

95, 197, 201-02, 206, 209, 213-28, 238, 306
    geological origins of, 174-76
    growth of population of, 193
    historical background of, 191-93
Long Island Sound, 5, 75, 143, 147, 175, 176, 193, 195
loons, 116-17, 284
Loran, 111, 286-87
Lucas, F. L., 307

Maine, 8, 9-13, 16, 26, 57, 61-65, 81; see also places within Maine
    people of, 59-60
maples, red, 92, 222
Marblehead, Mass., 75
Marconi Wireless Station, Cape Cod, 89-90
Martha's Vineyard, 80, 87, 113, 117-18, 182
    sand from, 168
Maryland, 247-56
Massachusetts, 8, 65-76, 77, 81-82, 130-31; see also places within Massachusetts
Massachusetts Audubon Society, 71, 95
meadowlark, 93, 277
Mellon, Paul H., 294
mergansers, red-breasted, 215, 300
Mitchell, Brig. Gen. Billy, 275
mockingbird, 127-28
Monhegan Island, Maine, 59
Monitor, U.S.S., sinking of, 282-83
Monomoy Island, Cape Cod, 88, 181
Montauk Point, Long Island, 102, 147, 149, 152, 169, 175, 176-77, 179, 180-82, 194
    climate of, 219-20
Montauk village, Long Island, 193-94
moonsnail, 146, 170, 235
Moose Island, Little, 50, 57

moraines, 80, 87, 117, 128, 130, 175-77, 178-79, 180

Morison, Samuel Eliot, 19, 103

Morro Castle, burning of, 238

Morton, Congressman Rogers C. B., 264

moss, Irish, *see Chondrus*

Mount Desert Island, Maine, 16-44, 50, 57, 206, 265, 311
  geological origin of, 13

Murphy, Robert Cushman, 192, 222, 284

mussels, 30-31, 147

myrtle, wax, 244, 255, 256, 273, 277, 279, 280, 283, 297

Nag's Head, the North Carolina Banks, 274, 278

Nantucket, Mass., 80, 87, 107, 113, 117-18, 145, 181-82, 234

Nantucket Historical Trust, 124

Narragansett Bay, 134-35

Nash, Ogden, 274

Nauset Beach and Marsh, Cape Cod, 88-89, 93, 94-95, 102

New Bedford, Mass., 81, 107, 131-34

New Jersey, 187, 232-43

Newport, R. I., 135-40, 206, 311
  sand from, 168

New York City, 191, 195-201, 225, 229-31

Nickerson State Park, Cape Cod, 86-87, 96

Northeast Harbor, Mount Desert Island, 37

oaks:
  bear, 91, 100, 125, 128, 178, 255, 260
  black, 85, 91, 100, 178
  laurel, 283
  live, 267, 273, 278, 279, 283, 297, 302

ocean, effect of on climate, 33-34, 219-20

Ocean Beach, Assateague Island, 250-52, 255

Ocean Beach, Fire Island, 225-27

Ocean City, Md., 247

Ocracoke and Ocracoke Island, 265, 271, 296, 298-99, 301-02

Odyssey, The, and Sonnet by Andrew Lang, 150

oleanders, 298, 299

Oregon Inlet, the North Carolina Banks, 276-77

Orient Point, Long Island, 175, 180, 193

Orleans, Cape Cod, 86, 97, 107, 123

Outer Banks, North Carolina, *see* Banks, the North Carolina

owls:
  short-eared, 277-78
  snowy, 71-72

oysters, and oyster-dredging and -tonging, 146, 203, 209, 256-57, 295

Palisades, the, N. J., 232

palmetto, saw, 283, 299

Pamlico Sound, N. C., 265, 268, 269, 289, 295

Panicum virgatum, see grass, switch

Parker River National Wildlife Refuge, *see* Plum Island, Mass.

Parvin State Park, N. J., 243

Payne, John Howard, home, East Hampton, 210

pea, beach, 69, 220

Peconic Bay, Long Island, 175, 177

Pelican, sinking of, 181

periwinkles, 31-32, 177

phalaropes, 117

pheasants, ring-necked, 211

Pilgrims, the, 101

Pilgrims Monument, Provincetown, 108

pine:
  loblolly, 244, 249, 254, 255, 260, 297
  pitch, 10, 43, 70, 85, 91, 92, 100, 123, 178, 222, 244
  white, 8, 9, 10, 64, 65

pintails, 68

plankton, 163

plover, black-bellied, 153

plum, beach, 69, 73, 177, 179, 220

Plum Island, Mass., 65-73

Poe, Edgar Allan: *A Dream within a Dream,* 166-67

Point O'Woods, Fire Island, 222, 226

ponies, wild:
  of Assateague, 254, 257, 262-63
  of Ocracoke, 263

Pope, Alexander: *Essay on Man,* 161, 165

Popham, Maine, 11

population, explosion and control of, 201, 204-05, 212, 223, 252, 309

Porcupines, the, Maine, 41

porpoises, *see* dolphins

Port Clyde, Maine, 58-59

Portsmouth and Portsmouth Island, the North Carolina Banks, 265, 271, 294, 299-300

Portuguese man-o'-war, 162

Potomac River, 203, 236

Prometheus, 159, 160, 307

Provincetown, Cape Cod, 87, 88, 101, 103, 104-08, 110, 123

quahogs, *see* clams

Race Point, Cape Cod, 102, 103-04

Raleigh, Sir Walter, 266, 271

raven, 24

reed (*Phragmites*), 147, 197, 233

Reston, James, 204

Rhode Island, 77, 134-35; *see also* Newport and Block Island

Richardson, Dr. Wyman, 93

Roanoke Island, N. C., 267, 269

Rockaway, Long Island, 195, 198, 234

Rockefeller, John D., 19, 35, 37

rockweed, *see* wracks

rocks:
  appeal of collecting, 57-58, 116, 128
  as the origin of everything, 51
  effect of waves on, 52-53
  varieties of, 141-42

Ronkonkoma, Lake, Long Island, 175-76

rose:
  multiflora, 220
  salt-spray, 64, 139, 220
  wild, 70, 177, 220

rush, black, 275

Sag Harbor, Long Island, 175, 192

sand, characteristics and components of, 166-70
  garnet, 168-69

sanderlings, 72, 208-09, 215

sandpipers, Western, 94

Sandy Hook, N. J., 118, 235

Sankaty Head, Nantucket, 102, 128-29

sassafras, 220, 222

Savannah, S.S., voyage and sinking of, 218

scallops and scalloping, 124-25, 132-33, 145, 203fn, 277

Schoodic Point, Maine, 44-46, 50

scoters, 179
  American, 45
  surf, 149
  white-winged, 116, 149
sea-lettuce, 63, 75, 170, 239, 245
sea-milkwort, 33
sea-oats, 267, 278
  planting of on Outer Banks, 292-93
sea-rocket, 33
Seal Harbor, Mount Desert Island, 37, 38
Searsport, Maine, 60
Shackleford Banks, N. C., 265, 289, 291
Shakespeare, William:
  King Lear, 166, 304
  Macbeth, 136-37
  Othello, 149
  Sonnet, 57, 182
shark-eyes, *see* moonsnails
Shelter Island and Shelter Island Sound, N. Y., 147, 175, 192
Shenandoah, C.S.S., 119, 122
Shinnecock Bay, Long Island, 177-78, 182, 208
Siasconset, Nantucket Island, 121, 125-28
silverling, *see* groundsel-bush
skimmer, black, 284
slipper-shells, *see* boatshells
smilax, 70, 273, 283
Smith, Captain John, 101, 104, 267-68
Smith, Logan Pearsall, 314
snails, *see Ampullaria*, moonsnails, periwinkles, whelks
Snake (Laurel) Hill, N. J., 232
Snoopy, destruction of, 282
Somerset, H.M.S., wreck of, 104
Somes Sound, Mount Desert Island, 38
Southampton, Long Island, 178, 206, 207
sparrow, song, 139, 253, 298

Spartina patens, see grass, high-tide
sponges, 146
spruces, 8, 9, 22, 23, 47, 65, 92
starfish, 146, 162, 203
Staten Island, N. Y., 80, 175, 197
Stick, David, 276-77
stones and pebbles, variety of from glacial till, 170-74
"Sunken Forest," Fire Island, 220-22
Sunken Meadows State Park, 147
Susquehanna River, 203, 236

taiga, *see* Canadian Zone
Taylor, Congressman Roy A., 252
teal, green-winged, 68, 211
thistle, 33, 220
Thomas, Captain Joseph Brown, 66
Thoreau, Henry David, 90, 92, 103-04, 161, 172
Thunderhole, the, Mount Desert Island, 26-32
tides, 185
Torpedo Junction, Battle of, Cape Hatteras, 282
Trollope, Anthony: Autobiography, 313
turnstones, ruddy, 244

Verrazano, Giovanni da, 104, 268
Verrazano-Narrows Bridge, 175, 231
Vikings, the, 17, 104
Virginia, 256-64, 267-69, 271
Virginia Beach, 267-68
vultures, turkey, 256

warblers, myrtle, 101, 148, 253
Waterway, Intracoastal, 238
waves:
  destructive power of, 52-53, 54-56, 57, 186-87

Waves (*continued*)

    effect of on coasts and shores, 56-57, 181-87, 288-89

    effect on of winds from different quarters, 150-57

    nature and behavior of, 53-54, 55-56, 245, 284-85

    sorting of materials by, 169-70

    "white horses" in, 157

Wellfleet, Cape Cod, 95, 96, 123

Wells, Maine, 64

whales and whaling, 107, 119, 120-22, 162, 192, 193

    blue, 122, 163

whelks, 145-46, 261

White Mountains, 13

Whitman, Walt, 192, 193

widgeon, American, 211

winds, character of:

    northwester, 72, 151, 245

    easterly, 153

    southerly, 156

    southeaster, 286

Wiscasset, Maine, 62

Woods Hole, Cape Cod, and Oceanographic Institute, 113, 128-30

worms, marine, 32, 162

wormwood, beach, 63, 69, 220

wracks, 27, 29

Wright brothers, 274-75

Wright, Frank Lloyd, 313

yaupon, 277, 279-81, 283, 297

yellowlegs, 153